# A THOUSAND LIES

In 1987 Sheila Shand was given a suspended sentence for murdering her father. At her trial, it emerged that she and her mother and sister had been forced to shield brutal sadist Leslie Shand while he subjected them to a reign of terror, daily beatings and sexual abuse.

Years later, investigative journalist Amy Vaughan discovers letters and a newspaper cutting about the Shand case while clearing out her late mother's flat. Concluding that she must be related to the Shands, she decides to visit Sheila's mother who is in a care home. As she pursues her investigation, Amy realises that there is more to the murder of Leslie than the police ever unearthed, including two long-buried skeletons in woods near the family's home.

# A THOUSAND LIES

## Laura Wilson

**WINDSOR**
**PARAGON**

First published 2006
by
Orion
This Large Print edition published 2006
by
BBC Audiobooks Ltd by arrangement with
Orion Publishing Group Ltd

Hardcover ISBN 10: 1 4056 1386 6
ISBN 13: 978 1 405 6136 6
Softcover ISBN 10: 1 4056 1387 4
ISBN 13: 978 1 405 61387 3

British Library Cataloguing in Publication Data available

Printed and bound in Great Britain by
Antony Rowe Ltd., Chippenham, Wiltshire

To Tim

# ACKNOWLEDGEMENTS

I am very grateful to Broo Doherty, Emma Dunford, Dean Fletcher, my dog Freeway, Major John Gilbert, Jane Gregory, Maya Jacobs, Claire Morris, Sara O'Keeffe, James Turner QC, Anna Valinger, June and William Wilson, and Jane Wood, for their enthusiasm, advice and support.

People saw in me weaknesses in themselves that they were afraid of—like fears that they could be broken down. It's hard for people to face that.

*Patty Hearst*

*When they asked me, 'Did you kill your father? Did you do it alone?' I said yes both times because that was what we'd agreed. I expected to go to prison. That didn't frighten me because I thought it could not be worse than my life already. The way I thought was, even if I am in prison, it will still be more freedom than before because it will be away from <u>him</u>. I was 36 at the time (1987).*

*I didn't believe that he <u>could</u> die. Even though I'd seen his body with the wounds it still took a long time to sink in. Mum and Mo were the same. In spite of telling the police that I'd done it on my own, they were both charged with conspiracy to murder, but the magistrate's court found them not guilty so they were free. My trial was about six weeks later, in November. I pleaded not guilty to murder but guilty to manslaughter, and I was given a three-year suspended sentence. The judge said (I will never forget this), 'In many ways your life has been a form of punishment.'*

*Sometimes I wonder what he would have said if I had told the truth.*

From Sheila Shand's journal, written in 1988

# CHAPTER ONE

Michael Farrow skirted the cricket pitch and sweated his way across Monken Hadley Common in the wake of his spaniel. As he went he cursed, in strict order of priority, the dog for needing a walk, his wife for wanting the dog in the first place, his children for providing the pretext for wanting the dog, and then the stinking hot July weather, his fatness, his headache, the bottle of red wine he'd had with last night's dinner and the brandies he'd consumed in front of the TV afterwards, and then—to round things off—the world in general.

It was all right for Honour, she'd grown up with dogs. Five of the things, rampaging round her parents' Dorset rectory and ramming their noses in his crotch whenever he visited. To be fair, it was usually Honour who took care of the walking and feeding, but this weekend she'd gone off to Hampshire to see an old friend, and, faced with the choice of entertaining Harry (four) and Eleanor (two), or traipsing through the wood with Gertie, he'd chosen the latter. At least it gave him a bit of peace and Eva the au pair had seemed happy with the arrangement—she didn't like the dog much, either. Shame Eva wasn't better looking, really. Not that he'd ever . . . and she probably wouldn't, even if he . . . All the same, Czech girls were supposed to be knockouts, weren't they? Like all those models. Trust Honour to pick a moose. Surely a pretty one wasn't too much to ask, especially as he was paying through the nose for it. Like the bloody house. He turned

3

back and squinted across at the elegant Georgian building with its portico and wisteria-clad wall. That was costing a fortune, too, the upkeep. At least he was going up to Scotland for a few days' golf with the boys on Wednesday—he'd insisted on that when Honour dropped her bombshell about leaving him alone with the kids for the whole weekend.

He turned round. Gertie was nowhere to be seen. That was all he needed, to lose the bloody dog. Not that he'd have minded, of course, but he'd never hear the last of it from Honour, and the kids were bound to start howling, and . . . Oh, sod it. 'Gertie!' That was loud enough—several of the cricketers near the pitch boundary had turned round to look—but the dog did not re-appear. Swearing, he hitched up his shorts and lumbered off towards the wood.

It took a good ten minutes of calling and tramping through nettles and once nearly getting his eye poked out by a low branch, before he spotted the black-and-white rump bobbing about among the trees. 'Gertie! Come here! *Now!*'

The dog continued to ignore him. Plunging after her through the undergrowth, he noticed piles of fresh earth. Must have been work done here, he thought—the council, probably. Hadn't Honour been going on about a swamp or something?

He came to the edge of a clearing. More piles of earth, a hastily erected wood-and-wire fence and a notice confirming that Barnet Council were carrying out drainage works and warning him to *Keep Out*. Gertie must have crawled in underneath somehow, because she was scrabbling at something in a deep ditch, earth shooting out on either side

4

of the blur of her stumpy tail.

'Gertie!' He went past the sign, hauled himself painfully over the wooden palings and bent down to grab her collar. She turned her head and snapped at him. He twisted the leather and yanked the snarling, choking dog back up to ground level. After a struggle, he attached her lead and slapped her, hard, on the bottom, but still she strained away from him, front paws beating at the air in the direction of the ditch.

He tugged the lead—for a small dog, Gertie was surprisingly strong—and began to drag her back to the fence, but his foot caught against a tree root and he lost his balance. He grabbed for the fence, but the dog made a frantic lunge towards the ditch, wrong-footing him so that he fell, heavily, onto his back, dropping the lead. Freed, Gertie bounded back into the ditch. Farrow groaned and levered himself into a sitting position. He just had time to blink before a scoop of earth thrown up by rummaging paws hit him full in the face. 'Shit!' He swiped at the muck around his eyes and lunged forwards to grab the end of the trailing lead. It was at that point that the dog moved sideways and Farrow got a glimpse of what she was trying to unearth. It was the skeleton of a human foot.


# CHAPTER TWO

'You're next,' Amy Vaughan told her reflection. She was sitting in a traffic jam on the Western Avenue, staring at herself in the rear-view mirror. Her eyes—the only bit she could see properly in the rectangle of glass—were dark blue, long and narrow with thick black lashes, and they looked tired and unhappy.

That was the thing about the death of a parent, especially one of the same sex: it put you right in the firing line. It didn't matter whether you'd got on or not, they were still the person who stood between you and the inevitable, and when they were gone it was your turn and there was nothing you could do about it. Everything would be so much easier, Amy thought, if I just knew where to find Dad. She'd tried to track him down in time for the funeral, but he seemed to have disappeared, which was, she had to admit, consistent—he had a knack of being unavailable during a crisis. In her darker moments during the last couple of weeks Amy had wondered several times if he was dead as well, and his current 'wife' (always their description, never his) either hadn't chosen to contact her, or—if he'd moved on since the last woman she'd met—hadn't known of her existence.

That aside, her mother's funeral had—all things considered—gone fairly well. What Amy had been dreading most was the next bit: clearing out her mother's flat. She'd put it off for a week already: she'd had to finish a long article about miscarriages of justice for the *Sunday Times*, and she was putting together another book proposal, and she'd spent half a day with her head under the sink, dismantling things because it wasn't draining properly, and . . . She knew she could have gone on adding to the list for ever, so, on Monday afternoon, she'd gritted her teeth, packed an overnight bag, and driven across London.

The lights changed from red to green and back

again several times, but the junction was jammed and the lines of cars didn't move. Amy stared out at the pitiless landscape of concrete and steel and corrugated iron and tried to work out where the house she'd lived in as a child—demolished in 1996 to make way for a never-built flyover—had stood. This wasn't a much happier subject, but at least the speculation took her mind off where she was (or rather, at the moment, wasn't) going, and the fact that she was slowly suffocating inside the sweltering car. She cranked down the window in an attempt to get some relief from the heat, but the exhaust fumes from the lines of trapped, frustrated vehicles seemed to bind the humid air to her skin. She wound it up again and turned to the Evian bottle on the passenger seat. It was warm to the touch—no relief there. She fluffed her short black ringlets away from her sticky neck, undid her safety belt and plucked at her sweaty T-shirt, trying to peel it away from her body, then gave up and slumped over the steering wheel, staring at the huge hoardings that lined the road, advertising cars that were newer and better and shinier than hers. The vision of speed and air-conditioned comfort was humiliating. I'm thirty-four, she thought, and I'm still driving a junk-heap. Bad thought—tempting fate: if the bloody thing decided not to start when the traffic ahead began to crawl forward she'd probably get lynched. 'Sorry, car,' she muttered. 'I didn't mean it.'

The Suburb that Failed. That was how Amy had always thought of the place where she'd grown up. This is the Family that Failed who lived in the House that Failed in the Suburb that Failed. She hadn't been in the least surprised to learn that the

7

entire row was being condemned. The Vaughans had moved into one of the Tudorbethan semis in 1974, when Amy was three, and her Dad had upped sticks six months later, leaving her and Mum with only the traffic for company. Admittedly, the cars—less than ten feet from their front garden—hadn't been too bad at first, but by the time Amy left for university in 1987, the endless rumble had made the window glass vibrate and coated it in greasy filth. When it rained, the spray flung up by the lorries turned everything brown. Amy remembered how she used to stare out of her bedroom window at the road below, watching the cars pass by en route for more desirable places, and promise herself that, as soon as she could, she would follow them.

And she had. Patti Vaughan, for some reason (nostalgia? stubbornness? masochism?), had chosen to remain on this congested, mismanaged stretch of tarmac. The A40 arterial road! Amy snorted. Anyone with an artery as badly clogged as this would have a heart attack within minutes . . . Unlike her mother, whose cancer (whether caused by heavy metals or some interior pollutant) had begun at fifty-seven and taken three and a half years to kill her. Initially, Patti had refused to move, even after the Department of Transport had served her with a notice of eviction, and the last time Amy had visited her at the old place, the row of once-neat houses had become the gutted backdrop to a landscape of feral mattresses, graffiti, nettles and broken glass. A year later, it had vanished, and Patti had grudgingly allowed herself to be installed a few miles up the road in a block of flats called Wendover Court.

8

The cars began crawling over the junction, then picked up speed before hurtling down towards Gipsy Corner. Amy threaded her way across to the outside lane where she drove along as slowly as she dared, trying to identify the turning. If she took the wrong one, she'd be lost for hours in a low-rise, primary-coloured landscape of warehouses, car showrooms and cul-de-sacs. Built in the thirties and miraculously undemolished, Wendover Court was the last remaining residential building on an industrial estate.

Amy found the right turning and parked. Then she peeled herself off the car seat, locked up, and climbed to the fourth floor, where she let herself into her mother's flat. The narrow, windowless hallway was dingy, and as Amy stepped forwards her knee thumped against something hard—a cardboard box, open and full of books. When she turned on the light, she saw that the topmost title was hers: *The Coffin Dodgers* by Amy Vaughan. Picking it up, she turned to the title page and saw her handwriting: *To Mum, with love and best wishes from Amy xxx*. The spine was unbroken. That wasn't particularly surprising—Patti had never been much of a reader, and Amy had to admit that her account of six months' working in various care homes for the elderly (*A compelling indictment of society's failure to address a growing social problem*) wasn't everyone's cup of tea. A sudden suspicion made her bend over for a look at the side of the box. Across the slogan for Walker's crisps was scrawled, in thick black marker, the single word *CHARITY*.

'Thanks, Mum.' Amy squeezed past the box to the kitchen. The books were obviously part of a

9

last, aborted clear-out before her mother went into the hospice for good. She must have had some help, Amy thought, because she'd have been far too frail to lug boxes around on her own. Amy'd had no reason to visit the flat since her mother had entered the hospice, since all the things that Patti Vaughan had needed for the last few weeks of her life—nightclothes, toothbrush, even her Will—had gone with her.

Surely she couldn't have left the book there deliberately, Amy thought. What *are* you supposed to do with your daughter's book if you know you've only got a short time left? Give it back? 'Stop making excuses for her,' she said, aloud. Her mother had known exactly what she was doing. *She thought I'd betrayed her and she couldn't forgive me, even when she was dying.* Face facts, Amy told herself—drugs or no drugs, Patti had known damn well who'd have to clear up after her, and she'd wanted it to hurt.

Amy took a deep breath and looked round the little kitchen. The bare worktops were covered in a fine layer of dust, and the place smelt musty. Five or six flies were circling aimlessly beneath the light fitting. Amy opened the window and took a pace back, almost deafened by the roar from the road. She closed it quickly and stood wondering where to start. She felt as if the flat itself was against her—there was something malevolent about the place. She'd spent the last week imagining finding her head slashed out of photographs by furious scissors, her few letters and postcards defaced with vicious scrawl, or turning on the stereo to a tape of curses: *You came between us, I wish you'd never been born* . . . Stop it, she thought. Don't cry. Keep calm. I'm going to put my head down and get through this, she told herself. I'm not going to get upset. Whatever happens, whatever I find, she is not going to win.

She went down to the car to pick up her groceries and overnight bag. Despite the humidity and the constant whiplash noise of passing cars, the air seemed fresh in comparison with the flat. When Amy had learnt that she was her mother's sole beneficiary, she'd thought there must have been a mistake, but when she discovered that all she was to have sole benefit of were a few sticks of cheap furniture and an unsaleable flat, it had made more sense. She'd have to put the place on the market at a bargain price and hope that someone was desperate enough to get on the housing ladder . . . If I'm lucky, she thought, looking up at Wendover Court, I might clear enough to pay off a chunk of the mortgage and—she glanced round guiltily at her car—buy something decent to drive.

She climbed back up to the flat. The fridge, she discovered when she went to unload her food, was switched off but not emptied. She dropped a bag of brown, liquefied lettuce into the bin, then turned her attention to a carton of near-solid milk. She upended it over the sink and tried not to gag as the contents flopped out onto the plughole and stayed there until she broke up the quivering, off-white mass with the handle of a wooden spoon.

She decided to make a start in the bedroom. It was at the back, as far away from the bad milk smell as possible, and the window could be opened without quite so much din, apart from the trains rattling past on the tracks behind the block. Patti Vaughan's bedroom was pink, dusty, thickly

11

carpeted, and very hot. Amy had the feeling that her mother was somehow present, lingering on in the backs of drawers and behind the rails of clothes in the wardrobe. She looked at the old-fashioned phone crouched on the bedside table and felt a sudden conviction that if she lifted the receiver her mother's part in every conversation they'd ever had would issue from it—the flat, cold denials, the shouted accusations, the whining emotional blackmail . . . She bent down, yanked the plug out of the jack, and trussed the phone in its own cord. 'That's shut you up,' she said. Beside it was the carved wooden box full of Patti's jewellery: huge dark beads, chunky bracelets and heavy silver rings. There was only one item she didn't recognise, in an oblong leather box with satin lining: an old-fashioned silver dress watch, far more delicate than the other items. She took it out and wound it, holding it to her ear to see if it still worked. She held it, momentarily, against her wrist, but the tiny tick seemed too much like a last weak echo of Patti's own pulse. Telling herself not to be ridiculous, she put the watch to one side. It looked as if it might be an heirloom, and she ought to keep one thing, at least.

Working fast, she upended drawers of clothing into bin-liners without so much as a glance at the contents. Then she turned her attention to the wardrobe, shucking armfuls of long dresses in swirling Indian fabrics, loon pants and gaudy blouses off their hangers and stuffing them into the bags. Those could go to the charity shop—with the boxes of books, there wouldn't be room in the car for the rest. She lugged the bags into the kitchen so as not to get mixed up, and set to work

12

on the shoes and handbags. Then she went through to the bathroom, emptied the contents of the cabinet into the miniature swing-bin and added that to the rubbish pile, together with the towels, the bed-linen and the bath mat. After a couple of hours, the hall carpet was entirely covered in bulging black plastic, and she began hauling the bin-liners out and down the stairs for the dustmen. By the time she'd finished it was nearly eight o'clock and she was limp and gritty with sweat and dust.

She went into the bathroom to wash her hands and splash her face with water, before getting herself a beer. At least she'd got rid of most of the things—good job it was only a one-bedroom flat. The house clearance people were coming tomorrow, for the furniture and pots and pans, but she'd wanted to dispose of all the other stuff herself. The act of bagging it and putting it out for the bin men had felt like a sort of exorcism. Now that most of the personal items were gone, the atmosphere in the flat seemed to have lightened a bit.

Even with the window shut she could hear the muffled whoosh-whoosh of the traffic. Amy felt an intense, almost savage, pleasure that the cars were eroding the landscape of her childhood. There had been a slightly wistful moment this afternoon when she'd noticed that the shop at Western Circus, where she'd spent her pocket money on Love Hearts and Fab ice lollies and *Jackie* magazine, was boarded up. *Jackie* magazine! She wondered how its agony aunts, Cathy and Claire, would have dealt with her problem, even if she'd been able to identify what it was, and—more to the point—

13

admit it to herself. Cathy and Claire would have thought she was making it up to get attention: the worst thing a mother could do in the *Jackie* universe was to stop you wearing high heels or embarrass you by picking you up from a party at 9.30. And even if someone—not Cathy and Claire, necessarily, but anyone—had believed her, it would have meant the fate worse than death: being *taken into care*.

Swiping angrily at the tears that pricked her eyes, Amy, collected more bin-liners and went into the sitting room. Most of the work had already been done: the shelves of the bookcase were bare, and a row of boxes marked *CHARITY* lined one wall. The cupboard with the CDs and videos had been cleaned out, and a paper carrier bag full of records was propped against the fireplace. In the middle of the coffee table there was a large rectangular chocolate box. Over the embossed curlicues of Terry's All-Gold had been stuck a white label: *AMY*.

The defaced photographs, the tape of her mother's final denunciation . . . Mouth dry, Amy hesitated. She didn't want to touch the box, much less take the lid off. She glanced at the roll of bin-liners she'd left on the bookcase. She could always throw it away without looking. But supposing there was a letter—an explanation—an apology—a stab at the truth, even? She'd be throwing away her only chance for some sort of reconciliation, even if it was posthumous . . .

The hope that had flared inside her died almost immediately. It's impossible, she thought. Dying, her mother had turned away from her. Every time Amy had come to see her, she'd looked up, hoping

14

for Dad, but when she'd seen her daughter she'd turned her face to the wall. Flashes of herself pleading with her mother came at Amy like shards of flying glass: *I'm doing my best to find him.*

One whispered word: *Liar.*

*Please, Mum, don't do this.*

*Liar.*

In spite of all the drugs, Patti had been lucid enough to hate, and even when her speech had left her she'd still turned away. Nevertheless, thought Amy, I have to open this box, or it'll drive me mad. Her mother's last, hoarse words rasped through her head. *Liar. You're keeping him from me. Liar.*

Hands shaking, she picked up the box and lifted the lid.


# CHAPTER THREE

Amy sat down on the carpet and examined the contents. Sellotaped to the inside of the lid was a white envelope with the words *George* and *Private* written across it in large letters. It was sealed with another piece of Sellotape, and had *Private* written again across the back. Amy turned her attention to the rest of the box, which contained a brown paper parcel and two photograph albums, one labelled *Patti & George*, the other labelled with her own name. Exiled to photographic Siberia. Oh, great. Amy sat on the floor, opened the first album and started turning the pages. Mum and Dad looking glamorous at the races, romantic at a restaurant, sun-tanned on a beach, he handsome, she beautiful, very Burton-and-Taylor, right down to

15

Mum's long black hair and Cleopatra eye make-up. You'd have thought it was a record of a couple's life together, even though Dad had probably spent a total of less than two years with Mum—on and off—since walking out when Amy was four. Flicking through, she noticed that some of the photographs were square and others rectangular. Thinking this was odd (surely photos used to be a standard size?), she looked closer and saw, in one of the square ones, the fingers of a child's severed hand—her own—clasped inside Dad's. Patti had neatly, surgically, sliced her off at the wrist.

Gasping, Amy shut the album and pushed it away. Being excised with such care and precision was worse than having your face scratched out in anger. It was the deliberateness of it that was so disturbing. It's all right, she told herself, desperately. It's only what you were expecting.

She'd spent so many years trying not to mind, not to acknowledge how much it hurt, masking the feelings with everything she could, but now, alone, and with a pain in her chest that felt almost like a wound, she started to cry. How long, she wondered, would Patti be able to make her feel like that? For the rest of her life?

She knew—Patti had told her when she was fifteen—that her mother hadn't wanted a child, and had only gone through with the pregnancy because George had insisted. Then—Patti hadn't said this, but by that time Amy understood it though she couldn't have put it into words—her mother had turned her into a means of controlling him.

Amy pulled the second album towards her, and

16

opened it. It was less a record of childhood than a case-study. Mum's version of the truth. The sequence of photographs gave a more distorted image than most, but then, Amy thought dully, who takes pictures of the row over dinner and the slapped toddler, or videos a funeral? The things we want to record are christenings, weddings, holidays and parties—the favourable reflections of family life. The photos in this album were intended to serve an entirely different purpose. They weren't a record of her growing up, they were a means to an end.

Patti had posed Amy carefully and posted the resulting images of a sickly creature, not long for this world, to her husband, hoping to blackmail him into coming home. Wiping her eyes, Amy turned the pages. From being a sturdy, grinning toddler, she saw herself mutate into a pale seven-year-old, propped up by pillows and smiling bravely but queasily (she'd been violently sick five minutes later); a stick-limbed nine-year-old, sprawled on a rug in the garden, a plastic hospital bracelet still round her wrist; and finally, at fourteen, a gowned, prone figure on a trolley in a hospital corridor. Amy couldn't remember that one being taken—perhaps she hadn't come round from the anaesthetic. She looked as if she were dead.

Exploratory surgery. It was always that. She rubbed her chest and stomach. The scars were still there—vertical and horizontal, neat and faint except for one botched job, where the skin had puckered around the incision.

There was no one else in the pictures. Even the baby ones didn't show either of her parents

17

holding her. There must have been at least one, Amy thought, but Patti obviously hadn't thought it worth keeping. Only Amy was left, sick and alone. But I did have friends, she told herself. She remembered them: Sandra Bailey and Katie Palmer from primary school, and then Jacqui Newstead, Lucy Davis, Susan Cooper . . . But there was no evidence of them here. And all the normal kid stuff like running and jumping and mucking about in sandpits and riding camels at the zoo, that wasn't here, either. Yet she'd done it, hadn't she? She remembered doing it—or bits of it—with a reasonable degree of clarity, or thought she did. But the invalid in the photographs made her think that she was wrong and Patti was right. That child couldn't have done any of those things: she was a wreck, and if her Dad didn't come home very, very soon, she'd die and then he'd never see his little girl again.

Don't let her get to you, Amy told herself. That's why she's done this. She. Is. Not. Going. To. Win. She closed the album, blew her nose, then picked up the brown paper parcel and felt it. Something solid and rectangular, like a book. Unwrapping it, she saw that it was an old-fashioned five-year diary, bound in shiny pink leather, with a strap and a lock. She looked into the paper bag—no keys. Amy tugged at the strap, but the book remained firmly shut. Odd, she thought, if it was her mother's—it didn't look like the sort of diary Patti would have, but then Amy hadn't known she'd kept one. She put it on her lap and stared at it for a long time. Did she really want to know what was in it?

Levering herself off the floor, she went through

to the kitchen and pulled the scissors out of the cutlery drawer. Weighing them in her hand, she thought, No. She didn't want to deface it, and in any case, she wanted to keep the lock—to shut Patti inside, if necessary. She fished in her handbag for the tweezers that she kept with her make-up. Back in the sitting room, she set to work picking the lock. After a few minutes of careful poking and twiddling, it yielded. Amy took a deep breath, opened the diary to its fullest extent, and shook it. A black-and-white photograph fluttered to the floor.

# CHAPTER FOUR

It was a baby. Just old enough to sit up, she—or possibly he—was dressed in a frilly white robe and posed against a traditional studio backdrop. Amy stared at the photograph. The baby had exactly the same wild black ringlets as she did, yet it wasn't her. The background and dress were too old-fashioned. She turned the photograph over, and read, *Maureen, aged 6 months.*

Who the hell was Maureen? Could Patti have had another child that Amy didn't know about? Perhaps she'd had Maureen as a teenager, and the girl had been adopted. 'For Christ's sake, Mum,' she muttered, 'this isn't *fair*.' She picked up the photograph album marked with her name, turned to the first picture, and compared them: identical.

Perhaps Maureen wasn't Patti's child, but a relative Amy hadn't been told about. Her grandmother and grandfather had both died before she was born, and, as far as she knew, Patti had been an only child. She turned back to the diary. The first thing she noticed was an address: Hadley Cottage, 89 Camlet Way, Barnet, Herts, written in an unsophisticated, backward-sloping hand—certainly not Patti's. She started flipping through it. The years covered were 1983 to 1987, and most of the pages had been filled until the entries stopped in mid-April 1987. The last entry was Saturday the 18th. That was—Amy checked the previous day's offering—the Easter weekend. The content was utterly banal.

*Sheila helped Dad mending the cupboard. It was a good job. Mr Drake came over from the farm and said, Your Dad is very clever with his hands. Angel Delight—'Butterscotch'.*

Perhaps the writer was Maureen herself. Obviously young, judging by the writing, the fact she appeared to live at home, and the mention of food. Amy turned back to the first entry: *Saturday, 1 January. New Year's Day! Started this diary. It will be interesting to have an account of our family life . . .*

*Sunday: Watched the New Year 'Special' last night on TV which was very good. We ran out of milk and the shops are shut so Dad sent Sheila down to the farm to borrow some.*

'Riveting,' Amy muttered.

*Monday: Back to work! Lots of tablecloths and restaurant stuff coming in after Xmas so we said we will do overtime because it pays well. We can get an evening meal at the café on the corner. Dad sent Sheila down to Mrs Drake with a bottle of milk. We will have to order an extra pint!*

So the diarist—supposing it was Maureen—

wasn't that young: she had a job. A menial one, by the sound of it, perhaps her first, but it meant she had to be over sixteen. Although why any teenager would want to record boring details about extra pints of milk . . . Sheila, Amy decided, must be the writer's sister. No mention of a mother, though.

She opened the diary at random, and read the entries for 14 to 16 June 1983:

*Thursday: My birthday today (30).* Thirty? Bloody hell, thought Amy, this is weird. *Dad said, What would you like, but I couldn't think of anything. I have got everything I want. Dad took us to the pub. 'The Talbot' this evening for 12 hour. We had a 12 lager and blackcurrant each. Then watched a 'Western' on TV and enjoyed it.*

*Friday: Mum*—so she did exist, then—*had a nasty fall. We took her to the hospital (Barnet General). They x-rayed and said her jaw is broken and they are worried because it might affect her brain so kept her in for tests.*

What sort of fall, Amy wondered, would result in a broken jaw? She read on.

*Saturday: We visited Mum in the hospital. She looked much better. Dad took flowers. He said, You are a silly thing, fancy having an argument with a door, and it made us all laugh. One of the other ladies said, Oh I wish I had a husband like that, he is so kind. Mum will come home tomorrow. We all miss her. Angel Delight 'Chocolate'.*

The 'argument with a door' sounded pretty suspect, especially as the day before it had been a 'nasty fall'. Amy shook her head and turned to the entries for the same period in 1984:

*Thursday: Dad came home with a new pet for us, a parrot 'African Grey'. He says they are the best*

21

*talkers of all parrots. I copied instructions from the pet care book and pinned them up in the kitchen so that we will know how to look after it. Sheila helped Dad making a perch. Unfortunately, Mum had an accident while she was making tea.*

*Friday: My birthday (31). Dad took Mum to the doctor for her burnt hand. After work, Sheila helped Dad outside and I did the ironing.*

*Saturday: Went to 'Spar' with Sheila. They didn't have the right toothpaste so we bought it at the chemist where we get the vitamins. It was 11p more than 'Spar'. Luckily, Sheila remembered to tell Dad. In the evening went to pub 'The Talbot'. Dad talked to Mr Drake and Mrs Drake came and sat with us. Mum made a stew for supper. Angel Delight 'Strawberry'.*

Amy thumbed through the diary looking for references to Mr and Mrs Drake and discovered that Mr Drake (first name unknown) was the farmer who employed the father. According to the entries, it was a pig farm, with the porkers under contract to Wall's, and it must have been fairly near if Sheila had been sent there to borrow a bottle of milk. She also discovered that the family's surname was Shand, the father's name was Leslie, and that the writer was, as she'd suspected, Maureen, known to her family as Mo. There was, however, no mention of Patti, and no hint of how the diary might have come into her possession.

Amy turned to the same period in June 1985:

*Friday: Mum went to Casualty this evening because her ear keeps bleeding. We don't know what caused it. They are closing the laundry in two months' time. We have been there longer than anyone, since we left school. So Sheila has been there*

22

*since 1965 and me since 1967! Dad said to find out if we will get a redundancy payment but nobody knows yet.*

*Saturday: We asked Dad what to do about jobs when the laundry closes, and he said he will ask at the Chase Lodge Hotel where Mum used to work. This will be good because it is not far to walk. Watched a war film on TV. Angel Delight 'Banana'.*

*Sunday: Mum's ear is a lot better now because the blood has stopped. We have got our fingers crossed about the hotel job.*

Amy started flipping back and forth through the pages: *Mum's been poorly again with her leg . . . Dad has been busy improving the kitchen . . . Visited Dr Renfrew for another prescription . . . Dad took us to the pub for 1/2 hour, with Honey . . .*

Honey, it transpired, was an Alsatian. She had no idea how old it was, but by 1986 it was dead. One of the striking things was the sheer number of animals that passed through the Shand household in five years: a dog, six cats, four canaries, one parrot and an unspecified number of rabbits. The worrying thing was the turnover. She kept coming across sentences like *Dad put the canary out of its misery* and *We had to get rid of the cat.* Either the Shands had spectacularly bad luck with their pets or there was a more sinister explanation.

Even more disturbing were the references to Mo's mother, whose name was Iris. When Amy went through the entries from 1983 to 1986, she counted a broken jaw, a broken wrist, burnt hands, bleeding ears and stitches to the head.

All these, according to the diary, were the result of accidents. Surely, thought Amy, someone must have noticed a pattern? Domestic violence hadn't

23

been particularly high on the police agenda in the early eighties, but surely the GP or the people at the hospital would have picked up on it? Then again, if they had asked, Iris might have been too afraid, or too ashamed, to tell the truth.

It wasn't clear whether Mo or Sheila were present when Iris's various injuries occurred, and the bland way in which they were recorded suggested that they were just run-of-the-mill events, like making tea or going shopping. It seemed impossible that Mo *hadn't* realised what was happening to her mother, yet that was how it appeared. The other odd thing was the complete absence of emotional content, which for a woman —even a rather dim one—was extraordinary. Apart from occasional comments about having enjoyed a film on TV or a visit to the pub, there was nothing—no negative remarks, no mention of arguments or worries—to show that Mo had treated her diary as a confidant. She never recorded much about her sister or mother, either, but there were frequent mentions of what Dad thought and said and did. The cumulative effect was eerie: the women in the Shand household were, effectively, silenced.

The sisters appeared to have no social life at all, unless you counted the occasional outing to the pub, accompanied by their father. These, with shopping trips, dog walking and visits to the farm on various errands, seemed to be the only times, other than work, when they were away from Hadley Cottage. Sentences like *We are lucky to have a nice home and wonderful parents* apparently indicated that they had no desire to leave it. They didn't appear to have any transport, either, or

24

holidays, or any friends of their own age. Amy found a couple of names—Pam and Allison—of fellow laundry workers, and, later on, several mentions of a Mrs Sandford who was the manager at the Chase Lodge Hotel, but that was all.

In 1987, Mo had been thirty-four, like herself. Amy thought of everything she'd done in the last five years: sold her first flat, moved in with Paul, married Paul, gone freelance, had her first book published, been on holidays, gone to parties and the theatre and art galleries and made new friends, got divorced and was now struggling with the mortgage on a doll-sized Georgian house in Islington . . . OK, it hadn't all been wonderful, but in terms of growing up and moving on and generally doing things, it was a *life*. In five years, Mo and Sheila had not, according to the diary, had so much as an outing to the cinema or a day-trip to Brighton. The highlights of their lives seemed to be an occasional fairy cake or éclair from the 'pig lorry' (whatever that was) and Angel Delight for pudding on Saturdays.

Perhaps they had had another life but, for some reason, it had gone unrecorded. Mo's fear of her father, perhaps? If he beat her mother, she must have been afraid of him. Perhaps he'd beaten her, too, and Sheila. But then, why not tell someone? It was one thing for a child to suffer in silence, but these were grown-up women. And why, why, *why* didn't they all just *leave*? Iris clearly didn't have a job, but Mo and Sheila did, so there was no financial incentive to stay, and they could have been re-housed or something.

Amy scoured the diary for more information about the farm, but found little. Mr Drake, the farmer, was mentioned a few times, but Mrs Drake, who—judging from the fact that she sometimes sat with Mo and Sheila in the pub— must have been the nearest they had to a friend, was barely mentioned before February 1987, when she left Mr Drake and Leslie joked that she had run off with the milkman. The two weeks after that were taken up with the Shand family's expeditions through a place called Hadley Wood in search of the parrot, Stanley, who had escaped. *Dad took his shotgun.* Amy raised her eyebrows. Perhaps he'd terrorised his wife with that, too.

A couple of entries in mid-September 1986 revealed that Mo had been to see the doctor. It wasn't the GP, Dr Renfrew, but someone at Barnet General Hospital. There was no mention of symptoms, but she'd spent two weeks as an in-patient in late October, and gone back for another week just before Christmas. There was still no named illness, just sentences like *They've given me a different sort of pill* and *This new treatment gives me headaches*, and a lot of stuff about the nurses being kind and how much she was missing her family.

Whatever was wrong with her didn't seem to have affected her handwriting, which remained almost painfully neat. Amy wondered about the treatment that gave her headaches. She'd made a definite distinction between 'pills' and 'treatment' so it must have been some sort of medical procedure. Psychiatric, perhaps? True to form, Mo hadn't recorded feeling unhappy in the months before her stay in hospital, only that she'd spent a lot of time lying on her bed. That might mean depression. Could Mo have been given Electro-

26

convulsive Therapy? Amy remembered footage she'd seen of electrodes fixed to people's temples, rubber bungs wedged in mouths, bodies thrashing as the shock hit them, talking heads saying they weren't sure how ECT worked or if it worked at all. It was still used, so Mo certainly could have had it in 1986.

Amy turned back to the beginning of the year and noted down references to pills. Dr Renfrew had prescribed some for Mo in May, and again in June and July, and she'd had the appointment with Dr Lovegood at Barnet General at the beginning of September. Assuming that was for the same problem, it meant that the GP's drugs weren't working. Could they have been anti-depressants? Surely depression alone didn't warrant a stay in hospital, unless, of course, Mo had been manic or suicidal. But it seemed unlikely that someone in that condition could have kept a neatly written diary about nothing much, and Mo hadn't missed a single day. And if Dr Lovegood at Barnet General were a psychiatrist, wouldn't he have asked her to explain what was troubling her? Perhaps she'd been too frightened to tell him. And why had she suddenly stopped writing? Suicide? Accident? Institution? And what did any of it have to do with Patti, and why had Patti left the diary for her?

Amy closed the little book. It was almost midnight. She felt exhausted. She took a glass of water through to Patti's bedroom, unfolded the sheet she'd brought with her onto the mattress, and undressed. The heat was stifling. Amy opened the back window, heard the clatter of an approaching train, and shut it again. She'd forgotten that the freight carriers ran all night.

Patti had never seemed to mind about the noise—
after so many years, Amy supposed, she'd simply
got used to it. Oh, well. She put the glass on the
bedside table, next to the mute, captive telephone,
lay down, and closed her eyes. The mystery would
have to wait until tomorrow.

# CHAPTER FIVE

Sheila Shand stood in the darkness and stared
through her bedroom window at the moonlit
common. The police cars were gone now. She'd
watched the men returning from the wood at dusk,
making their way across the grass behind the
cricket pitch in twos and threes. It must be, she
thought. It can't be anything else. The policemen
had been in the wood for hours—since half past
three, at least, when she'd come back from tea
with Bill and the first car had passed her on the
road.

In desperation, she'd concocted all sorts of
explanations, each more far-fetched than the one
before—somebody hurt, drugs, gangs, spies—but
she knew it was useless. They'd found it. They
must have.

It must be only bones by now. Would they be
able to find out who it was? It was all very high-
tech nowadays, she knew that from television, the
trailers for all those police serials she couldn't bear
to watch. There were no clothes, but what about
the teeth? And the plastic groundsheet? She had a
mental picture of men and women in scrubs and
fashionable glasses picking at a skeleton with

tweezers and talking about 'building up a picture'.

Perhaps it was someone else buried there. Or someone had died (but where was the ambulance?). Perhaps it was children messing around—Sheila gasped. What if a child had found it? No, she thought. Not a child. She couldn't bear it. It would be a dog. It was always a dog, you saw it on *Crimewatch*. And lots of people walked their dogs in the woods.

Perhaps it was the dog she'd seen this afternoon on her way to Bill's. The spaniel with the fat owner. She didn't know the man's name—she usually saw it with a woman—but the dog was called Gertie. She thought they lived in one of the big houses on the other side of the common.

She went to Bill's for tea every Sunday. She always took a Tupperware box with their favourite biscuits, and put her slippers, wrapped in plastic, in her handbag, because even in this very hot weather, the lane, neglected and terribly overhung with trees, was muddy. She couldn't understand why Bill never did anything about it, because his bungalow was always immaculate, inside and out. She did a lot for him, of course, cleaning and ironing, but he really was very good around the house, and he kept his garden beautifully. He just never seemed to notice that the lane, and what remained of the farmyard, were derelict, with the buildings almost falling down and rusty old bits of machinery just plonked all over the place.

As usual, Sheila felt herself tense as she threaded her way through the litter of implements in the concrete-covered yard. She hated that part—all the claws and prongs and bars made her think of instruments of torture, and if she'd ever

29

had to touch one (although she couldn't think why she would) she was sure she'd scream. The spikes seemed to encroach on her, hard and vicious, as if they were trying to impale or trap her, and her mind filled with pictures of vulnerable flesh that would only take a second to puncture, or gash open . . . She always breathed a sigh of relief as her foot alighted safely on the neat gravel path, and this afternoon she'd stopped for a moment to admire the rows of jolly red pom-pom dahlias on either side.

'Hello there.'

Sheila blinked. Bill Drake was standing in the doorway, natty in a checked shirt and tie, smart trousers with a knife-edge crease and highly polished leather slippers. His face, lined and craggy from years of work outside, was beaming.

'Pleasant journey?'

He said it every Sunday, and it always made her laugh. Recently, she'd thought of something to say in return: 'No traffic jams.'

'Jolly good!' He rubbed his hands together. 'Come on in.'

'I'll just take my shoes off.' She unlaced her shoes and stood on the hall carpet in her stockinged feet while she took her slippers out of their plastic bag.

'Why don't you go through? I'll make us a pot of tea.'

Sheila handed over her Tupperware box. 'Our favourites.'

'Oh, well done.' Bill made an appreciative gesture, as if bestowing a bouquet, and ushered her into the lounge.

The room was decorated in pale green (eau-de-

Nil, she thought it was called) and pink. Rosie's choice, of course, from years back, but it was still, with the sun coming through the net curtains, a bright, pretty room. There was a comfortable three-piece suite with the cushions arranged precisely across the back of the sofa, a vase of beautiful bronze chrysanthemums on top of a shining glass-fronted cabinet filled with Dresden shepherds and shepherdesses, and china collie dogs and Shire horses flanked the framed photographs on top of the stone-clad fire-surround.

Sheila put down her bag and settled herself carefully on the end of one of the sofas, sitting well forward so as not to disturb the plump symmetry of the cushions. Then, noticing a chip on the china hoof of one horse, she leant forward for a closer look, inclining her head slightly to avoid the eye of the redheaded woman in the photograph next to it. She was about to pick it up when Bill said, 'It's been a good few years . . .'

She turned and saw him standing in the doorway with a tray of tea, and realised he'd thought she was looking at the photo. 'Quite a time,' he continued, putting the tray down on one of the occasional tables. The happy lightness Sheila had felt in the air evaporated, replaced by a charge of the same lurching dread she used to feel on Saturday night, watching the clock for the time when Dad jerked his head for her to go outside.

Bill went over to the fireplace, and she tried to keep quite still and not flinch as he picked up the redhead's photograph. 'Eighteen years, now, since she left me.'

His words seemed to writhe in the air between

31

them like something impaled. Sheila stared at the mantelpiece, unable to answer, and, seeing a photograph of Mo and herself staring back, ducked her head, waiting with mounting anxiety for the inevitable. She felt as if she might be sick. Bill put the photograph back in its place and moved to stand directly in front of her so that, unable to meet his eye, she found herself staring down at the shiny toes of his leather slippers. She wished he wouldn't. She liked the tea and biscuits and their chats about gardening and pet programmes on the television and local politics and things like that, but sometimes, like this afternoon, their shared past and all the things they could never say ate into her like a tick burrowing under her skin.

'You know I'd never ask, Sheila,' he said, 'but I wish you'd change your mind.'

She swallowed, trying to force saliva into her mouth. He was too close, looming over her so that if she raised her eyes she'd have to look at his thighs, right in front of her face. He must know I hate it, she thought. He says he understands, but he still does it.

'I'm sorry, Bill,' she whispered. 'I can't.'

'I know how you feel, and I'd never put any pressure on you, but . . .'

'I can't.' She inched away from him, pressing her back into the sofa cushions.

'Sheila . . . If you ever do change your mind, you will tell me, won't you?'

'Yes.'

'I'm sorry. I shouldn't have brought it up. But you can't blame me for trying.'

She knew it was supposed to be a compliment

when he said things like that, but she hated it when he got *that* look on his face, or if any man did, even nice old Mr Bevan, the senior partner at work. It reminded her of Dad, and it was his voice she heard in her mind, trapped there as if it came from their old Dansette record player whose needle got stuck so often that she had needed to stand over it to keep the music flowing smoothly, as, on his instruction, she played the only two records in the house one after the other for hours at a time. 'The Laughing Policeman' and 'My Old Man's a Dustman'—both 45s—were badly scratched, and she knew exactly where the glitches were. The worst was in the middle of one of Charles Penrose's uproarious laughs, *Whooooah! Ha, ha, ha, ha, ha, ha, ha* . . . Her panicky fingers quivering over the arm to give it the tiniest nudge, so that it would not jump and make *him* angry. *He said, 'I must arrest you,' He didn't know what for, And then he started laughing, Until he cracked his jaw . . . Ah! Ha, ha, ha, ha, ha, ha, ha.* Thank heavens you never heard those songs nowadays. The first time Dad had cracked—or rather broken—Mum's jaw had been to the sound of the Laughing Policeman, who wouldn't have helped them, Sheila's seven-year-old self knew, even if he had existed. He probably would have found it funny. *Ha, ha, ha, ha* . . . The guffaws were lodged in her mind, like the words *he* had said when she was twelve, the first time it happened: 'Take your knickers off. Lie down and keep quiet.' They'd been in the old Anderson shelter, where he always did it. As the memories crowded in on her, she could almost smell the oil he used on the tools he kept there, and the thin, damp mattress. It was always

Saturday—as if it were a treat he'd been saving up for himself, and the build-up was part of it, she knew, as week after week, she'd counted off the days until it would happen again.

He'd issued other instructions, too, later, words she'd learnt to block out of her mind—if she wasn't quick enough, like this afternoon, they made her wince and turn her head away as if trying to escape a blow.

Bill said nothing, but she knew he was watching her. Usually, if this happened, she felt too uncomfortable to look at him, but this time she made herself. As their eyes met, she caught a flicker—just for a moment—not of sympathy, but of curiosity. Don't be stupid, she told herself. He's not like Dad. You're quite safe. Don't imagine things.

She stood up and busied herself with the tea things, while Bill told her about the trip he was planning to the garden centre to buy more goldfish for his pond. She tried hard to concentrate on what he was saying about the pros and cons of covering the water with a protective net, but she felt Mo's eyes, and Rosie Drake's, boring into her from the images on the mantelpiece, and keeping up her end of the conversation was a strain. Feeling the beginnings of a headache, she refused Bill's offer of a second cup, and, after only three-quarters of an hour, announced that she ought to go.

'I'll see you home,' he said, as he always did.

'I think I might go by myself this time, Bill, if you don't mind.'

'Not at all. I didn't mean to upset you, Sheila.'

'No, no, you haven't, it's . . . Really, it's fine. I'm

just tired.' She gave him a weak smile. 'It's the heat.'

She changed back into her shoes and made her way across the yard, trying not to flinch away from the machinery because Bill was bound to be watching from the window, and on up the lane.

Upset and anxious, she stumbled on a crust of dried mud, scraping the side of her shoe across the opposite calf and leaving a smear of dirt on her tights. Righting herself, she reached the gate just in time to see the blurred blue and yellow checks of a police car disappearing, at speed, down the road on the far edge of the common. Then another car came, and another. And they stopped, and the men got out and went into the wood. She watched them for hours, coming and going, turning their heads sideways to speak into their radios.

'Please God,' she whispered, 'let it not be her. Let it be someone else, not her. Please.' She felt as if she were speaking into a telephone with nobody at the other end of the line. It's too late, she thought despairingly. It's happened. There's nothing I can do.

# CHAPTER SIX

Amy woke at seven, groggy and thick-headed, and headed for the shower. She stared down at the cars from the kitchen window while she ate breakfast, and thought about the diary. Then she roused herself to bag the last odds and ends, made her last trips down to the rubbish bins, and spent a sweaty half-hour staggering down the stairs with the boxes of charity stuff, which she loaded onto the back seat of her car. By the time she'd finished she needed another shower, and she'd barely finished getting dressed again when the house-clearance men buzzed from the main door. She collected her things and told them she'd be downstairs if they needed her.

She made a last journey down to the car with her overnight bag slung over her shoulder and the big chocolate box with the photo albums and the diary under her arm. She didn't want to be in the flat while it was dismantled. It was one thing bagging clothes and little things and leaving them for the bin men, but the big, solid stuff, the furniture she remembered from childhood . . . that really was it: *final*. Now Amy was nearly at the end of the process, she wanted it over as quickly as possible, with the least fuss. Except for selling the place, of course, but sorting that out would have to wait till next week, at least.

Amy sat in the car, averting her face from Wendover Court, and only catching occasional glimpses of a bed frame, chair or gate-leg table as the men carried her mother's furniture out to their van. She busied herself with phone calls—work stuff, cheerful, brisk conversations about commissions, word counts and deadlines—until the foreman startled her by rapping on the window. 'All done,' he said. 'Want to come and check?'

Amy followed him back up the stairs and looked around the empty flat. It looked pathetic and unloved, with bare light bulbs, marks on the walls where the pictures had been, stained carpet and chipped paint. The dust raised by the furniture removers caught in Amy's throat as she walked round to inspect it.

'All right, is it?'

'Looks fine.'

'Good. There's a couple of forms to sign, then we're all set.'

Amy signed where she was told, then locked up. She wondered if she ought to get someone in to repaint the flat. She could clean it herself in a few hours, but the thought of spending an entire weekend—or possibly longer—camped out in the place was unbearable, and it was a bit much to ask her friends to give her a hand. She was just locking the front door when one of the house-clearers came back up the stairs, waving an envelope.

'The boss said to give you this. One of the boys found it down the back of a drawer. He thought you might want it.' It was a brown envelope, gritty with dust.

'Thanks.' Amy waited until he'd started down the stairs, then lifted the flap and took out two letters, flimsy pages folded in half, with faded handwriting, and a newspaper cutting. She let herself back into the flat and sat down on the sitting-room carpet for a proper look.

The first letter was dated October 1954. *Dear Kathleen*, Amy read. She turned it over to see who the writer was. *Your loving sister, Iris.* The Shands must be related to us, she thought. There's no other reason for Mum to have this stuff. *I hope you will forgive me for bothering you. Just to let you know we arrived home safe and sound and now we are back everything is fine again. It must have given you quite a shock us turning up like that but don't worry because Les will look after me now. Nice to see Pat,*

37

*what a lovely girl she is.* Pat must be her mother, so presumably Kathleen was her grandmother. Which meant that Iris—mother of Mo and Sheila—was her great-aunt.

Iris had obviously gone to Kathleen in a bid to escape from Leslie. Why hadn't Kathleen helped her? Christ, Amy thought, if I had a sister who had arrived on my doorstep with two babies, seeking refuge from a husband who beat her, I wouldn't hesitate. No one would. Kathleen could have phoned the police, and—Hang on, Amy told herself. No, she couldn't. It was 1954: a different world. She'd written articles about domestic violence, reviewed books, read the testimonies of battered women and seen the statistics. Special units hadn't existed in the fifties; the problem wasn't taken seriously, and the police wouldn't have intervened. The first women's refuge wasn't opened until the 1970s. It was all a far cry from posters proclaiming zero tolerance towards men who beat their partners.

Iris must have been desperate, Amy thought. It would have taken some courage to tell her sister. Maybe Kathleen had told Iris that it was her fault, that she'd provoked Les or failed in her domestic duties. Perhaps, being ten years a widow—Patti's father had been the first man who'd deserted her, dying on a European battlefield six months before her birth—Kathleen had told Iris to be thankful that she had a husband at all. You've made your bed, now lie in it. Or perhaps Leslie had turned up, smoothed things over, and taken Iris home with him. And she'd stayed. She'd colluded. Amy felt sick. She knew too much about collusion to start making snap judgements about other people—

except, she reminded herself, that I was a *child*. Iris Shand was a grown-up woman. And so, by 1983, when the diary began, were Mo and her sister.

Amy shook her head and turned her attention to the second letter. It was dated 28 April 1968.

> *Dear Pat,*
> *Thank you for coming to visit and for the flowers, you know how much I love them. Well Pat I'm sorry how this has turned out, I can't write much but you know how it's been in my mind about Iris and the girls. I hope you will try to keep in touch with them and see them sometimes if you can. Anyway keep the details in case something happens.*
> *My dear daughter love to you with all my heart.*
> *Mum*

Amy read it through several times, wondering whether Patti had done as requested and kept in touch with the family. If so, why had she, Amy, never been told about it? Kathleen might well have thought there was something shameful in Iris's situation, but Mum was a different generation . . . Amy wondered if she'd meant to leave the letters in the chocolate box with the other things, but had either forgotten about the envelope, or, more likely since it was found down the back of a drawer, mislaid it.

Maybe the newspaper cutting would clarify things. Amy unfolded it and smoothed it out. It was a piece from the *Daily Mail*, dated 24 November 1987.

# FREED: SEX SLAVE KILLER OF EVIL FATHER

Sheila Shand, who blasted her father to death after a lifetime of torment, was spared jail yesterday.

For years perverted sadist Leslie Shand kept Sheila and her sister Maureen virtual prisoners in their home, where he beat them and forced them to have sex with him.

If they tried to argue, he held a gun to their heads. From an early age they were forced to watch as he beat their mother and tortured the family pets. Sheila, 36, and Maureen, 34, had worked as chambermaids in a local hotel, but their father took their wages and gave them just £1.50 spending money each week. Food was rationed, and they had to obey his tyrannical rules or risk a thrashing, the court was told. Fifty-nine-year-old Shand told the sisters that he would kill their mother if they ran away from home.

Mr Justice Weatherly said that Sheila and her sister had been subjected to years of degradation, violence and fear, adding, 'In some ways, your life has been a form of punishment.'

Sheila's agony ended when she walked from Enfield Crown Court after being given a three-year suspended sentence for manslaughter. She was met by her sister Maureen and their 55-year-old mother, Iris.

The piece was accompanied by a photograph of two women, one dark and one fair, with the same

40

curly hair as Amy's. She stared at it, appalled. 'Fuck,' she muttered. 'Fucking *hell*.'

# CHAPTER SEVEN

Feeling queasy, Amy went through to the kitchen for some water. As there were no glasses, she stuck her mouth under the tap, but found that she could hardly swallow. Clutching the edge of the sink, she held the liquid in her mouth until it became thick and viscous, and then spat it into the sink.

Why hadn't Patti told her? And why hadn't someone done something to save Sheila and Maureen? Even if the police wouldn't intervene in a 'domestic', incest was still a crime. Then again, it was taboo. There was no Childline in those days, and the idea of an adult talking about the sexual abuse that he or she had suffered as a child was unthinkable. Perhaps Sheila and Maureen thought they wouldn't be believed if they'd told their mother or a teacher—and very likely, she thought grimly, they wouldn't have been. She wondered when Iris had discovered it, and, more, why the sisters hadn't left home at the first opportunity. That was what normally happened with victims of sexual abuse—and they could have taken Iris with them. And yet . . . Don't rush to judgement, Amy thought. It's too easy to condemn women who stay around to be battered or raped if you've never experienced violence yourself. She remembered something she'd once read: *To a terrorised person, an open door is not an open door.*

Clearly Patti, despite Kathleen's letter, hadn't

41

been able to help Iris. Amy wondered if she'd even tried. She went back to the sitting room. There was no address on Iris's letter to Kathleen, but when she turned the newspaper cutting over she found *Compton Lodge, Potters Bar, Herts* and a telephone number written in faint pencil. Perhaps, thought Amy, Mum meant to write *me* a letter about it, but she was too ill. Or—more likely—it was a way of saying, *You thought I was bad, now see what the rest of the family is like.*

It suddenly struck her that Leslie might have *made* Mo write the diary. He'd bought it for her, hadn't he? He couldn't run the risk that she would keep an honest account of what happened, the beatings and . . . She glanced at the cutting again. *If they tried to argue, he held a gun to their heads. From an early age they were forced to watch as he beat their mother and tortured the family pets.* Of course. Mo's diary was his proof that they were an ordinary family. Maybe he'd even dictated it—that would certainly explain the contents. The idea of him standing over the mentally sick girl, making her write down an official record of her happiness, was vile. Recalling what she'd read the previous night, Amy thought that it was the cosy domestic details that made the thing so disturbing: torture and television programmes, degradation and DIY, rape, beatings and Angel Delight. If Mo had been acting as Leslie's amanuensis, she decided, he had been eager to present himself, through the diary, as a dynamic man whose wife and daughters looked up to him and who was very much in control of things, a man whom other people (like his employer Mr Drake and the women in the hospital ward) admired and respected.

42

Presumably, Iris's injuries could not be left out because they were documented elsewhere, by the GP or the Casualty doctors. In which case, those times when the beatings weren't severe enough to warrant medical attention outside the home must have gone unrecorded.

Amy looked again at the pencilled address on the back of the cutting. Compton Lodge. The name rang a bell—an old people's home. Amy had considered applying for a job there when she was researching her book about the care of the elderly. If Iris, who must now be—Amy did a quick sum—seventy-three, was in a home, it meant she was incontinent or dotty, or both. Or it might mean that Sheila and Mo were dead and she couldn't look after herself. Mo might have given Patti the details, but when? And when had she given her the diary?

She took her phone out of her handbag and dialled the number. A professionally caring voice told her that yes, Mrs Shand was a resident. 'Are you a relative?'

'Yes. I'm her great-niece.'

'Oh, I see. Well, visiting hours are two till four and six till eight.'

'Would this afternoon be convenient?'

'Of course. I'll tell her you're coming. They're always pleased to have visitors. What name shall I say?'

'Amy Vaughan. You could tell her that I'm Patti's daughter—Kathleen's granddaughter. We've never actually met, you see.'

'Not to worry. To be honest, Ms Vaughan, she is a bit confused, so we're never quite sure . . . But as I say, they're always pleased to see people.'

Amy thanked her, took down the full address and switched her phone off, wondering if 'a bit confused' meant slightly touched or full-scale Alzheimer's. The memory of her six-month stint of research, working as a carer—the relentless physical slog, the hours spent sponging and dressing liver-spotted, age-slackened bodies and wiping elderly bottoms, and the never-ending, hopeless questions (When are we going? Can we go now?) depressed her. What if Mum hadn't had cancer? she asked herself. If she'd lived and got senile, what would I have done? And Dad, what about him? God, *Dad*. Had *he* known about the Shands? Perhaps Mum had told him, perhaps he'd be able to explain. But it was pointless to speculate, because he wasn't around to ask.

Amy took the *A-Z* out of the glove compartment and planned her route to Compton Lodge. There's bound to be a charity shop on the way, she thought, where I can drop off the books, and I ought to take some flowers for Iris. She coaxed her car into life and made her way through the industrial estate and back to the main road. Heat haze blurred the metal edges of the cars in front, and, despite her second shower, she felt sweaty again. The fan only served to pump in warm petro-chemical air that clung to her skin, and when she wiped her face with a Kleenex the crisp white tissue turned limp and grey. At Hanger Lane she turned onto the North Circular, then headed north, where the flats and Tudorbethan ribbon-development houses were replaced with green belt and new executive estates with raw brick edges, manicured lawns and skinny young trees.

Amy found a charity shop in Potter's Bar where

44

they were happy to take her boxes of books, and bought a bunch of bright yellow roses at the florist next door. The woman who served her seemed to know Compton Lodge well—funeral business, Amy reasoned—and gave her directions.

Compton Lodge itself was a Victorian mansion, huge and pompous-looking, with flat-roofed add-ons at the back. The old part had obviously been divided up with minimal sensitivity some time in the seventies and given a conference-centre colour scheme about twenty years later, and the whole effect was depressing. The bell was answered by an elderly black woman in a tabard emblazoned with the words *People Who Care*, who told Amy, in a strong West Indian accent, to take a seat. The place smelt faintly of cleaning fluids and the chemical flowers of a room spray—part of the constant battle to conceal the smell of urine and excrement. The wretchedness of it all, horribly familiar from her research, made Amy's heart sink. This bland, air-freshened world of buffs, pastel colours and cheerful attendants was death row, but here the inmates had no chance of appeal, and the only mercy they could expect came from drugs and the kindness of underpaid strangers. She wondered, for about the thousandth time, why anybody wanted to live longer if it meant ending up in a smelly fog of loose-sphinctered bewilderment.

The matron who came to greet her was tidy and self-contained, with discreet gold jewellery and a brisk, no nonsense kindliness. 'Ms Vaughan? I'm Sister Paula. Iris—Mrs Shand—is in her room. Most of the others are in the residents' lounge, and of course there are activities . . . We've tried to

45

encourage her, but she seems to prefer being alone. I must say, I was a little surprised when you called—Mrs Shand's daughter comes at least twice a week, but I didn't think she had anybody else.'

'I thought there were two daughters.'

'There's only one who visits.'

'Is that Sheila, or Maureen?'

Sister Paula's eyes narrowed almost imperceptibly. 'Sheila.' Amy, who regularly experienced everything from suspicious glances to naked aggression in the course of her work, knew that this was quite low on the scale, but reassurance was clearly needed, especially if—as she suspected—Sister Paula knew about Iris Shand's past.

'You did say that you were related.'

'I'm her great-niece.'

'So that's . . .'

'My grandmother was Mrs Shand's sister.'

'But you've never met her.'

'No, but I think my mother might have visited. Iris might not remember, of course.'

Sister Paula gave a faint smile. 'We have a lot of visitors here, Ms Vaughan. I'm afraid I don't know them all personally.'

'My mother was quite striking. You might remember—long black hair, black eye make-up, usually wore a lot of jewellery.'

'Doesn't ring a bell. She certainly hasn't been here in the last few weeks.'

'No, it wouldn't have been that recently.' Amy could see that Sister Paula was getting more suspicious by the minute. 'My mother died not so long ago, you see.' Noting that the matron had already shifted her gaze slightly, she carried on, 'I

46

found this address in her papers. I wanted to follow it up because I've been thinking of doing a family tree for some time, and I've got some fascinating stuff about one of my great-grandfathers who fought in the First World War, and apparently his mother had actually been a servant in—'

'How interesting,' said Sister Paula quickly. 'I'll get someone to take you up to Iris's room, shall I? I'm sure you'll have lots to talk about.' She turned away before Amy had a chance to reply. So far, so good, Amy thought. But if Sheila was the only visitor, what had happened to Mo?

The black carer, who looked old enough to be a resident, returned and, wheezing slightly, led her upstairs. The place looked clean, with fresh paintwork, and when an elderly lady pursued them down the corridor holding an empty commode shell and asking, plaintively, 'But what do I *do* with it?' the carer answered her patiently each time. Eventually, the old lady put the commode shell on her head and wandered off, apparently quite happy. 'That,' said the carer, as if it explained everything, 'was Martha.'

It was certainly a cut above some of the geriatric gulags Amy had worked in. She thought of the first place she'd gone to, where she'd managed to get four sets of dentures mixed up, and the woman in charge had sworn at her, then snatched up the false teeth and rushed round the room ramming them into the old ladies' mouths with the heel of her hand. When Amy tried to stop the assault, the woman had snapped, 'What's the matter? They don't know the difference.' Amy had waited until she'd gone and spent half an hour taking the teeth out as gently as she could, scrubbing them and working out, by a process of elimination, who owned which set.

Amy didn't imagine anything like that would happen at Compton Lodge. The carer, who'd become talkative after the Martha episode, said, 'Iris always stay in her room. Sister Paula doesn't like it. She says Iris getting institutionalised.' She stopped to catch her breath and fanned herself before continuing, 'They *all* institutionalised. What else you gonna be in a institution? Iris doesn't say much. Even when her daughter come she don't really talk. In a world of her own. Not your fault if she won't speak—just how it is.'

The carer stopped at the end of the corridor, rapped on a door and opened it, saying, 'Iris, there's someone here to see you.' There was no reply, and at first Amy thought there was no one in the room, but then she noticed a wing-backed armchair, set in front of the bay window, with a few candy-floss tufts of white hair protruding from one side.

The carer shook her head and led Amy across the room. 'Sit here,' she said, patting the window seat. Amy sat down, facing a tiny old lady, whose wraith-like body was pressed against one side of the armchair, and whose head was thrust forward, tortoise-like, over a photograph album that lay in her lap. She was wearing a pleated skirt of pale pink, a matching blouse with a pie-frill collar and black patent leather shoes. 'This is Miss Vaughan,' said the carer brightly. 'She's come to see you. You going to say hello?'

Iris Shand gave no sign of having heard her, but carried on gazing down at her photograph album, stroking one of the snapshots.

'She's brought you some lovely flowers, look.' No response. 'Give them to me, dear,' the carer said to Amy. 'I'll put them in a vase. Now then, you going to say hello, Iris? You can show Miss Vaughan—'

'Amy.'

The carer smiled and tapped her own chest. 'Clementine.' Then she turned back to Iris. 'You can show Amy your pictures. I'm sure she'd like to see them.'

Still no response. Clementine bent down and patted Iris's knee, but the old lady shook her head irritably and shooed her away with skinny, blue-white fingers. 'That's not very nice, is it? Amy's come a long way to see you.' Nothing. 'Well, what about some tea?' asked Clementine. 'I'll go and get some, shall I?' She turned to Amy. 'Won't be long. Try talking to her.'

'Does it work?'

Clementine shrugged. 'Sometimes.'

When they were alone, Amy stood up and went to stand beside Iris's chair. 'Can I look at your pictures?'

No response. The photo Amy could see most clearly was black and white: two little girls in bell-shaped frocks, round-necked and sleeveless, with wide sashes round their midriffs, standing in a back yard. Slightly severe haircuts, perhaps, but otherwise perfectly ordinary-looking kids, with white ankle-socks and plain dark shoes with one strap across. The smaller of the two held a piebald rabbit in her arms. The animal looked uncomfortable, but the children were beaming at the camera. Behind them were a hutch, the bottom

49

of a drainpipe, and the lower half of a sash window. A pencilled date above the photograph read, *June 1959.*

Iris stroked it again and again. This scene, Amy reflected—two kids and a bunny rabbit—must be replicated in millions of British photograph albums. An ordinary snapshot, except . . . A picture paints a thousand words, and in this case, all the words, like the ones in Mo's diary, are lies. The phrases from the newspaper cutting floated through her mind. *From an early age they were forced to watch as he beat their mother and tortured the family pets . . . perverted sadist . . . virtual prisoners in their home . . . forced them to have sex with him . . . degradation, violence and fear.* That was the truth. Having to pretend, to live the lie, must have been intolerable. If Mo had been depressed, it was hardly surprising—it was a miracle that they hadn't all ended up inside a madhouse.

*In a world of her own.* That's what Clementine had said about Iris. And who could blame her? Yet, even though the banks of switches inside Iris's brain were shutting down, and she could not—or perhaps would not—respond to words, the photo album, clearly, still had some significance. But what, exactly? What was going through her mind? Flickering images of a life she'd once had, growing fainter and fainter as they retreated into the inevitable darkness?

'What pretty girls,' she said. 'Are they Sheila and Maureen?' As she leant closer to point to the photograph, Iris flinched and clutched the album against her narrow chest. 'It's all right,' said Amy. 'It's yours, I know that. I'm not going to take it away from you.'

Iris raised her head, and, for the first time, made eye-contact with Amy. Then her face crumpled into tears. Guilty and appalled, Amy grabbed a box of tissues from the bedside table, and dropped a handful into the old lady's lap. 'Please don't be upset. I'm not going to hurt you, I promise. I just came for a chat. Look,' she said desperately, as the tears continued to flow, 'can I get you something? What about some water? Would that help?'

Iris shook her head. She hadn't touched the tissues, but her hands, still clutching the photo album, seemed to relax slightly.

'Would you like me to go now?'

Another headshake.

'I'm sorry,' said Amy, 'I haven't introduced myself properly. My name's Amy Vaughan, and I'm your great-niece. From your sister Kathleen. Do you remember her?'

Again, Iris looked directly at her. Behind the glitter of tears, her gaze was unnervingly shrewd, and Amy felt uncomfortable and vaguely ashamed. 'I just thought I'd come and see you,' she said. 'See how you are.'

'You were lovely,' said Iris, in a matter-of-fact voice.

'Do you mean,' asked Amy carefully, 'when I was a baby?'

Iris nodded.

'I didn't realise you'd ever seen me,' said Amy.

Iris nodded again, as if satisfied about something, then lowered the photo album and went back to staring at the photographs.

'Did my mother, Patti, come to visit you?'

No response. Amy glanced round the room, trying to think of something else to say. Everything was soft-edged and pastel-shaded, the metal and plastic props of old age covered by knitted cosies. On Iris's bedside table slumped a blue knitted rabbit, worn out with love, and on the shelf above the bed litters of china puppies and kittens frolicked in and out of a long row of greeting cards.

'Do you mind if I look at your cards?' she asked. 'They're super.'

Iris nodded, once, without looking up, and Amy went over to examine the collection. There were about ten cards, and they were all either Mother's Day or birthday cards. None was dated, so she had no way of telling whether they were in chronological order, but the four nearest the window were signed *With love from Sheila* or *With love from Mo,* whereas the others were signed *With love from Sheila and Mo.* The handwriting—Amy made a quick comparison—was Sheila's.

Mo seemed to favour baby animals, while Sheila preferred country scenes. The very last card showed a cornfield full of poppies and cornflowers, with a little rabbit peeping coyly out from behind the yellow stalks—a fusion of both tastes—with *Happy Birthday, Mother* embossed in copperplate across the top. The rhyme inside read:

> *Wishing you more happiness*
> *Than words could ever say,*
> *Hoping that your joys increase*
> *With every passing day,*
> *For you have always*
> *Been so kind,*

*So very thoughtful too,*
*That nothing but life's very best*
*Is good enough for you!*

Underneath, Sheila had written *We can never thank you enough for all you have done for us. Your daughters, Sheila and Mo (Maureen) xxx*

As if she'd been trying to remind Iris who they were, Amy thought. She wondered what was really behind the Hallmark sentiment and the oval plaque that hung on the wall above the cards, emblazoned with the words *The Best Mum in the World* inside a border of blue flowers. She remembered the newspaper cutting: *he beat them and forced them to have sex with him.* Iris hadn't protected her children. *From an early age they were forced to watch as he beat their mother.* Judging by this display of filial affection, they didn't blame her. Yet at some point Maureen had stopped writing her own cards. Why? Perhaps she was dead, but Iris hadn't been able to take it in, and so Sheila had signed both names in order not to upset her.

As she sat down again on the window seat, Amy noticed that Iris was poring over a different page of her album. A smiling couple, arm in arm. The woman was clearly a young Iris—the date 1958 was scrawled above the picture—and the man must be her husband. Leslie Shand's handsomeness surprised Amy, but then, she thought, what did I expect? People's faces weren't the indexes of their souls. He had high cheekbones and thick, dark hair, with a cowlick in the middle of his forehead. He was only a few inches taller than Iris, which meant, given that Iris must have shrunk a bit . . .

Amy calculated that he must have been a bit shorter than her five foot nine, but he had the broad shoulders and strong body of a manual worker.

The Shands were standing in what looked like a garden, in front of a low concrete building, like a pillbox, only smaller and with sloping sides. The entrance seemed low, as if the floor might be below ground level. Amy stared for a moment, mystified, and then realised that it was an Anderson shelter, left over from the war, which had been reinforced and concreted over. There was a large padlock hanging from the door.

She was wondering if it were just chance that Iris was stroking her husband's face when Clementine wheezed in with a tray of tea and biscuits neatly arranged on a doily. 'How are we doing?' she asked breathlessly. 'I hope you're looking after your guest, Iris.'

'Oh, yes,' said Amy. 'Everything's fine.'

'She talk to you?'

'Only a few words.' It felt wrong to be discussing Iris as if she wasn't there.

Clementine nodded. 'Some days she better than others.'

They both looked at Iris, who lifted her head and stared back for a moment, puzzled, as if she had no idea what they were doing in her room. Then her head drooped again and she carried on stroking the photograph.

Amy took Clementine aside and said, 'She says she's seen me before. When I was a baby.'

'Did she?'

Amy shook her head. 'I very much doubt it.'

'Could be dementia. You look like someone,

perhaps . . . Her mind come up with odd things from time to time, just random. We got a lot in here much worse.'

Amy nodded, remembering the surreal exclamations she'd heard during her research in care homes, snatches of conversation from long ago that had been thrown up by the scrambled circuits of a brain in melt-down.

'Leave you in peace,' said Clementine. 'You want anything, ring the bell.'

'Thanks.'

As Amy poured the tea, she reflected that this level of service, and the large private room with the bay window, must mean that Iris Shand was not an NHS patient. Which meant that her family—which, if Mo were dead, or living abroad, meant Sheila—could afford to keep her here, and that, she knew, would not be cheap.

Iris refused the tea, setting her mouth in a firm line and turning her head away as if she suspected that force-feeding was about to occur. 'It's all right,' said Amy. 'No one's going to make you drink it.' Iris blinked, and then, quite suddenly, the fluffy white head drooped down to her chest. After a couple of minutes, Amy realised that she had gone to sleep.

She met Clementine in the corridor. 'You leaving?'

'She's dropped off,' said Amy. 'I didn't like to disturb her. Thanks for the tea.'

'That's OK.' Clementine gave her a shrewd look. 'You coming again?'

'Yeah. I'll be back.'

'Good. Stairs on the right, that way.' She gestured down the corridor. 'I won't come down.

55

Too much.' She patted her chest again.

' 'Course. Thanks, Clementine.'

'You're welcome.'

Amy found Sister Paula in her office. 'Could I have a quick word?'

'Of course. Have you seen Iris?'

'Yes. She nodded off.' Amy gave what she hoped was the sort of caring smile that would mirror the matron's own. 'Didn't want to overdo it.'

'I see. How can I help you?'

'I wanted to ask you about Sheila Shand,' said Amy. 'I wanted to pay her a call, but I'm not sure if the address I've got is the current one, so—'

Sister Paula held up her hand. 'I'm afraid I can't give out personal information.'

'Oh, no.' Amy laughed, as if nothing had been further from her thoughts, and continued, 'I wasn't thinking of that. I just wondered if I could leave my address and telephone number for you to give her next time she comes.'

Sister Paula considered the request for a moment and then said, cautiously, that she supposed that would be all right. Realising that the word 'journalist' would probably be anathema to Sheila Shand, Amy didn't hand over a card but wrote her details down on a piece of paper, which Sister Paula accepted.

Crossing the carpark, Amy suddenly remembered Clementine's words: *You look like someone, perhaps.* Time was meaningless to a senile person—a twenty-year age gap wouldn't register. Iris, she realised, had thought that she was *Mo.*

# CHAPTER EIGHT

Returning from work, Sheila unlocked the door of Hadley Cottage and saw the local paper on the mat. This was the moment she'd been dreading all day—confirmation, in black and white, of what the police had found in the wood. It was like when she was at school: the mounting dread as the day drew to a close, and the desperate need to see Mum, coupled with the terror of what might happen in the evening. She'd tried to concentrate on her work, but it was impossible. She couldn't think, couldn't type, couldn't even manage the filing. In the end she'd pleaded a headache, and the senior solicitor, Mr Bevan, had let her go home an hour early. She fought the claustrophobia of the panic that seemed to close in on her and tried to breathe normally, but the fear was suffocating. It was the same as when *he* was alive and they'd waited for him to return from the farm, trapped in a house that seemed to grow smaller as the minutes ticked by and her mother, shaking inside, she knew, had pecked at her hair with jerky little movements, and prepared to smile and frame the cautious, practised question: 'How's your day been, love?' And then what she knew would follow—having to watch him hit Mum. He'd hit them, too, of course, but it was always worse for her. All they could ever do, once they were old enough, was to stand on either side of her and keep her upright while he punched her and kicked her with his heavy work boots. It was safer—he would get even angrier if she fell down, and there was always a risk that she

57

might hit her head or smash against a window.

She couldn't face the newspaper yet. There was a postcard lying beside it. Sheila picked it up and, unable to concentrate on the writing, looked at the picture. It was a Greek village: a donkey standing beside a little stone church. Sheila had never been abroad, even in the eighteen years since his death—unless you counted the Isle of Wight, which you couldn't, really.

It was nice of Carol to send the card. Stepping over the paper, she recited her schoolfriends' names: Carol Price, Helen White, Sandra Pascoe, Barbara Ellis . . . She'd never forgotten them. They were the only friends she'd had, apart from Mo. Not that she was ever allowed to go to their houses for tea—*he* wouldn't have it—and she'd known, without ever having to ask, that inviting any of them home was out of the question. She'd lost touch with them all when she left school, but Carol had written to her after the trial. She'd been ashamed at first, not knowing how to answer, but they'd exchanged Christmas cards ever since, and Carol never forgot to send a postcard when she was on holiday.

People's kindness still amazed her. Of course, most of the people she met nowadays had no idea about the past, but Mr Bevan knew, and he'd still been prepared to employ her when she'd completed her office management course. That had been a revelation—being able to go to work and actually look forward to coming home in the evenings, keeping her wages to buy new clothes in proper shops instead of having to root through rancid heaps in jumble sales.

The remand centre had been all right, too,

really, and even the police station—the first night she'd ever spent away from Hadley Cottage—when she'd been overwhelmed by it all, too stunned to speak. When they started to question her, she'd had a terrible pain in her chest and thought she was having a heart attack, then felt the terrible pressure of tears behind her eyes and burning her throat, and started to cry for the first time since she was a small child. But they'd been patient, and no one got angry. Instead, a policewoman handed her a box of tissues and a cup of tea, and everyone had been so kind . . . And all the things that had happened, buried inside her, had come to the surface and suddenly she wasn't numb any more, she was telling them all the things he'd done and made them do and how frightened they were. And then, for the first time in her life, despite the threat of prison, she'd actually felt free. But it won't be like that this time, she told herself. Not when they find out what really happened.

She went into the kitchen and raised the net curtain to look across the common. No one there now. Where had they taken the body? They must be doing the tests, finding out . . . She dropped the curtain and took Carol's postcard up to the storeroom, averting her eyes from the newspaper on the mat as she passed. She stepped noiselessly up the stairs, still, after eighteen years, avoiding the bits that creaked. It was a habit they'd all fallen into long ago, moving silently around the house because even the click of a light switch was enough to set *him* off, sidling round the furniture, handling plates and cutlery individually and deadening the sound of running water by placing a sponge under the tap.

Unable to move—they couldn't afford it—they'd reclaimed the house from *him* by redecorating it in the pretty colours they'd all secretly longed for, obliterating the drab, institutional shades he'd insisted on and replacing the cold, slippery lino with thick wall-to-wall carpets. The storeroom was the only part of the house they hadn't changed, apart from the khaki walls, which were now primrose yellow. They'd pinned up pictures and cards, too; it gave the place a more cheerful look. Sheila inspected the neat metal shelving and placed the postcard next to Carol's card from last year, a cat sitting on top of a sunny wall in another Greek village.

She delved into a cardboard box marked *Odds and Ends* for drawing pins. It was next to the padlocked iron deed box where they kept their journals—exercise books, jacketed in pretty wrapping paper. The counselling lady they'd seen after the trial had told them it was good to write things down, so they had. Mum had done it right up until she got ill and started filling up the lines with curved, elongated Vs that looked like flying birds.

They'd kept most of his things, tools and items like string that always came in handy, but they'd thrown away the hammer he had used to kill the rabbits, and the big saucepan where he had made Sheila and Mo (she glanced, involuntarily, in the direction of the common) drown Velvet. To prolong the death, he had ordered them to lift the lid slightly and then bring it down as the gasping, bedraggled cat scrabbled frantically upwards, trying to get a purchase on the stainless-steel rim. He had photographed them, too, holding the lid down as they felt Velvet's struggles grow weaker beneath it, until, with one last, desperate heave, they ceased entirely. 'Smile!' Sheila could still hear him say it, and see her mother framed in the doorway behind him, her face wiped of emotion. Experience had taught them that, whatever happened, they must not shed tears—that made him more angry than almost anything—but Sheila was crying inside, and she knew that Mum and Mo were, too.

How old had they been? Sheila couldn't remember exactly, just that she'd had to stand on a box to reach the top of the pot and that he had made Mo get up there with her because she wasn't strong enough to keep poor Velvet in the water on her own. The photograph was in Mum's album— not that you'd realise what you were seeing if you didn't know. Sheila and Mo's smiles for the camera, well practised, had been so convincing that it looked like a happy family snap: two little girls helping Mum make jam.

That was the reason she couldn't bear to have a pet. When Sheila's neighbour's cat had had kittens, she'd been offered the pick of the litter, but she couldn't take one. It was bad enough when flowers died—the thought of a cat or dog dying was unbearable. As a child, she used to think that the spirits of the animals he had killed must be still in the house, poor little ghosts, trapped, tormented and broken, and even now, sometimes, at night, she still thought she heard, faint but shrill, the shrieks of pain, and the frantic, useless scrabble of paws.

Sheila went across to the window and stared out at the garden, with its jolly geraniums and petunias spilling out of moulded plastic pots. In the centre of the lawn, where the old Anderson shelter had been, was a circular flowerbed full of roses. They'd planted a special one, Velvet Fragrance, in memory of their pretty black cat, but even that didn't comfort her now.

It's no good, she thought. I've got to know. She descended the stairs slowly, clutching the banister for support, picked up the paper, and started to turn the pages. There it was: '*SKELETON*'. She took a deep breath and forced herself to read it slowly.

## SKELETON FOUND IN WOOD

A man walking his dog in Hadley Wood has discovered human remains in a drainage ditch, it was revealed yesterday. Police have not yet identified the skeleton, which is thought to be female, but a spokesman said that it may have been buried for a number of years.

'No.' Clutching the paper, Sheila lurched into the kitchen, cannoning painfully off the doorframe, and lowered herself, shaking, into a chair. That was it. They'd found the body. And this time she was on her own, with no one she could turn to and nowhere to go. She buried her head in her hands.

# CHAPTER NINE

Sitting in the taxi waiting for the lights to change, Amy rubbed her eyes. She felt exhausted, and there was so much to do: a three-thousand-word article on the continued effectiveness of anti-social behaviour orders due tomorrow, two others for next week, reviews of books she hadn't even opened, and she was supposed to be giving a talk for a journalism course in Leeds somewhere, and . . . That's your life, she told herself, not all this other business, and you ought to be getting on with it. She'd been away from it for a single weekend, but it felt like months.

The dinner party hadn't helped, either. She'd completely forgotten about it until she returned home to an answerphone message reminding her that it was this evening. She was fond of Esmé and David, but she wished they wouldn't keep introducing her to 'wonderful men'. Tonight's offering had turned out to be a forty-something zoologist called John Carver, shiny-faced and bulging out of a pink-striped shirt. He'd alarmed the neighbours when his impression of a gibbon's mating call boomed out through the French windows, and his effect on her hadn't been much better.

Given that Esmé and David had so far tried to match her up with an eco-warrior, a professor of astrophysics, a celebrity hairdresser and a plastic surgeon, Amy supposed that a man who impersoned rutting primates and looked like Bagpuss was par for the course. Where do they find them? she wondered tiredly. She wished they'd stop. Since her divorce from Paul, the few relationships she'd had had been disastrous (her fault as much as theirs, she knew), and she wasn't ready for another.

She came to with a start as the cab driver said, 'Here we are, number seven. Having a kip, were you?'

He pulled up outside her doll-sized Georgian terraced house. She had just finished paying him when another taxi pulled up, and her father jumped out, waving a black fedora hat. 'Amy! There you are.'

Amy stared at him, astonished. 'What are *you* doing here?'

'Thought I'd pay you a visit, seeing as I'm in town.'

'I've been trying to get hold of you for *months*.'

'Well, now I'm here. I'm a bit strapped, though.' He gestured at the taxi. 'If you could just sort it out for me . . .'

Amy sighed. 'What would you have done if I hadn't been here, Dad?'

'But you *are*, darling, and it's lovely to see you.' George planted a kiss on her cheek and said, 'Now then, let's have your keys.' He whisked them out of her hand and scooted up the steps to open her front door.

His taxi driver was looking remarkably cheerful. She understood why when she read the meter: £32.40. 'Glad you're back,' he said. 'He's had me driving round in circles waiting for you. Not that I mind, of course.'

I bet you don't, thought Amy, as she turned her purse upside down and scrabbled for the last of her silver. 'He's quite a character, your dad,' said the driver. 'Told me all about you.'

'That's nice,' said Amy faintly. 'I'm afraid I haven't got enough for a tip.'

'Oh, not to worry. I'll just get the door for you.' He reached round and opened it. 'He's left a couple of things in the back.'

'A couple of things' turned out to be two extremely heavy suitcases. The driver watched while she heaved them up the steps and then called, 'Need any help, love?'

'No, thanks,' she panted, adding 'you bastard' under her breath.

Amy put the cases down on the hall floor and looked up to see her father lounging in the sitting-room doorway. George Vaughan was a big man, with a handsome, roguish face and a taste for handmade suits and fedora hats. He held an unlit Cohiba in one hand and a large brandy in the other.

'I see you've managed to find the drinks cabinet,' said Amy.

George raised his glass, said, 'Cheers!' and took a large swig. 'That's the stuff for the troops.'

'You've cleaned me out,' she said, holding out her empty purse. 'I suppose there's no use asking why you didn't just get out and wait like any normal person?'

'Oh . . .' He waved his cigar at her, eyes twinkling. 'You know how it is.'

'Not really, Dad, no. Perhaps you'd like to tell me?'

'Amy, don't be like that. Haven't you got a kiss for your old dad who's come so far to see you?' The brandy slopped dangerously as he flung out his arms.

'Not at the moment. And stop trying to soft-soap me.'

'That's no way to talk to your esteemed papa.'

'It is when he turns up unannounced in the middle of the night and makes me fork out for a whopping great cab fare.'

'Amy!' He gazed at her reproachfully. 'What am I going to do with you?'

'Judging by this lot,' indicating the suitcases, 'you're going to use my house as a hotel.'

'It's only for a few days. You might be a bit more welcoming, seeing as—'

Amy held up her hand for silence. 'Actually, Dad, I've got something to tell you.'

'Oh?'

'Yes. Just wait a minute while I get sorted out.'

As she headed upstairs, George called, 'Have you got any matches?'

'In the kitchen. Second drawer on the left. And for God's sake open a window. Those things stink.'

In the bathroom, Amy ran cold water over her wrists in an effort to calm herself. How dare he turn up *now*? It was so typical—he was never there when she really needed him, and now she'd have to tell him about Mum and listen to him get sentimental, and then, after a few brandies (it was always a few, never just one) sentimental would slide into maudlin and he'd cry and berate himself for how badly he'd treated them both. She groaned, splashed her face with water, and turned off the tap. Still, she thought, at least he's here. But what was all that business with the taxi? The last time he'd dumped himself on her, he'd been running away from someone. Would that be something else she had to sort out? Amy sat down on the edge of the bath, elbows on knees, head in hands. Why couldn't she have one *normal* parent? Their interaction had always been pretty superficial—Dad only had three modes for talking to her, after all: one was his default mode, I'm-great-you're-great-life's-great, when everything he said sounded like a toast, then there was the honest-businessman-doing-his-best-in-a-crooked-world shtick, and the other one, which was how he responded whenever Amy tried to bring up the past, was lachrymose self-recrimination. The last time she'd attempted a serious conversation with him, after she'd found out the extent of Patti's treachery and was hoping to reclaim one parent, at least, from the wreckage, had been the worst of all. If he tries that again, she thought furiously, I might just murder him.

She checked that the spare-room bed was made up, and then went downstairs. Her father was leaning against the doorway of her little conservatory, puffing blue smoke into the garden. 'Care to join me?' he said, as if it was his house and not hers. 'Have a nightcap, it'll do you good.'

'I suppose it might help cushion the shock of finding you on my doorstep.'

'Don't be ungracious. I'm surprised your mother didn't teach you better manners.'

'I'm not,' muttered Amy, as she headed to the sitting room to pour herself a tot of brandy.

'You might bring it out,' George called after her. 'I could do with a top-up.'

'Here.' Amy turned on the outside light, handed over the bottle and plonked herself down on the garden bench. 'What's going on?'

'Oh, just a spot of bother. Local difficulty—nothing to worry about. You put your trust in people . . .' He gave a world-weary shrug. 'What was it you wanted to tell me, anyway?'

'Mum's dead,' said Amy brutally. 'Two weeks ago.'

George, looking deflated, levered himself away from the doorframe and sat down beside her. Then he leant forward, elbows on knees, and began rolling his brandy glass back and forth between his hands.

'The funeral was last week. I couldn't tell you because I didn't know where you were.'

The brandy glass was in one hand now. The other was over his face. Amy caught the wet heave of a sob and felt a prick of irritation at her father's easy access to his emotions. 'You knew Mum didn't have long,' she said. 'I told you the last time I saw you. That was what—eight months ago? Why didn't you phone?'

'I . . .' he choked, 'I . . .'

'What? You could have rung her, Dad, or me. All you had to do was pick up the phone. It's amazing she lasted as long as she did.' To hell with it, she thought, why should I pull my punches? 'She kept asking for you. She was waiting for you to come.'

'I'm sorry. I honestly thought you had a number for me.'

'I did. It was disconnected six months ago.'

'Sorry about that. Look, I kept meaning to call you, but I just . . . I . . .' Her father's voice was quiet, no more than a whisper. He was staring down at the herring-bone brick paving. 'I wanted to remember her like . . . like she was. Before. I

68

couldn't bear to think . . . I know I should have got in touch. I'm sorry, Amy.'

'It's a bit late for that now. She was *dying*, Dad. You could have put someone else first for once in your life.'

'It wasn't like that, Amy. I've had a hard year. Business is getting tougher all the time, and I haven't been all that well myself, and . . .' His handsome profile crumpled into tears once more. 'I couldn't bear . . . Patti . . . she was so beautiful. The first time I saw her, and she . . .' The rest of it was overtaken by loud, harsh sobs. Amy sat back, sipped her brandy and watched. Knowing that he was genuinely upset didn't stop her feeling irritated that he was coating himself in self-pity. It's like quicksand, she thought, you try and walk over it but it sucks you in and you suffocate.

' . . . been much of a husband . . . father to you . . . why I came back. I was hoping . . . If she'd still been . . . make it right . . . too late.'

'Dad, stop. I can't hear what you're saying.'

He turned towards her, shoulders heaving, eyes wet and mouth silently blubbering. Reluctantly, she put her arms round him and rubbed him on the back. 'She always said no one would ever care about me as much as she did, and she was right . . . no one . . . not like her.' Amy shuddered, remembering Patti's endless protestations of love, the excuses she'd made for him, the mood swings—the black despair when he left, followed by the absolute conviction that he'd be back, and soon—how she'd made him responsible for her happiness. George must have felt her tense away from him, because after a moment he leant back, saying, 'I'm sorry, Amy. I don't blame you for being angry with me. I deserve it.'

Recognising one of his favourite ploys for dealing with angry women—give the party you've injured a chance to yell without defending yourself and she'll end up forgiving you, and apologising into the bargain—Amy said brusquely, 'Yes, you do.'

'I've let you down.'

'Yes, you have. And Mum.'

'You had to do it all on your own.'

'Yes, I did.'

'I don't mind if you want to have a go at me, you know.'

'I'm sure you don't,' said Amy coldly, 'but as it won't make one iota of difference to the way you behave, I shan't waste my breath.'

George sighed. 'Fair enough. But I know how you must feel.'

'No, you don't. You don't have a clue how I feel.'

'I've said I don't blame you, cherub.'

'Will you stop all this bollocks about not blaming me! It's like you're doing me a favour by allowing me to be angry—as if it's childish or self-indulgent or something. Well, it isn't. It's the rational response *to the shitty way you have behaved.*'

'OK, OK.' George put his hands up in a gesture of defeat. 'Well, now I'm here, maybe I can help a bit.'

'You could start by wiping your nose.'

'Sorry.' He plied his handkerchief. 'Better?'

Amy nodded, angry that she'd allowed herself to be goaded into an outburst. Having sidestepped the first trap, she'd promptly fallen smack into the second.

'Actually, Dad, there's not that much left to do.'

'What about the flat?'

'Well, I've cleared all the stuff out, and—Oh, before I forget, I've got something for you.' She ran upstairs and unstuck the envelope from the lid of the chocolate box. She debated showing George the photograph albums, but didn't trust his reaction—she didn't think she could cope with any crass, throwaway remarks. Glancing at Maureen Shand's diary, she decided now was not the time to mention that, either.

'Here. It's from Mum.'

George turned the envelope over as casually as if she'd just handed him a holiday postcard, and was about to open it when Amy said, 'I think you ought to read it on your own, Dad. It says Private.'

'Oh well.' He glanced at the envelope again and tucked it inside his jacket. 'You're probably right.'

She looked at him for a moment and then said, shrewdly, 'Sorry, I interrupted you. You were about to ask who gets the flat, weren't you? I do.'

'Well, that's only fair, sweetheart.'

'It's astonishing. Given that Mum had gone to the trouble of making a will, I thought she'd leave everything to you.'

'Of course she left it to you. It's only natural.'

'Not for Mum. You didn't see what she was like at the end, Dad. She wouldn't even speak to me. She thought it was my fault you weren't there.'

'Don't, Amy. I feel bad enough as it is.'

'Anyway, I'm going to sell it.'

'Well, I can certainly help with that. I know some good people.'

'No, thanks, it's all arranged,' Amy lied.

'I'd like to do *something*, cherub.'

'Well, if you're serious . . .'

'Tell me.'

'It needs a good clean, and I think it probably ought to have a lick of paint, as well.'

'Fair enough. Give me the keys, and I'll get on to it. To be honest, Amy . . .'

Here we go, she thought. 'Dad, I'm really tired, and—'

'I'm sorry.' George put a restraining hand on her arm. 'I know it isn't a good time to tell you this, but there's probably never a good time, so . . .'

'Tell me what?'

'Well, they've got to run some more tests, but . . .'

'What for?'

'Well, it's not confirmed, but they seem to think I might have . . . you know'—he lowered his voice—'cancer.'

'What sort of cancer? People can live for—'

'Pancreatic cancer. It's a nasty one, Amy. And if that does turn out to be the case, well, I don't want to be messed about with. I was thinking the other day about when you were a kid, how sick you were. Half the time I was sure that all the needles and muck they were putting into you were doing more harm than—'

'Dad! Don't you ever listen? I told you about that. It was Mum.'

'I know, chicky,' he said vaguely. 'Patti had some very strange ideas. But God, she was beautiful.' He smiled, a faraway look in his eye. 'Glorious. And sexy, of course. Do you know, the first time we—'

'Dad, stop it! I don't want to know.'

There was silence for a moment. George

sloshed more brandy into his glass and then, as an afterthought, offered the bottle to Amy. She shook her head. She was struggling with her feelings—embarrassment and bewilderment fought against anger and guilt (after all, he had been telling her he might be dying and she'd cut across him). Only Dad, she thought, could provoke such a clash of emotions. 'What were you saying about the treatment?'

'Just that I don't want any. I'm not going through all that.'

'How certain are they? I mean, you look fine, and you bounced out of that taxi like a spring lamb.'

He shrugged. 'Good days and bad days. It's the backache that really cripples you, but it's not so bad now. They've given me some stuff.' He got up and bent over to kiss Amy on the forehead. 'Now, if you don't mind, I'll take this'—he indicated the glass—'up to bed with me. Need some shut-eye. Where's the spare room?'

'Upstairs, at the back. The bed's made up. I'll bring your cases.'

He shook his head. 'I'll manage. Just need to take a few things out. I'm sorry about your mother, cherub. It's bad news all round, I'm afraid.'

'Yes. Are you sure there's nothing I can get you? A glass of water, or—'

'Never touch the stuff. You know what W. C. Fields said about water, don't you?'

'Yes, thanks.'

'Well, then. Don't worry, I'll be fine. Goodnight, cherub. Sleep tight.'

' 'Night, Dad.'

George removed himself with the stiffly

73

unstable gait of the slightly drunk, and Amy remained slumped on the bench, staring into the darkness beyond the circle of illumination from the garden light, too shocked to think properly. She wondered about the symptoms of pancreatic cancer. Back pain, she thought—Dad had mentioned that—and weight loss, although he didn't look thinner than when she'd last seen him. And what about jaundice? Or perhaps that came later on. Surely he wasn't supposed to be drinking—unless that was if you had liver cancer— but in any case, she thought, he wouldn't listen if someone told him to stop, so it wasn't conclusive. That remark about the treatment she'd had as a kid making her worse—he couldn't be turning the tables, could he? But he'd said he didn't *want* any treatment. The trouble is, she thought, you just never knew with Dad. Talking to him was like trying to catch bathwater in your fingers. But surely, straight after the news about Mum, pretending to be ill would be too much, even for him.

A surge of anger pricked her eyes with tears. She didn't know who she hated more: herself for thinking that her father might be lying, or him for giving her cause to think it. And as for that comment about her mother being sexy . . . He was never going to confront what her mother had done to her, even now. George wanted to stick to Patti's version of the story because it allowed him to wallow in self-pity. Talking about it properly was out of the question, because that would mean counting the true cost of his behaviour. Anyway, it didn't fit with how he'd decided to remember Mum. Patti, the beautiful, sexy victim, was set fast,

74

and Munchausen's could have no place in the picture.

# CHAPTER TEN

Amy knew she wouldn't be able to sleep. She spotted the brandy bottle just inside the conservatory door where Dad had left it, and decided she might as well have another, but as she stood up a squirt of something wet hit her on the cheek, making her jump. She spun round. It had come from the left—Mrs Buchanan next door. What on earth was she doing? She gasped as another jet hit her squarely between the eyes. She mopped her face, then padded across the flowerbed, put her hands on top of the brick wall— it wasn't that high—and pulled herself up to have a look. Instead of the sturdy, shelf-bosomed form of her neighbour, standing under the security light was—Amy blinked—a *naked man*. With (she couldn't help noticing) a very nice bum.

The man must have heard her, because he whirled round, and, before she had a chance to speak, pointed a gun at her. She ducked behind the wall, but not fast enough—something hit her just above the temple. She yelped, thinking she'd been shot, but it hadn't hurt, and when she put her hand up to her face she realised that the liquid trickling down her cheek was water, not blood. She scrambled up the wall again and shouted, 'Hey!'

The man put his hands up in a gesture of surrender, realised what he was exposing, and covered himself. Dangling from his finger and thumb was something pink and . . . wait . . . transparent . . . and *plastic*. A water pistol. Before she could say anything, he yelled, 'Oh my God' and dived out of sight through Mrs Buchanan's back door.

'Stop!' she shouted after him. 'What are you doing?' Moira Buchanan was made of stern stuff, but finding a naked man in her bedroom at gone two with a water pistol and God knows what intent might just give her a heart attack. Amy dashed into the sitting room to call the police, and was just about to dial the second 9 when the doorbell rang, and a man's voice called, 'It's me—from next door. It's all right.'

Amy put down the receiver and went out into the hall. George appeared in pyjamas at the bend of the stairs, and whispered, 'Don't open the door. Turn the light out.' He's frightened, Amy thought, really frightened. I can hear it in his voice. 'It's the man from next door, Dad,' she said. 'He knows I'm here.'

The words 'I just wanted to apologise' issued from the letter box.

'What does he want?' hissed George.

'I'm sorry I scared you,' said the voice, 'but it's all right, I've put some clothes on.'

'*What?*'

'Dad, it's OK. Leave it to me.'

The doorbell rang again. George muttered, 'For Christ's sake,' and retreated back up the stairs.

'Hang on a minute.' Without taking the chain off, Amy opened the front door and peered through the two-inch space. Standing in front of her, under the porch light, was a tall, well-built man, dressed in jeans and pulling a T-shirt over his head. When his face emerged, sunburnt and topped with dishevelled hair, his eyes locked on Amy's, and the change in the atmosphere was almost physical. Like a drop in pressure, she thought afterwards, that makes your ears pop. Without really knowing she was doing it, Amy unchained the door and they stared at each other for what seemed a long time before he spoke. 'I'm so sorry, I just wanted to explain. I'm Moira Buchanan's nephew, and I'm staying with her.' His voice was deep and thick, like chocolate. Get a grip, Amy told herself.

'I thought you might, you know, call the police or something, and I wanted you to know I'm quite harmless. Sorry, that sounds as if I've just escaped from a cage somewhere, but . . . Look, you can ring her up and check if you like. I mean, I'd rather you didn't, because she's asleep, but I know you know her because she's mentioned you, and . . . I'm sorry, I'm not making a very good job of this . . . If there's anything I can do to, you know . . .'

'Er, you might want to . . .' Amy gestured at his crotch.

'Oh, God!' He yanked the zip up so violently that she half expected a scream of pain.

'Can I ask you something?'

'Er, sure.'

'What were you doing, exactly? In the garden, I mean.'

'It's the cats.'

'Cats?'

'The bloody things keep crapping everywhere. I've been helping Aunt Moy with some digging, and I'd just had a shower when I saw one, so I grabbed the water pistol and went out—it went

77

towards your garden, so I thought a couple of warning shots—I didn't want to hurt it or anything—and then . . . Well, you know the rest. I'm truly sorry. You must think I'm mad—it's just I didn't think anyone would be around.'

'That's all right, it's fine, really,' Amy gabbled. 'Please don't worry about it.'

'I'll say goodnight, then.'

'G-goodnight.'

Amy closed the door, feeling drained and slightly hysterical. She could feel the bubbles of giggles bursting inside her. She knew that if she gave way to the enormous whoop that was trying to make its way upwards from her chest, she wouldn't be able to control herself, and knew, too, that the laughter was perilously close to tears. She stood beside the door with teeth, fists and buttocks clenched, willing herself not to erupt.

She'd just about managed a semblance of calm when the bell rang again, and a voice called through the letter box, 'I'm sorry, it's me again. I'm afraid I've managed to lock myself out, and—'

'Wait a minute.' Amy opened the door again.

The man looked, if possible, more dishevelled than before. 'I thought I might be able to climb over the railings and open a window, but the gap's too wide. You must think I'm a complete idiot, but if I could just nip over your wall . . . I left the back door open, you see.'

'Come in.'

As Amy led the way down the hall to the conservatory, her father re-appeared, looking worried and adjusting his pyjamas. 'What the hell's going on?'

'Dad, this is . . .'

78

'Charlie Deakin.'

' . . . from next door. He's locked himself out.'

'I'm terribly sorry to have woken you,' said Charlie.

'Not at all.' Relief gave George's voice a hearty, back-slapping quality. 'Don't worry. Done the same thing myself. I'll say goodnight, then.'

' 'Night, Dad.'

When he'd gone, Charlie said, 'I don't know what to say. I feel awful about this.'

'Don't be silly. He'd only just gone to bed. He doesn't live here,' she added, unnecessarily, 'he's just staying for a few days.'

'Oh . . . That's nice.'

'Yes, well . . . I don't get much chance to see him. I'm Amy Vaughan, by the way.'

'Charlie.' He held out his hand and retained hers for a fraction longer than was strictly necessary. After a slight pause, he said, 'Is it through here?'

'Oh. Yes. I'll show you.'

He refused Amy's offer of a ladder, said goodnight, then scrambled over the wall and disappeared, leaving her to lock the door and trudge upstairs to bed.

Dad's afraid, she thought again. She had a sudden, hideously vivid flashback of an excruciating encounter with one of her father's victims, an elderly author she'd met at a party who'd been induced to part with his life's savings. The memory of the gaunt old man with the blank, unmoving expression and shaking hands of Parkinson's disease, who'd taken four attempts to tell her—'Your father said it was a good investment, and I trusted him'—still scalded her

79

with shame. And, she thought, there are dozens more like him, not to mention bankrupted business partners and unpaid bills, and they aren't all defenceless pensioners, either. Some of them are downright dangerous. That was the reason for him not getting out of the taxi. But if he thought they'd follow him . . . Bloody hell. She jumped out of bed and ran downstairs to check that all the doors and windows were locked and the shutters barred.

Satisfied, she was about to return to her room when she caught sight of George's suitcases lying in the hall. Supposing he really is dying? she thought. I can't turn him out to fend for himself if he's got people after him. Firmly suppressing the thought that if those people (whoever they were) knew where he was, they might use her to get to him, Amy gingerly lowered the first case onto its side and sprang the catches. She lifted things carefully, looking for proof—pills, or a doctor's letter—but found nothing. Perhaps he'd taken his medicine upstairs. But surely he couldn't wash it down with brandy? And he'd refused her offer of water.

Amy had just got the second case open when a creaking from above made her look up. Her father was silhouetted against the landing window. She had no idea how long he'd been watching her. It was too dark to see the expression on his face, but before she could speak, he said, in a thick voice, 'Go to bed, Amy. It's late.'

He's been crying, she thought in astonishment. Not in front of anybody, not to any purpose, but on his own. Was it his fear, the illness, Patti, or everything? She snapped the locks on the second case, stood it upright, and went back upstairs to bed, where she lay for a long time, thinking.

# CHAPTER ELEVEN

'Thank you, Bill. I shan't be long.'

'Take as much time as you need. I'll be here.' Bill Drake settled himself into one of the armchairs in the foyer of Compton Lodge.

'I am sorry about this.' Sheila knew she'd told the lie several times already, but felt compelled to repeat it. 'As I said, I can't explain it but I had this funny feeling that I ought to see Mum this evening.'

Following Clementine up the stairs to Iris's room, the newspaper folded in her handbag, Sheila thought, it won't do any good, Mum won't understand me. But there was always a chance. Supposing somebody else showed her the newspaper, or talked about it, and Iris were to say something? Nobody would take the word of a senile woman, but all the same, you never knew what she might suddenly remember. Sheila had been thinking about it all day at work, and most of the previous night, the harsh clamour of panic mounting inside her until she thought she was going to scream. In the end, she couldn't bear it. She had to do something. And Mo . . . Oh, God, *Mo*.

She tried to be as calm as possible as she sat down beside Iris. To avoid looking at the ever-present photo album, she stared fixedly at the side of her mother's head while she told her what was happening at home—the new loose covers, how there were more birds in the garden since she'd put the new feeders out, how she'd heard a woman in the hairdresser talking about how birds can catch diseases from bird-tables and felt glad that she hadn't pushed the boat out and bought one of those. Her whole body seemed to ache with the effort of dredging the words up and getting them out of her mouth.

'Mo's keeping well,' she said, finally. 'She sends her love.'

Usually, Iris remained impassive when she said this, but this time, she'd nodded vigorously and said, 'She came to see me.'

'She . . . came to see you?'

'Yes,' said Iris firmly.

'That's nice,' said Sheila. Mum's imagining things, she thought. She must have had a dream. 'Mum,' she said, 'I've got something to show you.' She took the newspaper out of her bag and unfolded it at the right page. 'Look, Mum. There. "Skeleton Found in Wood." They've found her.'

Iris snatched the paper and clutched it to her chest, eyes angry, mumbling something Sheila couldn't catch.

She tried again. 'You can't keep it. I just wanted to show you—to make sure you won't say anything. If anyone mentions it, or if they ask, you mustn't talk about it.' A sudden vision of her father, towering over her, made her blink and lick her lips: *If you ever talk outside about what goes on in this family, I'll kill the lot of you.*

'Do you understand, Mum?' she asked. 'You mustn't tell anyone. Give me back the paper.' Sheila held out her hand. Iris drew back, hunching herself behind the wing of her armchair, and began keening, as if some long-dammed-up grief had suddenly been released. When Sheila tried to quiet her, the wailing only grew louder, welling up from somewhere deep inside her. 'Mum, stop. Please, Mum, please.' The sound was terrible. She couldn't bear it. 'Stop it!' she shouted into Iris's contorted face. 'Stop it!'

'You OK, Miss Shand?' It was Clementine. 'What's the matter?'

'I don't know,' said Sheila, in despair. 'I asked if I could have my newspaper back, and she just . . . She won't stop.'

Clementine knelt down beside Iris's chair. 'It's all right, darling,' she said. 'You can keep the paper. Come on, quiet now. No one gonna take it away from you.' Iris's howls subsided, and she blinked at Clementine, hiccupping slightly. 'There. That better. All better now.'

Clementine scrambled to her feet. 'Don't worry, Miss Shand. Just an upset. Let her keep the paper if she wants it.'

Sheila stared at her mother in horror. On either side of Iris's liver-spotted fingers, she could make out the words 'Skeleton' and 'Wood'. There's nothing I can do, she thought. I'll have to leave it with her. 'Goodbye, Mum,' she said helplessly. 'I'll come again on Saturday.' She remembers, Sheila thought. I've brought it all back. What if she starts telling people about it? I should never have shown it to her. I wanted . . . What had she wanted? Just to tell Mum. Not to have to go through it alone.

In the car, Sheila felt suffocated by a heavy grey pall of anxiety. It was like when Dad was alive, always trying to anticipate the things that would make him lose his temper: the television too loud or soft, a drawer left open, the curtains not closed exactly at sunset . . .

What would happen to her if they found out? And what about Bill? She watched him out of the corner of her eye, driving along, frowning slightly. Perhaps they wouldn't be able to find out whose body it was. She tried to comfort herself that it was a long time ago and the police might not bother in the way that they would over someone who had died yesterday, but it didn't help. Being a long time ago didn't make it right.

Refusing Bill's offer of a cup of tea, she asked him to drop her off in front of her house, and, moving like sleepwalker, unlocked the door and made her way into the sitting room. She stood for a moment, swaying slightly, in front of the mantelpiece, immobilised by a sudden physical memory: the deep, agonising hollow she'd felt inside after the first time *he* had done it to her. She was twelve again, tottering out of the Anderson shelter before collapsing like a newborn foal on the scrubby lawn, and then staggering up to the bathroom and trying to wipe the strange slimy stuff from between her legs with a hard sheet of Izal toilet roll, all the time knowing with a horrible, stomach-churning certainty that it was going to happen again and again and there was nothing that she, or Mum, or anyone else in the world could do to prevent it.

She picked up one of the silver-framed photographs—it was an effort to raise her arm— and took it over to her favourite armchair. It had been taken at Whitstable in 1988: their first holiday. Mo and Mum, smiling over vanilla ice creams with Flakes ('Ooh, go on, then') sticking out of the tops. They'd been all right then. A honeymoon period, the counsellor had called it. Before it all started to go wrong.

Sheila felt as if she were staring at the picture through a thick fog. She needed to lie down, but hauling herself up the stairs seemed an impossible task. Halfway up, the effort of holding the banister and keeping upright was so great that she thought she was going to faint, but somehow she managed the last, daunting steps, and shuffled across the landing and into her room, where she lay down on her bed, making no attempt to wipe away the slow tears that trickled across her cheeks and down into her ears.

She thought of the pills that she and Mo had stockpiled while *he* was alive, in case anything happened to Mum. Their escape route. She'd kept them—she'd never been quite sure why. Just a feeling, really—the insurance of a lethal dose being reassuring in a way she couldn't explain, especially as she couldn't use them. Not while Mum was alive, or Bill.

She was so lonely. It was like the feeling when Mum was in hospital for the night and she was at home with Mo and Dad. She knew Mum enjoyed it—the pain was worth it, with everyone being so kind and polite, treating her like a person—but she'd told them it would have been even nicer if she hadn't always been worrying about what was happening at home. Sheila hadn't grudged Mum those brief 'holidays', but she'd dreaded them because it made Dad more tense than ever, more ready to explode with anger at the slightest thing. And it meant he'd want sex from her, even if it wasn't Saturday. The stimulus of a sexy picture in a paper or a flirty woman on television would be enough to set him off, and she'd sit beside him through long, tense evenings in front of the box, praying that there'd be nothing suggestive. For some reason, comedy shows were the worst—most of the time she didn't understand the innuendos themselves, but the capering music of Benny Hill or a wave of smutty laughter always seemed to pursue her out of the door when he jerked his head for her to go out to the Anderson shelter.

The room seemed to darken and shrink, as if the ceiling had suddenly dropped by several feet, pressing down on her. In the past, she'd held these feelings at bay by watching a favourite film like *The Sound of Music*, or . . . What else had she done? She couldn't remember. I'm trapped, she thought. Stuck. I can't die, and I can't go on living, either. Not like this.

She glanced at the clock—20.45; then went to the bathroom to clean her teeth. She closed the bedroom curtains and undressed as she always did, taking off her outer clothes and pulling her pink cotton nightdress over her head before removing her bra and half-slip, then sat down on the side of the bed. She took two sleeping tablets from the drawer of the bedside table, washed them down with a glass of water from the jug, and tucked herself neatly under the covers. Her last image before the chemicals overtook her mind was of *him* slumped on the rug in the sitting room, head turned to the side and jaw slack, as if he were asleep. But his grey cardigan was unzipped, and the white vest it revealed was soaked bright red from the pulpy mess in his chest. She was standing

86

in front of him, staring, and from somewhere behind her (the doorway, perhaps?) Mo had whispered, 'Is he dead? Is he really dead?'

Yes, he's dead. Had she said that aloud, or just thought it? She could never remember.

# CHAPTER TWELVE

A knock on the study door made her jump. 'Amy?'

'Yes?'

Her father opened the door, dressed in a beautifully cut linen suit and carrying a tray of coffee, a cigar-stub clamped between his teeth. 'How's it going?'

'All right, thanks. Put it down there.' She patted a stack of papers.

'It's eleven o'clock.'

'It can't be.'

'It is. How about I take you out for lunch later? Cheer us up a bit, after last night.'

'Well . . .' Amy considered. The article was going better than she'd expected. 'If it's a late one.'

'Fair enough. You'd better choose the place, though. I don't know this end of town at all. But make it somewhere decent.' He lit the ragged end of his Cohiba and enveloped her in a cloud of smoke. 'My treat.'

'Can you afford it?'

'*Amy.*' He looked wounded. 'I've got plastic.'

'In that case, why didn't you go to a cashpoint last night? The taxi would have waited.'

'Not enough time.'

Amy pushed her chair back, exasperated. 'But

you were waiting for me, driving round in circles! We do have cash machines round here, you know. There's someone after you, isn't there?'

George coughed, and batted ineffectually at the smoke.

'That's why you were scared last night, isn't it?'

'I was worried about *you*, cherub. It could have been anyone out there. You ought to be more careful about opening the door. Who was that chap, anyway?'

'My neighbour. I told you. Don't change the subject. There *is* someone after you.'

George looked her straight in the eye. Great, she thought, he's going to tell me a thumping great lie.

'No, love. I was confused, that's all. Worried about Patti, and what I had to tell you. I wasn't thinking straight. To be honest, it didn't cross my mind. I was just concerned with getting to you.' He put his hands on the edge of the desk and leant over, eyes searching her face. 'You do believe me, don't you?'

Amy sighed. 'I don't have much choice, do I? Would you mind opening a window? I think I'm going to suffocate.'

He undid the catch and lowered the top half of the sash window. 'There you go. What about one o'clock for lunch? Would that be all right?'

'One thirty. Give me an extra half-hour.'

As she dithered over what to wear, Amy told herself repeatedly that she must, *must*, finish the ASBO piece in the evening, after she'd recovered from lunch (which, if typical, would last at least three hours and be super-alcoholic, because George was impossible to resist). Trying to find decent clothes—most of her favourite stuff needed dry-cleaning and the laundry was erupting out of the top of the basket—made her realise how much she'd let the domestic side of things slip since her mother's death.

She finally settled for a pale blue shift dress and kitten heels, which got an approving nod. The reasonably priced restaurant she'd chosen was not, however, what George had in mind. 'I said I'd take you to a restaurant, not a transport caff. Isn't there anywhere decent round here?'

'Decent' turned out to mean a modish, over-priced eatery, all blond wood and designer-clad waitrons who looked like resting models. Amy felt that she was clashing with the décor and wished she'd worn taupe. George, on the other hand, blended in perfectly, and seemed delighted by the whole thing.

He selected a table by the window, and they settled down to fois gras (him) and pear and pecorino with basil (her). George held up his glass of Claret to be clinked. 'Here's to us.'

'Dad?'

'Yes, my child?'

'I don't want to nag, but are you supposed to be drinking?'

'Mmm?'

'Haven't they told you to lay off a bit?'

'Wouldn't listen if they had. I told you, Amy, I'm not going to be mucked around with.' He raised his glass again. 'To my favourite daughter.'

'I thought I was your only daughter.'

'So you are. Mind you, I always wanted more children. Patti wasn't keen, though.'

'I'm not surprised. You are supposed to do a bit

more than be present at the conception, you know.'

He sighed. 'I know, sweetheart. That's why I'm here now.' He put his hand over hers. 'Let's enjoy it while we can, shall we?'

'Mmm.' Amy sipped her wine. 'Can I ask you something?'

' 'Course you can.'

'It about Mum's relatives.'

'I wasn't aware she had any. Apart from her mother, and she died years ago.'

'Did you know her?'

'I don't think I'd go that far. I met her a couple of times, but . . .' He shrugged. 'She and Patti weren't very close.'

'What was she like?'

'Beautiful, like Patti, or she had been. Sad, though. Depressed. I don't think she went out much. You know she topped herself, don't you?'

'No,' said Amy shortly, 'I didn't. Mum never really talked about her.'

'Overdose of sleeping pills. Patti said she never got over her father's death—Patti's dad, I mean, not her own.'

'When did she die?'

' 'Sixty-eight, I think, or 'sixty-nine.'

'Dad, when I was in Mum's flat, clearing up, I discovered this.' Amy fished the newspaper cutting out of her handbag and passed it across the table. 'It turns out that we're—well, you're not, but I am—related to these people.'

When he scanned the headline, his eyebrows shot up, and she could follow the points being made from his expression, as if she were reading along with him: *perverted sadist Leslie Shand . . .*

90

*forced them to have sex with him . . . From an early age . . . told the sisters that he would kill their mother . . . degradation, violence and fear . . .*

He put the cutting down. He looked confused, and Amy felt sick with disappointment. She realised that she had—in some vague, unspecified way, and despite all the evidence to the contrary—expected him to provide her with answers to her questions, answers that would help her make sense of everything, not just the Shands, but Mum, and all of it. She'd imagined herself on the cusp of some great discovery, and it wasn't going to happen.

'Jesus,' he said, 'but I don't see . . . Why do you think you're related to them?'

'Look at this.' Amy produced Iris's letter to her grandmother, and sat in silence while he read it. 'Kathleen didn't help her,' she said. 'She sent her away, or . . . I don't know. Something happened. But they went back to Leslie. And then I found this.' She handed over her grandmother's letter to Patti. 'It was obviously preying on her mind, and she wanted Mum to do something.'

George shook his head. 'I don't know what to say.'

Amy turned the letter round to face her, and re-read it. 'You don't think this was Kathleen's last letter, do you? Her suicide note?'

'It seems a bit . . .' He hesitated. 'I was going to say, it seems a bit prosaic, but then I don't know what a suicide note's supposed to look like. I've never seen one.'

'*I'm sorry how this has turned out*,' read Amy. 'That could mean . . . And the stuff about Iris means it must have been on her mind. Perhaps she felt guilty about it. Not helping them, I mean.'

'Maybe. But there was probably nothing she could have done, and . . . It's no good, cherub, I don't know.'

'So you keep saying. Did you really have no idea about this?'

'Nope. Not a dicky-bird. Patti never mentioned it.'

'Nothing in that letter I gave you?'

George shook his head.

'But it's terrible . . . it's . . .'

'I know, chicky.' He patted her knee. 'I know. It doesn't bear thinking about.'

'Dad, for God's sake! I have just discovered that I am related to the family from hell, and frankly, I'm finding it bloody difficult to think about anything else at the moment. I can't just dismiss it, can I?'

'I think I would, if I were you.'

'Well, you're not me, and I want to know what happened. I mean, why did Mum keep these letters if she wasn't going to do anything about it? And there's a diary, too, belonging to one of the daughters—when did she get hold of that? And why didn't she tell me about them?'

'No idea.'

'There's an address, though.' She turned the cutting over to show him. 'That's Mum's writing. She must have got this recently, because it's the care home where Iris lives. I went to see her.'

'Why?'

'Because I wanted to *know*. I feel responsible. Mum must have left those things for a reason.'

'But what can you do? The bloke's dead now, isn't he?'

92

'Yes, but all the same . . .'

George gave her a shrewd look. 'Be interesting to write about—family skeletons and all that.'

Amy felt uncomfortable. She couldn't pretend it hadn't occurred to her, but she'd shoved the thought firmly to the back of her mind. 'It's not about that, Dad.'

The waitress sashayed towards them to remove the plates, and the main course arrived.

'So,' asked her father, tucking into Queen scallops, 'what did you find out?'

'Not much. Iris Shand's pretty senile. But it's odd, because that diary I mentioned—it belonged to the younger daughter, Maureen—it's a sort of bowdlerised version. There's not a word about the violence, just a lot of stuff about the mother having accidents, and nothing about how frightened they must have been. I was wondering if Leslie might have forced Maureen to write it like that.'

George raised his eyebrows. 'That *is* odd. Will you go and see Iris again?'

'Yeah. I wasn't sure at first, but I think I will.'

By the time her father called for brandy and the bill, Amy, who'd picked at her lunch while somehow managing to put away three enormous glasses of Sancerre, was feeling a bit tipsy, but not enough to be surprised when the waitress put his card back on the table and said, 'I'm sorry, sir, but this hasn't been acccepted.'

George stared at her as if such a thing was unheard of, and said, 'Must be a cock-up at the bank. I've got another one somewhere.' He patted his pockets. 'Wretched people don't know what they're doing . . . I seem to have left my other cards at home. If you could just mop this up, cherub, we'll settle later.'

Amy sighed, pulled a card out of her purse, and plonked it down on the plate. Dad passed it up to the waitress, beaming. 'There you go.' She wished she'd asked for a brandy when she saw the amount on the slip.

'Nice place, this,' said her father. 'Might make it my regular while I'm here.'

'Not if I'm paying,' Amy said. 'I'm not J. K. Rowling, you know.'

'Oh, don't worry about that. I'll sort it out first thing tomorrow.' He looked round the restaurant and pulled out a Cohiba. 'We're the last ones here. You don't think they'd object to one of these, do you?'

# CHAPTER THIRTEEN

Amy sat up until almost two o'clock finishing her ASBO article, constantly distracted by thoughts of the Shands, then slept badly because of all the coffee she'd had to drink, and woke up the following morning feeling exhausted. Still, she thought, sipping water, at least I can sit out in the garden to look at those books I'm meant to review. They were on the kitchen table on top of a pile of papers; two glossy, doorstop hardbacks—*The Cultural State: A Biography of the Arts Council*, and a book about women in the trade union movement. Amy groaned. She'd really have to pay attention, especially to the second one—she was meant to be talking about it on *Woman's Hour*.

George marched in when she was halfway

through her breakfast. Wrapped in his handsome silk dressing gown, and already shaved, he looked relaxed, happy, and far better than he had done the previous morning.

'Coffee?'

'Wouldn't say no.'

'Well, the pot's there, and the mugs are in the cupboard.'

'What are you up to today?'

Amy flapped her hand at the books. He picked up the top one and perused it. 'Blimey. Not what you'd call light reading.'

'You can say that again. What are you doing to do?'

'Have breakfast. I'll do myself some eggs, if that's all right, and then I thought I'd go and see about that flat of yours.'

'You'll clean it?' asked Amy, incredulously.

'I'm not entirely useless, you know.'

'But you'll need *stuff*. You can't lug a Hoover all the way over there.'

'Leave it to me.' George tapped the side of his nose. 'Ways and means. Have you got the keys?'

'Well, if you're sure.' Amy, distracted, was glad to turn the problem over to someone else, even if it was her father, and dredged a set of keys from the bottom of her bag. 'How will you get there?'

'Train. Off you go, then. Don't want to hold you up.'

Amy carted the books and her laptop into the garden and settled down to read. Without the pressure of an immediate deadline, her thoughts kept straying to the Shands, and at half past four, unable to bear it any longer, she went indoors to phone Directory Enquiries in the hope of getting a number for Mo or Sheila. When she gave the names and the Hadley Cottage address, the operator told her that the number was unlisted and that he could not confirm whether the names she had given were those of the current occupants. Amy put the phone down, thought for a moment, then grabbed Mo's diary and her bag and went out to the car. She'd have to work late to make up for the lost hours, but what the hell. She wasn't going to be able to concentrate until she'd found out, anyway.

Parked in the full glare of the sun, the car was an oven again. Amy winced as her thin skirt rode up and her bare legs touched the seat, and rolled all the windows down as far as she could. The tarmac on Holloway Road seemed to be melting in a haze of heat and sluggish, irritable cars. Halfway down, she stopped at a photocopy shop and, feeling guilty, spent a fortune getting the entire diary copied. Driving away, with paper sliding across the back seat, she tried to rehearse what to say to the Shand sisters, always supposing that they, or one of them, still lived at Hadley Cottage. It would be interesting to see what the place looked like, in any case, and perhaps the farm was still nearby.

Amy got slightly lost on the outskirts of Barnet, and ended up doubling back and approaching Monken Hadley Common on the Great North Road. She was surprised by how affluent it looked. The swathes of grass, the trees and the pond were flanked by well-maintained Georgian houses with high brick garden walls and shining four-by-fours in the forecourts. Their occupants would be smug, sleek and moneyed. I bet the kids who grow up here have ponies, she thought, with a wistful, retrospective envy. Barnet—or at least this part of Barnet—was clearly the Suburb that Triumphed.

She parked her car by the church and walked through the old toll gate and round the corner to the common proper. More big houses, more bright paint and gleaming cars, a neatly marked cricket pitch, and Hadley Wood beyond.

Amy followed Camlet Way until she came to Hadley Cottage, which was set back from the road and announced itself from a round black plaque with letters embossed in gold round a Barbie-pink rose. It was a solid, semi-detached Victorian worker's cottage, uncomfortably adorned with a faux-Georgian portico, carriage lamps and shiny black town railings with gold tops. There wasn't much more to see: the front garden was tiny—a strip of grass edged with bedding plants—Venetian blinds hid what was presumably the kitchen, and lace-edged net curtains hid the front room.

Amy had expected to feel the same queasy frisson she'd experienced when, in 1994, she'd been sent to Gloucester to doorstep Fred and Rose West's neighbours in Cromwell Street while the police were tearing up No. 25 in search of bodies. That had been one of her very first jobs, and she'd never forgotten it. Hadley Cottage certainly didn't look like a house of horrors, and there was no atmosphere—but then, why should there be? Leslie Shand had been dead eighteen years, and the gentrification had obviously happened since then. I'm being stupid, she thought. Of course the Shand sisters had moved away. Nobody would want to stay in a place with such terrible associations. Was it even worth

97

ringing the bell?

She hesitated. I've come all this way, she thought, I can't just turn round and go home without getting something out of it. Perhaps the people who lived in Hadley Cottage would be able to tell her where the Shands had gone. I'll have a look round first, she told herself, putting off the disappointment.

Hadley Cottage's partner was called Dunster Croft, and next door to it was a primary school: low-rise, boxy buildings and a playground with primary-coloured markings. Amy skirted it, wondering if the Shand girls had gone there as children, and came to a rough path, overgrown by nettles and blocked off by a broken gate held in place by rusty chains and a padlock, with spars of wood nailed haphazardly across as a barricade. She thought she could see the grey edge of a building—a Nissen hut, perhaps—at the end of the lane, but the overhanging trees made it hard to tell. Was this the farm? If so, either it was long gone or there was another entrance. Amy decided to walk a bit further down the road, away from the common, to have a look.

The gate was incongrously ramshackle beside the neat school, but it was even more at odds with the buildings on the other side of it. Amy walked past tall laurel hedges, electric gates between pillars with urns on top and signs saying, *These premises are protected 24 hours* and *Private Driveway. No Turning.* From what she could see, peering between yews and cedars of Lebanon and monster rhododendron bushes, the objects of all the security were either sprawling ranch-style bungalows with stone cladding and triple garages, or crude mishmashes of Jacobethan and out-of-town supermarket, with gables, big windows and harsh red and brown bricks. Judging from the names—The Willows, White Walls, Five Oaks, Begma (Begma? Amy racked her brains to see if she could come up with an appropriate his 'n' hers fusion, and failed)—they were private houses, but from the size and appearance, half of them could just as easily have been conference centres or care homes like Compton Lodge. Their owners had arrived with a fanfare—serious money, coupled with seriously bad taste. The ranch-style ones could easily have been there since the seventies. In any case, even if the Shands had been an ordinary family, they'd have had nothing in common with these people. The occupants of houses like The Willows might have employed the Shand girls as cleaners, but they wouldn't have entertained them as friends.

Amy came to a bend in the road where the houses were set further back, and saw a large sign that read, WELCOME TO GOODMAYES FARM! VEG—EGGS—FRUIT—PLANTS, OPEN TUES-SAT 10 TILL 5. There was another long lane, flanked by hedges, with ranks of sorry-looking plants in black plastic pots with trays at their base, and the only building Amy could see was a wooden shed. The gates were locked. A notice was tied to them, covered in plastic to protect it from the weather. She went up to have a look. *We are doing renovation work. Ring the number below and we will gladly come and serve you.* Amy punched the number into her mobile. The woman who answered sounded anything but glad. 'What do you want? We haven't got much, not after the weekend.'

'I'd like some eggs, please.'

That cheered her up a bit. 'No eggs left.'

'What about fruit and veg?'

'Well, we've got a bit left. I suppose I'd better come up.'

A good ten minutes later a squat, weather-beaten figure clad in wellington boots, denim shorts and—no she wasn't, yes she *was*—a lacy, underwired bra, came stumping up the path, undid the padlock and ushered Amy into the wooden shed. Amy saw what she meant about lack of merchandise. The shelves were covered in cardboard boxes containing wizened fruit, yellow lettuces, sprouting potatoes and whiffy asparagus. She cast around for something she could reasonably buy, and came up with three onions and a jar of honey. 'I told you we hadn't got much,' said the woman triumphantly. 'That'll be seven pounds eighty.'

'*How* much?'

'Seven pounds eighty. It's all organic, you know. We do farmers' markets, mostly.'

A tiny opening. Amy made the most of it. 'Have you been here long?'

'Eight, nine years, something like that.'

'I thought there was a pig farm here.'

'That was up the road. Gone now, though.'

'When did it close?'

'About six months after we came. It wasn't much by the end. We rent most of the land now.'

'From Mr Drake?'

'That's right.'

'Is he still alive?'

'He was last week. Now, if you'd like to pay . . .'

'Does he live at the farm? I'd like to get in touch with him.'

'He's still there, yeah.'

'How do I get there?'

'The only way is down that lane at the top, but I wouldn't if I was you. He can be a bit . . . Well, let's just say he doesn't really encourage callers.'

Amy checked her watch as she walked back up the hill. Just because Mr Drake still lived in the farmhouse didn't mean that the Shand sisters still lived in their old home. In any case, it might have been a tied cottage. It was possible, of course, that Mr Drake might know where they'd gone. First things first. Amy took a deep breath, then opened the gate of Hadley Cottage and rang the doorbell.

# CHAPTER FOURTEEN

Amy heard the chimes inside the house—De-da, de-da, de-da, de-da. *O Lord our God, Thy chil-dren call, Grant us Thy peace, And bless us all.* She remembered the simple tune from Brownies. She heard noises inside, and then, after much fumbling with locks, the door opened about a foot and a slight woman with an anxious expression peered round it. 'Can I—' she began, and then froze, her hand covering her mouth, staring at Amy with unmistakable horror.

Alarmed by the reaction and afraid that the door would be slammed in her face, Amy heard herself babbling about how she was sorry to disturb her and she would have telephoned but couldn't get the number and as she was coming this way she thought she'd drop by and so forth. She was in full flow when she noticed that her listener's features had rearranged themselves into a look of contrition, which stopped her in mid-sentence. As the woman opened the door to reveal herself, Amy realised that she was looking at a junior version of Iris. The clothes were almost identical, except that the calf-length pleated skirt and matching blouse were pale blue, and the frill at the neck was augmented by a pussy-cat bow.

'I'm sorry,' she said. 'I just . . . well, for a second I thought . . . Silly. Anyway, how can I help you?'

'Are you Miss Shand?'

'Yes.' Her fair, soft curls bobbed as she nodded. 'That's right.'

'Miss Sheila Shand?' Amy hazarded.

'Yes.'

'Then I have come to the right place. I wasn't sure if you still lived here.'

'I don't really want . . .' Sheila Shand tailed off, looking for evidence of canvassing, charity or the hard sell.

Amy gave her what she hoped was a reassuring smile and said, 'It's all right, I'm not going to try and sell you anything. I came to see you because . . .' She launched into the explanation she'd prepared in the car, about finding the letters in Patti's flat and discovering relatives she didn't know she had, but leaving out the newspaper cutting. Sheila listened with an air of polite detachment, her face devoid of expression. 'And then,' Amy finished, pulling the pink diary out of her bag, 'I found this, and I thought your sister might like to have it back.'

When she held it out, Sheila recoiled, hands

held up in a miniature cameo of 'I surrender'. 'What is it?'

'It's a diary.'

'I don't think it's my sister's,' she said doubtfully, taking a small step backwards.

'It is.' Amy proffered the little book. 'I'm afraid . . . I thought it was my mother's, you see, so I started reading it, and it definitely belongs to your sister Maureen. It's an old one—1983 to 1987.'

Sheila seemed to freeze. Amy had the impression that some inner mechanism had suddenly jammed. She put her hand out—for the diary, Amy thought, but instead, the fingers fluttered against her arm. Sheila was shaking. 'Perhaps . . .' She hesitated, then stood back, flattening herself against the door as if to avoid contamination, and said, 'Would you like to come in for a moment?'

'Thank you.' Amy stepped past Sheila, who closed the door. Looking down at the hall carpet— wall-to-wall, pale cream, and bearing the marks of recent Hoovering—she said, 'Shall I take my shoes off? I've been tramping about a bit, and I don't—'

'What do you want?' Sheila interrupted, her voice tight. 'I haven't got any money.'

'Sorry?'

'I can't pay you. If you're thinking of going to the police—'

'Why would I go to the police? And I certainly don't want money.' Amy was baffled. 'I just thought your sister might like her diary back. That's all. You can take it.' She held it out. 'Unless you'd like me to send it to her—I mean, if she doesn't live here.'

Still, Sheila made no move to take the little

103

book. 'How did you find me?' she asked.

'There's an address in it. I thought you'd probably have moved, but on the off-chance—I was passing anyway,' Amy lied. '*Does* your sister live here?'

Sheila shook her head. 'I'll give it to her,' she said, taking the diary. Then, backtracking, 'It's very kind of you to return it.'

They stared at each other for a moment. After Sheila's outburst, the eyes that looked into Amy's seemed—unnervingly—uninhabited, as if she'd suddenly flicked an interior off switch.

'What did you mean about going to the police?' Amy asked.

'You know about us, don't you?'

'Yes. There was a newspaper cutting in my mother's flat. But that was the first I'd heard of it, and I don't see why you thought . . . Look'—Amy collected herself—'you're obviously upset. I think I should go.'

'No, please. I'm sorry. It's just that occasionally I've had journalists ringing up, and I get a bit nervous. Please,' Sheila laid what was clearly meant as a reassuring hand on Amy's arm, although the effect was marred by the fact that her fingers were trembling, 'do stay for a cup of tea. I've just put the kettle on.'

Amy thought she might as well. The afternoon couldn't get much stranger. 'That would be lovely.' She smiled. 'But I think I'd better take my shoes off.'

Sheila glanced down at the scuffed sandals— Amy found herself wondering how clean her feet were—and said, 'Well, if you don't mind.'

'Of course not.'

It was definitely the sort of house where people wore slippers. As she fumbled with the straps of her shoes, she glanced up and saw flowered pink wallpaper, an onyx and gilt phone console and a round wall clock mounted on a chrome star.

'The lounge is just through there,' said Sheila, motioning to her left. 'Why don't you go on in?' She disappeared into the kitchen.

The sitting room, decorated in shades of peach, was cluttered with occasional tables and old-fashioned pouffes in pale leather, and every surface was three-deep in china ornaments and framed photographs. It was spotlessly clean, and very tidy. Even the cushions along the back of the sofa were angled on their corners in a row of precise, plumped-up diamonds. The curtains had tasselled tie-backs, and the dazzling white nets had fussy scalloped edges.

Amy wandered over to look at the photographs on the mantelpiece. There were pictures of Iris, Sheila and Mo, both separately and together, enjoying a cream tea, outside a bingo hall and leaning against the wall of a promenade with the sea in the background. Judging by the women's clothing and youthful appearance, the photos had been taken in the late eighties. Only one, of Sheila with a man, smiling over drinks in the garden of a country pub, seemed more recent. Mo, though shorter and slighter, looked disturbingly like Amy.

She stood on the rug in front of the coal-effect gas fire and tried to gauge the atmosphere. The pastel colours had a muffling effect, so that Sheila's gentility and the curious interior stillness (until it had exploded so unexpectedly) was replicated in the house. The bright, just-this-side-

105

of-kitsch ornaments gave the place an artificial overlay of cheerfulness, which was, Amy felt, less to do with personal taste than with keeping something else at bay: it was the impression of a home, rather than the living stuff of one. Don't get carried away, she told herself. It's eighteen years since Sheila shot her father—don't fall into the trap of responding to the implications of the past. But then, what was all that business about blackmail and the police? Judging by her reaction, Sheila hadn't known that Mo kept a diary—odd, if it was written under Leslie's auspices as an official family document, that she was unaware of it. Perhaps Mo had been forbidden to tell her. But (and it always came back to this) she'd been thirty years old. Far too old to be threatened as a child could be threatened. Mo had struck her as strange, but not half-witted. It didn't make sense.

Sheila was worried about what the diary might contain. Something to do with Leslie's death, perhaps? There must be something Amy had missed, some significance she'd failed to grasp. She'd have to look at the photocopy and see what she could piece together.

She gave a start as Sheila deposited a tray on one of the occasional tables and busied herself removing cling-film from a plate of biscuits and positioning coasters. The entire tea-making operation had been conducted without any noise at all. Amy could easily have picked up a chink or rattle from the kitchen—the distance was small— but there hadn't been a sound.

With the same silent efficiency, Sheila arranged the cups and began to pour. 'How do you like your tea?'

'Just milk, please.'

Fearful of upsetting the pristine neatness of the room, Amy lowered herself gingerly into an armchair and accepted the delicate cup and saucer. Sheila poured a second cup for herself, then sat down on the sofa opposite. Each took a considered sip. Despite her care, the clink of Amy's cup descending into its saucer seemed to echo round the room as if she'd bashed a pair of dustbin lids together. 'This is lovely,' she said.

Sheila smiled politely and then, eyes down and using both hands, carefully edged her cup and coaster away from the little table's pie-frill surround until it was in the exact centre of the tooled leather, with the handle facing away from her. She seemed to have retreated back into herself, giving Amy the disconcerting sensation of being in the same room as an animated waxwork. And yet, behind it, Amy could sense that Sheila was taut, watchful. She suddenly remembered sitting through maths lessons at secondary school, trying not to draw attention to herself so that the sadist who taught them would have no excuse to single her out for humiliation. That's what it was: Sheila, through long practice, had succeeded in removing any vestige of 'self' while remaining super-alert.

'I went to Compton Lodge at the weekend,' Amy said, 'after I found out we were related. I left my number with Sister Paula. She said she'd pass it on.'

Sheila looked surprised. 'I was there yesterday,' she said, 'but I didn't see Sister Paula. Mum didn't mention you'd been, but her memory isn't very good these days.' She proffered the plate of

107

biscuits. After Amy had refused (the crunching noises and crumb spillage seemed too daunting), Sheila said formally, 'I'm sorry to hear about your mother. Had she been ill?'

'She had cancer.'

'That's terrible. She can't have been very old.'

'No. Sixty-one.'

After a pause, Sheila said simply, 'It was a long time ago.' Her face and voice were devoid of expression and Amy could get no inner reading from her at all, but she clearly wasn't talking about Patti's death.

'I wanted to ask,' she said, carefully, 'I'm not really sure how the diary came to be in Mum's possession, you see. Do you remember her at all, or my grandmother? Did they ever come to visit you?'

'Oh, no.' Sheila's tone was sardonic. 'There wasn't anything like that. But the letter you mentioned . . . I was very small when we met your grandmother, and I don't remember much about it. Mum told us about it when we were older.'

'That she'd brought you to . . . to see her?'

Sheila sighed. 'She'd taken us because she wanted—well, she hoped we could get away from Dad.' Amy tried not to betray shock at hearing the word 'Dad' on Sheila's lips. 'But then he came to fetch us. Mum hadn't told him where we'd gone, but he worked it out—he was clever, you see—and he made her come home. He told your grandmother Mum was imagining things.' Sheila gave a faint, hollow smile. 'When we got home he made her write that letter, saying it was all right.'

'Would you like it back? I haven't brought it with me, but I could—'

Sheila's 'No' was emphatic. 'It was all lies. Mum was so frightened, she couldn't . . .' She gave another sigh, perhaps at the hopelessness of trying to explain to an outsider, and continued, 'That was the problem. We didn't think anyone would believe us. And even if they had . . .'

Amy nodded. 'I understand.' No, I don't, she thought. How could I possibly? I can hardly begin to imagine the impact of the things that drove this woman to kill her own father. 'I'm sorry,' she said. 'I'm sorry that those terrible things happened to you—to all of you.'

Sheila inclined her head. 'Would you like a drop of hot water? If it's too strong . . .'

For a moment, Amy couldn't think what she was talking about. 'Oh, no thank you. It's fine.' Feeling it was called for, she picked up her cup for another sip.

'Your mother wrote to me,' Sheila said, in an even, remote voice. 'Last year. I wrote back to let her know how Mum was doing.'

When Patti knew she was dying, Amy thought. That must have been when she'd got the address of Compton Lodge.

'Did she ever come and see you?'

'A long time ago. Not here—it was when Mo was in hospital, in Barnet. Did Mo write about it in the diary?'

'A little. She said she missed you all.'

'I don't suppose she missed Dad. But it was kind of your mother to visit. She brought chocolates, but we had to hide them. Dad used to look in the cupboard by the bed, you see. To check.'

'Check? For what?'

'If she was hiding things. You know, if someone

109

had given her something. There was a man in there who used to come and talk to her. Dad said it was all she was good for, another loony, but he wouldn't have liked it if there'd been something between them.' She brightened. 'Those chocolates were *delicious*.' For the first time, in this small assertion of individual preference, Amy caught a glimpse of a bright, warm human being. 'I've always had a sweet tooth,' she continued. 'We all did.'

Amy remembered Mo's litany of buns and cakes. 'It says that in the diary. The Angel Delight on Saturdays.'

Sheila's start made her cup rattle violently in its saucer. Putting up her other hand to steady it, she said, 'That was in the diary?'

'Yes,' said Amy, surprised. 'All the different flavours.'

'The flavours . . .' It was a whisper, directed at her lap.

Amy stared at the carpet. She didn't know why, but such connection as there was between them had been abruptly and irretrievably severed. 'Look,' she said, gathering up her bag, 'I didn't mean to intrude. I'm glad we've met at last—if you ever want to contact me for any reason, Sister Paula has the details.' She stood up. 'I think I ought to leave you in peace now. Thank you very much for the tea.'

Sheila stood up, too, hands automatically smoothing her skirt, and accompanied Amy to the front door. 'Thank you for coming,' she said, without meeting Amy's eye.

Amy thanked her again, closed the front gate and began making her way across the wide grass verge that separated the cottage from the road. When she reached the bend she turned to wave, but the door was already shut.

# CHAPTER FIFTEEN

Amy sat in her car for several minutes, perplexed. 'What the hell was all that about?' she asked aloud. Sheila's demeanour, and the changes of tone and subject, bewildered her. I'm too used to being in control of the conversation, she thought. That's what's disconcerting—not having any idea of the agenda. As for Sheila's excuse about journalists bothering her, that must have been years ago, and in any case journalists weren't *blackmailers*, not in the sense of extorting money, at any rate. And why, for God's sake, had she got so upset about something as innocuous an Angel Delight?

Amy still felt positive that Sheila had been unaware of the diary's existence, yet what she'd said seemed to imply that she thought there could be something in its contents that might get her into trouble with the police. But Mo wouldn't have given her diary to Mum if there was anything incriminating in it, would she? Besides, Sheila had already been charged with killing her father—what more could there be?

But then, Amy didn't know Sheila, or Mo. She was assuming that they'd act rationally, and that wasn't necessarily the case. Perhaps, though, Sheila wasn't concerned about herself. Could that be the reason—that Sheila hadn't shot her father

111

at all? Maybe she'd simply held up her hands to it so that Mo—if she did have a history of mental illness—wouldn't end up somewhere like Broadmoor. But surely she must have realised that she was taking a terrible risk?

Amy looked at the clock on the dashboard: 18.25. Too late now to visit Iris at Compton Lodge. Not that it would be any use, but all the same . . . She was definitely curious. Perhaps she could make time to go there in the next few days.

Thinking about Iris reminded Amy of Sheila's reaction when she'd first opened the door. Unmistakable shock, as if she'd seen a ghost. Iris had appeared to think that she was Mo . . . Could Mo be dead? But if she were, how could Sheila return the diary? If Mo was dead, why not just say so?

Amy drove home abstractedly, turning her conversation with Sheila over in her mind, not reaching any conclusions. At home, after a single guilty glance at *The Cultural State*, she sat down at the kitchen table and set about reassembling the photocopied diary pages in the correct order. Then she fetched some Post-It notes and a pencil, poured herself a glass of wine, and settled down to read.

Now that she knew what had happened in the Shand family, she was even more struck by the bizarre contrast of banality and horror. But nothing leapt out at her, and she was beginning to wonder if she'd imagined the strength of Sheila's reaction when the phone rang.

'Hello?'

'Am I speaking to Miss Vaughan?' said an irascible male voice.

'Yes, this is Amy Vaughan. Who is it?'

'I'm a friend of Miss Sheila Shand.'

'Oh.' Ambushed, Amy couldn't think of anything to say.

'Yes, "Oh",' mimicked the voice. 'I understand you've been bothering her.'

'No, I—'

'I wouldn't normally call so late, but this is important. You weren't answering earlier.'

Hang on, thought Amy. If you knew I'd been 'bothering' Sheila, you must have known I wouldn't be at home to answer my landline. Deciding to let this go, she said simply, 'I was out.'

'I see,' said the man, as if he didn't believe her. 'Well, I understand you've been to Compton Lodge to see Iris Shand, without permission.'

'I wasn't aware that I needed permission,' Amy replied coolly. 'The matron seemed quite happy when I explained who I was.'

'I understand you told her you were a relative.'

'That's because I am. I'm Iris Shand's great-niece, Sheila's cousin.' Amy didn't think it was a good idea to weaken her case by adding the 'once removed' part. 'And I think that if you're going to start accusing me of things, you should at least tell me your name.'

There was a moment's silence, followed by some phlegmy throat-clearing. 'Name's Bill Drake. As I said, I'm a friend of Sheila Shand.'

Mr Drake the farmer, thought Amy, the man who'd employed Leslie Shand. He certainly didn't sound like the ragged recluse she'd imagined. 'Well, Mr Drake, as you know, I went to see Sheila with the intention of—'

'What? When did you see Sheila?'

113

'This afternoon. But you know that—I assumed that's what you meant when you said I'd been "bothering" her.'

'Well, that's all the more reason—'

'Did she tell you why I went to see her?'

'No. I knew nothing about it.'

'Well, in that case, I don't understand why you're so upset. All I did was to go and see Iris Shand and to leave my details with the matron, in case Sheila felt like contacting me.'

'I know. Sister Paula gave me those details while Sheila was visiting her mother. I haven't mentioned it to Sheila yet.' At least, thought Amy, that explains one thing, but why hadn't he mentioned it? He'd described himself as a friend—and he must be a close one if Sister Paula had given him her details to pass on—but why was he being so proprietary? Especially as Sheila, despite being upset herself, clearly hadn't seen fit to inform him about Amy's visit.

'Why did you want to see Sheila?' he asked.

'I had something for her.'

'What was that?'

'I think that's a matter for Sheila and myself,' said Amy firmly.

There was a moment's silence, followed by more throat-clearing, and then Mr Drake said, 'Look, Miss Vaughan, I'm sorry if I seemed a bit abrupt, but I'm very fond of Sheila. She's had terrible trouble with the newspapers in the past, and—'

'It's all right, Mr Drake. I know what happened to the family.'

'Well, then, I'm sure you'll understand that the last thing she needs is to have it all raked up again.'

114

'Mr Drake, I simply wanted to make contact with a relative I didn't know I had until about a week ago. I happened to be passing, so I thought I'd drop in. I wanted to find out more about my family. I'm sure you can understand that.' Even as she said this, Amy wondered why the hell she should be justifying herself (truthfully or otherwise) to a complete stranger.

'Would you mind telling me what it was you gave her?'

'I'm sure Sheila will tell you about it herself if she wants to.'

'I see. Well, I shall speak to Sheila about it, and if you've been pestering her . . .' He left the sentence unfinished. 'If you've nothing more to say to me, I'll bid you goodnight.'

'Goodnight, and—' The phone went down at the other end. 'And thanks so much for calling,' she said to the dial tone.

She replaced the receiver and took her glass into the kitchen for a refill. What on earth was going on? Mr Drake's threat, though unspoken, was definitely understood. And he'd trotted out the line about journalists, too. What was his interest? she wondered. He sounded like more than just a 'friend'. Perhaps he and Sheila were lovers. Amy couldn't imagine Sheila as anyone's lover, but that didn't mean it wasn't possible. One thing, however, was clear: she had, very definitely, been warned off.

# CHAPTER SIXTEEN

Sheila sat at the kitchen table, touching Mo's diary with her fingertips, not daring to open it. I can't, she thought. I don't want to know. Mo'd written about the Angel Delight. When the girl—Amy— had said so, Sheila'd thought she was going to faint. She remembered Mo in the kitchen on Saturday evening, hesitating over the different packets before selecting the flavour they'd have for pudding. Her moment of choice. Sheila flinched.

At first, it had been just that—before *he* got the idea of making a game of it. Sheila'd had her choice, too: the cakes from the pig van. Every week she'd gone down to the farm to meet the baker's lorry, loaded with all the stuff they hadn't been able to sell, which was to be mixed into the huge vats of pig swill. She'd been able to time her trip so that she was waiting for the driver to open the back doors and reveal the racks and racks of perfect Bakewell tarts and éclairs and buns and sliced white bread in waxed paper. They'd had two loaves every week, plus whatever she'd picked for their treat. She'd prized the small freedom—even when *he* took them to the pub he'd always told them what they must choose to drink—and looked forward to it. Mo must have looked forward to making her choice, too, and of course she hadn't understood.

They'd always been such good friends. All those years of whispered conversations in their bedroom at night, trying to comfort each other . . . Sheila groaned. 'I tried to protect her, Mum. I

116

tried so hard.'

Why hadn't Mo told her she was keeping a diary? Even if Dad had made her do it, surely she'd have mentioned it? Sheila stopped, remembering the things he had made *her* do that she'd never been able to tell Mo. Divide and rule, she'd heard someone say once, and it was true. Amy had said that Mo wrote the diary in the eighties: 1983 to 1987. That meant she must have written about Dad's death. Sheila wondered where Mo had kept the diary. She must have found another place, she thought, and not told me about it.

As children, when *he* had allowed them no toys, Mum had secretly bought them a blue woollen rabbit at a jumble sale. They'd called him Peter and hidden him under the floorboards in their room, filching bits of straw from the farm to make him a bed. At first he'd been merely a cuddly thing that helped Mo to sleep, but as they'd grown older he'd changed into . . . Sheila had found it hard to talk about what Peter had become, but the counsellor had said he was a symbol. Sheila thought he was more like a miracle, because they'd managed to keep Dad from finding him and ripping him limb from knitted limb. Coming home from school and, later on, from work, they'd checked, automatically, that he was still there, the comforting glint still in his glass eyes and the soft pink felt inside his long ears. In prayers at school assembly, she'd begged God to keep him safe. It had never occurred to her to pray for escape from Dad—that was unimaginable—and asking for the wellbeing of any of their pets would have been futile, but she'd hoped that because Peter wasn't actually 'real' keeping him hidden might not prove too difficult.

He'd been their secret. A *good* secret, not like all the terrible things they couldn't talk about to other people, or the things *he* had done to her that made her so ashamed for both of them that she'd never told Mum or Mo. She knew there were things that had happened before they were born, or when they were little, that Mum had written about afterwards and didn't want them to read, and Sheila never had. Mum hadn't read what she'd written, either. That was their agreement—the reason why they'd locked their journals in the box upstairs with two padlocks, one for each of them.

But *Mo* . . . She grabbed the diary, feeling suddenly furious. 'I protected you for years,' she told it. 'I let him do all those things to me so he wouldn't touch you.'

The thought of Mo writing in secret and giving her diary to Amy's mother made her feel sick with betrayal. Amy's mother was dead, but Amy had read it, and she'd . . . Sheila's stomach lurched as she remembered her words about money and the police—she'd been so frightened she hadn't known what she was saying, but now Amy would be suspicious. Supposing she came back to ask questions? Supposing the police . . .

Stop it, she told herself. You're not being fair about this. Mo's diary is private, same as Mum's journals, or mine. After Dad died, the counselling lady had told them to try and write down what they remembered about their lives with him, and Mo said she couldn't, because the ECT had taken away her memory. Perhaps that was why she'd written the diary—she was afraid of it happening when she

118

started the treatment. But if she'd wanted to give it to someone, why choose Patti Vaughan? 'Why didn't you trust me?' Sheila whispered. 'I can keep a secret, Mo. I've kept your secret for years. Years and years.'

She clutched the diary to her chest. What should she do with it? She couldn't lock it in the box with the journals—Mum had the other key. I'll hide it under our bedroom floor, she thought, in Peter's place. Peter didn't need it now—he was at Compton Lodge, with Mum. She was about to go upstairs and take up the loose floorboard when the doorbell rang.

The sun behind him, Bill Drake's dark shape seemed to loom over her as she opened the door.

'What's going on, Sheila?'

'Bill!' She jumped backwards and her elbow collided painfully with the doorframe.

He took a step towards her. 'Are you—'

'Please, I'm fine,' she said, desperately, and then, because she couldn't bear him to come any closer, she retreated into the kitchen, still clutching the diary.

Bill followed her. 'Are you all right?'

'Yes, I . . .' She swallowed. 'Would you like a cup of tea?'

'No. I just came to find out what's been happening.'

'I was just going to make some,' she lied, trying to ignore the edge in his voice. As she turned away from him to put on the kettle, the diary slipped out of her hand and fell on the floor.

'Let me,' said Bill.

'No, really, it's fine, I can manage.' Sheila bent down, picked it up, and—too late to hide it now—

119

put it on top of the bread bin.

Bill sat down and waited while she finished getting out the cups, then said, 'Amy Vaughan's been to see you, hasn't she?'

Sheila almost dropped the sugar bowl. 'How do you know?'

'She told me.'

'She told you? I don't understand. Do you know her?'

'Were you going to tell me about it?' For a moment, Bill's mouth seemed to be synchronised in time to her father's flat, menacing voice.

She shook her head. 'It was such a shock, Bill. She'd been to see Mum.'

'I know. I had a chat with Sister Paula while you were upstairs with Iris. She mentioned that Iris had had a visit from a woman called Amy Vaughan who'd left her details for you, so I told her I'd pass them on. I've just rung her up. She says you're related.'

'Why didn't you tell me?' asked Sheila.

'I didn't want her bothering you, but it turns out she already has. She said she'd given you something.'

'Yes. We are related. She's a cousin.'

'A distant cousin. And a busybody, by the sound of it.'

'She looks so much like Mo.'

'What did she want?'

'She gave me a diary,' Sheila said, 'an old one of Mo's. Amy's mother died recently, and it was with her things. She thought I might want it back. It was kind of her.'

'Her mother had your address, did she?'

'Amy said it was in the diary.'

'So she'd looked in it.'

'Mo was only little when she wrote it,' lied Sheila. 'There wouldn't have been anything . . . I mean, it couldn't have done any harm.'

'You're sure about that, are you?'

'Yes.' A second lie. 'I've had a look at it.'

'I see. Well, you won't be hearing any more from her,' said Bill. 'I've seen to that. It's for the best,' he added, more gently. 'I only want to protect you, Sheila.'

After he'd gone, Sheila ran upstairs and slid the diary under the loose floorboard. The frolicking puppies on her pretty blue walls were no comfort now. It wasn't as if she'd wanted to see Amy again—she'd been very nice, but the thought of questions, especially now, was unbearable—it was being so *alone*, and Bill driving the girl away like that made her feel even more isolated, as if there was a thick sheet of glass separating her from the rest of the world. She went to the window and stood staring out at the common.

## CHAPTER SEVENTEEN

Amy was dithering about food—she felt too churned-up to be hungry, but perhaps cooking something might give her an appetite—when the doorbell rang. The first thing she saw when she opened it was a policeman, and, behind him, Charlie from next door.

'Ms Vaughan?'

'Yes. What's happened?'

'It's about your father.'

121

'Oh, God, what's he done now?' Amy asked wearily, wondering if she could possibly afford to stump up bail—George was quite capable of doing a runner.

The policeman shook his head, making her feel instantly guilty for assuming the worst. 'It's nothing like that. I'm afraid he's been involved in an accident. It's nothing serious, but he had a bang on the head so they've taken him to hospital.'

'How did it happen?'

'He was knocked down by a car as he was crossing Essex Road. The driver didn't stop. We'll be making enquiries, of course, but so far we don't have a registration so it could be difficult.'

'Which hospital is it?'

'The Whittington, up at Archway.'

'I'll go there now. I've had wine,' she said, thinking aloud, 'I'll have to call a taxi.'

Charlie stepped forward. 'I'll take you, if you like,' he said. 'My van's just down the road.'

'Thanks, but I wasn't . . . I mean, why are you . . . ?' Amy stopped, confused.

'Why am I here? I saw it. I was a couple of cars behind.'

The policeman cleared his throat. 'If there's nothing else you want to ask . . . ?'

'No,' said Amy. 'Thanks for coming to tell me.'

'It's being dealt with at the station on Tolpuddle Street, if you need to get in touch, and of course we'll be speaking to your father.'

The policeman departed, and Charlie said, 'Come on. I'll drive you.'

'Are you sure?'

'Yeah, why not? I owe you one.'

'OK. Hang on just a sec.' Amy dashed into the

122

kitchen, grabbed her bag, and locked the front door. 'Thanks.'

Charlie's van was a big, old-fashioned Citroën, with *Deakin Landscaping* painted across the side. 'You're a gardener,' she said, as she clambered into the passenger seat. 'No wonder you feel so strongly about cats.'

'Yeah. I like them,' he reassured her. 'I mean, I'd never hurt one or anything. It's just the mess.'

Driving down Essex Road, he said, 'It was just back there. I didn't see exactly what happened—like I said, I was a couple of cars behind.' He frowned. 'It was odd, though, because it looked like this bloke—or it might have been a woman, I couldn't see—was going straight for him. I mean, it was a bit . . . To be honest, it wasn't a great place to cross the road, but the car seemed to be speeding up, not slowing down, and they didn't try and avoid him, either. He got out of the way pretty quick, and it looked like the bumper just caught his leg, but he fell quite badly, and I think he must have hit his head on the kerb, because it was bleeding. It's all right. He managed to get into the ambulance on his own, but he was a bit groggy. I'm sure it looked much worse than it is.'

'God, I hope so. Why didn't the car stop?'

'God knows. Perhaps it was nicked. Someone called an ambulance, and they wanted a name but your dad wasn't making much sense, so I had a look in his pockets and found a credit card—I'd thought he looked familiar but it was only when I saw his name that I realised who it was, so when the police arrived I told them, and I followed them up here, because I was coming back anyway, and that's it, really.'

'What did the car look like?'

'Dark saloon. Don't know the make. I'd have got the registration, but it happened so quickly. The police were still talking to some pedestrians when I left, so maybe one of them will have seen it.'

As they drove up the Holloway Road, Amy tried to keep a lid on the panic boiling up inside her—suppose Dad's skull was fractured, or he'd had a brain haemorrhage? And what about his illness?

Charlie's voice cut across the blurred montage of crash teams, flat lines on monitors and machines that made short bleeps, long bleeps, and then stopped altogether. 'We're nearly there.'

'I was so angry with him. I was all set to throw him out. Supposing—'

'I'm sure he's going to be all right,' said Charlie firmly. 'Don't beat yourself up about it.'

The bright A&E waiting room was almost empty. Amy looked around at the jovially menacing posters about flu jabs and stopping smoking, the drooping spider plants and the obese cleaner who was bumping her mop against a thicket of plastic chairs.

Charlie caught her eye. 'Someone'll be out to see you in a minute. Let's sit down.'

She took the chair next to his, and leant forward to pick up a curling copy of *Hello!* from the table. After a moment, she tossed it back again. 'Stupid. I can't concentrate. Do you think they'll come and get me if, you know . . . ?'

'I'm sure they would, but he's going to be fine. He's in good hands.'

Amy got up and prowled round the room, unable to keep still, feeling Charlie watching her.

When she'd completed her ninth or tenth circuit, she came back to sit beside him.

'What did you mean when you said, "What's he done now"?' he asked.

'What?'

'To that copper. You said, "What's he done now?"'

Shit. She *had* said that. 'Oh, it's just that I thought he'd got himself in trouble. It wouldn't be the first time. He's not a criminal or anything.' Even as Amy was saying this, she was thinking, No, that's exactly what he is. A criminal. 'He's got himself mixed up in a couple of dodgy things, that's all.' Downplaying it, as she always did in conversation. She'd never come clean about the extent (as far as she knew it) of George's activities to anyone, even her ex-husband.

Charlie didn't reply, and she spent the next five minutes fidgeting, churned up with worry and anger and wanting to yell at someone because she didn't know what was going on. When the doctor—or, rather, the schoolboy dressed up in a white coat and stethoscope—finally did push his way through the swing doors, she had to fight the urge to grab him by the lapels.

'Ms Vaughan?' he asked. He seemed tired and distracted, and Amy wondered how many hours he'd been on shift.

'Yes.' She stood up. 'I'm his daughter.'

'Dr Lorimer. We've stitched the head wound, but he's a bit concussed. The X-rays are clear, which is good, but I'd like to keep him in for observation, just to be on the safe side. If he's all right in the morning, he can go home. Does he live with you?'

'He does at the moment.'

'Good. You can ring in the morning and find out how he's doing. Would you like to see him now?'

'Yes, please.'

Amy was ushered through the swing doors and into a curtained-off cubicle. George was lying on a bed looking jowly and pale, his hair shaved elliptically round a line of butterfly stitches above his left ear. For a moment, Amy thought he hadn't recognised her, but then he swallowed, ran his tongue over his lips, and said, 'You're here.'

'Yes, I'm here.' She pulled up a chair to sit beside him. 'How are you feeling, Dad?'

'Bloody awful. What time is it?'

'Almost nine o'clock.'

'In the morning?'

'No, in the evening.'

'Oh.' He closed his eyes.

'Do you remember what happened, Dad?'

'Accident. Didn't see him coming.'

'Charlie said the driver didn't stop.'

'Who's Charlie?'

'From next door. He saw it.'

'No. My fault. Shouldn't have crossed.' He opened his eyes and gave her a weak smile. 'Sorry, chicky. Bit tired.'

'All right. I'll call tomorrow and find out how you're doing.' She got up to leave.

'Don't go. Not yet.'

'I can stay if you want.'

'Yes, please.'

Amy sat beside him until she could tell from his breathing that he was asleep, and then tiptoed out of the cubicle and went to find the doctor. 'He's fallen asleep. Is that all right? I mean, if he's

126

concussed?'

'We'll keep an eye on him, don't you worry.'

'I'm just a bit concerned because . . .'—she remembered her father's words about not wanting to be messed around with by doctors, and changed tack— '. . . because he hasn't been very well recently.'

'Has he had any falls?'

'Not that I know of. He's just been a bit under the weather.'

'Does he smoke?'

'Only cigars.'

The doctor raised his eyebrows. 'Mmm, I see. Drink?'

'That's one of the things I've been a bit worried about.'

'How many units, would you say?'

'Quite a few. Too many, probably.'

'It sounds as if he ought to cut down, and he should cut out the cigars altogether.'

Amy sighed. 'I know. Well, thanks anyway.'

Charlie was waiting for her, elbows on knees, staring down at the floor. 'How is he?'

'A lot better than I thought he'd be.'

Charlie grinned. 'Told you.'

'He's still pretty confused, though. He thinks it was an accident.'

'There are quite a few reasons why a car might not stop, Amy. If it's stolen, like I said, or the driver's been drinking, or doing drugs. It's not as if they were aiming for him deliberately.'

'You said the car speeded up.'

'I said I *thought* it did. But say the driver was pissed . . . Perhaps he or she was trying to slow down but pressed the wrong pedal.'

127

'Hard to do. Even if you are a bit out of it, you're still pretty much on autopilot.'

'Reflexes, though. If they were joyriders and they were off their faces, maybe they thought it would be funny to see some old bloke trying to jump out of the way.'

'Let's hope it gave them a good laugh.'

'Hey! I don't mean that *I* think it's funny, just that—'

'I know. Sorry, Charlie. I'm just tired, that's all. In any case, if they haven't got the number plate it's academic, isn't it?'

'You never know. Come on, I'll take you home. You can ring in the morning to find out how he's doing.'

'It's bizarre,' said Amy, as they drove back down the Holloway Road. 'One minute I'm so furious I want to kill him, and the next minute I'm practically hysterical because I think he's going to die on me.'

'You didn't sound it. And he's not going to die on you, is he?'

'Apparently not.'

'Definitely not. Why were you angry with him, if you don't mind my asking?'

'My mother died a couple of weeks ago. He wasn't there—left me to deal with it.'

'Does he often do things like that?'

'Not really. I don't have much involvement with him. He lives abroad.'

Even that was more than she usually said; she wondered why she'd said it. She changed the subject. 'Your van smells nice. Sort of . . . green. Earthy.'

Charlie laughed. 'Does it? I'm so used to it I

128

don't notice any more, not unless I've been carting sacks of manure.'

'It's very kind of you to give me a lift.'

'That's OK. Thanks for being so understanding, by the way. About the other night. I was convinced you'd call the police.'

'To be honest, I was about to. I didn't know Moira had a nephew, and it did give me a bit of a shock, seeing you like that, but when you came round, I thought, no one could make up a story like that, it's so . . .'

'Ridiculous? I know.'

Amy felt too tired to think, let alone carry on a conversation, and Charlie didn't volunteer anything else. When he pulled up in front of her house, she opened the door and clambered down onto the pavement. 'I'd ask you in for a drink, but I'm really . . .'

'I can see. Go on, get some sleep.'

'Good idea. 'Night, Charlie.'

She was about to close the door when he leant across the seat. For a moment, she thought he was going to kiss her, but he just touched the end of her nose, very lightly, with the tip of one finger, and said, 'See you.'

'Yeah.'

'Don't worry. Your dad's going to be fine.' He closed the door and she climbed up her front steps and let herself into the house.

Amy looked in the fridge. She wasn't hungry, but there was an open bottle of Chablis that would do nicely. As she poured the wine, the phone rang, and, thinking that it might be the hospital, she went to answer it. 'Hello?' Nothing. Not even breathing. 'Hello?' A click, and then the dial tone.

129

She put the phone down. 'I'm so sorry, I've got the wrong number,' she said to herself in an exaggeratedly polite voice. 'It doesn't take much, you muppet.'

Back in the kitchen, she took a swig, and then another, and another, until she'd finished the glass. That's better, she thought. Much better. Despite being exhausted, she knew she wouldn't be able to sleep. Mechanically, she gave herself a refill, and took it upstairs to her father's room. Expensive things were scattered about: a stack of Turnbull & Asser shirts, still in their laundry wrappings; handmade suits and shoes glimpsed through the half-open wardrobe door; a handsome toilet set; binoculars in a leather case hung with racecourse pendants; a box of his favourite Cohiba cigars; a cut-glass bottle of Trumper's Essence of Lime— expensive accoutrements, paid for, presumably, by the people he'd swindled over the years. One suitcase, the one she'd already examined, was empty, on top of the wardrobe. The other one was tucked under the bed. Maybe there was something in there that would give her a clue about what was going on and why someone had, apparently, tried to run him over, or about his condition.

She pulled the case out onto the rug and knelt down in front of it. Not locked. She lifted the lid and started to examine the contents, careful not to spill her wine or disturb the neatly folded clothes. Tucked into the pocket at the back was a letter from someone called Claire: *Darling, Thanks for your lovely note. It was sweet of you to write those things but I'm missing you dreadfully and you don't say when you'll be back . . .*

The date was March, and the address Zurich.

Amy visualised concrete tresses, rocking-horse eyes and a red-taloned claw round a glass of vodka, the ice and the costly bracelets clinking late into the night, next to a phone that never rang. Why had he kept the letter? Perhaps Claire was another dupe to be added to his roster for bi-annual visits and sponged off for as long as it was a useful massage to his ego and his bank balance. Amy shook her head and returned the letter to its place. Delving further, she unearthed an old Black Magic box, and when she opened it, she found herself looking at a child's drawing, in wax crayon, of a primary-coloured blob-and-stick family, floating, spindly fingers outspread, above a symmetrical house with a pointed roof and a cloud of smoke issuing from the chimney. The figures were labelled *Daddy, Mummy* and *Me*. Had she drawn it? If she had, she must have been more than four, surely, so Dad would have been gone by then, but she'd still pictured them all together. A child's idea of a proper family, graded in size: wish fulfilment—how things should be.

For a moment, Amy gave herself up to the luxury of self-pity, remembering how much she'd wanted the picture to be true, and the wild, desperate hope she'd felt, when Dad came back, that this time—*this time*—it would be for ever. *Please, God, please let it be, cross your fingers, cross your heart and hope to die.* But then there'd be the inevitable day when she returned from school and ran up the path and opened the front door and knew—always immediately, from the deadness in the air and the crying upstairs—that he'd gone. There was only Mum, inconsolable on her bed, breaking off from her noisy weeping just long enough to tell Amy that she couldn't understand and never would and to stop pestering and go *away*.

She found several other drawings, and a few letters. Patti's were pleading and threatening by turns, and there was a long screed from herself about a birthday trip to the cinema that ended, *Please come back to us soon, we love you, from Amy*, and then kiss, kiss, kiss, kiss, on and on down the page, ending in the shape of a heart.

She put everything back into the Black Magic box and scoured the rest of the suitcase for pills or prescriptions, but found nothing stronger than a tube of indigestion tablets. Perhaps he carries them around with him, she thought, if he takes them with meals. But he hadn't taken any at the restaurant, had he? She'd been to the loo a couple of times, so maybe he'd swallowed them then. But if they'd found something in his pockets at the hospital, surely the doctor would have mentioned it?

No last letter from Patti. That might still be in George's pocket. Not that I'd have wanted to read it, Amy told herself hastily. Nothing nasty from any creditors, either—but then George wouldn't be likely to keep those. She pushed the case back under the bed, glanced round the room to make sure everything was as she'd found it, and left, shutting the door behind her.

She went down to the kitchen for more wine, pushing away her guilt at rifling through George's things. She poured a final glass and threw the Chablis bottle into the recycling box, then sat down slumped forward, resting her head on her forearms. Impressions from the day chased each other across her weary mind: Sheila's distress, Mr Drake's anger, the policeman on the step and Dad in hospital, Charlie . . . Amy smiled, in spite of herself.

It all ought to mean something, she thought, or at least add up. Life would be so much easier if it worked like that instead of being a random, chaotic jumble. Like Iris Shand's brain with half its circuits missing. Poor Iris. Amy remembered the newspaper: *From an early age they were forced to watch as he beat their mother and tortured the family pets . . . held a gun to their heads . . . beat them and forced them to have sex with him . . .*

She finished her wine and went upstairs to bed, thinking, my problems are nothing. I don't know I'm born.

## CHAPTER EIGHTEEN

Amy revised this opinion—my problems may be nothing, but they're bloody well happening to *me*—when an insistent beeping pulled her out of sleep. For a moment, she thought it must be the alarm, but then she registered, firstly, that it was still dark outside, and, then, a split second later, that she could smell something burning. Yanking open her bedroom door—she must have forgotten to turn off the hall light before she'd gone to bed— she saw that the stairwell was hazy with smoke. Oh, shit. Shit, shit, *shit*! She slammed the door shut, grabbed the phone by her bed and dialled 999.

'Fire brigade, please.' She gave her name,

133

address and details.

'Can you vacate the house?'

'I'm not sure. The fire's downstairs, and the only way onto the street is through the front door. There's a back door into the garden, though. I can't see any actual flames but there's quite a bit of smoke.'

'Right. Well, if you can't get out of the front door, go into the garden. Don't worry, they're on their way.'

Throwing on her dressing gown, Amy took a deep breath and pushed open the bedroom door again. She was surprised by how calm she felt. First thing: get downstairs. The smoke wasn't too thick—she could see where she was going—and when she got down to the hall she realised that it was coming from a big dark patch in the centre of the coconut fibre mat in front of the door. Coughing, she dashed into the kitchen, smacked the light switch, and, cursing, heaved the plastic bowl full of dirty crockery from the sink, lugged it, slopping, across the kitchen and tipped the contents over the mat. There was a hiss and an instant, acrid reek that caught at the back of her throat.

As she was refilling the bowl, she heard sirens. Thank God. She rushed into the hall and opened the front door. Running out to meet the engine as it pulled up, she said, 'It's just inside. On the mat. I don't think you'll need hoses or anything.'

Within minutes, two of the firemen had removed the scattered plates and cups from the smouldering mat, manhandled it onto the front step and doused it with an extinguisher. The others waited by the truck. Amy, watching from the

134

pavement, felt she ought to apologise for calling them out over something so undramatic.

'I'm very sorry,' she said, when they'd finished. 'I don't know how it happened. I was woken up by the smoke alarm and it was . . . well, what you saw.'

'Looks like you've had something through your letter box,' said one of the firemen. 'See this?' He pointed to some flakes of ash on the step. 'Paper, by the look of it.'

Amy goggled at him. 'You mean . . . it was deliberate?'

'Somebody's idea of a joke,' said the fireman grimly. 'Better have a look around. You on your own?'

'Yes.'

She followed him into the hall. The smoke had begun to drift outside, but it still smelt awful and the walls on either side of the front door were dark with soot. One fireman stood on a chair to disable the smoke alarm, and the other steered her into the sitting room. 'It's not as bad as it looks,' he said. 'A bit of a scrub and a lick of paint should sort it out. Your insurance'll cover it.' He stopped, looked through the kitchen door and went to turn off the tap. The water had overflowed the bowl and was running down the front of the sink unit.

Amy, who'd followed him, stared numbly at the puddle on the kitchen floor and the tracks left by the fireman's boots. 'Sorry,' she said, pulling out one of the kitchen chairs and sinking into it. 'I'm sorry, I—'

'It just needs a mop-up, that's all. No harm done.' He opened the kitchen window. 'That's better. Give the place a bit of an airing.'

'Here.' His colleague handed her the battery

135

from the smoke alarm. 'You can put it back in an hour or so.'

'Can we come in?' A woman's voice, loud and confident, issued from the front steps, and Moira Buchanan, a mackintosh slung over her towelling dressing gown, swept into the kitchen, followed by Charlie in jeans and T-shirt. Amy stared at them.

'We heard the sirens,' said Moira. 'Thought we'd better come and see if you were all right.'

'It was deliberate,' Amy told her. 'Someone put paper through the letter box.'

'Is that right?' Moira asked the fireman.

'Looks that way. We do see a bit of it. Vandals and the like.' He turned to Amy. 'As I was saying, there'll be an incident report. It hasn't happened before, has it?'

'No,' said Amy. 'Never.'

'You'll be fine, then.' He gave her an encouraging smile. 'Nice place. You'll have it back to normal in no time.'

Amy gazed out at the mess in the hall. Now that the immediate crisis was over, she felt stunned, unable to move or speak. She heard the fireman ask Moira and Charlie if they'd stay for a while, heard herself thank him, and then Moira asked her if she wanted to come next door, and she said she didn't. She sat watching Moira make tea and mop up the kitchen floor. Charlie disappeared upstairs and returned with a blanket, which he draped around her shoulders.

'Doesn't smell too bad,' she said, sniffing it.

'It's better up there,' said Charlie. 'I've opened a few more windows—that should improve things.'

'There you are,' said Moira, handing her a mug of tea. 'Plenty of sugar.'

'Thanks,' said Amy, and then, because she couldn't get it out of her mind, 'It was deliberate. Somebody did it on purpose.'

'Vandals,' said Moira. 'No respect for other people's property.'

'I'm not sure . . .' said Amy, and stopped because the thought, half-formed, seemed so terrible that she didn't want to say it out loud. Dad. Could this be something to do with him? Getting run over, and now this. Suddenly feeling that she might be sick, Amy rushed upstairs to the bathroom and knelt, retching, over the loo. Bloody hell. She stood in front of the bathroom mirror, wiping her mouth with a shaking hand. Her reflection gazed back at her with glassy, glitteringeyes.

There was a knock on the bathroom door. 'Amy?' It was Moira. 'Are you all right?'

'Yes.' Amy opened the door.

'Did you throw up?'

'A bit.'

'It's the shock. Come on.' Moira put a firm hand under her elbow and steered her back down to the kitchen. 'Finish your tea. Charlie's finding you some brandy. He's going to spend the night on your sofa, so you won't be alone.'

Amy wondered whose idea this had been, but didn't ask. Moira had clearly placed herself in charge of things, and she wasn't in a fit state to argue. 'As long as he doesn't mind,' she said.

'Of course not. Anyway, he owes it to you. Rampaging about the place stark naked! He told me.'

Amy looked up to see that Charlie, who had re-appeared with the brandy bottle, was blushing.

137

Moira patted her on the shoulder. 'You're in safe hands. I'll come by in the morning, see if there's anything I can do.'

'Thanks.'

Left alone with Charlie, Amy felt awkward. Adjusting her dressing gown while he poured the brandy, she said, 'I really am sorry about this. Waking you up and everything, especially after you took me up to the hospital for Dad.'

'It's fine.' He sat down opposite her. 'Anyway, none of it is your fault.'

'I can't believe . . .'

'What? That people do things like that? God knows, there are enough morons out there. It's just bad luck that one of them happened to be passing your house.'

'I'm not sure.' Amy hesitated, then took the plunge. 'I'm not sure that it *is* just bad luck.'

'How do you mean?'

'Well, you know I said my dad's been involved in some dodgy things?' Before she knew it, Amy found herself explaining about Patti dying, and her suspicions about why George had suddenly appeared on her doorstep. 'I asked him if anything was going on—if he owed money to anyone—but he denied it, and . . . He says he's ill, I mean, *really* ill—cancer—but I'm not sure whether I believe him. I know that sounds terrible, but he's got a rather, well, unusual relationship with the truth.'

'But, even if he is ill, if what you've just said is true, he's putting you in danger.'

'That's what makes me wonder if it wasn't just kids after all. Dad's done some pretty awful things in the past, but I can't believe he's that much of a shit.'

'It couldn't be someone with a grudge against you, could it? Moy said you're a journalist. You haven't upset anybody, have you?'

'I don't think so. Even if I had, people write a letter to the paper. They don't try and torch my house.'

'Do you think you should tell the police?'

'Tell them what? They wouldn't be able to do anything, and anyway they might start asking questions about Dad, and I don't want to get him into trouble.'

Charlie thought for a moment, then said, 'Your dad—you said he'd done some dodgy things. Has he ever had people after him before?'

'I think so. I'm pretty sure he's come to me once or twice for a bolthole, but there's never been any evidence of it. I've never known that much about what he does, to be honest.' She laughed shakily. 'Never really wanted to ask. I know he's my father, but he's the sort of person who's better kept at arm's length.'

'What about when you were young?'

'He wasn't around that much. He left when I was small—I'm an only child, so there's no one to compare notes with—and he came back off and on, but never for long.'

'He must have been worried that people might come after you and your mum if he'd scammed them or something.'

'I suppose it was partly that, but the main reason he came back was to see me. I was always getting ill, and Mum kept telling him I might die, so . . .' Amy stared down into her tea. It was the first time she'd said even that much to anybody, but the urge to talk was overwhelming, and for some reason—

not definable, more of an instinct—she sensed that Charlie would understand.

'What was wrong with you?'

'Oh, God, everything. But it wasn't . . . It's hard to explain. Chronic headaches, lack of energy, blood in the urine, stomach bugs, that sort of thing. It never added up to anything, but I was always in and out of the doctor's, and going to hospital for tests and exploratory surgery and God knows what. I was a real poster girl for sick children, and Mum kept dragging me along to all these specialists, and she'd say, "You've got to make them understand what's wrong with you, we've got to get this thing sorted out." I knew that meant I had to exaggerate, because if I was very bad Dad would come home again, and that's what I wanted, so I went along with it. The worst thing was, when he did come back he was always on the verge of some huge deal that was going to make us all rich, and then he was going to take us off to Paris or Geneva or New York or somewhere, so that I could see a top specialist. He used to talk as if he knew these people, and I was terrified that I wouldn't be ill enough to pass muster. You know, that it would be some guy who looked like Einstein surrounded by test-tubes, and I wouldn't get the symptoms right, and then I'd have failed and Dad would never come and see us again and Mum would blame me.'

She paused. Charlie, sitting back from the table, was looking down at his lap, absorbing what she'd said.

'How old were you?' he asked, his voice carefully neutral.

I was wrong, Amy thought. It was a mistake to

tell him, and now he's humouring me. She'd grown increasingly aware, while she was talking, of how odd it must sound to another person. Charlie probably came from a happy, normal family—nice home, both parents, one point two kids, even a bloody golden Labrador. Oh, God. He thinks I'm mad, she told herself, or making it up.

Desperately, she ploughed on. 'It went on till I was about fifteen. That was when I realised that the fortune and the top specialist and all that was a figment of Dad's imagination, and after that I stopped co-operating with Mum as well. She never really forgave me. But I did think the illnesses were genuine—I mean, there was something wrong, but not as wrong as she'd have liked, if you see what I mean. And then I discovered . . .' Amy took a deep breath. 'I was at a party, and this bloke was talking about something called Munchausen's Syndrome by Proxy, parents or carers who make a child ill because they want the attention. It was like being hit by a train. I was twenty-six, and I had this blinding realisation. It was just . . . I can't explain. I went home and I couldn't do anything for about a week. I could suddenly see that *she* was the one who'd given me all the symptoms in the first place. It had started when I was very young—maybe even a baby. All those tablets she'd made me take, and what she called tonics—they were the things that had made me ill in the first place. And when I looked it up, it was classic—she was always studying the medical books, keeping up with the latest scientific discoveries and everything. It sounds mad, doesn't it? I've never told anyone about this before, but I'm not making it up, honestly.'

141

'I can see you're not,' said Charlie gently. 'I know it can happen.'

'I confronted her. She denied everything. I didn't *want* it to be true, but I knew it was. She went on and on about how many sacrifices she'd made for me, how she couldn't get a proper job because I was always off school and how difficult it was to bring up a child on her own—I can see that, because she never had much support from Dad, but all the same . . . She said she'd done her best, and if my life wasn't turning out the way I wanted, it wasn't her fault. Then she wrote me a letter, and . . .'—Amy shut her eyes tight, fighting back tears—' . . . and she said I was the reason Dad didn't stay with us, I was the one who'd driven him away. And that was it, really. I'm sorry, Charlie. Like I said, I've never talked about this before, and I'm not sure why I'm telling you now.'

'Shock, probably,' said Charlie. 'Sometimes it's easier to talk to someone if you don't know them. Did your dad have any idea about what your mum was doing?'

'I tried to tell him. Ages ago, just after I found out, the next time I saw him. I thought maybe he could explain, but he just pushed it away. You can't have a conversation with him on that level. I can't, anyway. God knows I've tried. When he arrived last night, he told me he thought he had cancer, and my first thought was, this is payback time. For what Mum and I had done.'

'You mean what *she* had done,' said Charlie. 'You weren't old enough to understand what was going on.'

'No, but . . . Anyway, I thought he might be making it up. Because of that. Because he needs

142

money, or help, or . . . I loathe myself for thinking like that. It's mean-spirited and paranoid.'

'But it's not surprising.'

'Isn't it?'

'No. Not the way you grew up.' He smiled at her. 'It's not your fault, you know.'

'I keep telling myself that.'

'Do you?'

'Yeah.' Amy shrugged. 'Perhaps if I repeat it for long enough, I might start to believe it.'

Charlie stood up. 'I think you ought to try and get some sleep. I'll just roll up on the sofa. I know where the blankets are.'

'Do you?'

'Don't look so alarmed.' He pointed to the blanket round her shoulders. 'I found that one, didn't I?'

'Of course.' Amy stood up, too. 'You can have it.' She pulled it off and gave it to him. 'Thanks, Charlie.'

'That's OK. By the way, I'd like to get to know you. And, for what it's worth, I don't think you're mad.'

Amy stared at him. Tears were pricking her eyes again. For God's sake, she thought, pull yourself together, or he really will think you're a basket case. 'That's a relief,' she managed. 'Goodnight. And thanks.'

'You've said that already.' Grinning, he said, 'Go on, then. Upstairs.'

Sitting in bed, Amy listened to Charlie getting the blankets out of the cupboard. It was odd, having told him. A release: she felt physically lighter, as if she'd put down a burden. He doesn't think I'm mad, she said to herself. Mind you, she

143

hadn't told him about the Shands . . . Oh, Christ, the Shands. 'Look,' she said, raising her eyes to the ceiling. 'If you're up there, I've had my lot for this week, OK? Enough already.'

# CHAPTER NINETEEN

When the alarm went at half past seven Amy reached over, turned it off, and went back to sleep. When she finally surfaced at twenty to ten, it took her several minutes to remember what had happened. She went downstairs to find a note from Charlie on the kitchen table.

> *Amy,*
> *Thought you needed to sleep. Moira will be round later to see how you're doing. I put the battery back in your smoke alarm. Call me if you need anything.*
> *Charlie x*
> *PS: I'll get rid of the mat.*

Next to the note was a business card with a mobile number. Amy had a bath and got dressed—the house smelt a bit better than it had the previous night, and her clothes didn't seem too badly affected. Most of them could go in the washing machine, but some would have to be dry-cleaned. Amy was wondering if that would be covered by the insurance, when the doorbell rang. George was standing on the front step, dishevelled, and, except for his head, unshaven. 'Thank God for that,' he said. 'Bloody places. They never let you sleep.'

'How did you get back?'

'Minicab.'

'Where is it?'

'Gone. It's all right, cherub, I paid him.'

'Oh.' Amy felt the familiar mix of irritation and guilt. 'Come on in.'

George shuffled into the hall and lowered himself onto the stairs as if he had neither the energy nor the will to go any further. Looking at the smoke-blackened walls, he said, 'What the hell's been going on?'

'Fire,' said Amy shortly. 'Last night. I'm just trying to sort things out.'

'Christ. How did it happen?'

Amy looked at his expression of slack-jawed amazement, and decided to leave that particular conversation until later. 'I think you ought to lie down,' she said. 'I've opened the window in your room, so the smell shouldn't be too bad.'

'Yes. In a minute.'

'Can I get you anything?'

'No, it's all right. I'm sorry, chicky. I can see you've got a lot to do.'

George took himself upstairs, and Amy phoned the insurance—that sounded pretty straightforward, thank God—and busied herself sorting clothing into piles, hanging the duvet and cushion covers on the washing line for an airing, cleaning up the mess in the hall and calling a couple of local decorators for quotes.

Moira Buchanan knocked on the door mid-afternoon with a scrubbing brush and a tin of sugar soap. 'Thought you'd like some help,' she announced.

'I'd love some,' said Amy, 'if you don't mind.

145

Would you like some tea first? I was just going to have a break.'

'Good idea.' Moira followed her into the kitchen. 'It looks a lot better already. And the smell . . .' She sniffed. 'Not bad at all.'

'It's mainly the upholstery I'm worried about,' said Amy. 'Curtains and rugs. And the stair carpet.'

'I'll help you get the curtains down,' said Moira. 'The dry-cleaners'll do those. And I know a good firm for carpets. One of those industrial shampoo things. Very reliable. I'll send Charlie round with their card.'

'He was really helpful last night.'

'He's always been kind. He's my sister's son.'

'He's a gardener, isn't he?' Amy fished.

'Yes. A good one, too. His father was dead against it, of course.'

'Why?'

'Thought Charlie ought to follow him. He was a judge, and a great bully.'

'Really?' Amy swung round, surprised. Moira had always seemed a die-hard, law-and-order Tory, with all trimmings.

'Oh,' Moira said, 'I'm not saying they're all like that, not at all. But Charlie's father was a thoroughly nasty piece of work. Never understood what my sister saw in him. Always despised Charlie because he wasn't academic.' Giving Amy a shrewd look, she said, 'Charlie's not stupid—far from it. Just didn't get on with books. Probably a reaction to his father, and, as I say, he's bloody good at his job. Chelsea Flower Show, all that. More work than he can handle—the reason he's staying with me at the moment is because some hotshot in

Highgate offered him a fortune to create an enormous garden from scratch.'

'Where does he usually live?'

'Sussex. On the downs. Lovely place. He's done well for himself.'

'That's nice.' Amy handed her a cup of tea.

'Charlie doesn't like talking about it,' Moira said. 'His father's dead now, so's my sister, but . . . It wasn't easy for him. His brother went into the law, so he was the odd one out.'

Amy wanted to hear more, but didn't see how she could continue the conversation without appearing to pry, so she said, 'My father's upstairs, by the way. Just got back from the hospital.'

Moira nodded. 'Charlie told me. All right, is he?'

'I think so. Just tired.'

'A good sleep ought to do the trick.' She put down her mug. 'Right. Where shall we start?'

That evening, after Moira had gone and Amy had ferried a car-load of things to the dry-cleaners, she went upstairs to look in on George. She'd expected to find him asleep, but when she peered round the door of his room his eyes were open.

'How are you feeling?'

'Bit better.' He sat up, adjusted his pyjama top, rubbed a hand over his face, then patted the edge of the bed. 'Come and sit down.'

'We didn't wake you, did we?'

'We?'

'A neighbour came to help me clear up.'

'How did it go?'

'It looks a lot better.'

'That's good.' George smiled at her. 'Bloody nuisance.'

'You can say that again.'

Why isn't he more curious? she thought. He hasn't asked me a thing about it. Is that because he's tired, or is there another reason? 'Did the police come and see you last night?' she asked.

'No. Well, not that I'm aware of. I wasn't really compos mentis.'

'Maybe they'll come tomorrow, then. The one who told me about it said they were following it up.'

'No point. It'll just be some kid who needs a search warrant to find his cock. In any case, it was an accident. Just bad luck.'

'Are you absolutely sure about that?'

George looked irritated. 'I've said so, haven't I? What are you implying?'

'The fire last night wasn't an accident.'

'Wasn't it? Easily done, you know. Cigarette in the rubbish bin, that sort of thing.'

'You may not have noticed, but I've stopped smoking. And the fireman said it was started deliberately. Paper through the letter box.'

'How did he know?'

'They see this sort of thing all the time.' Amy kept her eyes firmly fixed on his face.

'There you are, then. It was kids. Anti-social behaviour. You should know—you're always writing about that sort of thing.'

'So it was nothing to do with you?'

'Me?' George looked surprised, then put a hand on her knee. 'Look, Amy, you've got to understand. I might have pulled a few strokes in the past, but it's all above board nowadays. Legit.'

'Really?'

'Yes. I don't blame you for being suspicious, but

I promise you, there's nothing going on.'

Amy sighed, and stood up. 'If you say so. Look, I need to get on with some work.'

'All right, cherub.' He patted her on the bottom. 'Off you go.'

'Can I get you anything?'

'I'm fine.' George's smile had enough hint of suffering in silence to cause Amy a pang of annoyance.

'I'll look in later,' she said, and closed the door behind her. As she hadn't eaten all day, she made herself a large, messy sandwich and sat down in front of her laptop. Chewing, elbows on the desk, she gazed at the screensaver and wondered where, in George's make-up, the self-deluding fantasist ended and the manipulator began. He'd been concussed all right, but nothing else was certain. Maybe it was an accident. But the other thing . . . God, she remembered suddenly, the silent call. When she got back from the hospital—the person who'd just hung up. It could have been a wrong number, but supposing it wasn't? Supposing there were people after George and they knew he was here? They'd heard her voice. They'd known she was in, and done it anyway. And if they were the same people who'd tried to run George over, they hadn't stayed around to see the ambulance arrive, so presumably they thought he was here, too.

Hang on. The phone hadn't gone all day . . . Amy grabbed the study extension and dialled 1471. *Sorry, the last caller withheld their number.* What had she expected? She put the phone down. The police would be able to trace the number, but why should they? She hadn't anything to tell them apart from her suspicions about George, and it was clear he wasn't going to back her up. Perhaps it *was* just coincidence. There you go again, she told herself, trying to make patterns out of everything. Like a well-constructed article, topped and tailed. Life isn't like that.

After an unfruitful three hours, Amy closed *The Cultural State*, cast a last, despairing glance at her unfinished review, and decided it was bed time. She checked on George, found that he was fast asleep, and decided to spend the night on the sofa downstairs. She'd felt secure enough with Charlie in the house, but tonight . . . Probably stupid, but it was better to be on the safe side. She fetched her alarm clock, took her duvet and pillows from the line in the garden, made sure the phone was where she could reach it, and settled herself for the night.

She woke suddenly a few hours later and sat up, her heart pounding. Someone was in the kitchen. She pulled on her dressing gown and, holding the phone, tiptoed across the hall.

There were no lights on, just a spaceship glow from the corner furthest away from the window. As quietly as she could, Amy moved forward the last couple of feet and poked her head around the door. It was George, stark naked, bending over in front of the open fridge, staring at the contents, pallid buttocks backlit by the bulb inside.

'Dad!' Relief made Amy want to laugh. 'God, you gave me a fright! What are you doing?'

There was no response. 'Dad?' George neither looked up nor turned round. 'Listen, Dad, just stay there, and I'll fetch your dressing gown.' She ran upstairs and came back holding it in front of her like a screen. 'Come on, put this round you. You'll catch cold.' He made no attempt to help her as she

150

bent over and slipped the heavy silk around his shoulders, pulled him up gently and round to face her, pushed his arms into the sleeves and knotted the cord at his waist. At six foot four, with broad shoulders, George would always be big and pretty solid, but seeing him unclothed, Amy realised that age (and possibly illness) was sagging him, depositing small pouches of fat and stripping him of muscle so that he seemed feeble, almost like a baby. When she looked at his face, she saw that there were tears in his eyes.

'What is it, Dad? Do you want something?'

He blinked, but said nothing. The eerie fridge light gave his skin a sickly, greenish pallor.

'What about a drink of water?'

His face crenellated into a frown. 'Why?'

'I thought you might be thirsty.'

'I don't think so.'

'Why were you looking in the fridge?'

He looked at her as if this was a question which no reasonable person could be expected to answer. 'I *might* like some water,' he conceded.

'OK.' He stood back and watched closely while she took the bottle and poured a glassful, as if it were something he might be tested on later.

'Thank you.' He drank clumsily, two-fisted like a child, slopping water down his neck and onto his dressing gown. Amy wondered if she ought to call a doctor. The bang on the head had obviously affected him more than she'd thought.

Getting him to his bedroom was an uphill three-legged race, with George threatening to slither downwards and Amy trying to shore him up with one hand and dragging on the banister with the other. When she'd tucked him into bed, he asked,

'Can you stay for a bit?'

'Sure.' Amy sat down on the side of the bed. 'Are you going to be OK?'

'I think so. I was dreaming about Patti. I was going to see if she'd forgive me, you know. Take me back.'

'You know she would have. Why didn't you come sooner? You knew she was ill.'

In the moonlight—the curtains were at the cleaners—Amy could see that George's eyes were glittering with tears. 'That's why. When you told me she was ill, cherub, I couldn't stand it. Not again.'

'Again?'

'There was a woman in Switzerland. Young, beautiful . . . For the first time since Patti, I thought I was in love.' As he described the woman, Amy wondered if it was Claire and she'd got the wrong end of the stick. George was describing a competely different Claire from the one she'd imagined—his was a shampoo-ad blonde leaping gracefully down the side of a flower-covered alp, turning to smile winsomely over her shoulder, a soft-focus smile and a white sundress.

'I thought that was it,' he said. 'I thought we'd settle down and then . . . then . . . she got leukaemia, and I couldn't deal with it. She was so beautiful, and I left her. I ran away.'

'Why? And why didn't you tell me all this when you arrived?'

'I was tired, love, and I didn't want to upset you. You were so ill as a child,' he continued, reaching for her hand, 'and seeing you like that, in pain, with all those bloody tubes coming out of you, and knowing I couldn't help . . . Patti was always telling me how bad you were, and I couldn't bear it. I thought you were going to die, and I just couldn't . . . I had to leave.' He buried his face in his hands.

My God, Amy thought, it was all for nothing. Patti, who'd always said she knew George better than anybody else did and loved him more than any woman ever could, had got it so, so wrong. Talk about counter-intuitive. Amy didn't know whether to laugh or cry. That, she thought, was the reason they'd never been able to discuss the Munchausen's—it wasn't only death that terrified him, but illness, too. The only way he could deal with it was by running away.

It's only because he's still wobbly from that bang on the head that he's saying these things, Amy thought. It's as near as he's ever going to come to confronting any of it.

'What happened to the woman in Switzerland?'

'She died. About five years ago now.'

In the silence that followed, Amy thought, it can't have been Claire, then. 'Are you sure you're not running away from somebody?'

'No, chicky. I am in a mess, but it's not like that. I'm sorry. I know I haven't been much good as a father, I should have been there when you were ill.'

Amy looked down at George's hand covering hers, and had a sudden, tender shock of memory: her small hand in his as they swung along the pavement at Western Avenue, the two of them yelling at each other while the traffic hurtled alongside in a blur of trailing colour. When he'd been there, even a trip to the corner shop for a shared Kit-Kat had seemed like an adventure.

153

Then she imagined her mother's scissors cutting through her wrist to sever the connection between them as she had in the photographs. I'd bleed to death, she thought. Then: but you can't do that any more, Patti. You're gone, and we're still here. You made the mistake of leaving us together. Whatever's happened, whatever George has done, he's still my father, and I must look after him.

'You're welcome to stay as long as you want,' she said. 'Till you get sorted out.'

'Thanks, cherub.' George gazed at her with wet eyes. 'It's more than I deserve.'

'Yes, it is.'

'Give me a kiss, darling.' He tapped his cheek with a finger, and, when Amy leant down to give him a peck, he put both arms up and enveloped her in a hug, so that she lost her balance and ended up half kneeling on the side of the bed with her face pressed awkwardly against his. 'I know you've got your own life,' he said. 'I don't expect you to put up with me for much longer. But I've lost two of the women I loved, and I couldn't bear to lose you, too, not now.'

Amy closed the door. Standing on the landing, looking out through the staircase window into the garden, she heard 'Thanks, cherub. Sleep tight.' Fat chance, she thought, as she padded wearily down the stairs to the sofa.

# CHAPTER TWENTY

Amy finally dropped off at around five, overslept, and woke at twenty past ten. George emerged a couple of hours later, all smiles, and announced that he was taking himself off to the pub for lunch.

'Do you think that's a good idea?' Amy asked. 'You've just had a whack on the head.' She knew it was pointless bringing up the subject of creditors again—it would only lead to further denials, and she knew from years of observing Patti that the more she kept on about it, the less likely he was to tell her the truth.

'I'm fine.' George bent over and planted a kiss on the top of her head. 'No need to fuss. What are you up to?'

'Work.'

'Right-o. See you later.'

Hampered by constant thoughts of her father and the Shands, Amy's progress was slow. At half past seven, with mounting anxiety over George's whereabouts, she switched off her laptop and embarked on a tour of the local pubs, but nobody remembered seeing him. She walked back home, trying to keep a lid on all sorts of horrible imaginings about what might have happened to him, and was about to let herself in when Charlie's van pulled up next door.

'Amy. How are you doing?'

'I just wanted to say thank you for the other night. Staying with me, I mean.'

'Not at all. I was going to come round, actually. See if you were OK.' He looked at her for a moment. 'You aren't, are you?'

'I'm worried about Dad. He went out at half twelve, said he was going to have lunch at one of the pubs round here, and he hasn't come back. I've been asking, but no one's seen him.'

'He might have gone further afield.'

'It's possible. But seven hours is a hell of a long lunch, even for Dad. He was pretty odd last night, as well. I woke up at two and found him staring into the fridge. He didn't seem to know what he was doing.'

'Was he OK this morning?'

'He seemed fine, but he might have delayed concussion or something.'

'Isn't it more likely he's met up with some friends?'

'As long as they *are* friends, and not . . . what I told you.'

'Yeah.' Charlie frowned. 'Look, what are you doing this evening?'

'Nothing. Well, I ought to be working, but I couldn't concentrate. Dad'll probably roll up any minute, happy as Larry, but . . .'

'Would you like some company?'

'Only if you're not busy. I've already imposed on you enough as it is.'

'No, you haven't. I'd like to. I need to shower first, though.'

'OK. Great. Shall I order a takeaway or something? What do you like?'

'Anything. I don't mind.'

'Thai?'

'Fine. See you in about half an hour. And don't worry. I'm sure he'll turn up.'

They chatted for a while about George, and the garden Charlie was making in Highgate, and then, two glasses in, with the Thai meal spread between them on the table, Amy found herself talking about the Shands.

Charlie listened in silence while she explained about the diary and the newspaper cuttings and her visits to Sheila and Iris, and Bill Drake's phone call, and then he said, 'Leslie Shand must have been a worried man.'

'*Worried?*'

'Think about it,' said Charlie. 'It was him against the world. Keeping up appearances and making sure his family didn't say anything. Must have been a huge strain, especially when the girls got older. Boyfriends and all that.'

'I don't think he let them have boyfriends. Mo's diary certainly doesn't mention any. But you're right, I hadn't thought of it from his point of view—just Mo and the others'. What he did to them, why they stayed. I'd thought of him as someone all-powerful—a sort of ogre. But you can't simply say that someone is evil—it lets them off the hook. Means they aren't responsible for their actions.'

'He probably didn't think he was responsible,' said Charlie. 'Violent men blame their wives. If I don't get my dinner or my freshly ironed shirt or whatever I want right on tap, it's her fault—that's what she's there for and she's not doing her job. And the wives think they deserve it.'

Amy was taken aback by the flat authority of his voice. 'How do you know?'

'My parents.'

'*What?*'

'My dad used to hit my mum,' said Charlie, in a matter-of-fact tone. 'That's why I know about it. Don't look so shocked, Amy. It happens in nice, middle-class homes as well. Dad was a judge.'

'Moira told me.'

'Did she?' Charlie looked surprised. 'Did she tell you anything else?'

'She said he didn't like you doing gardening, and that you've got a brother who's a lawyer.'

'Yeah. We don't get on.'

'Is he older than you?'

'A few years. I didn't find out what was going on until I was about eleven. I'd been woken up a couple of times—bumping and banging downstairs. She always said it was nothing, but once I heard her screaming. I saw Dad come upstairs and I asked him what was wrong but he just told me to go back to bed. I waited until he'd gone into their room and then went down, and Mum was sitting there crying. He'd broken her arm. My brother was away at school, but when he came back in the summer I asked him if he knew what was going on and he said, "Sure." Really dismissive, as if it didn't matter. Mum never talked to us about it—I tried when I was older, but she insisted that everything was fine. When I went away to school I was always trying to phone her to make sure she was OK.'

'But your brother—didn't he *mind*?'

'I think . . .' Charlie looked down at his glass. 'He despised her. There wasn't anything we could do about it, so I suppose that was easier. Dad never hit us, but he was a bully. Verbally, I mean.

He could really humiliate you. We had a huge row when I said I wanted to go to horticultural college, and I left home and never went back. Mum came to visit me whenever she could get away, and I used to ring her when I knew he wouldn't be there.'

'Why didn't she leave him, Charlie?'

'Didn't want to break up the family. She'd never worked—she married Dad when she was nineteen and I suppose she didn't have much idea of living independently. By the time I left home, it was too late. We did talk about it once, after he died, and she said that she was too ashamed to admit it to anyone, so she made excuses for him. She didn't want us to know, because she thought it would be a bad example. And, like I said, she thought it must be her fault.'

'God.'

'Mum was a strong person in a lot of ways, not just a victim. That's the thing: when people haven't experienced something like that, someone who's been battered, they only see them as a doormat. It wasn't as if Mum was crying all the time—in fact, the broken arm was the only time I saw her in tears. She was very intelligent, she had a wicked sense of humour, and she was a brilliant gardener. Helping her was what got me interested.'

'Does Moira know?'

'I told her after Mum died. She said she thought there was something going on.'

'But she never asked? I mean, they were sisters.'

'She thought it wasn't her business. And Mum wouldn't have thanked her for interfering. It's difficult, Amy. I wanted to protect her so much—I used to sleep on the landing so I could rush

159

downstairs if I heard anything, because I knew Dad wouldn't hit her in front of me—but it was hard because she wouldn't talk about it, and I knew, when I was older, that there was no point in confronting him because they'd both have denied everything. I'm not condoning it, Amy, but things like that can be pretty complicated—people's feelings, and why they do things. A lot of the time they don't understand it themselves, so if you're coming from the outside . . . You can't just go barging into people's affairs like some sort of social worker, thinking you know best. That's why you ought to be careful about the Shands. I'm not saying you shouldn't have any more contact, but be careful. Don't go sailing in with a lot of'—he frowned, groping for the right words—'post-feminist assumptions.'

'I wasn't going to.' Amy was hurt. 'In any case, with the Shands it started happening in the fifties. There weren't any feminist assumptions in those days, let alone post-feminist ones.'

'It still happens, you know.'

'I know it does. That's why we have all those posters about domestic violence.'

'Yeah, those. But have you noticed that you see dozens of articles about it happening in other cultures—dowry deaths and so on—but not about Westerners? It's a new way of turning a blind eye. Western women—especially middle-class women —are supposed to be empowered and all the rest of it, so there's no reason to stay with a man who hits them, but they still do. I don't know why, but you never see articles about why people become victims of domestic violence. Why did my mum marry my dad? She told me she was in love with him, but he can't have just changed overnight, so the aggression—even if he wasn't expressing it—must have been there from the off. Perhaps it made him exciting. Do you see what I'm trying to say?'

'Yes. It's a pretty uncomfortable subject.'

'It's complicated, like I said. Just because you wouldn't put up with it—'

'No, I wouldn't.'

'—doesn't mean everyone's the same.'

'I do understand that, Charlie, but I think the Shands are an exceptional case.'

He nodded. 'Sounds like it.'

'I can't stop thinking about them. I decided this afternoon that I'd go and see the mother—Iris—again. Bill Drake can't stop me.'

'No.' Charlie frowned. 'But be careful. He sounds like he's got some sort of agenda.'

A loud crash against the front door made them both turn round. Charlie said, 'Wait here,' and went to open it. It was George.

For Amy, who could see from the kitchen, relief turned to embarrassed revulsion as she realised that her father was a whisker away from paralytic. She watched him sway forwards and then back on his heels in drunken push-me-pull-you fashion, as he continued trying to jab his key into a lock that was no longer there. After a moment he straightened up, peered at Charlie with intense concentration and muttered something. Then, trying to turn round, he lost his footing and fell heavily against the doorframe.

'It's OK, Dad.' Amy joined Charlie at the door. 'You're in the right place.' George squinted at her, then tried to shove his key into his jacket pocket.

He missed, and it fell through the railings and landed with a clatter in the basement area. Charlie raised his eyebrows. 'You'd better fetch it,' he said. 'I'll get him inside.'

When Amy returned, George was ensconced at the kitchen table, his nose in a glass of wine. She glared at him.

'Sorry,' said Charlie. 'He grabbed it before I could stop him.'

'It's OK.'

'Do you want some help getting him upstairs before I go?'

Amy shook her head. 'If I can't manage, he'll have to sleep on the sofa. I am sorry about this, Charlie.'

'Stop apologising. He's safe, that's the main thing.' Charlie put an arm round her waist and steered her into the hall. 'Listen,' he murmured into her hair. 'Three questions. Is it OK if I ring you tomorrow?'

'Yes.'

'What's your number?' He pulled his mobile phone from his jeans' pocket and keyed in the digits that Amy recited. 'Good. You've got mine, haven't you?'

'Yes, thanks. What's the other question?'

'Please may I kiss you?'

Amy turned her head towards the kitchen. George was slumped over the table, oblivious of what was happening behind him. 'Why not?'

# CHAPTER TWENTY-ONE

Amy closed the front door and returned to the kitchen, where she sat down opposite her father. 'Where the hell have you been?' she asked.

George raised his head and contemplated her blearily. 'Out.'

'Out where?'

'Out.' As he reached for the wine bottle, the elbow on which he was propped slipped off the edge of the table and he lunged sideways, narrowly preventing himself from crashing to the floor. 'Shlipt.'

'So I saw.'

Fumbling to re-light his cigar, he ignored her. The box fell from his hand, spilling matches across the table. 'Shurely,' he said belligerently, 'do gruj m'bi offun?'

'I don't begrudge you anything. Did you meet someone?'

'Offren.'

Amy mentally translated drunk-speak into English. 'An old friend?'

George nodded vigorously. 'Lover.'

'An old lover?'

Another nod.

'Dad,' she said firmly, removing the glass from his fingers, 'I don't want to know. Let's get you to bed.'

He scowled at her. 'Wafor?'

'Because you need to get some sleep. Come on.'

George rose, unsteadily, both hands on the table for support. He managed to extricate himself from the chair, then leant down at a dangerously oblique angle to scoop up his glass once more. 'Little lassht drop.' He took aim at his mouth without, apparently, even trying to swallow, and a trickle of red wine ran down his neck and soaked into his shirt collar.

'That's enough.' Amy caught his arm and steered him, lurching, into the hall and up the stairs. On the bend, in a farcical replay of the previous night, he began to subside, and there was nothing she could do to stop him. It was, she thought, as if he had sprung a leak and was going to spread out all over the carpet—she had an insane image of him splayed flat on the landing like a tiger-skin rug—and once his head was level with her knee, she knew there was no chance of getting him upright again. They finished the journey into the bedroom with George on his hands and knees, and Amy pushing from behind. A final shove got him lying on his side on the bed, and before she'd managed to get his shoes off his eyes were closing and he was breathing stertorously, as if sleep, too, were an uphill struggle. This is becoming a habit, Amy thought, as she returned to the kitchen to clear the table. She wondered what George's old flame was like. Probably a bit of a lush, to judge by the state of him.

In bed, she thought about Charlie. Moira said he didn't like to talk about his family, yet he'd said it all in such a matter-of-fact way. Still, now she thought about it, the confession made her uneasy. He'd said it partly to help her, she knew, but all the same, it was too much, too quick. And as for the things she'd told him . . . She felt shaken and off balance, as if there was only a tiny margin of safety, like the edge of a precipice, before a downward plunge to disaster. I don't know him, she thought, but then I don't know Dad, either. And she hadn't known Patti— certainly not what made her tick. As for the Shands . . . She'd surprised herself when she told Charlie she was thinking about going back to Compton Lodge to see Iris, but she definitely wanted to. I'll do it tomorrow, she decided. George can bloody well hold the fort. She suddenly remembered he hadn't told her what he'd done about Patti's flat or given back the keys. It felt like weeks ago. Nothing I can do now, she thought, and gave herself up to sleep.

The following morning, she got up early to finish her book reviews. Then she bolted a sandwich, left a note for George, gathered up the photocopied diary from the sitting-room floor and was on the road for Compton Lodge by half past one. On the way she stopped once for flowers— chrysanths, this time—and once at the library, where she took the diary in order to check the name of Mo Shand's specialist in the *Medical Directory*.

There was only one Dr Lovegood, with an address in Barnet, now working at University College Hospital, and, after his name, the letters MB, ChB, DPsych. She'd guessed right—Mo had definitely been admitted to Barnet General with mental health problems.

As before, Clementine answered the door at Compton Lodge. 'Miss Vaughan—back so soon? Iris will be pleased.'

165

'Hello, Clementine. Do you think so?'

'Oh, yes. She liked you. I can tell.'

She led Amy upstairs to Iris Shand's room and bore the chrysanthemums away to put them in a vase. Iris was sitting in the same place as before—the wing-backed armchair in front of the window—and wearing an almost identical outfit, this time in lilac. The photograph album was on her lap, and the blue knitted rabbit, which had lain on the bedside table during Amy's last visit, was propped beside her right knee.

Amy announced herself, but Iris did not look up, even when Amy sat down in the chair nearest hers. 'Has your daughter been to see you?' she asked. Iris didn't appear to have heard her. Amy tried again. 'Your daughter, in the photograph, has she been to see you? Has she been here?'

Iris looked up for a moment with a look of reproachful astonishment on her face, as if she couldn't understand why Amy was being so rudely persistent, and then bowed her head once more over her album.

Amy leant over and pointed a finger at the taller of the two girls. 'Has she been to see you?' Iris's skinny, liver-spotted hand moved with surprising speed, covering Amy's and placing it so that her fingertips rested on the shorter girl's face. 'That's Maureen, isn't it? Your younger daughter—you used to call her Mo.' Iris pressed down on her hand and moved it slightly, so that her fingers stroked the child's face. Iris's hand was light, almost weightless, yet Amy could feel a strong current running through it to her own, a tingling like a very mild electric shock. 'Mo,' said Iris.

There's no question about it, thought Amy, she

166

thinks that's who I am. She felt oddly guilty. She hadn't set out to trick Iris, but it seemed pointless to upset her by trying to explain, once more, who she actually was.

Clementine put her head round the door. 'I got your flowers,' she told Amy. 'You take them to her.' Iris nodded impatiently as Amy placed the flowers on the window ledge, and then, once she'd sat down, reached behind her and started scrabbling among her cushions, knocking the knitted rabbit onto the carpet.

She wants to show me something, thought Amy, with a surge of excitement. She had no idea what it might be, but when Iris produced what looked like a local newspaper she was disappointed.

Iris gestured at the paper, indicating that Amy should take it. It was folded to pages four and five, which, as far as she could see, were full of local news about parking schemes and proposals for playgrounds and anti-drug initiatives. She scanned the headlines, aware that Iris was watching her intently, head on one side like a little bird, until she came to the bottom of page five. 'Skeleton Found in Wood,' she read aloud. 'Is this what you wanted me to see?'

Iris leant forward, eyes anxious, her hands making little darting movements towards Amy's lap.

'You want me to put it in my bag? Yes? There, look, it's in the bag. It's gone.' Amy bent down and picked up the knitted rabbit.

Iris beamed at her and put the toy on the chair beside her, then sat back and leant her head against one of the wings, apparently satisfied. Her face, now in direct sun, was like crumpled tissue

167

paper. She's becoming transparent, Amy thought. Layer by layer, she's departing from life. 'Are you tired?' she asked. 'Would you like me to go now?'

Iris's eyes were closed, but her fingers, on the arm of the chair, fluttered slightly.

Amy took her hand, very gently, and got a faint squeeze in return. 'Thank you,' she said. 'Goodbye, Iris.'

She was desperate to get to her car so she could read about the skeleton, but she wanted to check something first. Sister Paula, looking through a pile of papers, looked less than thrilled to be interrupted. 'Sorry to bother you,' said Amy, placatingly. 'It's just a quick question. I was wondering if Iris might like something to read, but I don't know what to get, and I thought maybe you could help.'

She had the distinct impression that if Sister Paula hadn't been on duty she would have laughed. 'I'm afraid she's a wee bit beyond that.'

'That did cross my mind,' said Amy innocently, 'but she had a copy of the local paper, so I assumed . . . I mean, one can't always tell.'

'I daresay her daughter left it. She was here a couple of days ago. We only take *The Times* and the *Mail*.'

'Oh, well, never mind. I'll have to think of something else. Now, I mustn't take up any more of your time.' Sister Paula was re-immersed in her papers before Amy had left the room.

OK, thought Amy, so Sheila had brought the paper. As soon as she was safely locked in her car, she pulled it out of her bag.

## SKELETON FOUND IN WOOD

A man walking his dog in Hadley Wood has discovered human remains in a drainage ditch, it was revealed yesterday. Police have not yet identified the skeleton, which is thought to be female, but a spokesman said that it may have been buried for a number of years.

She read it several times. It's Mo, she thought, remembering Sheila's horror on seeing her standing on the porch at Hadley Cottage. Mo is a ghost. Iris hadn't reacted in the same way, but then, even if she'd been told Mo was dead, the concepts of life and death might no longer hold any meaning for her. If Sheila had killed Mo, and Bill Drake knew, it certainly went a long way to explaining their behaviour. What if Sheila had carried the can for Mo over the killing of Leslie, and then, overcome by remorse after the trial, Mo had told Sheila that she was going to confess? That would make some sort of sense—if that had happened, Sheila would have been in trouble for perverting the course of justice, and Mo would undoubtedly have ended up in a secure unit. A mercy killing? Amy pictured the immaculate cottage and its genteel occupant with her curiously absent personality. Sheila hadn't seemed off her rocker, but . . . You couldn't really blame her if she was, thought Amy. She stuffed the newspaper back in her bag and started the engine.

# CHAPTER TWENTY-TWO

In spite of the tablets, Sheila slept badly. First she dreamt that their parrot, Stanley, was in the bedroom, malevolent eyes swivelling at her as he strutted up and down on his perch and repeated phrases he'd learnt from her father. *You useless cow, I'll give you a hiding, you thick bitch* . . . Over and over. Pinioned by the sheet, she couldn't make him stop, and woke at three, sweating and flailing in a tangle of sheets. When she dozed off again, just before dawn, she dreamt of *him*. She was holding his hand, as she'd often done when he had his bad times and would sit, depressed in front of the electric fire, telling her how miserable he was. In the dream, she did what she always did at those times, putting her arm round his shoulder and saying, mechanically, 'It's all right, Dad, you'll be all right,' over and over, but when she let go, he lolled backwards and she saw the wounds on his chest and knew he was dead.

For the first seconds after she woke, she felt as shocked as if it had just happened. He was always saying he wanted to die: *You don't know what my life is like. I'd kill myself if it wasn't for the three of you.* When Mo told him she wanted to commit suicide, he'd said that if she did it he would kill her and Mum as well; and she'd had a suicide pact with Mo in case anything happened to Mum. Sometimes, in brief, objective interludes, Sheila could see their situation as a black farce, and now, lying in bed, the Laughing Policeman broke through the surface of her mind in an explosion of raucous derision: *Whooooah! Ha, ha, ha, ha, ha, ha, ha!* She got up and ran across to the bathroom, but the hard, shiny porcelain intensified the noise to an incessant, jangling clamour.

The laughter followed her downstairs to the kitchen, where the small amount of soft morning light that filtered through the blinds gave the fitments and furniture fuzzy, comforting outlines, so that the din inside her head lost its sharp edges and the throbbing reduced itself, gradually, to a dull ache.

Silently, Sheila made herself a cup of tea. At least it was her day off and she didn't have to face anybody. She knew that her father had often been unhappy, and she knew, too, that he'd been weak in some ways, afraid of the dark, not wanting to be left alone. He'd never tried to dominate other people in the way he did them. He'd say things behind their backs ('If I had power, they'd be in the gas ovens') but never to their faces. And, even though he was always telling them how much he'd enjoyed the army and wished himself back there (why had he ever left?) he'd been almost shy with other men—in fact, she'd often noticed that he didn't much enjoy their company, never visiting the pub alone or taking the dog on the commonwhen the cricketers were there. There had been moments, growing up, when she'd understood that, despite his terrible hold over them, he was childish and pathetic, as dependent on them as they were on him. But they were only moments: the rest of the time, his power was entire and overwhelming.

She dragged herself back upstairs to get washed and dressed, and by the time she returned to the kitchen in a neat cotton frock she felt calmer and was able to cook herself some breakfast—tomatoes on toast. Halfway through, she heard the *Mail* thudding onto the mat, but only when she'd finished eating did she go into the hall and collect it.

She poured a second cup of tea, opened the blinds to the sun, and sat flicking through the pages, scanning the headlines for anything about a body, but there was nothing. She checked twice, three times, her fingers scrabbling at the paper, the black type a blur in front of her eyes. But soon, it would be soon. And this time . . .

In a single, violent movement, Sheila pushed the paper away, not registering as the wedge of pages connected with her saucer and the cup clattered sideways, slopping tea across the formica table top. Elbows on the table, knuckles scraping together, she rocked backwards and forwards. 'No, please, no, no . . .'


# CHAPTER TWENTY-THREE

Amy drove home, fruitless thoughts circling, never connecting, and reached the phone just in time to take a call asking her to write an article about fetish parties for the over-seventies. Cheered by the prospect of chatting with corseted and rouged geriatrics over post-flagellation cups of Horlicks, she returned to work with renewed energy, and was halfway through roughing out an overdue piece on the success of the government's childcare policy when George appeared, shaved, dressed, and looking remarkably spruce.

'Hello, chicky. Sorry about last night. Can't remember much, to be honest.'

'That's probably just as well.'

'That bad, eh? Have to make it up to you, then. Are you doing anything this evening?'

'Working.'

'Because if you've nothing planned—'

'Apart from work.'

'That can wait, can't it? I want to take you out to dinner.'

'You mean you want *me* to take *you* out to dinner. You still owe me for that lunch, remember?'

'Of course I remember. How much was it?' He put his hand into his jacket pocket and, with a conjurer's flourish, produced a wad of notes secured in a silver clip.

Amy's eyes bulged. 'Where did you get all that?'

'Chap owed me some money. Saw him yesterday and he paid me back. Got a new mobile, too, by the way. Here's the number.' He handed her a slip of paper. 'Now then, where's the bill?'

Astonished, Amy rooted in her purse for the receipt. 'There you are.'

George glanced at it—'Not much of a tip'—then peeled off two fifty-pound notes and put them down on the desk. 'There you go. Keep the change. You should have a bit more faith in your old dad, you know. Now, about this evening: there's someone I'd like you to meet. Someone special.'

'It's not the woman you were with last night, is it?'

'How do you know about that?'

'You told me.'

'Did I? God.' He shook his head. 'I can't remember a bloody thing.'

'You said she was an old friend, and that you'd been lovers.'

'That's right. Lovely woman. One of the best.'

'What's her name?'

'Claire.'

The same Claire, presumably, who'd written the letter. 'Is that why you came back, to see her?'

George shook his head. 'She lives in Switzerland. I didn't even know she was here.'

'Then why *did* you come?' Amy persisted.

'To see you, darling. And because of Patti. I know you find it hard to believe, and I don't blame you, but that's the truth.'

Amy sighed. 'OK. Did Claire give you that money?'

'No! Somebody owed me. Anyway, what about tonight?'

'You don't really want me there, do you?'

'Claire wants to meet you.'

'To be honest, Dad, I'm a bit worried about leaving the house empty. I know you keep saying there's no one after you . . .'

'There isn't. You know something, Amy'—he moved behind her chair and put his hands on her shoulders—'you've got to start trusting people.'

It was an effort to keep her voice level. 'I don't think you're in any position to talk to me about trust.'

'Don't be upset, chicky.' His thumbs kneaded the back of her neck. 'I know it's your job to be suspicious and ask questions and things. All I meant was that you've got to relax as well. You're so tense. Anyone would think you were seventy,

174

not thirty-five.'

'Thirty-*four*. And I'm tense because you're hurting me.'

George took his hands off her shoulders and walked round the desk to face her, shaking his head sorrowfully. 'That's what I mean. You've got to learn to loosen up and enjoy life. There's nothing going on, I promise you.'

'So you keep saying. Look, I'll think about it.'

'That's more like it.'

'You're OK to go out to dinner, are you?'

'Never better. Pretty rough this morning, though.'

'I'm not surprised. I think you ought to go easy on the drinking, especially if you think you might have cancer. You've got to start looking after yourself better, and . . . Well, it's not a good idea.' Amy could have gone on, but she'd run out of steam and finished with a defeated gesture. George opened his mouth to reply, but she was buggered if she was going to be subjected to another life-is-for-living riff, and waved a hand in dismissal. 'Dad, if I'm going to come out with you, I've got to get on.'

'All right, I'll leave you to it. Taxi at seven. Wear something presentable—we're going to Simpsons.'

Left alone, Amy stared at the screen of her laptop for five unproductive minutes. It had been going so well, but now she felt unsettled and angry. How dare George lecture her about trust? He'd barged back into her life, conveniently too late to say goodbye to Patti or help with the funeral arrangements, and very possibly bringing dangerous thugs in his wake, and now he was telling her not to be suspicious. 'What the fuck do you expect?' she muttered. 'A fatted calf?'

She wondered if she ought to ring Charlie and ask him if he wouldn't mind keeping an eye on the house while they were out. It seemed a bit much—he wasn't an emergency service, after all. Perhaps I'm getting all this out of proportion, she thought. Perhaps it's just my frame of mind—Mum's death, and having mixed feelings about it, discovering strange new relatives, George . . . Maybe his accident really had been an accident, and the burning paper through the door was kids. And perhaps, she thought, Iris Shand giving her the newspaper article about the skeleton was just random. She might even be overreacting to Sheila and Bill. She sighed. After the continuous head-spin of the last week, it was quite possible. She was starting to feel that nothing would surprise her ever again.

She shook her head vigorously and started to read over what she'd written to try to pick up the threads.


# CHAPTER TWENTY-FOUR

George was in jovial mode as he handed her out of the taxi onto the Strand and ushered her through Simpsons' revolving doors. He greeted the staff like old friends and—as always happened—they reciprocated with genuine warmth.

Claire was waiting for them upstairs, in the Knights Bar. 'George, darling!' Heads turned as she rose and sashayed down the long room to meet them, laced with clinking gold. She was slim, with immaculate hair and make-up, designer clothes and alarmingly good legs shown off by a short skirt and high heels. As she got closer, Amy realised that her line-free brow and tight jaw were owed to Botox and a recent face-lift, and wondered if the neck was going to be next. When Claire threw her arms round George, Amy caught sight of a superb manicure, which made her want to jam her own hands into her pockets and keep them there.

'Darling.' Claire's voice was a sexy purr. Detaching herself from George, she said, 'And you must be Amy. How lovely. George has told me so much about you. Come on, come and have a drink.' She put her arm through Amy's and led her to a table with three round-backed leather chairs. Close up, she smelt of Chanel 19, with a top-note of gin.

Once they were seated, Claire said, 'Well, I don't know about you, but I'm going to have another dry Martini. Ronnie—my late husband, darling—always used to say that dry Martinis are like breasts. One is too few, three are too many.' She summoned a waiter. 'What about you, Amy?'

'Gin and tonic, please.'

'I'll have the same,' said George.

Claire leant across the table. Her expression had the sort of heat-seeking-missile quality that made Amy certain that she was about to gain a self-appointed new best friend. She uttered a silent prayer that none of the intimacies she was undoubtedly about to learn would involve George. 'Marvellous dress, darling,' said Claire. 'Who is it?'

'Nicole Fahri.'

'Gorgeous. Such a wonderful designer—really knows how to make clothes for women, not like all those queens who design for twelve-year-old boys. I don't believe half of them even know what a naked woman's supposed to look like.'

Amy managed something in return, then sat back to listen as Claire began expounding on her favourite designers. By the time the drinks arrived, she'd moved on to anecdotes about people she and George knew, and Amy had an idea that the confessions were just round the corner. She'd realised, about five minutes in, that although Claire's chatter was largely directed at her, all the body language from the waist down was concentrated on George: her knee was pressed against his, and her hand, out of sight under the table, seemed, judging from the slight arm movement, to be stroking his thigh.

Amy sat responding minimally and trying not to notice what was going on, until a waiter summoned them to the restaurant, whereupon Claire insisted on linking arms with her and continuing the girls-together theme with comments like 'Men! Can't live with them, can't live without them.' Her speech was slightly slurred, and Amy wondered how many drinks she'd consumed before her second Martini.

As the maitre d' ('Wonderful to see you again, Mr Vaughan') steered Claire skilfully across the room, Amy, trailing in her wake, looked around at the glossy, dark panelling, the crystal chandeliers hanging from the ornate plaster ceiling and the silver-domed trolleys. Restaurants like Simpsons—traditional British fare in cathedral-like surroundings, shining, and stiff with white napery—were, she knew, her father's favourite hunting grounds. She wondered how many lunches and dinners there had been in this room when, over potted shrimps and roast beef, and without any noticeable transition, he had managed to turn possibilities into probabilities and then, by the time the treacle tart arrived, inevitabilities. She suddenly wondered if old-friend-and-lover Claire, who clearly wanted to rekindle the flame and looked as if she wasn't short of a bob or two, was tonight's mark. It seemed odd to bring your daughter along as a stooge if you were scamming somebody, but if that person had asked to meet her she supposed George hadn't had much option. He seemed pretty relaxed about the whole thing, but . . . Oh, bollocks, she thought. I'm not his keeper. Since I don't have a bloody clue about anything, she decided, sliding onto the banquette next to Claire, I might as well try and enjoy myself for one evening, at least.

Unlike when they were in the bar, George did most of the talking. After the wine had arrived and the orders were taken, Amy expected him to start spieling about some golden investment opportunity, but he didn't. After a spot of general state-of-the-nation address, during which Claire seemed riveted, and kept up an enthusiastic chorus of agreement, he turned the conversation to Amy. 'I keep telling this one,' he said, reaching across the table to pat her hand, 'that she's got to learn to trust people more. I don't want her to end up hard as nails like all those other women who write for the papers.'

'Quite right,' said Claire approvingly, grasping her other hand. 'Must keep in touch with your feminine side, darling.'

Amy, pinioned to the table like a butterfly on a

board, asked irritably, 'How many journalists do you two actually *know*? Some of them are very nice.'

George let go of her and picked up his glass. 'They may seem all right,' he said darkly. 'But you don't want to get paranoid, that's the thing. Sends people off the rails. I don't know if I ever told you this, but I used to know a man who was convinced that his wife was having an affair with a cabinet minister. Kept putting her knickers in envelopes and sending them to Scotland Yard as evidence.'

'What happened to him?' asked Amy.

'Divorced. Terrible mess. She thought he'd been pinching them to wear.'

Claire, who'd been tucking into the wine with gusto, was still laughing when the first course arrived. Other anecdotes followed, more wine was ordered, and by the time the carver, wearing a tall chef's toque, appeared with his trolley and began to cut slices of lamb, Amy was starting to feel a bit more relaxed.

When George excused himself—'Just leave you two girls alone for a minute'—Claire gazed fondly after him and said, in a husky whisper, 'Such a sweet man. And a *wonderful* lover.'

Amy narrowly avoided choking on a mouthful of Merlot. When she recovered, she tried to head Claire off by asking what she was doing in London, but it was hopeless. The woman seemed irresistably drawn to the subject of George's sexual prowess (Amy wondered how recently all this love-making had taken place—after all, he was supposed to be ill), and when she wasn't dwelling on that she was grilling Amy about her private life. 'Are you married, darling? But you've got a lover?

Well, in that case, I know the perfect man—'

'Has he asked you for money?' Amy hadn't meant to ask so bluntly, and in the silence that followed, subjected herself to a catechism of recrimination.

'Money?' The single word seemed to drift in the space between them before being borne away on a roar of laughter from the table behind.

'Yes.' I've started, thought Amy, so I might as well finish. 'Has he asked you for any?'

'Why? Does he need some?'

'Well . . .' Amy shifted uncomfortably, feeling disloyal. 'I think he might be in a bit of a mess. He was broke when he arrived, but when he came home yesterday he was flush. He said he'd seen you, so I thought perhaps . . .'

'Nothing to do with me.' Claire shook her head emphatically. 'What sort of mess?'

'I'm not sure. He seems a bit down on his luck, and he's not been very well recently.'

'I see.' Claire drew out the words slowly, then toyed for a moment with the stem of the glass. She seemed to be gathering herself together for something. 'You know, darling, he did warn me about this.'

'About what?'

'That you might . . . Well, that you might be a wee bit jealous.'

'*Jealous?*'

'Sweetheart, I know that your mother's just died, and I do feel for you. But it's dreadful for him, too. Bereavement is bloody. I remember how I felt when my husband died. He'd been everything to me—an absolute rock.'

'Mum wasn't a rock for Dad,' said Amy.

181

'Yes, she was, darling. In an odd sort of way.' She did some more glass-twiddling, then said, 'I understand George.'

'Not you as well! Mum used to say that, and it wasn't true.' Amy knew that she sounded like a petulant schoolgirl, but she no longer cared. 'His past is littered with women who thought they understood him, and men who trusted him, and—'

'Amy, stop. Let me explain.' Claire's sexy kitty-cat voice took on a sharpness that hadn't been there before. 'Your father doesn't know it—or maybe he just won't admit it—but I've got his number. My Ronnie was the same. More successful—how do you think I got all this?' She indicated her jewellery. 'But he sailed just as near the wind. Nearer, in fact—he went to prison a couple of times. How do you think I got to know George in the first place? Believe me, darling, I've been around men like that for long enough to know how they operate, and I've always liked them. *Much* more fun than the other sort.'

She paused, and gave Amy a shrewd look. 'It was George who told me you might be jealous, but I can see you're not. You know'—she patted Amy's knee—'you remind me of my son. Straight as an arrow, always worrying about us. He's never said as much, but I think he might have been just a teensy bit relieved when Ronnie died—no more anxiety about what the old man would be up to next. But I never felt like that. I miss him, miss the excitement.' She looked round, and said abruptly, 'Change the subject. He's coming back.'

Before Amy could think of anything to say, her phone rang. 'Shit!' Bateman cartoon time. 'Sorry.' She dug it out of her bag and looked at it. *Charlie*

182

*Mob calling.* 'I'd better get this.' She answered, said, 'Hang on,' and ran past George and out across the hall to the Ladies'.

'Hello?'

'Amy? It's Charlie. Sorry to bother you, but there's been a break-in at your house.'

# CHAPTER TWENTY-FIVE

'That was the guy next door. I need to go home right now—he says I've been burgled.'

The two faces swivelled towards her, shocked.

'I've a feeling this is something to do with you, Dad,' she said sarcastically, 'so you might want to come with me.'

Ignoring her tone, George said indistinctly, 'Of course I'm coming.' He slid to the edge of the banquette and began scanning for a waiter.

'Absolutely.' Claire drained her glass. 'We can't let you do this on your own.'

Amy looked at her. Half an hour ago, she thought, I'd have moved heaven and earth to get away from her, but now she feels almost like an ally.

'You girls grab a cab,' George instructed. 'I'll settle up, then I'll be right with you.'

Waiting in the taxi the doorman had flagged down, Claire asked, 'Why should the burglary be anything to do with George?'

'He's been up to something. He's denied it, but I'm sure someone's after him. He got knocked down by a car a few days ago—hit and run—and then someone tried to burn down my house.'

Claire raised her eyebrows. 'How?'

'The firemen said it was burning paper through the letter box. My neighbours didn't see anyone, but I'm pretty sure it's something to do with Dad.'

'Well, darling, if that's what you really think, he can always come and stay with me. I'm at the Dorchester.'

Amy looked at her incredulously. 'Are you sure?'

'Sweetheart, I don't mind a bit. It'll be just like the old days. Besides, what can happen in a hotel?'

'You're mad.'

Claire laughed. 'That's what my son always says. Such a shame he's already married—you'd get on like a house on fire.'

Claire held George's hand and prattled about her son—the youngest board member of a 'top-flight' pharmaceutical company—most of the way home, while Amy closed her eyes, rested her head against the side window, and wondered what had been nicked and what sort of state the house would be in. Charlie had said it was the sitting-room window—of course she'd forgotten to close the bloody shutters—and that was in full view of the road, which was pretty risky, because it wasn't late, and anyone passing would see. Besides which, there was the burglar alarm, which had been whooping away all the time she'd been on the phone to Charlie, and there was no way out of the back garden unless you scaled a high wall, which— even for an athletic person—would be pretty hard if you were carrying a DVD player or a laptop. But then, she thought, if it's something to do with Dad, they wouldn't want those things; they'd just trash the place in order to make a point.

184

To stop herself imagining smashed computers and crapped-on bedsheets, she tried to focus on the practicalities. Charlie said Moira had called the police when they'd returned and spotted the broken window, so they might have arrived already. And people were bound to come out and see what was going on after a while, because of the noise, so there wasn't much chance of whoever it was coming back. It would probably mean another insurance claim, and she hadn't completed the first one, yet. Oh, *Christ*.

She took a deep breath and said, 'Dad, Claire says you can stay with her at the Dorchester. I'd like you to pack up—if there's anything left to pack up—and go there tonight. I really have had enough.'

George leant across Claire and put a hand on her arm. 'Chicky, I promise you it's nothing to do with me.'

'Stop it.' Amy shook him off.

'I don't know how many times I can say this—'

'Then don't.'

'—but there is no one on my back.'

Charlie and Moira were waiting on the front steps when they arrived. Amy rushed inside to turn off the alarm, then went on a tour of inspection. Apart from the broken window, the sitting room looked pretty much as she'd left it, and so did her bedroom. Her jewellery was still in its box, and her Tiffany lamp was on the dressing table. George's room was similarly untouched, but the study— Amy gasped—was in chaos. The desk looked as if it had been disembowelled, with drawers pulled out and papers, computer disks and splayed files all over the floor, with a sprinkling of pens, pencils and multi-coloured paperclips providing a metallic garnish across the top. It took a moment for her to register that her laptop—buried under a heap of books and telephone directories—was still in its place, and so was her printer. She righted the big Anglepoise lamp, which was reeling drunkenly against a bookcase, and ferreted about for her passport—still there—and her new digital camera, which was intact in its case.

'Bloody hell,' George was standing in the doorway. 'What's missing?'

'Nothing, as far as I can see. Your room looks OK, too.'

'I haven't got much in the way of valuables.'

'I don't think they even went in there.' Amy surveyed the chaos once more, then shook her head. 'I don't understand it.'

George put an arm round her shoulders. 'Neither do I, cherub. Why don't you leave all this till tomorrow, and go downstairs? Your neighbour . . . ?'

'Moira.'

'Yes. She's made some tea, and Charlie's looking after the window. I'll be down in a minute.'

Charlie was kneeling on the hall floor, dismembering a cardboard box. 'I'll put this over the broken pane for tonight,' he said. 'Your burglar must have been pretty small, otherwise he'd never have fitted through.'

'Kids,' said Moira, pressing a mug of tea into Amy's hand. 'They rob people and mess up their houses and take pictures of themselves doing it to send to their friends. I've read about it.'

'It's possible,' said Amy doubtfully, 'but it seems like a big risk with the alarm going, and nothing's

186

actually missing.'

'Nothing at all?' asked Charlie.

Amy shook her head. 'Not as far as I can see.'

'That's lucky.'

'Drugs,' said Moira. 'Must have been off their heads.'

'That doesn't make sense,' Charlie objected. 'If they'd been on drugs they'd have taken stuff to sell.'

'Drunk, then.'

'I don't think so,' said Amy. 'I think they were looking for something.'

'Have you got an ashtray, darling?' Claire appeared in the kitchen doorway with a brandy balloon in her hand.

'Try the dishwasher,' Amy told her.

'Thanks. Do you want some of this?' She held up the brandy.

'I'll stick with tea, thanks.'

'Are you sure? You've had a dreadful shock.'

'It's not as bad as I thought it would be. I was just saying, my study's pretty messy, but nothing seems to have gone.'

Claire settled herself at the kitchen table and lit a cigarette. 'What about George's things?'

'Didn't look like it. I think he's checking now.'

Claire exhaled thoughtfully, head on one side. 'So it might not be anything to do with him after all.'

'They might have thought he'd hidden something in my study,' said Amy defensively. 'Perhaps he did.'

Claire raised her eyebrows.

'It's possible.' Amy massaged her temples. 'I don't know,' she said wearily. 'I just don't know.'

187

'He'd never put you at risk like that, darling. He loves you too much. He's always talking about you.'

'Is he?'

'He adores you. He used to tell me all about how brave you were when you were ill.'

'You've known him since then?'

'Oh, yes, years.'

'Then you'll know he always gets sentimental when he's pissed.'

'Yes,' said Claire, 'that's when it comes out. But it doesn't mean he doesn't think about you, darling. Anyway, this burglary, and the fire—'

'And Dad being knocked down.'

'—and that. It's probably nothing. Bad luck, coincidence. They say trouble always comes in threes. But if you still want me to take him off your hands, I will.'

'I think so,' said Amy. 'I seem to have rather a lot to contend with at the moment.'

'Right.' Claire stood up. 'I'd better go and help him pack.' As she passed Amy's chair, she murmured, 'Charlie's rather dishy, isn't he?'

# CHAPTER TWENTY-SIX

Despite everything, the house had somehow taken on a party atmosphere by the time the police arrived, with everyone—egged on by George and Claire—sitting round the kitchen table drinking brandy. Even Moira, who had initially demurred, had joined in and was regaling Claire with stories about her childhood in Kenya.

Amy found she didn't mind when Claire rolled her eyes and flashed her legs at the two young officers, who looked terrified, or when George tried to insist that they each accepted a cigar. She noticed, too, that Moira appeared—very discreetly—to find it funny. The policemen took statements from her and Charlie, told her that there would be an incident report and that she should telephone the station immediately if she found that anything was missing, and departed with evident relief.

George and Claire left soon afterwards, in a taxi. George told Amy he'd carry on sorting out Patti's flat. 'I wish I could be more help, angel. I don't like leaving you like this, but if it's what you want . . .' His eyes looked moist.

'It is what I want.'

'I don't know why you won't believe me. None of this has anything to do with me. You will come and see me, won't you?'

'At the Dorchester? Try and stop me,' said Amy, trying to make light of it.

Claire kissed her. 'Don't worry, darling. I'll see he doesn't get into trouble.'

Amy watched them down the road, waving madly from the back of the cab, Claire shouting something that she couldn't catch, and went back inside with an obscure feeling that she was missing something.

The place seemed rather flat after they'd left. Moira and Charlie, who'd gone back to the kitchen, were tidying up, and Amy, suddenly exhausted, slumped in a chair. 'You look shattered,' Charlie told her.

'I feel it.'

'We'd better let you get some sleep. Are you going to be OK on your own? I've closed the shutters in the sitting room, so you'll be quite safe, but I'll stay if you want.'

'I'll be fine,' said Amy. 'I've caused you enough disturbance as it is.'

'Tell you what,' said Charlie casually, 'if you really want to make it up to me, why don't you let me take you out to dinner? You can listen to me rabbit on about gardening.'

Amy looked over at Moira, who was briskly washing up, her back to them. 'I'd like that,' she said.

'I'll ring you tomorrow, then. We can arrange it.'

As they were leaving, Moira said to Amy, 'Are you interested in gardening?'

'Oh, yes,' said Amy solemnly. 'Very.'

Moira winked at her. 'That's good. Now, I'm off home, and you two can say goodnight.'

When Charlie had gone, Amy gathered up some of the papers in her study—the bank statements and credit-card bills seemed to be all there, which, she supposed, ruled out identity theft—and thought about what Claire had said. Dishy. Amy grinned. She hadn't heard the word since the seventies, but she supposed that, being an ex-pat, Claire's slang was a bit fossilised. Anyway, she thought as she shovelled the paperclips back into their jar, she's right: Charlie is dishy.

Cleaning her teeth, Amy reflected that the brandy and the cigar Charlie had accepted from George had given him the same smell when he kissed her, which, while not unpleasant, was slightly disconcerting. Supposing it is all coincidence? she thought. George's sudden riches

190

might be some long overdue loan, and the broken pane was, as Charlie had pointed out, too small to admit an adult man, and certainly not the bull-necked thug of her imagining.

Lying in bed, she found herself thinking about how Claire had pretty much admitted to being a danger-junkie, and remembering the women she'd once interviewed for an article about women who marry lifers. Armed robbers, rapists, even serial killers: dangerous men, contained. Notorious men. She remembered how the women had spoken, even boasted, that these men had opened up to them as to no one else, and that they—that bloody word again—*understood* them. What Charlie had said about his parents, his father's latent aggression being exciting to his mother, what attracted Claire to George, and, presumably, Iris to Leslie Shand, must be part of the same thing. Now she came to think of it, it probably had a lot to do with why Patti had waited for George all those years. Bloody hell. But then again, she thought, already roughing out an article in her head, women have always been attracted to bad boys. She recalled her own three-month dalliance, aged sixteen, with a leather-jacketed tearaway who'd later ended up in Borstal for stealing cars: her first lover. She hadn't liked the sex much, but she'd been infatuated with the idea of him—and part of the appeal, of course, was Patti's hysterical, almost operatic, disapproval. And what about highwaymen? They'd been popular—all those ballards and rogues' biographies—and Victorian novels peopled with Heathcliffs and Rochesters. But most of us—this would be the conclusion—draw the line at violent Neanderthals or out-and-out conmen. Really, she thought, as she drifted off to sleep, I ought to be writing this down . . .

When she considered it the following morning, over toast and phone calls to glaziers, the article didn't seem such a good idea. For one thing, it was tantamount to saying that some women courted violence, and that was bound to cause trouble. Erin Pizzey, founder of the first refuge for battered wives, had said it, because so many of the occupants returned to the men who'd abused them, and she'd got a hell of a lot of flak for it. Perhaps, thought Amy, she'd be able to understand better when she got to know Sheila Shand. *If* I get to know her, she told herself—if Bill Drake lets me. She was wondering if she should call Sheila—and, if so, what she might say—when the phone rang.

'Miss Vaughan? This is Bill Drake.'

Amy gasped, recovered, and then said tightly, 'What can I do for you?'

'I believe I owe you an apology. I've spoken to Sheila, and it seems I rather overreacted.' He cleared his throat. 'I wondered . . . We'd appreciate it if you would come to visit. I know that Sheila would like to see you, and I feel I ought to apologise in person. We thought—if it's convenient for you, of course—that you might like to come and have tea with us this afternoon.'

Amy did a few seconds' mental juggling with schedules, then said, 'Yes, I don't see why not.'

'Excellent. If you don't mind coming to my house . . . it's next door to the school, and there's a gate there. The lane's in a bit of a state, I'm afraid, so you'll need to park at the top and walk down. Shall we say four o'clock?'

# CHAPTER TWENTY-SEVEN

Remembering Charlie's warning about Bill Drake's agenda and the article mentioning the skeleton in the wood, Amy decided that it would be a good idea to tell somebody where she was going. George, who'd rung at midday, hadn't sounded as if he was capable of taking that much information on board, so she rang Charlie before setting off, left a message of explanation, and, thinking that he was bound to check his phone every so often, asked him to give her a call in a couple of hours' time.

She stopped en route to buy some flowers for Sheila, squaring away the photocopied pages of Mo's diary, which were still strewn across the back seat, so that they wouldn't get wet from the damp wrapping paper.

She parked outside Sheila Shand's tiny front garden, made her way past the school, squeezed, with difficulty, round the sagging gate, and picked her way between the stagnant, khaki-coloured puddles in the rutted lane. She hadn't been sure what to expect—the condition of the lane, and the description given by the woman in the farm shop had made her think that Bill Drake's house must be a rural slum, but his voice had sounded too brisk and clipped to inhabit such a ramshackle place. She found herself on the edge of what seemed to be an agricultural graveyard—rusting farm skeletons with spikes and claws that threatened her skin and skirt as she wove her way through the carcasses of tractors, harrows and feeding apparatus. Perhaps it was intentional; a burglar deterrent. In contrast, the modern brick bungalow that stood on the other side was, like Sheila Shand's cottage, tweely immaculate, and the man who answered the bell was pinkly scrubbed and check-shirted, with natty twill trousers—no stubble or bailer twine in sight. More ex-army than farmer, Amy thought, noting the sleeves rolled up in perfect symmetry and the highly polished chestnut brogues.

Surprised, she took a step back and bashed her head against a hanging basket full of violently coloured petunias and busy lizzies. It hurt, and he must have realised it, but they both pretended it hadn't.

'Miss Vaughan? Nice of you to come at such short notice.'

'Thanks. Please, call me Amy.'

'Amy, then. I'm Bill Drake. Do come in.'

The sitting room had the same fussy ornamentation as Sheila's, surrounded by a striped wallpaper of pink and pale green. Design tips from *Woman's Own*, Amy thought—all wrong for Bill.

'Sit down. I'll go and rustle up some tea.' Amy, who'd presumed that Sheila was silently preparing a tray in the kitchen, was nonplussed. Bill didn't initiate any conversation through the open kitchen door, and the cloying pastels and self-conscious gentility of the room, coupled with a mounting anxiety over Sheila's whereabouts put paid to any attempts on her part. Instead, she sat in silence, staring at the row of china flower-baskets on the window ledge and the photos on the fire-surround, wondering if the redhead with the outdoor complexion was—or had been—Bill's wife. The woman who, according to Leslie Shand, had run off with the milkman. Humiliating, Amy thought, and then wondered if Bill had been more interested in Sheila, even then.

Beside the redhead stood a picture of the Shand sisters, similar to the one she'd seen on Sheila's mantelpiece. She felt uneasy about Bill discovering her inspecting his photographs, so she contented herself with leaning forward for a closer look at the redhead: the picture, she decided, wasn't recent.

'Here we are.' Bill re-appeared and Amy watched in silence as he fussed with the tea things. His plate of biscuits, like Sheila's, was covered in cling-film, and Amy had the odd feeling that it had been wrapped solely for the short journey out of the kitchen.

Her feeling of tension grew while Bill fiddled with cups and saucers, made an elaborate ceremony of the right amount of milk and sugar (in lumps, from a china bowl with tongs), and insisted on fetching a paper napkin to protect her knees from crumbs. When he finally settled on the armchair opposite hers, she said, indicating the bouquet, 'I thought Sheila might like these. Will she be here soon?'

Bill stirred his tea with immense concentration and a delicately womanish wrist movement, then paused for a second, spoon aloft, before tapping it twice on the edge of the cup and laying it to rest in the saucer. Amy, mesmerised, began to wish that she hadn't chosen the seat furthest from the front door, and wondered if there was a back door through the kitchen.

After what seemed like a very long minute, Bill

looked up. 'She's not coming. I thought you and I ought to have a chat.'

'What about?'

'The diary.' The calm flatness of his voice was worse than overt hostility, and the dainty china and fussy presentation of the tea seemed to accentuate the menace.

'Why? It's not really any of my business.'

'I'm sure you made it your business.'

'As I've already explained to Sheila, I thought it belonged to my late mother. There was no name on the front.'

'So you read it.'

'Some of it, yes.'

'Do you think that was right, reading someone else's private diary?'

'For heaven's sake,' said Amy, exasperation overriding her nerves, 'I've told you. I found it when I was sorting out my mother's things. It was an old diary—it could have been anyone's. Then I found a newspaper cutting about the . . . what happened to Leslie Shand, and I realised whose it was. Look, what is this about?'

'What was in it?'

'Just ordinary stuff. Work, home.' Amy shrugged. 'You know.'

'Work?'

'Yes. At the hotel. You should be asking Sheila about this, not me.'

'I have asked Sheila. She said it was written when Mo was small, but that wasn't true, was it?'

'Look.' Amy stood up. 'I've no idea what's going on, but I don't want to be the cause of any trouble between you. I admit I was curious—you can hardly blame me for that—but I just wanted to return the diary to its original owner.' As she started to cross the pink Chinese rug, heading for the door, Bill got out of his chair and stood in her path, teacup still in one hand. 'I want to know,' he said, stiffly, 'what you—'

Footsteps on the path made them both jump. Amy could feel her heart pounding as they stood facing each other. Bill looked at her, and then down at the teacup, which was rattling in its saucer; his hand was shaking. The doorbell rang, and somebody tapped on the window. Amy stepped to one side and raised the net curtain. Seeing two men, one in a dark-blue uniform, she said, 'You'd better get the door. It's the police.'

For a second, Amy entertained the wild idea that Charlie must have sent them; nothing else seemed to account for their sudden presence. Whatever the cause, though, she couldn't deny that it was a relief. Now, she'd be able to leave without any . . . well, any anything. She stayed in the living room while Bill went into the hall. She heard him open the front door, and then a male voice spoke. 'Are you William Drake?'

'Yes, that's right.' Bill sounded cautious. 'How can I help you?'

'I'm DI Bainbridge of the Thames Valley Police. May we come in for a moment?'

Bill must have nodded assent because Amy heard the scuffing of feet being wiped on the mat.

'What's this about?'

'You may have heard about the body that was discovered in Hadley Wood. Do you know anything about that?'

My God, thought Amy, the skeleton. What the hell was going on?

197

'Well,' said Bill, 'I saw the policeman up there, but I don't see what it's got to do with me.'

'We have reason to believe that the remains are those of your wife, Rosemary Drake.'

# CHAPTER TWENTY-EIGHT

Amy felt as if she'd been given an electric shock. It wasn't Mo at all, but Mrs Drake. So much for running off with the milkman. Thinking she'd better announce her presence, Amy went to the door of the sitting room.

'But she left me.' The puzzlement in Bill's voice sounded genuine. Turning to Amy, he repeated, 'Rosie left me.' He looked completely bewildered.

The plain-clothes policeman—presumably DI Bainbridge—turned to Amy. 'And you are, miss?'

'Amy Vaughan. Just visiting. Perhaps I should leave.'

'Wait.' Bill flung out an arm to block her path. 'You've got to tell Sheila.' He stared intently at her, as if he was trying to convey some meaning beyond his words.

'Sheila?' asked DI Bainbridge.

'Sheila Shand. She's a neighbour.'

'I see.' The younger, uniformed policeman produced a notebook and started writing. 'And where does she live?'

'By the school. Hadley Cottage.'

'We're not charging anyone at the moment,' said DI Bainbridge, 'but we think you'll be able to clear up a few things for us, and it might be better'—he glanced at Amy—'if we did it down at the station.'

'I'd better come out with you,' said Amy. 'I'll go up and see Sheila now.'

'Thanks.' Bill held out his hand and Amy, surprised, shook it automatically. She felt as if she'd just sealed a bargain, but had no idea what it was.

They left together, walking in silent single file up the muddy lane, and Amy watched the police car depart round the bend of Camlet Way before pulling out her mobile to ring Charlie.

'I was about to phone you. Is everything OK?'

'Not really. Well, I'm fine, but I went to see Bill and Sheila, like I said—at least, I *thought* I was going to see both of them, but Bill was on his own, and he started grilling me about the diary, when was it written and what was in it. I told him he ought to ask Sheila, and he said she'd lied to him. I don't know why, but she'd told him the diary was written by Mo when she was small. I didn't tell Bill the dates, but I said something about her writing about work, so he knew . . . I was going to leave, I'd stood up, and he stood up, too, and I thought he was going to try and stop me, but then the police arrived.'

'The *police*?'

'Yes. They said that the body—'

'What body?'

'They found a skeleton buried in the wood near where Bill and Sheila live. I went to see Iris yesterday—God, it feels like years ago—and she gave me a local newspaper with a piece about it. It was obvious that she wanted me to see that particular bit, but I didn't know why. The matron told me that Sheila must have brought the paper with her, because the home didn't get it. I meant to

199

tell you, but what with everything else . . . Anyway, the police said that it was Bill's wife.'

'Did they arrest him?'

'No, they just wanted him to answer some questions. "Clear a few things up" was how they put it.'

'Do you think he killed her?'

'I don't know. He seemed really shocked when they told him. He kept saying that his wife had left him—and that's what it says in Mo's diary.'

'He must have been trying to find out what she'd written about it—if he'd seen the bit in the paper, he'd have realised they'd found her, and wanted to make sure.'

'That would only make sense if they both knew something about it. When I read about the skeleton I thought it must be Mo. The only thing I could think was that Sheila had killed her, and that was why she was so freaked out when I said I'd read the diary—except that it doesn't even hint at trouble between them. I've got no idea where Mo is. All Sheila told me was that Mo didn't live with her, but she'd pass on the diary. Bill did seem genuinely bewildered when the police told him, Charlie. I don't think he's that good an actor. He asked me to go and tell Sheila what's happened.'

'Perhaps they're in it together.'

'Sheila isn't that sort of person.'

'How do you know?'

'Well, I don't, really, but given that the woman's endured a lifetime of sexual abuse from her father, she's hardly likely to want to embrace a substitute, is she? Bill's older than her, and he acts like he owns her.'

'That might be the reason she's drawn to him. I

200

know it sounds sick, but it is possible.'

'All right, but if Bill and Sheila murdered Bill's wife so that they could be together—which I'm not convinced they are, by the way, not in a sexual sense—why would Sheila show the paper to her mother?'

'Perhaps she just happened to take it with her, not knowing what was in it, and the mother spotted the article.'

'Iris Shand's senile. She can't read a word.'

'So how did she manage to show it to you?'

'It was folded open at that page—and Sheila could have told her about it.'

'I'm worried about you going to see her, Amy.'

'Why? It's not as if I *know* anything. I mean, if she's that worried, she'll have read the diary by now, won't she? She'll know there's nothing in it.'

'I suppose so.' Charlie sounded doubtful. 'You'd better give me her address, just in case. Wait, I'll get a pen.' He jotted it down, then said, 'OK. But ring me when you've talked to her. And don't switch your phone off.'

Amy pocketed her phone, then walked over to Hadley Cottage and pressed the doorbell. Sheila opened the door. 'What are you doing here?'

'Could I come in?'

'Yes, I suppose . . . but Bill said . . .'

'I've just been having tea with him.'

Sheila looked confused. 'I don't understand. Please.' She stepped back and Amy walked past her, into the sitting room.

'It might be a good idea,' she said, 'if you sat down.'

'Why? What's happened?'

Amy explained. Sheila Shand stared at her for a

moment, then made a faint sound in her throat, swayed, and collapsed on the carpet.

# CHAPTER TWENTY-NINE

Amy knelt down and undid the top button of Sheila's blouse. Sheila opened her eyes. 'I'm sorry,' she said weakly. 'I just felt a bit dizzy.'

'You fainted. I think you ought to stay there for a moment and let the blood get back to your head.'

After several minutes, Sheila allowed Amy to help her to her feet and steer her to an armchair. Amy knelt beside her and put a hand on her arm. Desite the heat, Sheila was icy. 'I'm going to get you a blanket. Is that all right?'

'Yes.' A whisper. 'Upstairs. On the shelves.'

'Don't try to move. I shan't be a minute.'

Amy passed up the stairs and across the landing. Four doors, all closed. The first she opened must have been Iris's bedroom. It contained a double bed with a pink buttoned headboard and flowered bedspread, and above it a framed, blown-up photograph of three kittens peeping coyly out of a wicker basket. There was no dust on the sheet of glass that covered the top of the dressing table, but the air had a still quality, as if it was rarely disturbed. The next room, done out in pale blue, had twin single beds and photos of puppies on the walls. Sheila's room, Amy thought, once shared with Mo.

The third room was a bathroom, and the fourth a storeroom: green lino flooring, racks of metal shelving, plastic containers and cardboard boxes neatly labelled in biro on white stickers. Despite the primrose-yellow walls and the large, framed photographs (fluffy chicks and a flotilla of ducklings crossing a village pond), Amy's immediate reaction was that this must be a hangover from Leslie's time. It wasn't the items themselves—after all, she thought, plenty of people have toolboxes and torches and reserves of loo paper—it was the arrangement and volume of things that made it seem like an army store. Or, she thought, noting the rows of tinned and dried food, the axe, the coiled rope and the box of candles, a person living in a state of siege. Leslie must have kept his gun here. She found herself glancing around for it, before remembering that it would have been taken away by the police as evidence at Sheila's trial.

Was it only her knowledge that made the tools look so menacing? Amy shivered, imagining Leslie running his hands over the tools, testing the blade of an axe, the weight of a hammer, the point of a knife. His malevolent spirit seemed present in each crude, hard thing and in every piece of the ugly metal racking erected by his calloused worker's hands, with little Sheila standing by as his helper. No amount of pretty pictures or bright paint could exorcise it.

An iron deed box caught her eye, with two padlocks hanging from the hasp. Amy wondered why Sheila had taken the precaution of locking it twice. What was in it? The secret of Rosie Drake's death, perhaps. 'What do you know, Sheila?' she muttered. Something too terrible to be spoken? But what on earth could be more terrible than the situation Sheila had endured for so many years?

Turning away from the deed box, Amy found herself facing, at eye level, a label reading *Angel Delight*. Separated from the other food, the cardboard box stood alone on its section of metal racking. Angel Delight. Amy remembered Sheila's sudden and complete withdrawal at the mention of it. She opened the box: Strawberry, Banana, Butterscotch, Chocolate. All the flavours mentioned in the diary. She picked out one of the packets. The best-before date was March 1988. I don't know how long this stuff keeps, she thought, but it's a fair bet that it's got enough preservatives in it to last at least six months, if not more. Which probably meant that the packets had been bought before Leslie Shand's death in November the previous year.

But they were no use now, so why had Sheila decided to keep them? Unless she was a compulsive hoarder. Amy went over to the rows of tinned food. There were no faded labels and the cans she checked were all well within their shelf-life. That wasn't it, then: unless Sheila had simply forgotten to throw it out, the Angel Delight must have some particular significance. Maybe she'd be able to work it out from the diary.

She found five spare blankets folded in plastic zippered bags at the far end of the middle row of shelves, and took two of them downstairs. Sheila sat passively, barely seeming to notice when Amy shook them out and tucked them round her. 'I'm going to make you a cup of tea with plenty of sugar,' Amy said.

Crossing the kitchen to fill the kettle, she realised that she was moving on tiptoe, and had been ever since she'd entered the house. All her movements, in fact, had been consciously quiet and controlled—as if I'm afraid of disturbing something, she thought.

She shuddered, wondering if the 'something' might be Leslie's vengeful spirit, and, turning to plug in the kettle, saw that Sheila was standing in the doorway. 'I'm sorry,' she said, 'but would you mind . . . I think I'd like to go upstairs and lie down.'

'Of course. I should have thought. I'll bring your tea up.'

'Thank you. You're very kind.'

When she'd gone, Amy realised that to take an unadorned cup of tea upstairs would be an affront both to the house and to Sheila, and hunted around until she found a little tray and a pretty embroidered cloth to spread on it. She took extra care going upstairs, so as not to spill any tea into the saucer, and was about to transfer the tray onto one hand in order to knock on the door when she saw that it was wide open. She'd been right about the sleeping arrangements: Sheila was sitting up in one of the twin beds, looking frail and childlike, wearing an old-fashioned cotton nightdress, high-necked and patterned with tiny pink rosebuds. The sudden, powerful thought came to Amy that it wasn't Leslie's spirit she was afraid of disturbing, but Sheila's sanity.

Watching Sheila sip her tea, Amy wondered about her interior life. The suppression of emotion—and, presumably, the memories that prompted it—the reliance on tidiness and order, the ladylike manners, the house with its carefully chosen cheerful colours and patterns and 'nice things' was Sheila's means of keeping a measure of control—however shaky—over her mind. That, in itself, was an extraordinary feat. Mo, wherever she was—or wasn't—didn't seem to have managed it, and as for Iris, her decline into senility might have been inevitable, but all the same, Amy couldn't help thinking that the darkness it brought with it might also draw a welcome veil over things that were simply too painful to recall.

'Would you like me to stay here for the night?' she asked. 'I don't think you should be by yourself.'

'Yes.' Sheila's whisper barely reached her over the china rim of the cup. 'Thank you.'

'We don't have to talk if you don't want to.'

'Will they let Bill go?'

'I'm sure they will. They only wanted to ask him some questions.'

'When will he come back?'

Amy wasn't sure of the answer to this, but she didn't want to diminish Sheila's faith in her by admitting it. 'It'll probably take a couple of hours.'

'I think I'd like to sleep,' said Sheila. 'I've got some tablets.' She nodded in the direction of a pill bottle and Amy shook two out and handed them over.

'I'm sure Bill will phone, but you'll be asleep by then, won't you?'

'Yes.' Sheila sounded relieved. 'I think so.' She was silent for a moment, and then said, in an agitated voice, as if fearful of punishment, 'I haven't cleaned my teeth.' Her face creased in anxiety. 'I ought to brush them.'

'I don't think it'll matter. Not this once.'

Sheila handed over her cup and lay back on the pillows, apparently satisfied with the dispensation. 'The first time you came,' she said, 'your hair . . .'

'I know. Like Mo. I saw the pictures on your mantelpiece. I'm sorry, I didn't mean to frighten you.'

'Bill's done so much for me, you know. For us.'

'Did you know about Mrs Drake, Sheila?'

Sheila shook her head, her eyes anxious.

'Did Iris know?'

'No. We thought . . . like Dad said. She'd gone away with a man. That's what we thought.'

'That's what it says in the diary.'

'Does it?'

'Haven't you read it?' asked Amy, surprised.

Another head shake. 'I couldn't bear it, going back.'

'So you know Bill didn't have anything to do with it,' said Amy soothingly. 'You don't need to worry.'

'They won't arrest him, will they?'

'Not if that's the truth.'

'It is, Amy. Bill had nothing to do with it.'

Sheila closed her eyes again, and Amy saw tears trickling out from under the lids, and had to restrain herself from taking Sheila in her arms for a hug. 'I'm sorry,' she said. 'I shouldn't have asked. Would you like to go to sleep now?'

The eyes didn't open, but there was a whispered 'Yes.'

'I'll be downstairs if you need anything.' She picked up the tray, turned off the lamp and was about to close the door on her way out when Sheila whispered something else. 'I'm sorry,' said Amy, returning to the bed. 'I didn't hear you.'

'Will you leave the door open?'

'Yes, of course, if that's what you want. Goodnight, Sheila.'

'Bill will come back, won't he?'

'Yes. They won't have any reason to detain him.' Unless, Amy thought, he confesses to murdering his wife. She wondered why Sheila was so positive that he hadn't. Love? Loyalty to a friend? Or—and her behaviour with the newspaper and her reaction to Amy's announcement both pointed to this—she knew what had really happened. But in that case, why was Bill so keen on finding out what was in Mo's diary?

'Goodnight,' said Sheila. 'And thank you for staying.'

'That's all right. I'll see you in the morning.'

No wonder she doesn't want the door closed, Amy reflected as she tiptoed downstairs. The woman's been in prison. Eighteen years ago, but still, and before that . . . *virtual prisoners in their home where he beat them and forced them to have sex with him.* In this very house. Perhaps where I'm standing now, Amy thought, as she crossed the threshold of the spotless kitchen. *From an early age they were forced to watch* . . . The two young girls in their summer frocks and white ankle-socks, side by side, blank-eyed as a hazy-bright summer day erupted into violence. Standing rigidly to attention, watching in silence as their father pummelled, head-butted and kicked their mother until she grovelled on the floor, begging for mercy.

Amy washed up the tea things as quietly as she could and put them away. Then she fetched the photocopied diary from her car, sat down at the kitchen table and started searching for mentions of Rosemary Drake. She'd thought there weren't very many, and she was right. There were a few references to her talking to the Shand girls in the

208

pub, and then, on 13 February 1987:

*Friday: When Dad came back from the farm he told us that Mrs Drake has left. He said Mr Drake should have clipped <u>her</u> wings, because she has probably gone off with the milkman! 'Stanley' has not come home.*

Stanley, Amy remembered, was the Shands' African grey parrot. She looked at the entry for the day before.

*Thursday: Our parrot 'Stanley' escaped through the back door this evening while I was cleaning under the perch. We couldn't catch him! Dad says when we get him back he will clip his wings.*

That explained the reference. On Saturday, the day after Mrs Drake's apparent defection, Mo had written:

*Sheila said she could not understand why Mrs Drake wanted to go away because Mr Drake is such a nice man, which is true because he has been very good to our Family. But then Mum said that Mrs Drake has a fancy man, they have been seen together and lots of people know about it. Except poor Mr Drake, he didn't know and Dad says he is very cut up, so he told Mum she ought to go and talk to Mr Drake so that he knows his wife is no good after all and if she has gone it's good riddance. Mum said that was a good idea so Dad took her down to the farm and she told him. Later Dad took photographs of us in the garden, and Sheila took a picture of him and Mum together.*

It was quite a lot more than Mo usually wrote, spilling over into the space for Sunday, for which there was no separate entry. Amy cast her mind

209

back to her conversation with Sheila, trying to recall the exact words. *We thought like Dad, she'd gone away with a man.* But according to the diary, it was Iris who knew about the 'fancy man'. Leslie had merely joked about her running off with the milkman, and it was only when Iris mentioned Mrs Drake's affair that he'd suggested that she go and break the news to Mr Drake. Escorted her to the farm, in fact. *And* the entry was unusual in that it recorded opinions expressed by both Sheila and Iris. Unless Leslie had, via Mo, put words into their mouths.

In any case, if Mrs Drake had run away with another man, surely she'd have left a note? Amy scanned through the pages until she reached July, but there was no mention of a letter or phone call—which of course there wouldn't be if she hadn't gone anywhere. But what about her clothes, jewellery, make-up? A woman leaving home would take something with her, surely? Maybe she had. So how had she ended up buried in the wood? Had Leslie had something to do with it? Perhaps he'd had an affair with her, or she'd found out how he treated his wife and daughters and threatened to blow the whistle. But if that were the case, she'd hardly have accompanied him across the common to be strangled or shot or whatever it was. And it must have been murder—dead bodies don't bury themselves.

Her mind felt like a disintegrating jigsaw puzzle. She massaged her temples and then, for lack of anything better to do, and to stop herself thinking in circles about Sheila and Bill and Bill's dead wife, decided to apply herself to solving the mystery of the Angel Delight. She'd assumed that, in such a

210

regimented household, the different flavours would be served up in strict rotation, but she hadn't checked to see if this was the case.

It wasn't. Beginning in January 1983, she jotted down each Saturday's flavour in her notebook and got: Chocolate, Butterscotch, Banana, Banana, Chocolate, Strawberry, Banana, Chocolate, Butterscotch. No discernable pattern. Perhaps Iris had simply used the first packet that came to hand. There was something significant about it, Amy thought, remembering again Sheila's sudden, strange emptiness. A code, perhaps? But the stuff was real enough, she'd seen it in the storeroom.

Going in circles again. Amy glanced up at the wall clock (a seated tabby cat with the hands set in the middle of its chest) and saw that it was almost 7.15. She was about to ring Charlie when she heard the doorbell. Lifting the net curtain, she saw Bill Drake standing on the front step.

# CHAPTER THIRTY

Amy shoved the diary pages into her bag, took a deep breath, and went to open the door.

'Amy!' He looked haggard, but his relief was evident. 'I'm glad you're still here.'

'I'm going to stay the night.'

'Are you?'

'Yes,' said Amy firmly. 'I am. You look exhausted. Perhaps you should go home and get some rest.'

'Is Sheila all right?'

'Shocked. She fainted. She's asleep now.'

211

'I see. Can I come in for a moment? I'd like to talk to you.'

'I don't really see how I can help.'

'Please.' Bill looked desolate. 'I'm sorry about this afternoon. Sheila's been through such a lot, and I've always tried to protect her. I went the wrong way about it. But now, this business about Rosie . . .'

'All right. Come in.' Bill followed her into the kitchen, and sat down at the table. Amy picked up her bag. 'I'm just going to make a phone call,' she said. 'Then I'll make you a cup of tea.'

Amy went to the back door and let herself into the garden. There was no sign of the Anderson shelter, just a manicured lawn with carefully tended flowerbeds and profusions of colour—shrill and clamorous, even in the evening sun—erupting from white plastic urns. Not a garden to relax in, Amy thought, as she dug her mobile out of her bag. She remembered Iris's photos, the grey hulk of the Anderson shelter, the patch of scrubby grass, the sickly rose bushes, the knocked-together rabbit hutch with its doomed occupants quivering in semi-darkness, stale bread and cabbage stalks strewn over cracked concrete and maybe a dog on a chain just out of shot. A miserable garden, where nothing could grow or flourish. Its replacement was relentlessly bright and vigorous, keeping the past at bay.

'Charlie?'

'What's happening? Are you out of there?'

'No. I'm going to stay the night. Sheila took it badly, and I don't think she ought to be on her own. She's asleep now—or I hope she is, she took some pills—and Bill's just arrived. He says he

212

wants to talk. He's here now. That's why I'm ringing. He seems pretty subdued, and he apologised for this afternoon, said he'd overreacted, so I don't think . . . I think he'll be all right, but I just thought I should let someone know.'

'Right. Will you ring me when he's gone? Whatever time it is, let me know you're OK.'

'All right. Thanks, Charlie.'

Feeling considerably more secure, Amy returned to the kitchen. Bill was sitting where she'd left him, his head in his hands. Waiting for the kettle to boil, she took the seat opposite his and said, gently, 'Would it help to talk about it?'

Bill rubbed his face hard, as if he were trying to sandpaper his chin. 'Can I trust you?' he asked.

The phantom of George flickered, and died, in Amy's mind. 'Yes,' she said. 'You can trust me. Can I trust you?'

'Yes. I swear I don't know anything about it, but it's Rosie. My wife. She's buried in the wood.'

'How do they know it's her?' Amy hesitated for a second before taking the plunge. 'I saw it in the local paper. It said the body was a skeleton.'

Bill sighed. 'Her sister read about it. She's the one who called the police. Said she hadn't heard from Rosie since she left me, and she thought it might be her. Maggie—that's Rosie's sister—we never got on. They got hold of the dental records.'

'Weren't they destroyed?'

'They usually are. Amazing for anyone to keep them this long, apparently, but for some reason the local practice never got round to it. Anyway, there's no doubt.'

'Did you know they'd found a body?'

213

Bill shook his head. 'I knew the police were up there—you couldn't miss it. It's true I hadn't heard from Rosie, but it never occurred to me that she might be dead.'

'Didn't she leave you a note?'

'No.'

'I don't understand. If she'd just disappeared into thin air, surely you called the police at the time?'

'No. That's what I've been trying to explain to them. We hadn't been getting on too well. Arguing. I'd begun to wonder whether it was worth carrying on. We were both miserable. I didn't like the idea of divorce—never have—but it got to the point when I thought, it's got to be better than this. And I suppose . . . Well, when Iris told me Rosie was having an affair, it made sense. I thought I must be a laughing stock—the last to find out and everyone else knowing. Iris tried her best to soften the blow, but that was what it amounted to. It was humiliating. After that, I just wanted to keep my head down. And, to be honest, it was a relief, her not being there and us having rows all the time. Meant I could have a bit of peace.'

'So you weren't suspicious? Even though she'd vanished without taking any of her things?'

'Oh, she did. She took a couple of suitcases. Clothes, jewellery, stuff from the bathroom.'

'Did you tell the police that?'

'They didn't believe me. They said they hadn't found anything like that. Then they told me there was a baby.'

'A *baby*?'

'Buried next to Rosie.'

'Was it hers?'

214

'They kept saying it was. I told them it couldn't be, because we'd tried to have a baby and we couldn't. They said she'd left because she was pregnant by another man. They kept on asking who he was. I told them I didn't know, but they didn't believe me. They said they'd be doing tests—I said fine, go ahead, I offered to have a test myself—DNA or whatever they wanted—but then they changed the subject and started asking about guns.'

'Was she shot?'

'I suppose so. I asked, but they wouldn't give me a straight answer, just kept asking where I kept my gun and who knew I had it and was it locked up. I told them I'd got a licence, but they made it sound as if it was a crime. It was like a nightmare. I couldn't think straight. We went round and round in circles, and I kept thinking they were going to arrest me. I didn't do it, Amy. I can't believe it. She's been there, all this time . . .'

'Do they know how long?'

'Years, they said.'

'I'm so sorry, Bill. The baby, was it a boy or a girl?'

'They didn't know.'

'Perhaps it wasn't full term. A miscarriage, or an abortion.'

'They didn't mention anything like that. I feel as if I'm going mad. They told me not to go anywhere.' He stared at her, utterly defeated. 'You believe me, don't you?'

'I think so, yes.'

'Does Sheila? What did she say when you told her?'

'She said you didn't do it.'

215

'It's true!' Bill got up, shaking, and began blundering around the room, running his hands over the surfaces like a blind man trying to find something. 'I didn't kill Rosie, I wouldn't, there was no reason.'

'Come on.' Amy got up and guided him back to his chair. 'You stay there, and I'll make that tea, shall I? Or maybe something stronger. If there is anything, I mean. I'm sure Sheila wouldn't mind.'

'In the storeroom,' said Bill. 'Key's in the drawer by the sink.'

'Key?'

'There's a cupboard up there. Sheila keeps it locked.'

Amy found an old-fashioned iron key under a stack of spotless table linen and tiptoed upstairs with it. She found a small wooden cabinet on one of the lower shelves. Turning the key in the lock, she thought of the 'tantalus' contraptions used by Victorian housewives to stop their servants taking a nip while no one was looking, and decided that this, too, must have been left over from Leslie's day. She picked out a bottle of brandy, then padded across the landing to check on Sheila, who was, mercifully, fast asleep. Listening to the faint snuffling of her breath, Amy wondered if she ought to show Bill the diary. He seemed to be telling the truth—if he wasn't, he was a bloody good actor—and there might be something in Mo's account that would help him. But Sheila, despite not having read the diary, had lied about it to Bill, so, clearly, she didn't want him to see it. And if Bill had had no involvement in Rosie's death, and didn't know that it was her body in the wood, why had he been so keen to know what was in it?

216

Rosie might have been killed by the man she supposedly ran away with, only no one seemed to know who he was, and Bill had obviously washed his hands of the whole thing and never attempted to get his wife back. And the baby . . . Bill had denied all knowledge of it. She stared at Sheila's curls, spectral in the dim bedroom. 'Was it yours?' she murmured. If it was, who was its father? Or perhaps it was Rosie's and Leslie was the father—and Leslie had killed them both. But if that was the case, why the hell was Sheila still trying to protect him? And if Leslie had killed Rosie and Sheila had known about it, why hadn't it come out at her trial?

Feeling as if she'd stumbled into a maze, Amy went back downstairs, found a tumbler, and poured out a double measure. 'There you are.'

'Thanks. I'd like to see the diary, Amy. Do you know where it is?'

'I think you ought to ask Sheila about that.'

'It isn't hers.'

'No, it's Mo's. And Mo gave it to my mother, presumably because she didn't want anybody else to see it.'

'You read it,' he accused.

'Yes,' said Amy patiently, 'I know. But that was a genuine mistake—all right, perhaps I shouldn't have *gone on* reading it, but I didn't know who it belonged to. Look, as I said this afternoon, I'm an outsider in all this. I don't know why she lied to you about it. Do you?'

Bill's gaze shifted. 'We've always . . . looked out for each other. She was trying to protect me.'

'From what?'

'The business in the past. Leslie. I felt terrible

217

when I found out what he'd done. The man worked for me—we were neighbours—and I'd had no idea about any of it. Nobody did. I remember people here talking about it afterwards. No one knew what to say. Everyone thought they should have realised. Paid more attention. You read about things like that, but you never think you're going to find it onyour doorstep.'

'Do you think Rosie knew? Before, I mean?'

'No! She'd have told me.'

'Didn't you ever wonder about them? Two women still living at home in their thirties, no boyfriends?'

'We used to talk about it sometimes. We just thought they were different.'

'How do you mean?'

'The way they dressed. They didn't have a lot of money, but they were always well turned out. Old-fashioned-looking. All the young people in those days were scruffy—they didn't look as if they'd seen a bar of soap from one year's end to the next—but Sheila and Mo were always neat and tidy. Rosie used to say it was odd they never seemed to have boyfriends, but I can't say I ever gave it much thought. It sounds as if we didn't care, but we didn't think it was any of our business, if that was what they wanted.'

That, thought Amy, was where Leslie Shand had been so clever: Sheila and Mo might have seemed 'different' but they were grown women, and people had assumed that they were free agents.

'I'd known them a long time,' said Bill. 'Leslie came to work for me when they were about ten or so. I was in my twenties then—I'd inherited the place when my father died. I just assumed they preferred to live at home. Leslie wasn't much of a talker, but you couldn't fault his work, and I never saw a sign of his temper.'

'What about Sheila and Mo? Did you see much of them?'

'Not really. They came down to the farm sometimes, but they were very quiet. Sheila'd talk a bit, but Mo was very shy. Jumped like a rabbit if anyone spoke to her. Iris was always pleasant, though. When we saw them up at the pub, she had more to say than he did.'

'What did you talk about?'

Bill frowned. 'The usual things, I suppose. I can't really remember. She and Rosie would have a bit of chit-chat—just passing the time of day. We knew Iris had to go up to the hospital sometimes, and I remember Rosie mentioning something about women's problems, but that was all.'

'You don't think,' said Amy, picking her words carefully, 'that Sheila didn't want you to see the diary because she thought there was something in it about Rosie? She hasn't read it, by the way—I asked her.'

'I don't see how she could have known anything,' he said, frowning. 'She'd have told me, wouldn't she?'

'Would she? If it was something to do with Leslie?'

Bill looked surprised. 'Why should it have anything to do with Leslie? He was a bastard, all right, but that was all to do with his family.'

'There wasn't anything going on between them?'

'Rosie and Leslie? God, no. She didn't even like him much. Said he gave her the creeps.'

219

'When was that?'

Bill thought for a moment. 'Quite late on, I think. A week or so before she went.'

'Did she say why?'

Bill shook his head, remembering. 'It was one evening before he knocked off. He'd come up to the house for a word about work. We were standing at the back door and then he went home. When I went through into the lounge Rosie was standing at the window, watching him go up the lane, and she told me he gave her the creeps. I was surprised because I didn't know she felt like that.'

'Did she say anything else?'

'No. She started nagging me because I was still in my overalls.' He smiled. 'She was always house-proud. Poor woman. I suppose this man she went off with must have done it.'

'What you said—Iris telling you about him— that was in the diary.'

'Was it?'

'Yes.' Seeing the look on his face, Amy relented, opened the bag, and pulled out the photocopy of Mo's diary. 'Look,' she said, 'I'm not sure about this, and I don't want to cause problems, but it seems to me that you're entitled to see the relevant bits.' She found the page and passed it across the table.

'You copied it,' said Bill.

'Yes. I know I shouldn't have, but I was interested.'

'I see.' Bill frowned, but didn't say anything further. He read the entries, then looked up, clearly puzzled.

'Is that how you remember it?'

'Yes. Except . . .'

'Except what?'

'It says here that Leslie told them about Rosie on the Friday. *When Dad came back from the farm he told us that Mrs Drake has left.* That's what she's put. But he wasn't there when I discovered she'd gone.'

'Are you sure?'

'Yes. I went over and over it with the police, and I'm positive. I'd been off the farm myself—a tractor broke down, and I had to get a part for it. Rosie must have waited until I'd gone out before she left, you see. We were barely speaking, so . . . I'd have thought she'd have left some sort of note, but she'd taken her things, so it was fairly obvious what had happened. Anyway, I managed to get hold of this part, and then I went straight to the yard because I wanted to sort out the tractor. It was February, and it must have been after five, because I remember I rigged up a light on a cable, to see what I was doing. I suppose it must have taken an hour or so to get it fixed. But the point is, Leslie'd already gone home.'

'So he was gone by the time you came back?'

'No, he was just finishing up. Him and Chalky, the other man who worked for me. I remember because one of them asked if I wanted a hand.'

'Which one?'

Bill thought for a moment, then shook his head. 'It's gone. Anyway, I told them I could manage and to get off home.'

'Did they mention Rosie?'

'No.'

'So they didn't know she'd left?'

'No.'

'Are you sure about that?'

'I can't see why they'd lie about it. In any case, they might not have seen her leave. There used to be a lot more buildings than there are now—Nissen huts and pigsties and so on—away from the main yard, so they wouldn't have known about it.'

'But they'd have heard a car?'

'They might have. Depends where they were and what they were doing. There's only one exit from the farm. There used to be a track through the woods behind the school to Leslie's back garden—it's overgrown now, of course—but the way you came in is the only access to the road. It wasn't as if Les and Chalky were looking out for Rosie or anything—no reason why they should—but I'm sure they'd have told me if they'd seen anything odd. So this'—he tapped the diary with a finger—'doesn't make sense.'

'I suppose it might be a mistake,' said Amy thoughtfully, 'if Mo was writing it after the event. Are you absolutely sure about the date?'

'Yes. That was the reason I had to go for the part. The shop wasn't open on Saturday, and I needed the tractor at the weekend.'

'Did Leslie and Chalky work on Saturdays?'

'Yes. Alternate weekends. It was Les's turn.'

'And you told him about Rosie?'

'Couldn't avoid it. Rosie used to come out with a cup of tea in the mornings. I think I told him she'd gone out shopping or something, but when she didn't come back he started saying things.'

'What sort of things?'

'"She's been a fair old time" or something like that. In the end I thought, I'll have to tell him.'

'How did he react?'

'I can't really remember. Just the usual stuff, I

suppose. I was . . . Well, I felt pretty stupid, to tell you the truth, and I was angry that she'd gone off like that. Thought I'd be a laughing stock.'

It struck Amy that that was the second time he'd mentioned being a laughing stock, as if the disappearance of his wife was painful for him not of itself, but because of how other people would react. And that, presumably, was the main reason he hadn't pursued her—fear of humiliation.

'Do you remember what time Leslie went home on Saturday?' she asked. 'It's just that Mo says they took photographs in the garden, and if he'd put in a day's work and then brought Iris down to see you and taken the pictures after that, there wouldn't have been a lot of light left.'

'I suppose not. It's hard to remember.' Bill sighed. 'Iris said she didn't know the man's name. Can't ask her now, of course.'

'Sheila might remember something if Iris told her about it.'

'She's never said anything to me.' Bill looked hurt.

'Then maybe she doesn't know,' said Amy hastily. 'Or she wanted to spare your feelings, like you protecting her. Perhaps you should ask. What about the other man?'

'Chalky?'

'Is he still around?'

'Lives round the corner.'

'Why don't you talk to him? He might remember something.'

'I suppose so.' Bill stood up. 'I wish I knew what the hell was going on.'

'You need to get some sleep,' said Amy.

'You'll tell Sheila, will you, in the morning?'

Following him to the front door, Amy decided to ask the question that had bothered her, on and off, all evening. 'Bill, where was Leslie Shand shot?'

'In the chest.'

'I meant, was it in the house?'

'Oh, yes. In there.' He jerked his head in the direction of the sitting room.

'Does the cottage belong to you?'

'Yes. It's part of the farm.'

'You let them stay here.'

'It's their home—Sheila's now. For as long as she wants it.'

'That's kind of you.'

'Least I could do.' Bill sounded dismissive.

'Do you pay for Compton Lodge, too? For Iris?'

'I help out. Not cheap, that sort of thing. Sheila couldn't manage on her own.'

That, thought Amy as she closed the door, was why Sheila hadn't moved house. She wondered if it had been Bill's suggestion that Iris go to Compton Lodge. With Iris gone, and no Mo (where *was* she?), Bill had Sheila to himself, living in a house provided by him. A benevolent despot—unlike Leslie—but a despot, nonetheless.

She rang Charlie—no response—and left a message. 'Bill's left. I'm fine—about to go to bed. Too much to tell you now, just that it's getting weirder by the minute. Hope everything's OK.' It struck her that Charlie might be investigating another break-in at that very moment, hence the answerphone. 'If not, let me know. I'll give you a call tomorrow.'

She sloshed some brandy into Bill's empty glass and leant against the sitting-room doorjamb, drink

224

in hand. Had Sheila really shot her father in this prissy, over-decorated little room? She imagined blood splattered across the genteel wallpaper with its discreet pattern of raised trellis, spraying the ceiling and dripping off the light shade, and Sheila, primly garbed, standing over her father's prostrate body with the shotgun while her mother and sister stared. Don't be stupid, she told herself. The place had obviously been redecorated since then, and anyway she had no idea how much blood there would be from a wound in the chest. All the same, she thought, I'm not sleeping down here. It would have to be Iris's bedroom. She picked up her handbag, turned off the lights, and tiptoed upstairs. In the bathroom, she splashed her face with water and rubbed toothpaste round her gums with a finger. Then, in Iris's bedroom, she peeled the blankets off the bed and lay down under a single sheet. Her nakedness, in this place, felt wrong, vulnerable, and, despite the heat, she longed for a T-shirt. She switched off the bedside lamp (pink pleats with gold tassels round the bottom), and turned onto her side. Despite being tired, it took a long time, staring into the darkness, before she fell asleep.

# CHAPTER THIRTY-ONE

Sheila glanced at her bedside clock. Twenty past five. I shan't get back to sleep now, she thought. She turned her head and looked at the empty bed beside her, wishing that Mo were in it. The old Mo, the one she'd trusted. Confidante, comforter,

225

comforted, as it had been, before. But even that wouldn't do any good. This was something she had to do alone. It wasn't Mum's fault, or Mo's, that they had never been strong enough; that was the way it was, and she had to look after them. That had been true eighteen years ago, when she'd confessed to killing *him*, and now it was even more so.

Something—a slight sound or vibration, was it?—told her that she wasn't alone in the house. Sheila started, then remembered: the girl from yesterday. Amy, that was it. Patti Vaughan's daughter. She eased herself out of bed, wriggled her feet into her slippers, and passed noiselessly out of her room and down the stairs. Seeing the empty lounge, she realised that Amy must be in Mum's room. It upset her to think of someone else sleeping in Mum's bed, but she supposed that it was only the beginning of all the things that were going to happen now the police knew about Rosie. Suppose they'd already arrested Bill? I'm trapped, she thought. There isn't a way out.

Her vision blurred by tears, she blundered across the room, barking her shin on the coffee table, and curled herself in a ball on the sofa, trembling, one fist jammed into her mouth to keep from screaming, rocking back and forth, *I can't bear it, I can't bear it any more, it's too much, I can't bear it.*

The sudden metallic sharpness of blood in her mouth came as a relief. She withdrew her hand and examined the raw knuckles for a moment before sucking them, calf-like, for comfort, until the bleeding stopped. She plodded back upstairs to the storeroom, and stood in front of the deed box.

She ought to take the journals out and burn them. That's what she'd do, when Amy had gone. Burn them. Then no one would ever know.

She fingered the two padlocks. One key was in her bedside table, the other was with Iris at Compton Lodge. The locks weren't very strong— she could break them. She looked round at the row of tools hanging from the wall. But she'd promised to look after them, hadn't she? Even if she didn't read what Iris had written, it would still be a betrayal, a repudiation of all they had suffered together. Mum's mind had betrayed their shared past, and so had Mo's, but they couldn't help that. She, the sole custodian of the truth, couldn't do the same. She couldn't destroy Mum's words.

She let go of the padlocks and stood staring down at her hands, the fingers rigid, stiff like flippers, trembling. 'Oh, Mum,' she sobbed. 'Help me. Please help me.'

# CHAPTER THIRTY-TWO

When Amy woke up, it took her a moment to remember where she was. She dressed quickly, and, after splashing her face with water in the bathroom, went to check on Sheila. Seeing the bed empty, she went downstairs, expecting to find her in the kitchen. She checked the other downstairs rooms and was about to go into the garden when she realised she hadn't tried the storeroom.

She found Sheila sitting on the floor, wrapped in a blanket. 'Good morning.' Amy knelt down beside her. Sheila seemed to be in a trance of misery.

'This floor's pretty hard, isn't it?'

When Sheila didn't respond, she tried again. 'Wouldn't you be more comfortable downstairs? Or you can go back to bed, if you like.' Amy shifted round so that she was directly in front of Sheila, but the blank expression didn't change. 'It's still early. I can make you a cup of tea—or coffee, if you'd prefer it. Would you like that?'

Sheila let out a groan, as if in terrible pain. Awkwardly, Amy shuffled forward on her knees and put her arms round her. 'Come on, Sheila.' The groan mutated into a keening wail that seemed to go on and on. 'It's all right, Sheila, it's all right.' Even as she spoke, she realised the futility of saying those words to someone for whom nothing, ever, had been 'all right'—whatever that meant—and the utter impossibility of making it so. But Sheila didn't attempt to disengage herself, and, after a few minutes, the meaningless repetitions seemed to quiet her, so that she sat passively in Amy's embrace. After a few more minutes, she let Amy help her up, adjust the blanket round her shoulders, and coax her back across the landing and into bed.

'That's better, isn't it?' Amy tucked in the sheet. Sheila lay like an obedient child while Amy fetched tissues and a flannel from the bathroom, wiped her face, and tidied her hair. 'Now,' she said, as gently as she could, 'I want you to close your eyes and rest, and I'm going to make you a nice hot drink.'

Christ, she thought on her way downstairs, the woman's falling apart in front of my eyes and all I can do is offer platitudes and cups of tea. She prepared a tray and took it upstairs to Sheila, who was lying exactly as she'd left her, staring blankly across the room. 'I thought you might like some toast,' she said. 'I found some napkins, so you don't have to worry about crumbs.'

'Thank you. Did Bill come back?'

'Yes. He told me what happened.'

'What's going to happen to him?'

'I don't know. But if they're going to investigate, they might want to talk to you.'

'I know.'

'There's something else, Sheila. Bill told me that when they found Mrs Drake there was another skeleton. A baby.'

Sheila gasped, and her body went so rigid that Amy thought she was about to have some sort of fit. 'Sheila? I'm sorry, I didn't mean to frighten you. Here, give me your cup, and let's—'

'There can't be,' said Sheila. 'There wasn't a baby.'

'What do you mean?'

Sheila collected herself with obvious effort, and said, 'There can't have been. Rosie didn't have a baby.'

'Are you sure?'

'Yes. There wasn't a baby.'

'They found one, Sheila.'

'Do they know about it?'

'Whose it was? No.'

'Then . . . then . . .'

'Was it yours, Sheila?'

'No!' Sheila's eyes filled with tears.

Amy handed her a fistful of tissues from the box on the bedside table and waited for the sobbing to subside. 'I'm really sorry, Sheila. I want to help, but I don't know what's going on. Perhaps if you could tell me—'

'I don't know!'

'About the baby?'

'Any of it.'

'But you knew that Rosie—Mrs Drake—didn't have a baby.'

'Yes. Will they come today?'

'The police? I don't know.'

'Will Bill come?'

'I should think so.'

'I don't . . . I can't . . .'

'You don't want to see him?'

Sheila shook her head. 'Will you stay with me for a while?'

'If you like. Look, why don't you try and get some more sleep? If there's anyone you want me to ring for you—work—I can tell them you're not very well.'

'Please. Bevan & Marks. The number's by the phone.'

At Sheila's request, Amy doled out another of her pills, then sat with her while she drifted towards sleep. She found a neatly printed list of numbers by the telephone, headed by Bevan & Marks, Solicitors. She noted a number for Compton Lodge, one for Bill, doctor, dentist, hairdresser, and a few others, but nothing for Mo. After she'd made the call, she settled down at the kitchen table to try and think what to do. She couldn't, in all conscience, leave Sheila alone, especially as she'd said she didn't want to see Bill—who, given that she'd suggested he ask Sheila about Rosie's disappearance—would probably be round sometime today. She'd have to ask Sheila if there was anyone else who could come and be with

230

her—which might, of course, be a good way to bring up the subject of Mo. As she was considering this, Sheila's phone rang.

It was Sister Paula, the matron from Compton Lodge. 'Am I speaking to Sheila Shand?'

'I'm Amy Vaughan, Iris's great-niece. We met a few days ago.'

'I remember. May I speak to Miss Shand, please?'

'I'm afraid she's asleep at the moment. She hasn't been very well.'

'I really do need—'

'She's just taken a sleeping tablet, so it might be difficult.'

'I see.'

'I can take a message, if you like.'

'I'm afraid I've got some bad news. We found Iris this morning. She's passed away.'

# CHAPTER THIRTY-THREE

Amy said stupidly, 'You mean, she's dead?'

'I'm afraid so. The doctor thinks it was a stroke,' said Sister Paula. 'Very quick. She wouldn't have known anything about it.'

'Poor Iris. I'll tell Sheila as soon as she wakes up.'

Putting the phone down, Amy sat on the stairs. Sheila was in enough of a state as it was, and with no chance to say goodbye—if you could say goodbye to someone like Iris in any meaningful sense—and all this business about Rosie Drake . . . 'Oh, shit,' she muttered. She really couldn't

231

abandon the woman now.

Her mobile warbled inside her bag, and she went into the kitchen to answer it. 'Charlie?'

'How's it going?'

'It's like being in somebody else's nightmare.'

'Tell me.'

'I've just taken a call from the care home to say that Iris has died.'

'Have you told Sheila?'

'Not yet. She's asleep. Last night was, well . . .'

Charlie remained silent during Amy's résumé, then said, 'You don't think Sheila could have killed Rosie, do you?'

'I'm hardly going to ask her. The woman's mother's just died, for God's sake.'

'I wasn't suggesting you should ask her. I just meant, because of Bill.'

'I suppose it's possible. But it doesn't seem likely—it's not in character.'

'You've only met her twice, Amy. You can't know that. She killed her father.'

'Yes, but that was different. And anyway, if Rosie died on the day she disappeared—or soon after—Leslie was still alive then, and I can't see Sheila taking Rosie out to the wood and killing her while he was around.'

'Why not? Perhaps her plan was to kill Rosie first, then him. You don't know *when* Rosie was killed. Or the baby. There's nothing to say that she and the baby died at the same time, is there?'

'I don't know. It's probably quite hard to find out with bones. But I hadn't thought of that. Sheila was genuinely shocked when I mentioned the baby, Charlie. She said, "There wasn't a baby," and when I asked her what she meant, she said that

232

there couldn't have been because Rosie didn't have a baby. But I did wonder if that's what she actually meant, because it was so vehement—as if she'd seen the grave, so she knew the baby wasn't in it.'

'There you are, then. You could be looking after a murderer.'

'I seriously doubt that. Anyway, she's in no state to murder anyone at the moment. She's just taken another sleeping pill, and she's asked me to stay, so—'

'Because she doesn't want to see Bill.'

'She seems almost afraid of him. Surely that means they can't be in it together.'

'Not necessarily. I really think you ought to get out of there, Amy.'

'Don't be stupid. Someone's got to tell her about Iris.'

'Perhaps you should call the police.'

'And tell them what, exactly? That Bill swears he didn't do it, and Sheila swears he didn't do it, but she seems to know more than she's letting on?'

'What about the diary? You said according to that the Shands knew about Rosie leaving before Bill told Leslie.'

'Rosie might have confided in Iris if she'd been seeing someone.'

'But it was Leslie who told them she'd gone.'

'Yes. Oh, I don't know. It's an old diary, and I don't even know where Mo is or if she's still alive.'

'Doesn't matter. I'm surprised Bill didn't want to take the diary to the police. I would, if I was trying to clear my name.'

'He's still trying to protect Sheila.'

'From what? If she knows who killed his wife,

233

and if she's so fond of him, she ought to suggest it herself.'

'She hasn't read it, and she's in no state to suggest anything. It's up to the police to find out, and they know where she is. I'm just praying they're not about to come banging on the door.'

'Why?'

'Because the poor woman is drugged to the eyeballs and her mother's just died, that's why. I told you what she's been through, Charlie, and she's in pieces. This just doesn't seem *fair*. You probably think I'm being naive, but both she and Bill strike me as decent people. I told you, Bill seemed genuinely—'

'You *are* being naive, Amy. Or . . .'

'Or what?'

'You haven't got some mad idea that you can solve this murder, have you? I know you're a journalist, but—'

'Of course I bloody haven't. I'm worried about Sheila, that's all. She's still in shock from yesterday, and in a couple of hours' time she's going to wake up and I'll have to tell her that her mother's dead. It's broad daylight, for God's sake, and Sheila is a petite fifty-something woman in a fragile state. I'm at least six inches taller than she is, twenty years younger, much stronger, I'm wide awake, I've got a phone and the car's just outside.'

'All right, but what about Bill? He's a farmer, he must have a gun.'

'For heaven's sake, Charlie! Bill's in enough trouble as it is. You didn't see him last night—he was completely bewildered by the whole thing. I've no idea whether he's got a gun or not, but he isn't about to kill me, or Sheila, or anyone else.'

234

'You're sure about that, are you?'

'As much as I can be.'

'I find it a bit odd that you were the one getting paranoid about George and the arson and the burglary—your house is fine, by the way—and now you seem perfectly happy to find yourself in this situation.'

'Hardly happy. But, as you say, I am *in* this situation, and I'm not getting up and walking out and leaving a distressed, bereaved woman. Please don't let's have an argument about it, Charlie.'

'I'm worried about you, that's all.'

'I'm not going to stay here for ever. Apart from anything else, I've got work to do.'

'I know. But will you phone me later to let me know you're OK? And if anything happens—anything—just call the police and get out of there. Remember what I said about my mum—seeing people just as victims. It's more complicated than that, Amy.'

'I know. Look, I'd better go. I've got some calls to make about work, and I ought to ring George.'

'All right. Give him my regards.'

'Will do. Bye, Charlie.'

'Bye. And take care.'

Amy took her bag and phone into the garden, where she sat in the sun, made calls, and thought about families. It was the conflict of loyalties that made it so difficult. God knows, it had been—still was—hard enough in her own family, but loyalties in the Shand family—not to mention Bill—were clearly a minefield. She just wished she understood why.

She tried George's mobile.

'Hello, cherub.'

235

'How are you doing?'

'Fine. Claire's taking good care of me.'

'Glad to hear it. I thought you were going to call yesterday.'

'We had a few things to sort out. She's got me in to see some fellow she knows in Harley Street.'

Thank God, thought Amy. 'That was quick,' she said. 'Who's paying?'

'She is.'

'That's nice of her. Is she there?'

'Gone shopping.' George chuckled indulgently, as if it was his money Claire was spending, not her own.

'Well, thank her from me, will you? And let me know how you get on.'

'Will do. Bye, chicky.'

At one o'clock, she prepared a lunch of salad and cold meat. Not feeling much like eating, she put some on a tray with a cup of tea and was about to take it upstairs to Sheila when the phone rang.

'Is that Amy?'

'Bill?'

'Yes. I've just spoken to Chalky. He says he wasn't on the farm that afternoon. He'd got another job on the side, painting—farm work's not the best paid—and the woman was on at him to get it done, so he thought, as I wasn't there, he'd go and finish it. So it means that Leslie was on his own at the farm with Rosie. Chalky said he'd told Les he was going, and Les said he wasn't bothered.'

Amy decided she'd better let Bill finish before she broached the subject of Iris's death.

'Chalky said Les didn't say anything about Rosie when he came back. But it still doesn't make sense,

236

Amy. Rosie'd packed her suitcases. She was going, Iris told me. She wouldn't have lied. And if Les knew about it, why the hell didn't he tell me? That's what I don't understand. I can understand her confiding in Iris—another woman—but not *him*—unless he knew about this affair she was having because Iris had told him, and he'd been laughing behind my back all the time. I can't help thinking Sheila must have known something about it. I need to talk to her, but the police want me to go to the station for the DNA test this afternoon. That'll prove I've got nothing to do with the baby, but they still think—'

'Bill, listen to me. Sheila's not in a fit state to talk to anyone at the moment. She was really distressed when I told her about the baby, she's completely exhausted—she's asleep at the moment—and a couple of hours ago Compton Lodge phoned to say that Iris died this morning.'

'My God. We knew it was coming, but . . . That's dreadful. Poor Sheila.'

'She's taken some sleeping pills—I don't know how long they last, and I think it's better if I leave her to wake in her own time, but I was just going up to see how she's doing.'

'That's terrible . . . Terrible news, and after all this other business. I don't know what to say. You can't imagine how much Iris meant to her. She'll be devastated. I'll come over. Don't worry, I won't ask her about the other business, not now, but I ought to be with her.'

'No, Bill. Absolutely not. You need to get down to the station and give them your blood or whatever it is they need. That's the most important thing. You can ring when you get back.'

237

She put the phone down, asking herself what the hell she was doing. Protecting Sheila, yes—against what, she wasn't sure—but what about Bill? She still didn't know why he'd been so eager to know the contents of Mo's diary in the first place. I'm getting too close to all this, she thought. I can't see the wood for the trees.

Amy put the tray on the dressing table and stood looking down at the sleeping woman. Sheila was lying on her side, her left hand pushed under the pillow. Her face, in profile, with its fluffy halo of fair hair, looked soft and peaceful. Amy couldn't bring herself to wake her. She was about to go back downstairs when Sheila stirred and turned her head. For a moment, she looked groggy, and then her face snapped into taut lines, eyes like a cat on instant alert. 'What's happened?'

'How are you feeling?'

'Something's happened, hasn't it? Is it Bill?'

'No. Bill's fine.' Amy sat down on the side of the bed. 'There was a call from Compton Lodge.'

'Mum's dead, isn't she?' said Sheila in a toneless voice.

'Yes. I'm sorry. They think she had a stroke.'

'Her blood pressure was high,' Sheila said. 'They told me.'

'That can cause a stroke.'

'Yes. You know . . .' Sheila looked round like an actor expecting a prompt. 'It's strange,' she said, after a moment, 'but I always thought this would be the worst moment of my life, and it's not. Isn't that strange?'

Amy shook her head. 'It's the shock.'

'Yes.' There was wonder in Sheila's voice. 'I suppose it is. I've been dreading it for so long, and yet it's nothing like I thought.' She shook her head. 'I can't explain it,' she continued softly, almost to herself. 'It's not how I imagined it at all.'

'They said it happened very quickly. She didn't suffer.'

'She . . . didn't . . . suffer,' Sheila repeated slowly, as though she was trying to understand the full significance of the words. 'That's good,' she said finally. 'I'm glad she didn't suffer.'

'Yes, it is good. Very peaceful.'

'I'd like to see her.'

'I can take you, if you like.'

'Thank you.' Sheila pushed back the sheet, swung her legs off the bed, tried to stand up, and swayed for a moment before sitting back down again. 'It's really not how I expected,' she murmured, 'not at all.'

'Would you like me to help you get dressed?'

Sheila shook her head. 'Please, I'd like to be on my own.'

'There's some lunch there. Just in case . . .'

Sheila turned her head, as if in slow motion, and gazed at the tray of food as if it was a curious artefact she'd never encountered before.

'I don't think so, thank you. I just want to see her.'

When she walked into the kitchen half an hour later, dry-eyed in a peach-coloured summer dress, with neat hair and a trace of powder on her cheeks, Amy was struck by Sheila's *amour propre* and quiet, graceful movements. She hasn't taken it in, Amy thought. It's as if she's suspended somehow, floating. Seeing Iris's body will bring it home to her.

In the car, Amy asked, 'How did you know

239

something had happened?'

Sheila thought for a moment, then said, 'It's hard to explain. It wasn't your face, but . . . I feel changes. We got used to watching each other, you see, in case . . .'

'Because of your father?'

'Yes. If there was anything that might make him angry.' After a moment, she added, as if Amy had asked a question, 'Mum was very good to us.'

Remembering the cards in Iris's room, Amy said, 'You love her very much, don't you?'

'Yes,' said Sheila simply. 'She was a good mother. And,' she added with sudden, fierce determination, 'I'm not having her buried anywhere near *him*.'

# CHAPTER THIRTY-FOUR

Sitting in the lobby, while Sister Paula escorted Sheila upstairs to see Iris, Amy wondered about their relationship. How had Iris felt about being a sexual rival to her own daughters? Or possibly—if Leslie had not continued to require sex from her at all—about being supplanted? The remembered potency of Patti's anger—her fury at being trapped (as she saw it) in a situation where she was forced to use her daughter as bait—made Amy flinch. None of it had been her fault, yet Patti's spite had been directed at her, not George. And sex hadn't even come into it.

Clementine appeared with a cup of tea. 'Here you are.' She handed it to Amy and sat down on the sofa next to her, fanning herself while she caught her breath.

'Thanks.'

'I'm sorry about Iris.'

'Were you the one who found her?'

'Yes. Sittin' in her chair. She looked so peaceful. All happen very quick—the bes' way.'

'Yes, it was.'

Clementine leant towards her, one hand on her chest. 'I know about it, what happen in the family. Iris blame her daughter.'

'She blamed *Sheila*?'

'Iris show me the pictures, long time ago. She talk more when she first here. She said, "I have one good daughter, but I never know what happen to her." So then I ask someone what it about.' Clementine shook her head. 'Terrible story. But Iris'—she tapped her temple—'got mix up in here. Those pictures . . . When Sheila come, she don't want to look. When I find out what that man done, *I* don't want to look. But Iris confused. She think they her memories. Happy family, you know?'

Amy nodded.

'That man deserve to be shot.'

'Yes, he did. It's just a shame Sheila waited so long to do it.'

'Not for her,' said Clementine, seriously. You gotta understand—things change. When I first come here, nineteen fifty-seven, it was, from Trinidad, and my husband look for work, they put COL on the record, for coloured. Any job, the employment people say, "Will you take a black man?" and they say, "Oh, no, we got women workin' here." And when you look for a room, in the windows, big signs: No Irish, No Black, No Dog. One place we go says, "No coloured", but

241

they spell it KOL. My old man say, "These people don't want us, and they can't even spell!" Them so ignorant, you have to laugh, but that's what I'm sayin' about change. Sheila kill him before, she be in prison. Long sentence. Well . . .' She hoisted herself upright, and said, 'Got to get on.'

She's right, Amy thought. Attitudes have changed. And the judge in Sheila's case had been pretty enlightened. But what was that business about 'one good daughter'? Presumably Mo was the good one because she hadn't killed Leslie, who, in Iris's jumbled mind, had mutated into the exemplary father of a loving family.

Amy rose to meet Sheila and Sister Paula at the foot of the stairs. Sheila, grasping her handbag as if it were a lifebelt, looked as though she were about to collapse. Amy put an arm round her and was about to take her out to the car, when Sister Paula stopped her. 'We just need to have a word about the arrangements,' she said, putting a firm hand under Sheila's elbow. 'Shouldn't be too long.'

Reluctantly, Amy removed her arm. 'Take as long as you like,' she said. 'I'll wait here.'

'Thanks.' It was a whisper. Sheila's free hand closed on Amy's. 'Do you want to go up and see Mum?'

She wants me to, Amy realised. She nodded. 'Don't worry,' she said to Sister Paula. 'I can find my way up there.'

'Very well. We'll be in the office.'

Amy stopped outside the door of Iris's room. She didn't want to open it, not from squeamishness (after all, she'd seen a corpse before), but because death was on the other side. She raised her hand to knock, realised it was absurd, and, closing her eyes for a second to compose herself, turned the handle.

The curtains were drawn, and the room was full of soft, dim shapes—the wing-backed armchair where Iris had sat, the tea table, a dressing gown on a hook, a sponge bag, cushions and valances. The cards and trinkets on Iris's special shelf looked forlorn in the half-light, and above them, the pinks and blues of the oval plaque (*The Best Mum in the World*) had taken on the grey, granular quality of a headstone. Below it, Iris, washed and combed, was laid out on her bed in a clean white nightdress. A sheet covered the lower half of her body, and her hands were crossed on her chest. Her eyes were closed, and her face, the yellowish-white of ivory, wore an expression of repose. She's tiny, Amy thought. A husk. Uninhabited, like a shell. It was an uncomfortable reminder of what she'd thought when she'd first met Sheila. A part of her was dead, too, a spark that had been crushed by Leslie's boot before it had had the chance to grow into a living flame.

She stood looking down at Iris, unsure what to do. A prayer seemed appropriate, but since she wasn't a believer it would be hypocritical. Remembering that Iris had been a church-goer, Amy shook her head. Imagine believing in a God who let you in for all that! 'If He exists,' she told Iris, 'I hope you give Him what for.'

The photograph album lay on the bed at Iris's feet. Amy stared at it, thinking of tombs she'd seen—little dogs at the feet of stone effigies of knights and ladies in crypts. Faithful unto death. Had one of the carers put it there, she wondered, or had Sheila? Was it to be buried, or burnt, with her?

'Excuse me, Iris,' she murmured. Careful not to untidy the sheet, she picked up the album. It didn't seem right to turn on the light, so she took it across to the window and pulled the curtain slightly so that she could see the pictures. She glanced through the first pages quickly—Sheila and Mo as babes in arms, posing with pets as toddlers, Leslie with his arm round Iris, Iris and the girls, everybody smiling fit to bust, an idyll of family life where the sun always shone.

The change to colour came in 1966. Amy flipped through to the last few pages of the album. 1984: Stanley the parrot, a large, handsome bird, eyed the camera, flanked by the now grown-up Mo and Sheila. 1986: Sheila and Mo sitting on the sofa, dressed identically in striped cardigans. Was it her imagination, or did their smiles look more hesitant? 1987: mother and daughters in the garden, posed in front of the Anderson shelter, looking pinched and cold, their body language definitely less convincing than before. The photograph, which cut them off at the knees, showed Mo staring at the ground, Iris in the middle looking nervous, and Sheila, an awkward couple of feet away, forcing a grin. Perhaps that was the photograph Leslie had taken after Iris had been to the farm to tell Bill about Rosie and her lover.

The last picture showed the whole family. Leslie, smart in a suit and smiling proudly, was standing, chest thrown out, with one arm round each of his daughters, and Iris seated on a chair in front of him. They were posed in front of a pub fireplace, its wide oak bressummer and supports

244

hung with horse-brasses, warming pans and other bits of olde-worlde set dressing, a round table with beer mats and pint glasses glimpsed to one side. He looked like a man who'd achieved something in life (which, in his warped way, Amy supposed he had). Sheila, as usual, was doing her best to look happy, but Mo, her arms limp by her sides, looked apprehensive. Iris, her ankles crossed demurely, was the image of maternal pride.

Amy wondered who'd taken it. The landlord, perhaps, or a fellow customer? Some pub chum of Leslie's who, in a haze of beer and goodwill, hadn't noticed Leslie's thick fingers digging into his daughters' arms, their bruising pressure a taste of things to come if they failed to comply with his wishes? There was a calendar in the right-hand corner of the snap, pinned to the brickwork of the chimney piece. April. How long after that had Sheila picked up her father's gun and emptied it into his chest?

Amy closed the curtains, replaced the album on the bed and reached over to touch Iris's hand. It felt icy, like marble. 'Did you lie for him, Iris?' she asked.

Too late now. Iris was empty, and in any case she'd forgotten her secrets long before she died. 'Goodbye, Iris. Wherever you are, I hope it's peaceful. I'll do my best to help Sheila, I promise.' She stood, silent, in awkward, self-conscious reverence, for another minute, and was about to leave when she noticed something blue sticking up in the gap between the bed and the bedside table. It looked nubbly, like something knitted. Careful not to disturb Iris's hair, she stuck an arm down and tugged it free. It was the blue rabbit she'd seen on her previous visits, old and worn, ears flopping. Its remaining button eye seemed to stare back at her. She poked a bit of kapok back through a hole in one of the seams and then, on an impulse, pushed the toy into her handbag.

Sheila seemed agitated on the drive back to Hadley Cottage, picking at her clothes and responding to Amy's attempts at conversation with distracted monosyllables. As soon as they were inside, she said, abruptly, 'There's something I have to do,' and ran up the stairs.

Amy was sitting in the kitchen listening to her phone messages when she heard a thud from upstairs, followed by the repeated clang of metal glancing off metal. When she went to investigate, she found Sheila in the storeroom, standing in front of the locked iron deed box with a hammer and chisel in her hands, the dark severity of the tools incongruous against her pastel-coloured clothes.

'What are you doing?'

'Look.' Sheila, who seemed astonishingly composed, pointed to two opened padlocks on the shelf beside the box. 'They were very cheap,' she said, in a matter-of-fact way.

'What's in there?' asked Amy.

Sheila bowed her head for a moment, as if in silent prayer, then lifted the hasp and opened the lid. Amy took an involuntary step back, half expecting to be engulfed by an evil miasma, but Sheila bent forward and took out a bundle of school exercise books, neatly wrapped in clear plastic. 'These are our journals,' she said. 'The counselling lady said it might help us if we wrote things down about our lives with Dad.'

The topmost book was marked *Iris Shand (Mrs)* in crabbed, elderly handwriting. 'The others are mine,' said Sheila.

Amy looked into the box and saw another pile, marked *Sheila Shand (Miss)*. 'What about Mo?' she asked.

'She couldn't remember properly,' said Sheila. 'It was the ECT. Mum and I never read each other's diaries. She had the other key. I was going to take it from her room, but I couldn't find it. We agreed we wouldn't read them, but we wanted to have a proper record, because . . .'

'Because of Mo's diary?'

Sheila stared at her for a moment, her face expressionless. 'Because it was important,' she said flatly. 'I didn't know about Mo's diary.'

'You remember that letter Iris wrote to my grandmother? You said it was all lies, because Leslie made her write it. I know you haven't read Mo's diary, but I think it's the same.'

Sheila frowned, then said, 'If Dad had told her not to say anything, we wouldn't have known.'

'She didn't tell you afterwards?'

Sheila shook her head. 'I don't know why. But if that's true, it's like all those photos.'

'Iris's photos?'

'Yes. Mum got confused. She kept looking at them, saying we were happy and Dad was good with us. But I knew it was all in here.' She tapped the pile of exercise books. 'This is how it was.'

'Where is Mo, Sheila?'

'In a . . . place.'

'You mean some sort of unit?'

'She's not locked in or anything. They can come and go—it's really more like a hostel, with wardens

247

to look after them. She had a breakdown a couple of years after Dad died. I'll have to tell her about Mum, but I don't want to do it on the phone. And I want to look at these first. For Bill.'

Amy thought of the claim in Mo's diary that Leslie had broken the news about Rosie's disappearance to his family a day before Bill told him about it, of Leslie alone on the farm with Rosie, of Iris explaining to Bill, ever so gently, about Rosie's lover, of the vanishing suitcases full of clothes, of Iris thinking Amy was Mo and handing over the newspaper. 'Did Leslie kill Rosie, Sheila?' she asked.

Sheila's reply was a whisper. 'Yes.'

'Why?'

'Because she knew. She found out about us.'

'Did Iris cover up for him?'

Another whisper. 'Yes.'

# CHAPTER THIRTY-FIVE

'Have you known since it happened?'

Sheila nodded.

'Why didn't you tell the police when you . . . when Leslie died?'

'Mum said we shouldn't. And I didn't want to, in case she got into trouble.'

'I didn't tell you, but I went to see Iris a second time. She gave me the newspaper with the piece about the body in the wood.'

Sheila looked alarmed. 'Did you tell Bill?'

'I said I'd seen the paper. I didn't tell him anything else. But you've got to tell the police,

Sheila. For his sake. You don't have to say you knew about it, just that you found it here.' She pointed to the notebooks.

'I know, but . . .' Sheila swallowed. 'The baby. I think it's something to do with Mum. I wanted to look yesterday, but I couldn't. Not while she was still alive.'

'Do you think it was her baby?'

'It must be. There's no one else. Will you help me?'

Amy stared at the notebooks, fascinated and repelled at the same time. 'If you want me to.'

'You go downstairs, then. I want to unwrap these. I shan't be a minute.'

Preparing a tray of tea while she waited downstairs, Amy realised she'd done this automatically, as if she'd become attuned to Sheila and Bill's rituals. Once, she would have scoffed; now she recognised that the carefully prepared tray, the coasters and napkins, the neatly arranged biscuits, were, like the fussy décor with its plethora of 'nice things' and the luridly cheerful garden, vitally important.

They sat, one on each side of the kitchen table, the steaming pot and the pile of notebooks between them, ready to begin. 'Are they in sequence?' Amy asked.

'Not really. We just wrote when we remembered things, and when we'd filled up one book, we started another. That's what I did, so I suppose Mum must have done the same.'

'Have you any idea when it might have happened?'

'When we were young. There were some things we didn't talk about.' Sheila lowered her eyes. 'We couldn't.' She smoothed the cover of the topmost book for a moment, then pulled it towards her, indicating that Amy should do the same.

*The first time Leslie hit me was about a month after we were married. That was in 1949, in October. It seemed to come from nowhere and I didn't understand what I'd done wrong. He burst my lip and I had a nosebleed but he didn't say he was sorry, just told me to clean myself up. I thought he would apologise in the morning but he didn't, in fact we never talked about it at all.*

*I was ashamed and I begged him to keep his voice down and not shout because we lived in a flat then and I didn't want the neighbours to hear. After the first time he began to do it often. He hit me and if I fell down he would kick my stomach and back where it would not show with clothes on.*

*Sometimes he said he loved me. I thought of this when I was miserable and it made me feel better but I dreaded him coming home from work and when I heard his feet on the stairs I would shake from fear.*

*I often thought it must be my fault for not being a good wife to him. I always tried to do what he wanted and never left our house without asking him first, but he had a terrible temper. The worst was the old gas mask. He taped over the eyes and air holes and put it on me so I could not breathe. That was my worst fear, that he would kill me and sometimes I thought it would be better to die but then what would happen to Sheila and Mo? But I did not dare tell anyone, even when I found out how bad he really was. I could not run away because he was not frightened of anyone, even the police. He said if we ran away he would always be able to find us wherever we went and then he would kill us so we would die slowly and suffer. He was very strong from the work on the farm and I am not a big woman. There was only one way in our house and that was his way. I did not have money or a family who would help me, and he wouldn't let me make friends with others, so I had to make the best of things.*

The handwriting was cramped, but the simple words, set down in ordinary exercise books with ruled lines and margins of the type that Amy remembered from her school days, had a fluency and life of their own. The style was plain and the vocabulary simple, yet the narrative—bizarre juxtapositions of domestic detail with refinements of sadism that would have awed a professional torturer—was utterly alien. Amy looked up several times in shock, but Sheila's gaze never seemed to falter, and the only sounds in the sunny room were the turning of pages and the faint tick of the tabby-cat clock.

Amy was in the middle of her fourth notebook when Sheila said, 'It's here.'

'Show me.'

Sheila turned the notebook round and pushed it across the table.

*. . . he was very angry and told me I couldn't keep it. I could not have an abortion because in those days it was against the law and I didn't know anyone who could help me. Leslie said, If you have it, you'll have to kill it. I told him I could not do that and I would be able to manage with three so it would not be a nuisance to him in any way, but he would not change*

251

*his mind. I was very frightened and unhappy. When the baby began to show I spent most of the time in the bedroom. Sheila was four or five at the time, it was when Leslie was working at a different place and we lived in a flat round the corner from here. If anyone asked Leslie (why didn't I go to the shops) he said I was poorly and under the doctor but it would get better. He would not let the girls come in to see me for the last months. It was like a prison then, all the time staring at the walls and wondering what would happen because I knew I could not kill a baby and I thought he would kill me, and I was so frightened for Sheila and Mo, what would become of them if he did? It was like a person being condemned for doing something when they haven't done wrong, only being deceived by him into marrying him because I thought he was a kind man when all the time he had such a violent temper. If he wasn't there the girls would come up and we would whisper in case he came back suddenly and caught us. I didn't tell them what was happening. I felt so sorry for them, the poor little things were distressed enough without knowing about that as well.*

*I had the baby in our bedroom at home. I was frightened because I had a bad time before with Sheila and Mo and they were born in hospital. Leslie bought a medical book to see what to do when the time came. He said it would be all right because he had delivered animals on the farm many times. I tried to tell him it wasn't the same but he said he would use disinfectant and I was worrying over nothing. It took a long time and I suffered terrible pain but I couldn't cry or make any noise in case of upsetting the girls. It was always in my mind about what would happen if something went wrong.*

252

*I never knew if it was a boy or a girl. I heard it cry, but he wouldn't let me see it or hold it, just wanted me to smother it as soon as it was born but I said No. He saw I was too weak so he said he would do it himself. He said he would fetch the girls (before he did it) but I begged him not to make them watch. I pleaded with him and he agreed but only because they might say something and it would cause trouble for him. Then he put a pillow over its face.*

# CHAPTER THIRTY-SIX

Amy read it through twice, trying to take it in. Leslie had killed Iris's child. *His* child. He'd wanted his two young daughters to watch him murder it. 'Perverted sadist', or whatever it had said in the paper, didn't even come close to describing him. Leslie Shand was a man who was capable of anything—anything at all—and Iris had known it.

Looking up from the exercise book, her eyes met Sheila's. Amy saw no surprise there, or shock, but more a sort of weary recognition.

'Do you understand now?' she asked. 'That's how he was.'

'Why did you think . . .?' Amy gestured at the notebook. 'Did you remember something?'

'Not exactly. Dad told me about Mum being ill, but I didn't know what was wrong with her. When you told me about the baby, I had a feeling . . . I remember I thought she'd got a bit fatter, but, well, I was too young. I didn't understand. You know, I used to think sometimes that one day people would read about us in the paper, how Dad had killed us all. But now you can understand about Mum, can't you—what it was like for her?'

Amy thought of Iris, bloody and exhausted after a long labour, lying on the bed upstairs, her face grey with grief and shock, unable even to see the helpless little creature that Leslie had pulled out of her. Had she, all along, been nursing the forlorn hope that when he set eyes on his third child he might, miraculously, change his mind and let her keep it? She pictured him, sleeves neatly rolled up like Bill Drake's, drying his hands methodically on a towel before wrenching a pillow from beneath his wife's weak head and placing it over the tiny, scrunched-up face.

'I suppose,' said Sheila matter-of-factly, 'it was just as well, really. It would have had a horrible life.' The shock must have registered on Amy's face, because she added, more gently, 'I wouldn't want anyone to have a life like ours.'

'I can understand that.'

'That's why he buried Rosie where he did. The same place.'

'I think,' said Amy, 'that perhaps that's the reason Iris gave me the newspaper. Because she remembered the baby.'

'Yes. It ought to be buried with Mum. Do you think they'll let us?'

'I'm sure they will. When they've finished investigating.'

This is extraordinary, Amy thought. I'm in shock, and God knows Sheila must be, yet we are sitting here talking about this calmly. How the hell do police officers manage? 'Sheila,' she said, keeping her voice as light as she could, 'can I ask you something?'

'What is it?'

'Why were you so sure it was your mother's baby? I know you said it wasn't yours, but what about Mo?'

'He didn't do it to Mo.'

'Never? But it said in the paper—'

'Only once. He never tried again. I don't know why, but I thought, if he was doing it to me, he wouldn't want it from her as well.'

'So . . . with you, did he take precautions?'

'Oh, yes.' Again, the voice was matter of fact. 'Durex. Mum used to get them from the chemist.'

'*Iris* bought them?'

The corners of Sheila's mouth curved upwards in a faint, hollow smile. 'He'd never have bought them himself,' she said. 'Mum always left a packet for him in the Anderson shelter. That's where he did it,' she explained. 'It was a bomb shelter, left from the war. He used to keep some of his tools in it, and there was a bed in there. It was always on Saturday. I used to hate Saturdays.'

Amy remembered the photograph of Iris and Leslie standing in front of the Anderson shelter. He had posed himself and his wife in front of the place where, every Saturday, and with her knowledge, he'd raped his eldest daughter—the audacity of it was incredible. 'When did Iris find out?'

Sheila fiddled with her teacup for a moment before answering. When she spoke, her voice had a flat, neutral tone, as if she were recounting events that had happened to somebody else. 'She always knew. He told me he was going to do it, you see, about two weeks before. That was one of the worst times, waiting for it to happen. In fact . . .' She considered for a moment, then said, 'I think the waiting was worse, because I was so frightened.'

'So Iris knew he was going to rape you?'

'Yes.' Sheila sounded mildly impatient. 'There was nothing she could do. At first she said, "He couldn't do *that* to you," but I think she knew he would, because if he said something, he always did it.'

'But didn't she try to stop him?'

'I think she did say something, but she was so frightened. He had the gun, and he'd threaten us with it.' And, thought Amy, he'd already murdered her baby. 'I think it was worse for Mum,' Sheila continued, 'because she wanted to stop him and she couldn't.'

'*Worse?* How old were you?'

'Twelve.'

Amy stared at Sheila, appalled, trying to digest what she'd heard. Her imaginings had been bad enough, but actually hearing it . . . My God, she thought, if I'd had a gun and I'd known what that evil bastard was up to, I'd have killed him myself. Willingly. And I'd have started by aiming a bloody sight lower down than his chest, as well.

'Did you understand what he was going to do to you?' she asked.

Sheila hesitated, then said, 'I did know a bit. I knew it was wrong. We were in the garden when he said it, feeding the rabbits. I used to help him. It must have been in the summer, because it was in the evening, but still quite light. We'd fed them, and I was helping him with the water, getting the bowls. He didn't like it if any water got spilt, if it made a mess. That's when he told me. I was

256

holding the bowl under the tap and I must have moved it because my shoes and socks got splashed and I thought he was going to be angry about that, but he just said it again, that he wanted sex with me.'

'What did you say?'

'I told him I didn't want to. He put his hand in the hutch and grabbed one of the rabbits. It was a little black one—Mo's favourite. He held it up by the ears, and then he swung it against the wall, hard, on the bricks, and killed it. That was to show . . . if I said anything or made a fuss . . .'

'*Jesus!*' Sheila frowned at her. 'Sorry, I didn't mean to. It's just . . .'

'We had it for dinner,' she continued, in a remote voice.

'You ate the rabbit?'

'Oh, yes. It wasn't unusual. Dad did kill them, sometimes, and Mum would prepare them. We ate quite a lot of rabbit, because we didn't have much money, but often when he killed them it was a way of . . .'

'Making a point?'

'Yes, to make a point. Mo was upset because it was her favourite, and she couldn't eat it. He kept saying, "What's the matter with you?" You know, that he put good food on the table and she wasn't grateful, and all the time I was thinking about what he was going to do to me. Mo blamed me because she thought I must have done something wrong to cause it.'

'Did you tell her?'

Sheila shook her head. 'She was so upset, it wasn't fair. And she was younger than me. I thought she might not understand, and I wanted to

257

protect her. But I think Dad thought it would be all right, because he'd told me, so he thought, you know, that I could get used to the idea. I couldn't concentrate at school because I was waiting for it to happen. That was part of it—how he was with us. Like the photos.'

'How do you mean?'

'It was before he was going to hit you, or . . . Well, he always took a lot of photos on Saturdays. If we were at the pub, or watching television, anything that looked natural. Always before . . . Or straight after. He made a lot of it, getting it right, and if he didn't think we were smiling enough, he was furious.'

Amy thought of Mo's diary entry for the Friday when Rosie Drake had disappeared. *Later, Dad took photos of us . . .* 'He took a picture after Iris told Bill about Rosie's boyfriend, didn't he?'

'Yes,' said Sheila. 'In the garden.'

'Why did he take it? Because he'd killed her?'

'No. Not then. Not . . . then.' Sheila began to cry, covering her face with her hands. Amy leapt from her chair and stood behind her, rubbing her back as she rocked to and fro, keening, shuddering with grief. 'It's my fault,' she wailed. 'All my fault.'

'Sheila, none of it's your fault, you did your best. Have a tissue.'

Sheila wiped her eyes half-heartedly, hiccupping out disjointed words between her sobs. 'Sorry— such—long time—so tired.'

'I'm not surprised. Why don't you go and lie down for a while? The police can wait. I'm sorry, I shouldn't have asked all those questions.'

'Yes, I think I will.' Sheila stood up, blew her nose, smoothed her skirt automatically, and moved wearily towards the door.

'Wait a minute.' Amy pulled the blue knitted rabbit out of her handbag. 'I found this stuck down by your mum's bed. I thought you might like to keep it.'

'Oh.' Sheila smiled. 'It's Peter.'

'Is that his name?'

'Yes. Peter Rabbit. He was ours when we were little. Thank you.' Tucking the toy under one arm, she mounted the stairs.

Amy helped her undress and put on her nightie, then helped her into bed. Her face against the smooth white pillow looked grey and doughy, and her eyes dull and unblinking like two marbles pressed into Plasticine.

She's wiped out, thought Amy. 'Do you want me to go on looking through Iris's notebooks?' she asked. 'We need to find the bits about Rosie's death.'

'Yes. What time is it?'

'Half past eight. If you go to sleep now, I'll take you to the police station first thing tomorrow, but I'm going to have to dash home now and get some clothes and things. I won't be fit to be seen otherwise.'

Sheila sat up, looking alarmed. 'Bill! I don't want . . .'

'I'll ring him,' said Amy, 'and tell him not to disturb you. I shan't tell him anything else if you don't want me to.'

'No. Please.'

'All right. I'll go and phone him now, shall I? Don't worry, I'll be back later.'

Sheila looked at Peter Rabbit, who was sitting on the bedside table, then back to Amy. 'Will you sleep in this room?'

'If you like.' Amy squeezed her hand. 'Have you got spare keys?'

'In the storeroom,' said Sheila. 'The hook behind the door.'

'Right. I won't be long, I promise. And no one's going to disturb you.'

Amy went downstairs, composed something suitable to say to Bill, found his number on the list, and picked up the phone.

'Hi, it's Amy. How did it go at the police station?'

'Not too bad. At least they were efficient about it.'

'Did you say anything about Leslie?' she asked.

'Didn't get the chance. It was just a duty doctor I saw, not a policeman. Why? Has Sheila mentioned something?'

'No,' Amy lied. 'And this really isn't the time to discuss it. I've just put her to bed. She's exhausted.'

'I'm not surprised,' said Bill. 'How did she take it?'

'It's hard to know. I don't think it's really sunk in about Iris. And she's so churned up about this other business. It's going to take her a long time, Bill.'

'I know. To be honest, it's only just beginning to sink in about Rosie.' He sighed. 'I just wish I knew what was going on.'

'Why don't you try and get some sleep?'

'Yes,' said Bill hopelessly. 'All right. I'll talk to you in the morning.'

As Amy drove back to Islington through the thinning rush-hour traffic, she wondered whether Iris had known where her baby was buried, and

260

what Sheila had meant when she'd said it was her fault. She must have known Rosie's body was somewhere in the wood, otherwise why give the cutting to Iris? Whatever her involvement, her need to protect Bill—and the concomitant inability to tell him the truth—must have grown stronger as the years passed. Bill might understand rationally what Sheila had done, but emotionally . . . And yet Sheila appeared to understand that Iris was powerless to protect her from Leslie, without resenting her for it. That might change now that Iris was dead—the grieving process could hardly be uncomplicated. And it would be the same for Bill. He'd seen Rosie as a wife who deserted and humiliated him, and the Shand women as victims, but now, if he found out that Sheila and Iris—and possibly Mo—knew, he must surely recast them as betrayers. And she was slap in the middle of it.

Once indoors, she listened to her messages—no weird silent ones, thank God—made notes, left messages in answer, dealt with her e-mails, and shoved some clean clothes and washing things into a holdall to take back with her. Then she ran herself a hot, scented bath and lay staring at the ceiling until all the bubbles had dissolved.

There was a knock on the door as she was drying herself. When she opened it, Charlie was standing on the step.

'Sorry,' he said, seeing her bathrobe and turbaned head. 'Bad timing. I saw your car and I wanted to check you were OK.'

'Come on in. It won't take me a minute to get some clothes on.'

Back in the bathroom, she checked her watch. Sheila was bound to be fast asleep by now—she'd taken another of her tablets—so there'd be time for a drink with Charlie before she returned to Hadley Cottage. She rubbed her ringlets furiously—they were always better left to their own devices—threw on underwear and jeans, and, cursing herself for not doing the washing, scrabbled through her cupboard until she found a clean top. She fluffed her hair at the mirror, splashed herself with perfume, and ran down to Charlie, who was standing uncertainly in the hall. 'Would you like a drink?'

'I'd love one. Then you can tell me what's been going on—if you want to, of course. I'm sorry if I went on a bit before, but—'

'It's OK, Charlie. I understand why, but it's really not like you think. White OK?'

'Fine.'

'Good.' Amy collected a bottle, an ice bucket and two glasses. 'Come into the garden.'

'This is lovely,' said Charlie, looking round.

'I haven't done much to it.' Amy poured wine. 'Just the pots and climbers. I'm not much of a gardener, really.'

'It's great. South-facing—you can grow pretty much anything. How's your dad?'

'Seems OK. I phoned him this morning. God, it seems like years ago. At least I haven't got him to worry about. Sheila was asleep when I left. I'm going back tonight.'

'Is that a good idea?'

'Yes. You don't know the half of it, Charlie. The baby was Iris's. It was born at home, and Leslie smothered it.'

'*Christ.*'

'Nobody knew. It was in one of Iris's notebooks.'

262

'Notebooks?'

'For therapy. After Leslie was shot they all went to counselling. Sheila's kept all these books they wrote, full of stuff about their lives.'

'So she must have known all along.'

'No. She was very young when it happened, and they didn't read each other's notebooks. That was the point—writing down things they couldn't say. I haven't seen Sheila's. Iris's are bad enough, but hers must be . . . He raped her, Charlie, every Saturday, since she was twelve. I mean, I knew that from the paper, but hearing her talk about it . . . You can't imagine.'

'How old was she when she shot him?'

'Thirty-six.'

'Was he still doing it?'

'I think so. She didn't say he stopped.'

Charlie shook his head. 'I know what I told you about my mother, but that is just . . . God, I wish I still smoked.'

'Me too. It gets worse, though. Iris knew what Leslie was up to, right from the start. She was too frightened to do anything about it. And Sheila says Leslie killed Rosie.'

'Why?'

'She found out what he was doing to Sheila. I suppose she threatened to go to the police. Or tell Bill.'

'The police wouldn't be much of a threat. After all, Sheila was grown up by then. And if she was as much under Leslie's thumb as you say, they'd both have denied it.'

'But Bill would have believed her.'

'Not necessarily. You said the marriage wasn't working. If Rosie had told Bill, he might have

263

thought she was saying it to stir things up because she was jealous of Sheila. Didn't Iris write anything about it?'

'If she did, we haven't come across it yet. I'm going to read the rest of the notebooks when I get back.'

Charlie took a sip of wine and stared down at his feet, frowning.

'What is it?'

'Look, Amy, people like that can be very manipulative, and you're getting sucked into a situation that—'

'Hang on.' Despite her anxieties, Amy was instantly defensive. 'I know about manipulative, Charlie. I grew up with it, remember? My mother was the high priestess of manipulative, and George isn't exactly a beginner. These people are trying to *protect* each other. Leslie was the manipulator in that family—there wasn't room for anyone else. The bastard's been dead nearly twenty years, and they're still in his web. Believe me, Sheila is *not* manipulative. She spent years letting Leslie screw her to stop him turning his attentions on Mo, and now she's trying to protect Bill because he's been good to them.'

'You said she was afraid of him.'

'She was afraid because of Leslie—Bill finding out that she knew. But she's agreed to come with me to the police station tomorrow, to show them what Iris wrote.'

'Are you sure it's the truth?'

'Well, the whole exercise was supposed to be about confession—getting things off their chests— so I don't see why Iris would write down a pack of lies.'

'What about Sheila? If she knew from the off about what Leslie did to Rosie, she's going to be in trouble. I imagine she could be charged as an accessory. And so could Mo, if she knew about it.'

'Mo's in some sort of secure home. Well, warden-assisted or something. As far as I can make out, she's away with the fairies. And she was having ECT and God knows what else for a good year before any of it happened. It says so in her diary. And I'm sure they'll be lenient.' Amy realised, as she was speaking, that she wasn't sure of anything of the kind.

'No, you're not.'

'You're right, I'm not. But it all seems so unfair, Charlie. The poor woman's been through so much already, and her mother's just died, and now this.' Amy felt tears welling up and turned her head away.

'You're really involved, aren't you?'

'Of course I'm bloody involved!' Amy wiped her eyes. 'I can't help it. Sheila and Bill are good people.'

'Yes, you said. I know you want to help. I'm just saying that it might not be as straightforward as you think.'

'I *know* it's not straightforward. That's the problem. I feel as if I'm trapped in a maze, and talking about it just makes it even more confusing. And now'—she drained her glass—'I need to get back to Sheila.'

Charlie stood up. 'Right. I'll go.'

Amy followed him into the hall. Charlie paused in front of the door, and said, without looking at her, 'I'm not trying to interfere in your life, Amy. This is an odd situation. We don't know each other

that well, and yet we've told each other things that
. . . Well, I don't know about you, but I never talk
about my parents, and I suspect you don't, either.'

'Never.'

'I'm sorry if I upset you. I'm going to go now,
and if you want to phone me, phone me. I hope
you will, but it's up to you.' He gave her a peck on
the cheek, and left.

# CHAPTER THIRTY-SEVEN

Amy let herself into Hadley Cottage, feeling like
an intruder in the dark, silent house, and tiptoed
upstairs with Iris's stack of exercise books. She
undressed in the bathroom before turning off her
mobile phone and slipping quietly through the
open door of Sheila's bedroom. Sheila was
comatose, her anguish temporarily subdued by
drugs and sleep, as if it was being held down, a
monster strapped to a table.

Leslie Shand is the monster, Amy thought. He
did all this. Perhaps she'd find the reason in one of
Iris's journals. She switched on the Anglepoise
lamp on the bedside table, and got into the narrow
bed. As she folded back the eiderdown and pulled
back the sheet she wondered, briefly, why it was
made up. Surely Bill had never slept here? Was it
because Sheila was expecting Mo to return one
day, or simply habit?

Sitting up in bed with the first of Iris's journals
propped open on her knee, Amy felt like a hospital
nurse keeping a night vigil. The pale blue walls
made her small pool of lamplight shine hygienic

white, and gave Sheila's sleeping face a waxy cast. Even the baggy green T-shirt she'd brought to wear to bed looked clinical, like a surgeon's scrubs. There was the pain, too, Leslie's legacy of torment, heavy in the air. You could trap it with medication, or dull its edge with manufactured sleep, but it was always there, waiting.

*He got very angry if things were not arranged the way he liked. We had to fetch a ruler and put the mug of water and ashtray on his bedside table at exactly four inches away from the side and make sure they were lined up. Also the mug must be filled to within half an inch of the top.*

Amy shook her head, astonished. You couldn't make it up. Leslie had devised rules for when his family should wash their hair, how they should walk down the street (no hands in pockets), how the table should be laid, how the girls should sweep the garden paths (dirt must be brushed away from the house), how ornaments should be arranged on the mantelpiece, and the order in which tools should be cleaned and put away after use. To make it worse, the list of regulations, with its bewildering and pointless detail, had been subject to sudden, arbitrary changes: *it was an excuse to punish us if we forgot something or did not get it right.*

The obsession with obedience and order was interesting. Amy discovered that Leslie had done National Service and, according to Iris, enjoyed it. She wondered why he hadn't stayed in the army; a soldier's pay wasn't great, but it had to be better than a farm worker's.

Iris had also chronicled Leslie's growing reliance on alcohol, his black moods (*you have no idea what suffering is, you lot have everything you want*), and his terrifying drunken paranoia:

*He made us fetch wooden boxes from the garden and Sheila and I had to stand on top of them while he sat opposite in the armchair with the gun held against the back of Mo's leg. He said we'd betrayed him by talking outside the house and that he was going to shoot her in the knee to teach us a lesson. Sometimes this lasted for hours but eventually he would get tired and fall asleep and Sheila could take the gun out of his hand and put it away.*

What Amy hadn't found, after forty minutes' reading, was any reference to Rosie Drake.

Iris thought that Leslie had picked her because she was quiet and unassertive. At first, she'd thought the beatings were her fault, a view her mother and stepfather had reinforced (*they told me I must be doing something wrong*). Then she had tried various means of avoiding the violence (*I would always agree with him and try to change the subject if I thought something was going to make him angry. It was hardly ever successful*), but eventually —aided, presumably, by Leslie's threats against her and her children—she seemed to have accepted it as inevitable.

In the last notebook, Amy read Iris's attempts to analyse his behaviour and find reasons for it:

*Leslie's stepfather was a farm worker, too. They lived in a tied cottage with no electricity or gas, and water taken from a well. Leslie started helping on the farm when he was quite young. He was the middle one in his family. It was a big one with stepchildren on both sides, and all the boys a good bit taller than him. The eldest boy was the father's son from his marriage before and he was always at Leslie, tripping him up and blowing his nose into his food even when he was quite old and about to leave home. If Leslie tried to get back at him, his stepfather would slap him for playing up and then his mother would start on the stepfather because Leslie was her favourite. They always finished up shouting at each other and the stepfather getting rough with Leslie, using his fists. That wasn't like my family at all. We were very quiet. Leslie never wanted to see his family after we were married and I did not mind because I do not like arguments and fighting but then I realised the true reason, that he did not want anyone to see how he was with me.*

*Before we were married I did see something between Leslie and his older brother (a disagreement) and I think this was one reason why he was so hard on me. I was in the passage with his mum while the men were eating their dinner and I happened to look round the door when the brother (Alan) slapped him on the face. Perhaps Leslie was getting back at me for bad things that were done to him.*

*At the time I met Leslie I wanted to leave home because my mother married again after my father died and my stepfather made it clear that I was not wanted in the home. My stepfather was a strict man and I thought Leslie was different because he was Romantic to me, but that all changed soon after we married. My mother was like me, she always put the man first and had told me that I should get married*

269

*and leave. After the first few times when Leslie hit me, I asked her what I should do about it. She told this to my stepfather and he said I must put up with it because we were married and so that was that. So my mother said she was sorry for me but there was nothing she could do.*

Most telling, Amy thought, was the phrase *getting back at me for bad things that were done to him.* She wondered if Leslie had been sexually abused as a child, and, if so, who'd done the abusing. If it had been his mother, it might explain his treatment of his wife and family as a form of revenge.

Reading on, she came across a passage that made her gasp:

*There was one very strange thing he said (I thought it was strange) about a man in the Talbot who was talking about his bad luck when a horse didn't come in. Leslie said, 'What's he got to complain about? He's tall!' It was such an odd thing to say that at first I thought I must have heard wrong, but he repeated it. Leslie was not tall, although to me he seemed tall and big because I was so frightened of him and also being a small made woman. But I couldn't believe that someone would have such a bad temper because they thought they were too short.*

Amy almost laughed. Had Leslie Shand really become a poisonous sadist who inflicted daily humiliation and unspeakable cruelty on three innocent women just because he was *short*? But then she flipped back to what Iris had written before; *all the boys a good bit taller than him.* And they'd picked on him, hadn't they? So perhaps

270

there was something in it.

She eased herself quietly out of bed and tiptoed downstairs to fetch a glass of water. Carrying it back upstairs, she reflected on the truism that the perpetrators of the greatest evil do it for the most banal of reasons. Perhaps, if you were that way inclined, you found yourself an excuse and got on with it. It put Patti's behaviour in the shade, and for a moment she felt almost warm towards her mother.

Sheila was still deeply asleep. Amy got back into bed, settled the notebook on her knees, and carried on reading. Both Leslie's mother and stepfather sounded violent. The stepfather had clearly been a drinker (*his mother had to be quick on Friday night to get some of the wages before he went into the pub*). Leslie had been—by the end, at least—a heavy drinker, so perhaps his real father had, too. He wasn't mentioned, so presumably Iris hadn't known anything about him. Maybe he'd died, or left when Leslie was very young. It was a pretty primitive way of life, Amy thought. Tough. She remembered from the newspaper cutting that Leslie had been fifty-nine when he was killed, and did a quick sum: he'd been born in 1928, before the welfare state. With no safety net, the family, with mother fighting to stop father drinking away his meagre wages, would have been perilously near starvation—not much room for love and affection and finer feelings when it's a daily struggle just to stay alive.

There was still nothing about Rosie Drake. Amy came to Iris's description of the death of her baby. Reading on, it became clear that Iris had not known where it had been buried.

*I asked Leslie what he was going to do. I was hoping that he would bury it in the garden so that I could plant something and it would be like a proper grave, but he said he would take it into the woods. I was afraid that he might take Sheila with him to help, but he didn't. It surprised me because Leslie did not like being alone, especially when it was dark (it was about two or three a.m.). I hoped it was because of his conscience, that he felt sorry for what he had done, but I don't think it was because afterwards he was just as bad as ever. He never mentioned the baby. He didn't say, 'We are not going to talk about it.' I knew that as far as he was concerned, that was the end of it, but I never forgot my poor baby.*

Amy rubbed her eyes. Reading about Leslie Shand's relentless cruelty and violence was bad enough: what on earth must it have been like to live through it? She started reading Iris's description of her escape attempt, when she'd taken the babies to her sister and begged for help:

*I felt bad about troubling Kathleen because she didn't have much money, only enough to manage for herself and little Pat. I didn't leave a note for Leslie to say I was going there, but he knew. I don't know how. I suppose he worked out that she was the only person I could have gone to. It made me think if I went anywhere in the world he'd still be able to find me. He was kind to me in front of Kathleen and charming and nice to her (he said I was imagining things because I'd been ill and wouldn't eat) but when we came away from the house he told me I had betrayed him and he would never forgive me. I*

272

*thought he was going to kill me that night. I was shaking while I was putting the girls to bed because I knew he was downstairs waiting for me. I don't think there was any part of me not bruised. Afterwards he pulled me upstairs by my hair. He said, 'If you go behind my back again, I'll kill you.'*

Amy remembered the letter Iris had written to Kathleen at Leslie's bidding: *I hope you will forgive me for bothering you.* It didn't explain why Kathleen still had Iris on her mind all those years later, unless . . . She turned the page. *I did write again to my sister when Sheila told me Leslie wanted sex from her. I hoped that Kathleen could help us (although I did not know how). I did not know how to explain how bad things were. I never had a reply. Maybe Kathleen thought I was imagining it because that's what Leslie told her before.*

My God, Amy muttered. How ironic. Her grandmother had written that letter to Patti not because she was worried about Leslie, but because she was worried about *Iris*. She'd thought that her sister was mentally ill, and had been too afraid of possible contamination to contact her, especially as the insanity seemed to be taking the particularly unpleasant form of accusing her husband (so charming, so patient) of unnatural practices.

Leslie Shand, thought Amy, was a genius: every single base covered. Add to that the good manners of non-interference, and squeamishness, shame and social taboos . . . She remembered the tiny, frail figure hunched in an armchair at Compton Lodge. Iris Shand hadn't stood a chance.

She read the last few pages then sat, arms round her knees, thinking. There was nothing about

273

Rosie's death, and nothing about Leslie's death. Given the simple frankness with which Iris had described everything else that had happened to her, it didn't fit that both these events had gone unrecorded. One of the books must be missing—there was no point in Sheila asking her to read them if she knew she wasn't going to find anything.

Moving as quietly as she could, she got out of bed and went across the landing to the storeroom. The curtains were open, and the iron deed box gleamed in the moonlight. She eased the lid open, praying that it wouldn't creak, and peered inside. Sheila's notebooks were there, but nothing else. She couldn't break Sheila's trust, not now. She lowered the lid of the box, and tiptoed back to bed.

# CHAPTER THIRTY-EIGHT

Sheila woke at dawn. Sitting up in bed, she was conscious first of a pain in her chest, and then of black, numbing misery. Mum was gone. She lay picturing Iris as she'd been when they were children, the warmth of cuddles snatched behind Leslie's back, the watchful eyes always ready to signal in case they put a foot wrong and made him angry, the way she'd sidle into their bedroom to tuck them up while he was downstairs, and how she always tried to deflect his anger, her quick fingers lining a tin with pastry, knitting, decorating the house with threadbare tinsel foraged from a bin outside a shop because he wouldn't let her buy Christmas decorations. She'd always done her best for them, always.

'What shall I do, Mum?' she asked aloud.

Mo. Look after Mo. Glancing towards the other bed, the tangle of black ringlets on the white pillow—even though she knew it wasn't Mo—made her heart thud in her chest. 'I'm frightened, Mum,' she whispered. 'I'm so frightened.'

She looked at the exercise books scattered across the foot of Amy's bed, and then felt under the pillow for the one she'd purloined while Amy was downstairs making tea. Despite what she'd told her about the journals not having an exact chronological sequence, she knew that they'd both written about Leslie's death early on—independent attempts at exorcising the man who'd visited them in nightmares, bent on revenge and destruction. And he'd succeeded. They'd been united, and he'd turned them against each other. When she'd seen, on the first page, *We are going to write down what happened*, she'd known that was the book she had to hide.

She got out of bed, took the exercise book into the bathroom, and locked the door. Sitting on the bath mat, she began, slowly, to turn the pages. Fragments of sentences caught her eye:

*Leslie said it was Mrs Drake's fault said she was mad*
    *she would turn the girls into lesbians if she was*
*not stopped*
    *spread lies about us          he'd do it quick, so she*
*wouldn't suffer          He made us stand there*
          *I was frightened for Sheila, what he would do*

It was kind of Mum not to mention it being her fault, but it was still true. Of course, Mum hadn't known the whole story—neither she nor Mo had told her, and, for some reason she didn't entirely understand, Leslie hadn't, either. Shutting her eyes tight, digging her nails into her palms, she forced herself to remember the evening when Mrs Drake—Rosie—had seen them coming out of the Anderson, seen Leslie doing up his fly in the light of the back window and Sheila follow a moment later, adjusting her clothes. They hadn't known she was there—she'd hardly ever come up to their house before, only once at the weekend and never at night—but a minute later she'd knocked on the back door, to see Mum and return a borrowed baking tray. She'd come through the back way, the path behind the school, with a torch, which was why she had gone to the back door, not the front. Mum had been polite, taking her into the kitchen and offering a cup of tea, while she and Mo sat rigid on the sitting-room sofa with Leslie glaring at them to keep quiet or they'd get it later. Sore from Leslie's assault on her, listening to her mother's calm dissembling, and conscious that her inner and outer worlds were separated by a mere five feet of carpet, Sheila had thought that her body would snap with tension. She knew that Leslie, like her, was wondering if Mrs Drake had seen them leave the Anderson, and, if so, what conclusions she might draw.

Frantic for Mrs Drake to leave, but dreading what would happen when she did, Sheila had fixed her eyes on a small brown mark on the pale green lino. The air seemed alive with the electric current of her father's anger, so that she almost expected to see sparks as, at the corner of her vision, his fist clenched and one of his legs began to twitch and judder with a life of its own. Finally, giving them both a fierce nod, he'd got up and gone into the kitchen. 'Are you coming through, love? Your favourite programme's on in a minute.' Speaking nicely, as if he was unperturbed by the interruption to their Saturday night's viewing.

She'd heard Mrs Drake say she was sorry for the intrusion, heard Leslie's offer to accompany her back to the farm ('It's dark out there, you never know what you might bump into') and her polite refusal. Then, still not daring to raise her eyes, she'd been aware of the three of them passing down the hall, and heard the final pleasantries and the opening and closing of the back door. They heard their mother's faltering explanation ('Leslie, love, it was for the church—she was making cakes for the sale—I couldn't say no'), but they hadn't moved until Iris, white with terror and propelled by Leslie's sharp jabs to her back, had tottered into the sitting room. Then, rising together, they'd taken their positions on either side of her as he began, silently and systematically, to lay about her with his fists, feet and head. Sheila had flinched at each blow as if she'd been hit herself, but she knew that she must watch in order to anticipate Iris's fall, so that she did not dash her head against the mantelpiece or the lethal edge of the glass-sheeted coffee table. Then, with Iris curled in a corner, trying not to whimper in pain, he had calmly sat down and told Sheila that if Mrs Drake ever asked what they were doing in the Anderson shelter, she must say that she'd been helping him mend a broken shelf bracket. Punctuating his message with smacks of his fist in his open palm, he'd told them that they were never to lend anything to anyone again. 'If she asks for something, you're to say no. I

277

don't care what it is, you'll say we haven't got it. Is that clear? Well, is it?' They'd nodded, dumbly. 'And if any of you ever speak about what goes on in this house, I'll shoot the lot of you.' Only then had he allowed them to help Iris upstairs to the bathroom and tend to her bruises. That time, Sheila remembered, she'd been lucky and nothing was broken.

For the next few days, the atmosphere had crackled with tension, with Leslie even more volatile than usual, and the three women creeping around him in terror, hardly daring to open their mouths. Sheila recalled the hours she'd spent at work, counting out toilet rolls and sachets of complimentary shampoo, barely able to concentrate for thinking about what Mrs Drake might have seen and what she might say. Mo had been even worse, her hands shaking so much that one day she'd spilt a whole bottle of cleaning fluid on the carpet in the Sassoon suite and it had taken almost an hour to remove it.

They'd walked home after their shifts, trembling in anticipation of the news that might be waiting for them, and she'd put her arm round Mo's waist and supported her up the hill, blank-faced and muttering, 'I can't go on, Sheila, I can't.' The feeling of being on the edge of an abyss, of wanting it all to end but being impossibly enmeshed in a web of shame, deception and dependency, came back to Sheila so sharply that, for a moment, she thought she would be sick.

Swallowing the vomit that was rising in her throat, she sluiced her mouth out with water and breathed slowly, trying to calm herself. The next part had been the worst, when she'd gone down to the farm to collect the weekly ration of treats from the pig lorry and seen Mrs Drake in the yard. She'd wanted to turn round and go straight back home, but the certainty of Leslie's fury if she returned empty-handed kept her rooted to the spot.

Mrs Drake had stood close beside Sheila as, not daring to look round, she'd picked out unblemished Bakewell tarts and iced buns from the trays in the back of the van and placed them carefully in two brown paper bags so that they'd reach Hadley Cottage in the immaculate condition that Leslie demanded. When she'd finished, Mrs Drake had asked if she wanted a cup of tea. She'd tried to get away, stammering that she needed to get home, but Mrs Drake had insisted and Sheila, heart thumping, had no choice but to follow her into the house. She'd stood in the kitchen while Mrs Drake made tea, her mind racing as she rehearsed the lies she must tell in order to keep them all alive.

Then came the moment she'd dreaded most of all, when Mrs Drake motioned to her to sit down, and, leaning across the table, asked gently, 'Have you ever had a boyfriend, Sheila?'

'N-no.'

'Wouldn't you like to? You might meet someone and get married. Wouldn't you like a family of your own?'

Head bowed, heart pounding, and unable to speak, she'd merely shaken her head.

'Why not? It's quite normal. It's what most women want.'

'Well . . .' Sheila had swallowed, trying to force saliva into her mouth. 'We're not interested in that. We like to stay at home.'

Then Mrs Drake had smiled and said, quite kindly, 'It's none of my business, but when I came up to your house on Saturday, I saw you. With your dad. You know what I mean, don't you?'

Sheila remembered the quality of the silence, heavy and loaded, and how, powerless to prevent what was happening, she'd felt a deep, telltale blush suffuse her face. Hanging her head, she blurted out Leslie's prescribed words. 'We were fixing the bracket. Mending it. It was broken.'

'What, in the dark? Your dad was putting his trousers on. I saw him.'

'We were doing repairs,' Sheila stuttered. 'Your clothes . . . they get messed up.'

'Your dad was doing up his fly, Sheila. And you were pulling down your jumper, adjusting your skirt. You're grown up, Sheila. I can't stop you if that's what you want to do. But there are men out there, you know.'

'It's not like that!' Sheila burst out. She'd meant to add that they really had been making repairs to the shelf, but the words got stuck in her throat. 'I . . . I . . .'

She remembered Rosie's wide, puzzled eyes, the new mood in the room that she couldn't control, the feeling of slipping, the agony of exposure as, for the first time in her life, her inner and outer worlds seemed to be touching, overlapping in the terrible silence that grew and grew. And then, with Rosie's sudden look of understanding, they came together, and everything went into slow motion as her stomach churned, sweat poured from her armpits, and the blood pounded inside her head, battering at her like her father's words: *If-you-ev-*

*er-speak-about-what-goes-on-in-side-this-house* . . .

As she gazed at Rosie in terror, and heard the slow, measured words coming out of her mouth—the words that could kill them all—Sheila had felt the grip of a panic so strong that she couldn't move, couldn't talk, could do nothing except sit there and shake and stare into the sympathetic face that was inviting her confidences, the words that she would never be able to speak.

'It's not what you want, is it?'

'No!' she blurted. 'No!'

'It's what your Dad wants, isn't it? He's been messing you about.'

'No! That's not what I meant, it's not like—'

Rosie's voice, deadly calm, cut in: 'How long has he been doing it?'

'We were mending the bracket. We had to do it!'

She'd gazed at Rosie, transfixed, hearing *his* voice—*I'll kill you! I'll kill the lot of you!*—thudding inside her head as if he were hitting her.

'You don't have to—'

'It's not like that, it really isn't. There's nothing like that. We're just . . . just a close family, that's all.'

'That's one way of putting it.'

She hadn't understood, then, that Rosie had said that as a joke. She'd never heard anyone joke about it before, although she did later, when she was on remand, and couldn't understand how anyone might find it funny. She'd stumbled on, trying to convince Rosie that she was mistaken, knowing it was hopeless.

'When did he start doing it to you, Sheila?'

'He doesn't . . . You mustn't tell anyone, Mrs Drake. Please.'

'It's not right, what he's doing. There are people who could help.'

'Please, Mrs Drake. I have to go now. Please don't say anything.'

She remembered that she'd thought, afterwards, as she ran back up the drive, that she shouldn't have said those things, but she'd been so confused and frightened, terrified that Mrs Drake might tell Mr Drake or the police, or come up to Hadley Cottage and confront Leslie, or . . . With a thousand horrible possibilities, any one of which would lead to Leslie murdering them all, racing through her mind, and clutching the bags of treats, she'd scarcely felt the hard white glaze on the Bakewell tarts buckle and crack in her shaking hands.

At Hadley Cottage, Iris had gazed at the squashed treats with their crumbling pastry and then, with trepidation, at her trembling, stammering daughter. 'Sheila! What happened?'

She remembered Iris holding her and stroking her hair as she tried to explain what Mrs Drake had said, how her mother's soothing voice—'It's all right, love, it's all right'—was belied by her shaking hands, so that they ended up shivering in each other's arms while she'd whispered, 'I'm sorry, I'm so sorry,' over and over again.

At the bang of the back door—as if using some demoniac form of telepathy, Leslie had been ten minutes early—they'd broken apart and sprung to assume their positions in front of the kitchen units so that, sergeant-major-like, he could inspect them.

'What's this?' Picking up the mangled cakes they'd been too distressed to remember to hide, he'd hurled them at the wall so hard that one glacé cherry stuck, as if embedded, next to Sheila's neatly printed list of curtain-closing times.

'What's going on?' he'd shouted. Then, rounding on Sheila, 'She's said something, hasn't she?' He'd grabbed her by the upper arms and thrown her across the room. She'd felt her head hit the corner of the table and thought she must have blacked out for a moment, because the next thing she knew, he was standing over her, his heavy work boots inches away from her ribs. 'What did you say to her?'

'W-what you told me, Dad. We were mending the bracket.'

'Did she believe you?'

'Yes, Dad.'

'Did she?'

'Yes! Dad, I couldn't help it, please—'

'Of course you could bloody help it, you useless cow!' As he dragged her, cringing, to her feet, she heard her mother's voice, soft and placatory, 'Leslie, dear—'

'DON'T TELL ME WHAT TO DO!'

Dizzy, aware of the blood from her cut head trickling down the side of her neck, Sheila had watched her father advance on Iris. Knowing that anything but doglike submissiveness would invite more violence but somehow unable to stop herself, she'd cried out, 'Dad, please!'

'Shut up!' And then, for the first time that she could remember, Sheila had seen him make a deliberate attempt to check himself, arms rigid at his sides, clenching and unclenching his fists. They'd stood, not daring to look at each other but keeping their eyes fixed on him, while he stood

283

ramrod straight, as if on parade, battling what they knew to be a desperate inner compulsion to smash them all to the ground, and—miraculously—conquering it, contenting himself merely with thumping the table so hard that it jarred their teeth. 'Listen,' he said, in a low, thick voice, 'if she says anything, I'll shoot her. Do you understand? One word, and I'll kill her. And that's the same for all of you. Now, get this place cleaned up.'

Then he'd gone. Ashen-faced, they'd stood in astonished silence, not daring to believe that that could really be it, that he wasn't going to re-emerge, like the end of one of his beloved horror films, a malevolent whirlwind of fists and feet. Then they'd watched, still in silence, as the single glacé cherry unstuck itself from the wall and slid down to the floor, leaving a red smear on the olive-green paper.

Later, in the bathroom, as Mum sponged her bleeding head (they hadn't dared ask if she might go to Casualty), and applied witch-hazel, they'd held a whispered conference.

'Do you think he means it?'

'Yes.'

'We can't let him kill her.'

'We can't stop him.'

'If we took the gun and hid it somewhere, or . . .'

Sheila couldn't remember which one of them had said it, but they'd avoided each other's eyes while the shared, unspoken thought—that they could kill Leslie—seemed to fill the little room. They'd discussed the subject before, vaguely, never coming to any resolution, their talk being less a practical exchange about how and when than the reiteration of a simple wish that Leslie would, in some unspecified way, disappear. This time, however, with an urgency and focus that was absent before, they began, tentatively, to form a plan.

'When he's asleep.'

'We could use the gun.'

'It's right by the bed. He'd hear us.'

'Not if he'd been drinking. Then he wouldn't.'

'If we were quick . . .'

She'd known that *we* meant *her*, because she was the one Leslie had taught to shoot, taking her into Hadley Wood and making her fire at a piece of board nailed to a tree. She'd always hated the noise the gun had made, and the shoulder-bruising shock of the recoil, but she'd learnt how to fire it, and learnt, too, how to load and clean it.

'We couldn't,' she said. 'It's murder.'

'But we can't let him kill Mrs Drake. It's wrong.'

'We could do it on Saturday.'

'He won't wake then.'

'Supposing something happens before then? It's only Wednesday.'

'It won't. There's other people around. He wouldn't do anything with Mr Drake and Chalky there.'

'What if Mrs Drake says something to him?'

'I don't know.'

'Supposing she comes here?'

'We'll have to try and stop him somehow.'

'We'll just have to hope.'

Sheila remembered, as they filed downstairs, the tacit acceptance that a decision had been reached. In a way it had been a relief, but the tension of the next two days was almost unbearable. Time dragged, and Mo, the worst affected, seemed to be sleepwalking through the days, barely noticing when Leslie caught her a hard blow on the side of the head (his preferred target because the bruise wouldn't show under the hair) after the parrot, Stanley, had escaped.

'Everything's black,' she'd told Sheila, as they lay side by side in the darkness, holding hands across the strip of carpet between their narrow beds. 'It's like being buried alive. I can't get out.'

As Sheila murmured words of comfort, she had wondered, just as she had all day, if, when Saturday night finally came, she'd be able to go through with it.

Leaning over the basin, Sheila stared at her reflection for a moment, then picked up Iris's notebook and, opening the airing cupboard, slid it between a pair of sheets. It's today, she told herself. We're going to the police. I can show them what Mum wrote about the baby, but what about Rosie? I've got to tell them, for Bill's sake. Something—not the whole truth—but something. I'll say Mum told me, she decided. Yes. Mum told me Dad killed her, because she found out about us. They've got to believe me. They must.

# CHAPTER THIRTY-NINE

Amy awoke to find Sheila sitting on the bed, watching her. She looked pale, but composed, and the first words she said were 'I'd like to go to the police station this morning. I'll show them what Mum wrote about the baby.'

When they'd washed and dressed and had

breakfast, prepared by Sheila, they drove the short distance to Barnet High Street, where Amy found a parking space at the shopping centre. Sheila, very calm, led the way to the police station, where Amy waited while she spoke to the desk sergeant. Ten minutes later, a plain-clothes policeman appeared. Amy recognised him: DI Bainbridge, who'd come to question Bill.

'Miss Shand?'

Sheila stood up, nervous but resolute. 'I'll like to speak to you in private, please.'

'Of course.' He ushered her through the double doors into the back of the station.

Almost three hours, and two cups of poisonous coffee from the vending machine later, Sheila re-appeared. She shook hands with DI Bainbridge, and, turning to Amy, said with a new lightness of tone, 'Can you take me home now?'

In the car, Amy asked, 'What did you tell him about Rosie?'

'Dad killed her,' said Sheila flatly. 'I made a statement.'

'But surely they'll want . . . I mean, aren't they going to charge you with anything? I thought . . .'

'I said I didn't know about it at the time, that Mum had told me afterwards.'

'I suppose they can't prove . . .'

'They believed me,' said Sheila.

'Are you sure?'

'They know about Dad. What he was like. I didn't remember Mr Bainbridge, but he remembered me. He said it rang a bell when Bill mentioned my name.'

'I don't think it's going to be quite that simple, Sheila,' said Amy, carefully. 'Will they test you, to

287

see if you're related to the baby?'

'I expect so, but that's OK, isn't it? Because I am.'

'Did you tell Mr Bainbridge why Leslie killed Rosie?'

'Yes.'

'But if she knew . . . what Leslie was doing to you, why didn't she tell Bill?'

After a moment, Sheila said, haltingly, without a trace of her former assurance, 'I begged her not to. I was so frightened. You don't know how it was, Amy.'

Amy took her hand off the wheel and patted Sheila's. 'It's very hard to imagine. But I'm on your side, Sheila.'

As soon as they opened the door to Hadley Cottage, Amy smelt burning. Looking down the hall, she could see, through the glass panel in the back door, a haze of smoke in the garden. She heard Sheila cry out behind her, and raced down the passage. Yanking open the door, she saw a smouldering garden incinerator on the immaculate lawn and a woman bending over it, poking the contents with a stick.

She turned back to Sheila, who was tottering in the doorway, her hand at her mouth. 'Mo!'

The woman turned towards them, stiffly graceful, like an elderly ballerina, and Amy gasped. She was looking at a spectre of herself— older, rail thin, dressed in jeans and a T-shirt, with the same dark-blue eyes and thick dark ringlets, though hers were streaked with grey. But as she came closer and the eyes in the gaunt, downy face fixed on hers, Amy saw that they had no more human presence than those of a fox. 'What are you

288

doing?'

Mo's face was mask-like. 'What does it look like? You're Amy. You took my diary.'

'I . . .' Amy stammered. 'How do you know who I am?'

'Patti showed me a photograph. You're Amy. I want my diary back.'

'It's in the house,' said Amy. 'You can have it. But what are you doing?'

'Burning Mum's notebooks. I saw the paper.'

'No!' Sheila stumbled towards Mo and stared at the charred fragments in the incinerator. 'What have you done?'

'It's all right.' Mo's voice was robotic. 'It's under control. The house won't burn down.'

Amy stared at her. '*You!* It was you, wasn't it? What about my house? You—'

'You had no right to take my diary.'

'Patti's dead, Mo,' she said brutally. 'I had to clear up her things. If you knew where I lived, why didn't you just ask for it?'

'I didn't trust you to give it back.'

'I gave it to Sheila. I didn't know where you were.'

'Patti had my address.'

'There was no name in your diary—how was I supposed to know it was yours? You tried to burn down my house. Did you break in, too?'

'I wanted my diary. I needed it.'

'Burning the place down wasn't going to get it back for you, was it?'

'No, just get rid of it. Then I came back and tried to find it, but you'd hidden it.'

Amy took a deep breath. In the face of Mo's warped logic, rational argument was hopeless.

289

'How did you find out where I live?' she asked.

'I got it from Patti.'

'So she gave you my address?'

'She had it by the telephone.' Mo looked triumphant. 'I copied it when she wasn't looking. She said the diary would be safe, but I didn't trust her. And I was right, wasn't I? I only gave her the diary in the first place because I don't trust the people where I live. They've got keys so they can search my room.'

'You mean the wardens?'

'Yes. Spying on me. That's why I couldn't take it back. I thought Patti was my friend, but when I tried to phone, she wouldn't speak to me.'

'She was in a hospice, Mo. She was dying, for Christ's sake!'

'Amy.' Sheila put a hand on her arm. 'Don't. She's not . . . She can't . . .'

'I can see that.' Amy rounded on her. 'Why didn't you tell me she's insane? She could have killed me.'

'I thought she was being looked after,' said Sheila desperately. 'I had no idea. Why are you doing this, Mo?'

'You betrayed us.' Mo pulled a stick out of the fire and brandished the burning end in Sheila's face. Sheila backed away, dragging Amy with her. 'You looked in Mum's notebooks.'

'I had to, Mo—for Bill. They found Rosie Drake's body. He was going to—'

'Because you went with him. You betrayed us.'

'No! Mo, I didn't, I swear I didn't. I haven't—'

'Liar!'

'Stop it!' Amy shook off Sheila's restraining hand and caught hold of Mo's wrist, knocking the

290

stick to the ground and stamping hard on the glowing end.

'Don't.' Sheila clawed at her arm. 'She can't help herself. She doesn't know what she's doing. Let's go inside. We can't save Mum's notebooks now.'

'She tried to kill me, Sheila.'

'You told her.' Amy felt warm spray on her cheek as Mo spat the words at Sheila. 'You told her about us.'

'No. I had to help Bill,' said Sheila. 'I went to the police. I had no choice, Mo. Please . . . Mum's dead.'

'You're lying.' Mo backed away from them, her eyes wide.

'No.' Sheila was pleading now. 'She died yesterday, at the home. I was going to tell you. Please, let's go inside.'

Amy, who'd braced herself for a violent reaction, was surprised when Mo rubbed her face in a sudden, childish gesture, like a little girl after a playground scrap. 'Is it really true?' she asked.

'Yes. I'm sorry, Mo. That's why I looked at her notebooks. I told the police Dad killed Rosie,' Sheila said. Her voice was deadpan, but her eyes were alive with a message that Amy couldn't read. 'I told them. You remember, Mo—Dad killed her.'

Mo's eyes flickered towards Amy, then back to Sheila. 'No,' she said. 'He didn't.'

Amy looked from one sister to the other. Both faces were blank. Once more, she thought of the two little girls standing side by side, watching in silence as their father battered their mother. 'Who did kill Rosie?' she asked.

'Can we go inside?' asked Sheila. 'I'd like to sit down.'

# CHAPTER FORTY

When they were seated round the kitchen table, Amy said, 'You told me it was your fault, Sheila, but if Leslie *made* you do it—'

'No,' Sheila interrupted. 'It wasn't like that.'

'What was it like?'

'There was another notebook,' said Sheila. 'I hid it.'

'Where?' asked Mo.

'In the airing cupboard,' said Sheila. 'You can burn it, if you like, Mo, but it won't make any difference. I can't do this any more. All these lies . . . I thought, if I told the police,' she continued, wearily, 'what I told them, it would be all right, but it won't, and I can't go on any longer, Mo. I realised when I saw you in the garden. I can't bear it. What we've done is wrong, and—'

'No.' The robotic tone was back in Mo's voice. 'No, no, no, no, no, no, no.'

'Don't, love.' Sheila took her hand. 'Don't make it worse. I've tried so hard,' she told Amy, 'but if this is what the rest of my life is going to be like, I can't go on any more. It was like I told you, Amy. Rosie Drake found out about Dad—what he was doing. I tried to tell her it wasn't true—I was terrified he'd kill us all—but she didn't believe me. Dad said he'd kill Rosie, and we were so scared. We talked about it and decided we'd have to do something.'

'You decided,' said Mo.

'Mum and I decided, really. We thought we could get the gun, and . . .' She swallowed. 'We said

292

we'd do it on the Saturday, when he'd been drinking, but we never got the chance. Rosie went to Dad on the Friday and asked him about it—she didn't realise there was no one else on the farm, you see.'

As Sheila began telling the story, Amy kept expecting Mo to protest, but she slumped in withdrawn silence as her sister talked, never interrupting or even altering her expression. It seemed that, returning from work on the Friday when Rosie disappeared, Mo had drifted upstairs, as usual, to lie down on her bed, and Sheila had found Iris in the kitchen, in tears.

'Mum, what's happened?'

It took some time, between sobs and gulps, for Iris to tell her that Leslie had arrived home unexpectedly in the middle of the afternoon, announcing that Mrs Drake had accused him of raping Sheila, and that he'd knocked her unconscious, bound her with bailer twine, gagged her, carted her round to their garden in a wheelbarrow, using the back way, and locked her in the Anderson shelter.

Sheila was stunned. 'But how could he, Mum? Didn't anyone see?'

'There wasn't anyone there. Mr Drake and Chalky were off the farm, and he'd come up by the back way.'

'Is Mrs Drake still in there?'

'Yes.'

'We've got to rescue her, Mum.'

'We can't. He's got the key.'

'I'll get the gun. We'll wait until he comes back, and then—'

Iris's voice was dull with despair. 'He's taken it

293

with him.'

'But when Mr Drake comes back, he'll want to know where she's gone, won't he? He'll come up here, and we can tell him.'

'No.' Iris started to cry again. 'Your dad made me go back to the farm with him and pack some of her things in suitcases. He said I'd know what to take. He's brought them back here so it looks as if she's left him. I felt terrible doing it, I told him I wouldn't, but he . . . he . . .'

'It's all right, Mum, I know. Is Mrs Drake all right? Did he hurt her?'

Iris shook her head. 'I don't know. I just don't know.'

They were making tea in the kitchen when Leslie had walked in with the gun broken over one arm, jubilant, as if he'd been out for a successful day's shooting. He'd insisted on a photograph, posing them all in the garden, in front of the Anderson shelter, where, feet away, they knew that Mrs Drake was bound, gagged and helpless.

Sheila remembered the gleeful note in his voice afterwards as he told them what happened, the gloating words. 'Tried to tell me how to treat my family . . . I told her, "I'll do what I like with my own daughter." Told me I wouldn't dare try anything. I said, "Why not? There's no one here." That scared her. Silly bitch didn't know it was just her and me. Thought she could come and throw her weight about, didn't she? Kept whining, asking where Chalky was, but I shut her up pretty quick. Now she's in there'—a jerk of the head towards the back of the house—'and that's where she's staying.'

Then her faltering question: 'What are you

294

going to do?'

'I'll sort her out later. And,' he'd rounded on her, 'I'll sort you out, too, if you don't shut your trap. All this is your fault!' Snapping the two parts of the gun together, he'd levelled it at her. From long practice, she'd kept quite still as he moved towards her until the muzzle was touching her left breast. 'You useless cow. Getting us all in trouble with your big mouth.' He jabbed the gun into her. 'If any of you try and help her—if you say anything—you know what you'll get.' Then, turning to Iris, 'Where are the suitcases?'

'B-behind the couch.'

'Get them in here. Put them on the table.'

Leslie inspected the contents, fingering items of clothing, pocketing jewellery and setting aside the toothpaste and talcum powder that Iris had hastily collected from the Drakes' bathroom. 'Those can go upstairs. We'll burn the rest.'

Even when she heard this, Sheila still couldn't—wouldn't allow herself to—believe that Leslie intended to do more than frighten Mrs Drake, but then she saw her mother's expression. She didn't know then, about him killing the baby, but Mum did, and that's why she knew he'd go through with it.

Picking a bottle of perfume out of the jumble of clothes and smiling the smile of a benevolent father conferring a treat, he said, 'Hold out your wrists,' and, gun in one hand, scent in the other, he had anointed their upturned arms, awkwardly, sloshing on too much so that the rising fumes pricked their eyes. Sheila could still remember the unfamiliar sensation as her flesh was doused (he'd never let them have things like that) and the

295

cloying smell. As if officiating at some bizarre ritual, Leslie told them to bend their heads forward while he dabbed the perfume, with an odd, rough tenderness, behind their ears. Then, closing the suitcases with a snap, he said, 'Right. Get these out of here and get the supper on.'

He was strangely jubilant all that evening, as if there was something to celebrate, and she found this more unsettling than the familiar time-bomb of his anger. After dinner, when they'd settled down to an evening of TV, he laughed, cracked jokes, and even permitted them one small glass each from the brandy he kept locked away in the storeroom. When Iris asked, tentatively, knowing that to question was to risk a beating, if they might take out some supper for poor Mrs Drake, he merely replied that it would be a waste of food.

After the television had finished, he ordered them to stand, faces to the wall, in different corners of the lounge, positioning himself in his chair in the middle, beneath the single naked light bulb, the gun across his lap. Sheila, her nose almost touching the wallpaper so that its pattern of lime and brown squares blurred before her eyes, went over and over her conversation with Mrs Drake in her mind. It's all my fault, she told herself. When she asked me about Dad, I should have been different. Calm, like Mum. Polite. *Different*. It's my fault that this has happened.

Her ears like antennae, alert for any change in breathing that would indicate he'd gone to sleep, she waited in an agony of anticipation for the moment when she could turn round and gently remove the gun from his lap. Then, she thought, dizzy with fright, I'll have to do it.

Experience (he'd done this before) had told her that he would, at some point, drop off, and she'd stood, hardly daring to breathe, anticipating the moment. The silence in the room—broken only by the cars that passed less and less frequently as each crawling hour elapsed—seemed to hammer inside her head. To keep herself from screaming, she employed a remedy she'd often used before, of counting up to one hundred, and then to one thousand, but still Leslie didn't fall asleep. One thousand and one, one thousand and two, one thousand and three . . . She'd never got this high before. Why didn't he go to sleep? Although she longed for it to happen, she dreaded the moment. It would have to be the chest, she decided. She'd have to place the gun as close as possible, so as not to miss.

The room, once the radiator had gone off, was cold. The occasional bang told her that, despite Leslie's laborious round of venting the week before, there was still air in the system. Sometime before dawn—she'd lost all track of time—she heard Iris gasp, and saw, out of the corner of her eye (she dared not move her head), her mother begin to sway, then double over and fall to the floor.

'Get her up!' Turning, Sheila saw the gun pointed directly at her. 'Get her up!'

Bending over Iris's sprawled body, hearing the laboured breathing and seeing her face, grey with exhaustion and fear, she replied, simply, 'Dad, she can't.'

'She bloody can if she wants to. Get her on the couch.' And, turning to Mo, he snapped, 'Don't just stand there, you thick bitch. Help her!'

Following his instructions, they half dragged, half carried, their mother to the sofa, and settled her there, pillowing her head with cushions to make her as comfortable as possible, and then returned to their corners, where they stayed until half past four in the morning, when Leslie had told them they could go up to bed for an hour before walking down the hill for their early shift at the hotel. 'Don't worry,' he said, almost kindly. 'I'll stay down here with your mother.'

Sheila stumbled upstairs behind Mo, her calves aching as if they were on fire, and they went to their room and sat, wordlessly, taking it in turns to rub each other's legs and feet, before huddling up in the same bed for comfort. As Mo fell into an exhausted sleep, Sheila told herself again and again, *You failed. You should have got the gun off him, but you failed.*

When they padded silently down into the hall in the morning and looked through the doorway of the lounge, Leslie, the gun across his knees, was nonchalantly smoking a cigarette while their mother slept, curled in a ball on the couch. He lifted his head and smiled at them—or, not quite. Less a smile, Sheila remembered, shuddering, more of a grin, as if he were suddenly transformed into a malicious child.

She couldn't believe, now, that she'd managed to get through the following day and appear normal, yet it must have happened. It was Valentine's Day, and the hotel was preparing a special dinner menu, but the flowers, heart-shaped balloons and silver and pink decorations seemed to be part of another world. She kept thinking about Mrs Drake, alone and afraid in the darkness of the

298

Anderson shelter, and of what Leslie was going to do. Everything seemed mad, the manufactured romance in the air at the Chase Lodge as incomprehensible as the situation at home. She remembered one terrible moment when Mrs Sandford, the manageress, had asked her if she was all right, and she'd replied merely that she thought she had a cold coming, but other than that, she could recall nothing except the sight of her mother's shocked, haggard face when they returned home.

Swapping her coat for an apron, she automatically began helping Iris to make supper while Mo drifted into the sitting room to lie down on the couch.

'Where is he?' she whispered.

'At work.'

'Is she still there?'

'Yes.'

'Did he take the gun with him?'

'Yes.'

As they cooked mince and boiled potatoes for cottage pie, Iris quietly explained that Leslie had made her tell Mr Drake that Mrs Drake had been having an affair. 'Seeing another man. I had to say she'd run off with him. Otherwise . . .'

'Oh, *Mum!*'

Again, as Sheila was peering into the oven to check that the fluffy potato topping was progressing satisfactorily to the perfection of golden crispness that Leslie expected, they asked each other the futile question 'What can we do?' and shook their heads in despair.

When Leslie returned, there was an undercurrent of agitation below his forced calm.

He seemed like an officer in one of the war films he loved to watch, about to lead his men over the top. He even put on the combat jacket he'd bought from the military surplus shop, and after the usual Saturday meal with a pudding of Angel Delight, the women leaving their food almost untasted, he produced a list of items for them to assemble, 'At the double!' as if it really was the army. They ran up and down stairs, piling the things on the kitchen table with trembling hands, not daring to question or even meet each other's eyes, concentrating on maintaining the absolute silence he demanded for carrying out household tasks: heavy torches, spare batteries, a balaclava helmet, a butcher's knife, a rope, plastic sheeting, a blanket and Iris's hooded winter coat.

After checking each item as if he were performing a kit inspection, and ticking off the list with ferocious concentration, the gun always at his side, Leslie, in a few staccato words, ordered Mo and herself to change out of their work clothes (white blouse and black skirt) and into dark trousers and jerseys, and then to put on coats and wellington boots. Then, after sending Sheila upstairs for the brandy bottle, he lined them up with cups in their hands and doled out a double measure for each of them, commanding that they drink it in one go, so that Mo choked and Mum had to pat her on the back.

At midnight, after distributing the items for them to carry, and with a final threat ('One sound out of any of you . . .'), he led them, single file, into the dark garden. 'Now, torches.'

In the two quivering beams of light, they could see the door of the Anderson with its heavy padlock. Leslie produced the keys from his pocket and motioned Sheila forward. 'Give me the torch. Now open it.' She remembered staring through the door into the darkness below, the smell of damp cut with the sharper odours of sweat and urine, the scuffling noises, and then the sight, as Mo's torch shone in from the doorway, of Mrs Drake's blinking, watery eyes above a gag of heavy electrical tape. For a moment, they looked hopeful, trusting; and then, as Leslie climbed down the steps behind her. Sheila saw the reassurance replaced first by accusation and then by terror. She'd lowered her head in shame—not just on her own behalf, but for all of them.

Mrs Drake was lying on her side on the thin mattress, her knees up against her chest, her ankles tied together with orange bailer twine, and her hands trussed behind her. She was wearing jeans and a woollen jumper and her feet were bare. Her body jerked from side to side as she tried to pull herself into a sitting position. Leslie prodded her with the gun, 'Stay where you are,' and then, to Sheila, 'Untie her hands.'

Dry-mouthed, she managed, 'What are—'

Jerking the gun upwards, he jabbed her in the ribs. 'Do it!'

She bent over and fumbled with the spiteful knots in the thin plastic string, seeing, in the torchlight, the rawness on Mrs Drake's wrists where the twine had bitten into them.

'Now tie them in front of her.'

'Dad, please. It's wrong.'

'Shut up!'

Mrs Drake's hands were freezing, white and bloodless, but as Sheila tried, awkwardly, to drag her arms forward, she started to make numb, puppet-like movements, trying to shake her off.

'That enough!' Leslie pointed the gun at Mrs Drake's head. 'Keep still.'

As Sheila's trembling fingers reached for Mrs Drake's hands, he said, 'Wait. Get that coat in here.' Silently, Iris passed it through the door.

'Put it on her.'

Mrs Drake didn't resist when Sheila pulled her into a kneeling position and pushed her stiff arms into the sleeves of the heavy coat, which was too small and would not do up at the front.

'Now the hands.'

Again, she struggled with the twine, tightening it round Mrs Drake's wrists until Leslie was satisfied.

'Get her shoes on, then loosen the legs so she can walk.'

While Sheila worked on the twine she tried, surreptitiously, to rub Mrs Drake's ankles. They were swollen and scored with ugly red weals, and her feet were mottled blue from cold and lack of circulation. As Leslie turned to check on Mo and Iris, Mrs Drake had turned to look at Sheila. When their eyes met, she could read the expression of betrayal. *I tried to help you.* If she'd shouted it, the meaning couldn't have been clearer. Ducking her head, Sheila concentrated desperately, fitting the shoes on Mrs Drake's icy feet and tying the laces.

'Put this on her.' Turning towards Leslie, who was holding out the balaclava helmet, she recognised the rapt, intense expression that darkened his eyes to blackness—it was the one he wore when he was killing their pets. She fitted the balaclava over Mrs Drake's head, trying to keep the hair smoothed back from her eyes when she pulled it down ('Get on with it!'), arranging the neck so that it covered the tape of the gag and then putting up the hood of Iris's coat as Leslie instructed.

'Get her on her feet.' Mrs Drake's numb legs buckled, and she fell against Sheila, knocking her painfully into the rows of spiky tools. 'Now get her out of here.' Bent almost double, the pair of them had staggered to the doorway, and Sheila managed, somehow, to propel Mrs Drake up the few steps and onto the lawn, where both of them collapsed.

Kneeling on the grass beside Mrs Drake, heart hammering in her chest, Sheila watched Leslie pick a shovel off the rack and hand it to Mo. Then he turned to Iris, who was swaying slightly, as if in a trance, and, taking her by the elbow, shoved her roughly through the door of the Anderson. 'You're staying in here,' he said, and then, to Sheila, 'Give me the keys.' Closing the padlock, he turned the torch beam full on her face, blinding her. 'That's so you don't try anything.' She could hear the excitement in his voice and see, as the torch swung away and the halos of after-spots danced in front of her vision, that his black eyes were shining with a powerful, malicious glee. She thought, *He is the Devil. There is nothing I can do.*

Looking down, she saw that Mrs Drake was trying to crawl away on her knees and elbows, her bound hands stuck out in front of her. Leslie, like an executioner, took one pace forward and stuck the muzzle of the gun into the back of her head. He's going to do it, Sheila thought. He's going to kill her now. She closed her eyes. Behind her, Mo

303

began to cry.

Then Leslie jerked his head at Sheila. 'Get her up!'

She bent over Mrs Drake and attempted to get her into an upright position. Mrs Drake beat at her with her pinioned hands and kicked out with her hobbled legs, tripping herself and pulling Sheila down onto the grass with her.

Leslie gave Mo a shove in their direction. 'Help her. Go on—make yourself useful for once.' Training the torch beam on them, he watched impassively until, eventually, they stood upright, panting and shaking, in front of him. Despite her distress, Sheila heard his voice in her head— 'Smile!'—as if he were taking an imaginary photograph, with Mrs Drake standing between herself and Mo, head drooping, the fight gone out of her.

Leslie gestured with the gun for Mo to stand aside. 'She's coming with me,' he told Sheila. 'You go first, with her.'

'W-where are we going?'

'Into the wood. If you try anything—*anything*. Do you understand me?'

'Yes.'

'Yes, what?'

'Yes, Dad.'

Then, in a voice that was strangely kind and reasonable, he said, 'I'm doing this for you.'

No, Sheila wanted to shout. *No!*

'Remember, I'll be right behind you.'

He told Mo to pick up the other torch, and they set off, Sheila supporting Mrs Drake round the waist and tugging her arm so that she shuffled forwards. It seemed an age before they reached the road, and stood, shivering with cold, waiting to cross. A car sped past, Mrs Drake made a convulsive movement towards it, and Sheila had to pull her sleeve to stop her toppling forward onto the tarmac. As the lights of a second car swept around the bend, she could see the streaks of tears on Mrs Drake's cheeks. 'I'm sorry,' she whispered, almost inaudibly. 'I'm so sorry.'

Leslie's voice—'Now cross'—accompanied by a shove in the small of her back, set them going again, inching across the tarmac with agonising slowness. In silence, their breath showing white in the crisp night air, they made their way across the cricket pitch and into the wood. The walk, stumbling over tussocky grass and roots, their way lit only by the pools of light from Leslie and Mo's torches, seemed endless. Sheila had no idea where, or how far, they were going, and after a while the cold seemed to close around her, numbing her emotions as well as her hands and feet, so that she felt as though she were in a dream. It helped her to shut out any thought of what was about to happen and concentrate only on moving forwards. She heard an owl hoot, and the occasional rustling of small animals in the undergrowth, and, as they moved away from the track, ducking beneath branches, with the ground growing damp and yielding underfoot, her own stifled sobs.

They arrived in a small clearing and Leslie told them to stop. Mrs Drake had slumped to the ground, pulling Sheila down beside her. Leslie handed her the torch. 'Leave her to me. You keep watch.' Then, as she hesitated, 'Go on—over there!'

Sheila heaved herself to her feet and backed a

few paces towards the trees. 'Further!' Leslie motioned with the gun. She took a few more steps. 'Stop. Now turn round.' Sheila tried to recall what had passed through her mind, but there was only a sensation of utter, blank helplessness, as if she wasn't a human being at all, but a mere *thing*.

Leslie said, 'It's time you pulled your weight around here.' And then, 'Give me the torch. And the shovel. Now take it.' He was giving the gun to Mo. 'Take it!' He was giving her the gun. Mouth dry and heart pounding, her mind seemed to clench round the thought that Mo must kill Leslie. Keeping the torch beam trained on the brambles in front of her, not daring to turn round, she tried desperately to communicate with her sister. Do it, she willed Mo. *Do it*. Shoot him. Shoot—

Then the explosion. Ears ringing, she fell forward onto her knees. More deafening, even, than the report of the gun was the fierce cry of relief in her head: She's done it. Mo's done it. She's killed him.

And then she heard Leslie's voice, framed in the silence that followed the roar of the gun. 'Good girl. Now do it again.'

Kneeling, she turned and saw Mo fire, without hesitation, a second shot into Mrs Drake's prone body. Sheila felt as if she were screaming, but she knew it was only inside her head; she was locked inside her own body, incapable of movement or speech.

Leslie and Mo turned, as one, to face her. She remembered the expressions on their faces. On Leslie's, pure triumph, and on Mo's—for a mere second, a barely discernable flicker—pride.

306

# CHAPTER FORTY-ONE

There was silence in the kitchen, but Amy could almost hear the tension, as if there was a taut, humming wire strung between Sheila and Mo.

'I killed her,' said Mo calmly. 'Not Sheila. I did it.'

'And you never told Iris?'

The sisters shook their heads—one fair, one dark—in unison. 'We didn't want to upset her,' said Sheila.

'Why did you do it?' Amy asked Mo.

'Because Dad told me to.'

'But you had the gun.'

'He chose me,' Mo said. 'He never chose me. He always chose *her*.'

'Was . . . was that why you were proud? Because you'd helped him?'

'Yes.' Mo gave Sheila a look of defiance. 'He chose me. Not her. *Me*.'

Amy gasped. 'You were jealous.'

Jealous of Sheila: Sheila the chosen one, the one picked to help feed the rabbits, help with the DIY, the recipient of sexual attention. Amy'd wondered about Iris feeling jealous, but she'd never thought of *Mo*. The terrible, twisted logic of it, and the way Leslie had, instinctively, understood and played on it, made her feel sick. The idea that Mo had seen rape as a form of affection, that she felt she'd failed because her own father didn't want her sexually . . . Sheila had said he'd tried it once with Mo and then never again. Had Mo's mental instability been noticeable even at twelve or thirteen? *All she's good for is another loony.* That's what Leslie had said. Mo had felt rejected by him. Shooting Rosie had been her chance to prove her worth. Amy thought of all the times she herself had been trailed round to doctors, how she'd exaggerated her symptoms to please her mother, how happy she'd felt going home, when Patti, satisfied, and, in her own mind, vindicated, had rewarded her with an ice cream. Pleasing Mummy by telling the doctors. Making it right. Like Mo.

'The diary,' she said. 'Leslie didn't make you write it, did he? You wrote it *for* him.'

'Yes,' said Mo simply. 'That's right.'

'You wrote it for him,' Sheila repeated dully. 'You wrote . . .'

'Yes.' Mo gazed at Sheila, triumph in her eyes. 'I did. It was our secret.'

Looking at Sheila, Amy thought she'd never seen so much anguish on a human face. 'Sheila,' she said. 'It's like you said, Mo can't help herself. She doesn't know what she's saying.'

Sheila shook her head. 'I never realised how much . . .' she whispered. 'I didn't know.' She got up and stood at the window, looking out over the common. Mo, sitting straight in her chair, stared at her sister's back with gimlet eyes. Amy couldn't look at her. She went to Sheila and put an arm round her. 'You tried to protect her,' she murmured. 'No one could have done more.' Sheila's taut body seemed to vibrate with pain. Freeing herself from Amy, she turned to face Mo. 'I'll tell you the rest,' she said quietly.

She remembered the remainder of the night only in flashes. She and Mo had taken it in turns to dig the grave, and when Leslie decided that it was deep enough they had undressed Rosie Drake. She recalled the cold, blue-white density of the dead woman's body, the smeary look of her flesh once it was swathed in the thick groundsheet, the soft black forest earth showering down on strands of Mrs Drake's coppery hair, and trickling down across the sculpted surface of her plastic shroud before coming to rest in the creases.

As they walked back, in silence, she'd wondered, dully, if anyone would come—it wasn't likely, because people often went shooting rabbits and no one paid much attention. She found she didn't care much one way or the other—prison couldn't be worse, and besides, they deserved it, all of them, for what they'd done.

When Leslie released Iris, trembling with cold, from the Anderson shelter, she just had time to exchange a look of futile sympathy with Sheila before Leslie ordered her and Mo into the house. Thrusting the bundle of clothes into Iris's arms, he said, 'Sort them out. We'll burn hers with others.'

When they'd gone, he jerked his head at Sheila. 'In there.' Oh, no, she thought. No, please. Surely he couldn't want *that now*? It was as much as she could do, in the cramped, smelly darkness, to take off her boots and trousers. Lowering her knickers over her hips, she'd heard him come down the steps behind her, the scrape and clank as he'd hung the shovel back in its appointed space. 'You can clean it tomorrow,' he'd said, as if conferring a treat. Lying on her back on the mattress, she'd seen muzzy blue spots as the torch beam penetrated her closed eyelids, and felt his breath as he bent down close to her and asked, in a casual

309

fashion that wasn't casual at all, 'What flavour was it?'

She couldn't remember. Supper was a lifetime ago. She pictured Iris in the kitchen, making the desert, and tried to 'see' the colour of the packet opened by her mother, but it wouldn't come.

'What was it?'

'B-butterscotch, Dad.'

He'd slapped her hard, open-handed, across the face. 'Don't lie to me. It was chocolate.' Then— and she heard the pleasure in his voice—he said, 'Turn over.'

# CHAPTER FORTY-TWO

Sheila stumbled out of the kitchen. Amy heard her running upstairs, and, seconds later, vomiting. She sat quite still, remembering the Angel Delight in Mo's diary, every Saturday; the way Sheila had reacted when she'd mentioned it; the packets in the box upstairs. Mo sat impassively, staring at her.

'When you had Angel Delight,' she asked, 'who chose the flavours?'

Mo's giggle scrabbled inside Amy's head like a trapped rodent. 'I did,' she said. 'It was my treat. Sheila had the pig lorry, I had the Angel Delight.'

Her face had a guileless look. It was like her odd, babyish gesture in the garden—a sudden reversion to the child she had once been. For a moment, Amy thought that she, too, might be sick. For Mo, the Angel Delight had represented the pleasure of choice—a single act of autonomy in an otherwise prescribed existence. She'd had no idea that the flavours she'd chosen each Saturday had determined Sheila's sexual fate.

'Did Sheila ever try to influence you—tell you what to choose?'

'Sometimes. I told her it wasn't fair. I never told her which cakes to bring back.'

'Was that when you were actually making the choice?'

Mo shook her head. 'Before. She never said anything in front of Dad.'

'So he was there when you chose?'

'Oh, yes. Always. He'd put the packets out in front of me, on the table, so I could pick one.'

Oh, God. Amy felt her stomach lurch, imagining the ritual on Saturday evening, Sheila, on a rack of tension, watching Mo, and Leslie watching Sheila to see how she'd react to the choice of flavour. The ultimate sick refinement in a sadistic sexual game that had gone on for years and years.

'You wrote it down in your diary.'

'Yes. I showed him. He thought it was funny.'

Of course he did. The idea of Mo keeping a record, unwittingly and in code, of the different ways in which he'd raped Sheila must have tickled him to death.

'You stay here,' Amy said, and she dashed up the stairs to the bathroom. Sheila was kneeling on the mat, mopping her face with toilet paper. When she saw Amy, a violent blush suffused her pale skin. 'I'm sorry,' she whispered. 'It's just . . . All these years, I've tried not to believe it. I kept telling myself that Mo shot Rosie because she was too frightened not to do what Dad said. But it wasn't true, was it?'

'It was true in a way.' Amy pulled Sheila to her

311

feet and hugged her. 'And it wasn't your fault. None of it was.'

'We fell out,' said Sheila into her neck, 'after Dad died. When she got ill. I knew how she felt, but I never realised it was that . . . that *bad*. I can't bear to think of it, Amy. I've always tried to protect her, always.'

'I know.' Amy rubbed Sheila's back.

'She was so depressed, and it was so brutal, what they did to her. It changed her.'

'It wasn't the treatment, Sheila. Perhaps that didn't help, but—'

'It's my fault, I know it is. I should have realised.'

'No, you shouldn't, and it is absolutely *not* your fault. I can't imagine how I'd have coped in your shoes. You're a very brave woman.'

'Tell me,' she said, as Sheila splashed her face with water, 'Did you tell your mother about the Angel Delight?'

'No.' Sheila caught Amy's eye in the mirror, and dropped her gaze. 'I was so ashamed. We knew he was bad, but . . .'

'You were trying to protect her, too. And him, in a way. Weren't you?'

'Yes. I couldn't tell her. Nobody knows except you. Please, Amy, don't tell anyone. I couldn't bear it.'

Even if I did tell someone, Amy thought, they wouldn't believe it. She could hardly believe it herself. The idea that the woman in front of her, with her ladylike manners and old-fashioned clothes, had been forced to endure such an ordeal was monstrous.

'Why did you keep the packets?' she asked.

'Mo and Mum always liked Angel Delight. They'd have thought I was mad if I'd thrown it out, and I couldn't tell them. Then, when Mum got ill and started saying that Dad was all right with us, like a normal father, and some of the things Mo said, especially with the gaps in her memory . . . I used to wonder if it hadn't really been so bad at all, and I'd just imagined it. Sometimes I thought I was going mad and I couldn't trust my memory, either, so then I'd go up to the storeroom and look at those packets, just to confirm I was right, and it was like I remembered.'

'It was proof.'

Sheila nodded.

'We have to do something about Mo,' Amy said gently. 'I know you want to look after her, but you can't, Sheila, not while she's like this. She needs help.'

'She's got help. It's a special place—'

'It's not secure. You said she can come and go as she likes. And she needs *proper* help, Sheila. She's dangerous.'

'You can't call the police. Dad made her do it. She couldn't help it.'

'Maybe not, but she's a danger to other people. How did she get in here, by the way?'

'She's still got a key. Her and Bill, they both have.'

'You'd better get it off her. You still don't realise, Sheila. She set fire to my house—she could have *killed* me—and then she broke in, looking for her diary, and now she's burnt your mother's journals.' A sudden thought stopped Amy in her tracks. 'Wait a minute.' She nipped out of the bathroom and into the storeroom, where she looked in the iron deed box.

It was empty. 'She's burnt yours, too.'

Sheila came up behind her. 'She can't have.'

'Well, they're not here. Did you move them?'

'No.'

'She must have. She sees them as competition, Sheila. She's not interested in the truth about what happened—she doesn't want any version of your story to exist except hers.'

Sheila wheeled away from her and ran down the stairs.

Amy followed at her heels. 'Sheila, stop! She's dangerous, she—'

Sheila stopped dead in the kitchen doorway, and Amy cannoned into her, almost knocking her over. When Sheila recovered herself, Amy saw, over her shoulder, Mo, standing in front of the draining board, quite still, her eyes unblinking in a mask-like face, and Bill Drake, pointing a shotgun at her.

# CHAPTER FORTY-THREE

What Amy remembered afterwards was how normal Bill looked, with his immaculate clothes, neat hair and shiny shoes. Her mind whirled—should she grab Sheila and make a run for it? Bill would get to them before they opened the front door, and the hallway was too long to risk it—he could shoot them both in the back before they reached the door. Her mobile phone was in the kitchen; she could see it sticking out of her bag by Mo's feet. Sheila's phone was just by her elbow. If she could pick it up . . . She slammed an arm into Sheila's midriff, shoving her backwards, and with her other hand grabbed the phone.

'Bill,' she said, trying to keep her voice steady, 'put down the gun. If you don't put it down, I'll have to call the—'

Bill glanced round, then turned back to Mo. 'I will shoot her,' he said, his voice loaded with menace. 'I mean it. Put the phone down.'

Amy put the phone back on the hall table, and held up her hands. 'See?' she said. 'It's gone. You can put the gun down now, Bill.'

'Shut up! I want to talk to Sheila.'

Amy felt, rather than saw, Sheila edge out from behind her, and before she could do anything to stop her, she had shot across the kitchen to stand in front of Mo. 'Don't hurt her, Bill. Please.'

'I didn't know she was here,' said Bill, his voice cracking, 'but she's who I want. She killed Rosie. I know.'

Sheila stared at him. 'How?'

'I came up here this morning. While you and that'—he jerked his head at Amy—'busybody were out. I found your notebooks, Sheila, and I've read them. When I thought about it last night, I knew she was lying for you.'

'We went to the police station,' Sheila said quietly. 'I told them about the baby—it was Mum's baby, Bill, and Dad smothered it. Then I told them about Rosie. I said that Dad killed her.'

'*She* killed her.' Bill's face was rigid.

'Dad made her do it. She had no choice. None of us did. If you want to blame someone, blame me. I should have stopped him.'

'How could you have stopped him? He gave her

the bloody gun. She could have shot him, instead.'

'You know what he was like.'

'She didn't have to do it! She wanted to kill Rosie because she had some sick obsession about her own father. It was in your notebooks, Sheila. She's perverted, can't you see that?'

Sheila's face flushed, but she held Bill's gaze. Amy, moving her weight slowly away from the doorway and towards the kitchen wall, willed her to keep looking at him.

Sheila said, in the same quiet voice, 'You don't understand.'

'Damn right I don't understand. Do you understand, Sheila? Do you? Do you think it's right?'

'No. I never said it was right.'

Amy measured the distance between herself and Bill. Ten feet? Twelve? It seemed like a football field. If she could grab a chair, she could—Her foot squeaked on the lino, and Bill whirled round. The twin barrels where pointing at her chest. 'Don't move!'

'OK, OK.' Amy put her hands up in surrender.

'Come in here where I can see you. Sit down.' He indicated a chair on the far side of the table. 'Don't try anything. Keep your hands where I can see them.'

He turned back to Sheila and Mo. Sheila was shaking, but Mo was quite still, her face devoid of expression. 'You knew,' said Bill, 'and you didn't tell me. You let me go on thinking Rosie had run off with another man. How do you think that feels, Sheila, believing that? And Les telling everyone, making me a laughing stock. Why didn't you tell me?'

'To protect you, Bill.' Sheila was staring at him with intense concentration, as if she were attempting telepathy. 'I wanted to protect you, just like you protected me.'

'I saved you, Sheila, but you chose to protect *her*, not me. Don't you think I deserved to know?'

'I thought it was for the best.'

'The best!' Bill's bark of laughter ricocheted round the small room. 'How do you feel now? All those years, letting him do it to you, to save her, and all the time, she wanted it. Or did you secretly enjoy it, him fucking you? Are you as sick as she is?'

'No, Bill, please.' Sheila's voice dropped to a whisper. 'I felt so guilty. I'm sorry.'

'It's too late for that. Get away from her.' He took a step towards Sheila, who spread out her arms to shield Mo.

'Please, Bill. She's all I've got left.'

Amy found her voice. 'Bill, this isn't doing any good.'

'Shut up!' Bill was staring at Sheila. 'What about me? How can you put her before me after what she's done?'

'She needs me, Bill.'

'No! She's thrown it all back in your face. I told you, I read what you wrote—every word. You did it because he made you, but she did it because she wanted to. Stand away from her.'

Amy saw tears slide down Sheila's face, heard her say, 'I'm sorry.' She hesitated—the air seemed to vibrate with purpose, and Amy realised what she was about to do a second before she did it and screamed, 'No!' as Sheila, with a sudden sideways jerk, broke away from Mo.

317

There was a pause—a heartbeat—then Amy was almost knocked off her chair as the roar of the shotgun slammed through her, deafening her. Regaining her balance, ears ringing, she turned and saw Sheila crouching on the floor, and Mo, blood spreading across the front of her pale T-shirt, slumped against the base of the wall beneath the tabby-cat clock, her thin legs folded underneath her. Bill was on the other side of the room, the gun still in his hands. He looked punch-drunk, swaying on his feet, his face slack. He muttered something Amy didn't catch, then ran from the room. She heard the front door slam, and then everything seemed to go into slow motion, as if she were under water.

Sheila's voice floated towards her in a bubble, isolated from the reverberation of the front door. 'He shot her. He shot her.'

'Yes,' said Amy, pulling herself out of her chair. 'I'll call . . .'

'He shot her.'

In the hall, with hands not her own, she picked up the phone and dialled 999.


# CHAPTER FORTY-FOUR

Afterwards, Amy found that, try as she might, she had no precise recollection of what happened next. She had an impression of herself huddled in the corner beside Mo, swabbing her chest with a tea-towel, picking up a skinny arm and being astonished by its heaviness, then feeling for a pulse that wasn't there while Sheila rocked backwards and forwards on the floor, her arms round her knees, blood on her face and her pretty cotton dress, asking, over and over again, 'Is she dead? Is she dead?' She remembered, too, seeing blood smeared on the lino as she levered herself to her feet to answer the door when the police came, and then their bulky, uniformed authority filling the kitchen, radios crackling, the ambulance men bending over Mo, heads shaking, and then saying her own name, and Mo's, and Sheila's, and Bill's, and later a group of faces—neighbours, she supposed—staring while she was escorted outside to the police car, and feeling the light pressure of a hand on top of her head as she climbed into the back.

They took away her clothes. She was surprised by the amount of blood on them, and on her hands and knees when she tried to clean up in the cloakroom at the police station, scrubbing herself with harsh paper towels from the dispenser. She wondered why she should be so surprised, because Sheila had blood on her, too. A policewoman helped her dress in a white paper boiler suit that tingled against her bare skin as if her arms and legs had been rubbed with metholated spirits. At some point she asked if she might make a phone call and spoke to Charlie. She remembered the texture of the inkpad against the tips of her fingers, the smell of disinfectant, the starkness of the interview room with the wooden table and chairs, and DI Bainbridge asking questions in a low, calm voice, going over and over the events of the last week because they wouldn't come back in any sensible order. She told them everything she knew— omitting only one detail—and then sat for what seemed like hours with a silent police officer before DI Bainbridge returned and told her that Bill had returned to his own house and shot himself before the police arrived.

'What happens now?' she asked.

'We'll need to contact you again, and I'm afraid we'll have to hang on to your clothes and your handbag, but you're free to go.'

'What about Sheila?'

'She can go, too.'

'She can't go back to Hadley Cottage.'

'Not today, I'm afraid. The forensic team are still there. I've sent a WPC to collect some clothes for her. Sorry we can't do the same for you.'

'That's OK. Can Sheila come home with me?'

Bainbridge smiled. 'I think that's probably the best option, don't you? By the way, your friend arrived about an hour ago. He's been waiting for you.'

A policewoman handed Amy the contents of her handbag in a clear plastic wallet and escorted her to the reception area. Charlie was standing by the desk, talking to the sergeant. He took her in his arms.

Amy clung to him wordlessly for a moment, then looked up at him and said, 'Please don't say I told you so.'

'I wasn't going to.'

'I didn't mean you to come all this way.'

'Don't be stupid,' said Charlie. 'I was worried about you.'

'You must have been waiting for ages. I didn't realise . . . You shouldn't have. My car's outside Sheila's. I'm sure they would have given us a lift, and I could have driven home.'

'Oh, really? You look shattered.'

'I am pretty tired. And'—she looked down at herself—'the abominable snowman.'

Charlie put his head on one side and pursed his lips. 'Oh, I don't know,' he said. 'Smart but casual. You're not coming home like that, are you?'

'No choice. They're keeping my clothes. But we need to wait for Sheila. She's coming with us.'

Charlie lowered his voice. 'They're not charging her with anything? Perverting the course of justice?'

'Apparently not.'

'What about Bill?'

'They found him at his home. He'd shot himself.'

'Christ. So she's the only one left.'

'And me.'

'You said on the phone that Mo killed Rosie.'

'Yes. It was horrible, Charlie. I can't tell you . . . unbelievable. And when I saw Bill was there, with the gun—I was upstairs with Sheila, we didn't hear him come in—I didn't know what to do. I told him to put the gun down, but he . . . Sheila told me he had a key, but it didn't really register at the time. We thought Mo had burnt Sheila's diaries, as well, that's why Sheila went downstairs, to ask her about it, or at least I think it was—perhaps she heard something, I don't know.'

'Sssh.' Charlie stroked her hair. 'It's over.'

'I don't think it'll ever be over.'

'You know what I mean. Sorry, Amy, I just don't know what to say. Do you know how Sheila is?'

'No idea. They brought us here in separate cars and I haven't seen her since.'

'Is she on her way?'

'I think so.'

'Right. I'll go and get the van.'

'Thanks, Charlie. I really do appreciate this.'

He kissed the top of her head, and left. After a moment, DI Bainbridge appeared with Sheila who, though conventionally dressed, looked bewildered and very frail. They stared at each other for a moment before Amy gave her a hug. Her body, under the thin papery stuff, was full of sharp little bones, and Amy held her gingerly, almost afraid to break something. 'You're coming home with me,' she said. 'For tonight.'

They were silent on the way back to Islington, Charlie driving, Sheila sitting in the front, looking straight ahead of her, and Amy, dull with exhaustion, doing her best to keep upright on a sack of sharp sand in the back.

'I've explained to Aunt Moy,' Charlie told her as he was helping her inside. 'Enough, anyway. She's waiting for us.'

Moira must have been looking out of her front window, because she appeared as soon as Charlie pulled up to the kerb. Amy, blinking at the light as he opened the back of the van, said, 'Talk about lowering the tone. First the fire brigade, then the police, and now this. I'll never live it down.'

'I shouldn't worry. It's dark, and anyway Aunt Moy plays bridge with half the neighbours—if anyone starts complaining, she'll soon sort them out.'

Once inside, Moira took charge, taking Sheila straight upstairs to the spare room and producing an enormous, tuna-coloured nightdress from her bag. Amy, trailing after her, was grateful to abnegate responsibility in the face of such sensible bossiness, and let herself be shooed away to change into her own clothes. Sheila, silent and withdrawn, meekly allowed herself to be put to bed. When Moira announced that she was going to fetch a doctor, Amy—who didn't see how such a thing was possible, even if you were a registered patient—didn't resist this, either. She went into the spare room and found Sheila sitting upright in bed, plucking at the sheets. 'Can I get you anything?' Amy asked. 'A cup of tea?'

Sheila's eyes, dark and empty, seemed to be straining to focus, as if she'd just come out of a fit. The not-quite-human look reminded Amy, horribly, of Mo. 'I'll bring you something anyway,' she said, 'then you can decide for yourself.' She retreated and closed the door, feeling a guilty relief at leaving Sheila's eerie non-presence.

Charlie was waiting for her in the kitchen. 'How is she?'

'I don't know. Gone. She's not talking, just staring into space. It's frightening. I couldn't stay in there, Charlie. I couldn't.'

'It's all right,' said Charlie gently. 'Moy's gone to fetch George Waterlane.'

'Who's he?'

'GP. One of her bridge lot. Lives round the corner.'

'Oh. Let's hope he's at home, then, because Sheila's in a really bad way, Charlie. I'm worried about her sanity.'

'It's hardly surprising, given what she's been through, but you can't do any more for her now.'

'I said I'd take her a cup of tea.'

'I'll put the kettle on. By the way, this was on the draining board.' He handed her a bunch of keys and a heavy cream envelope with *Amy* scrawled across it in her father's big, flamboyant handwriting. She opened it, and took out three sheets of notepaper.

*Dear Amy,*
*Thank you for your hospitality. I'm off to Switzerland with Claire. I can't think why she puts up with me, but she wants me to live with her, so I'm going. There's nothing for me here apart from you, darling, and I don't want to be a nuisance. To be honest, I thought she was after me because she was kind enough to lend me some money in the past and I wasn't able to repay her, but she says she's in love with me. She even hired a private detective to find me—how's that for enterprise? I hope you will forgive my taking off like that, but I think it will be for the best.*
*I know you think I haven't been honest with you, Amy, but I can promise you that neither the fire nor the burglary was anything to do with me. Whatever I may have done in the past, I never endangered your safety, nor would I. I can understand why you don't trust me; I haven't given you much reason to do so. Neither, I'm afraid, did Patti. It breaks my heart to think that you were on such bad terms when she died. I'm sorry I wasn't there. Claire has given me hell for it, and she's right. But I wasn't lying about the cancer. I did think I was in trouble there. As I told you, Claire carted me off to a tame quack in Harley Street, and we got the all-clear this morning. That was another reason I came to see you. I know my*

324

*actions may not have shown it, but I loved Patti very much, and I love you, too. Please don't think too badly of me.*

*We'll be in touch very soon. Claire's going to put her address and phone at the end of this.*

*With much love,*

*Dad xxx*

*PS: Some friends of mine have been staying at Patti's place. I hope you don't mind. I don't think it will be for long.*

*PPS: If you look in the fridge, you'll see we've left you a present.*

That was all, apart from the address and a scribbled line from Claire: *Don't worry, darling, I'll look after him. You must come and visit us soon, and make sure you bring that gorgeous man with you! C x*

'Bad news?' asked Charlie, when she looked up.

'It's Dad. He hasn't got cancer, which is great, but he's managed to sublet Mum's flat to some dodgy pals of his. That's why he was so flush, all of a sudden. He must have had keys cut, and everything. God knows how he did it in the time. No mention of a contract, but I suppose that would be too much to ask, and I shouldn't think I'll be seeing a lot of the rent, either.'

Charlie, in search of milk, was staring into the fridge. 'There seems to be rather a lot of champagne in here.'

'What?'

'Look.' He opened the door wide. The fridge was stacked, floor to ceiling, with bottles. Frowning, Amy went over to the bin and lifted the lid. In the bottom, jumbled underneath a pile of fag ends and crowned with a cigar butt, were her

325

milk, butter, eggs and other groceries. She started to laugh. 'Dad said they'd left me a present. Unfortunately, they've chucked everything away to make room for it.'

Charlie peered over her shoulder. 'Shit! So they have.'

'I think there might be some UHT in the cupboard, if they haven't filled that with chocolate or something.'

Amy sat watching Charlie make Sheila's tea, feeling dazed and only coming to her senses when a rap on the door announced Moira and an elderly man with an avuncular manner who introduced himself as Dr Waterlane. 'You stay where you are,' Moira told her, taking the tea from Charlie. 'We'll sort this out.'

'What about you?' said Charlie, when they'd gone upstairs. 'Tea, or something stronger?'

'I don't think there's any brandy left.'

'Scotch?'

'I hate it.'

'Have to be champagne, then.'

'Nothing to celebrate.'

'You're alive. So's Sheila.'

'Yes, but what's going to happen to her? She's alone. The sole survivor of the wreckage. If she is a survivor.'

'She's got you.'

'Yes,' said Amy, heavily. 'She's got me. You were right, Charlie. I shouldn't have got involved. I thought I was helping, but it didn't do any good, did it? And now . . .' She tailed off. Sheila's future, and her role in it, were too much to contemplate.

Charlie leant across the table and took her hand. 'Don't go there,' he said. 'Not now.'

'No. Not now.'

Amy watched Charlie go to the fridge and wondered if he really wanted to be with someone who had so many things to sort out. He's got his own life, she thought, he doesn't need all my problems as well, even if they are second-hand. I got myself into this—with a little help from Patti—and I need to deal with it before—Stop it, she told herself. Don't run before you can walk. Think about it tomorrow.

Charlie popped the cork, and poured two glasses. 'Let's drink to survival.'

'Pretty double-edged.'

'Nevertheless.'

'OK.' Amy raised her glass, said, 'Cheers, then,' and burst into tears. Charlie charged round the table and put his arms round her, and that was how Moira and Dr Waterlane found them when they came downstairs.

# CHAPTER FORTY-FIVE

One Saturday morning, seven months later, Amy left her house and walked down the road and across the canal bridge in the lashing March rain to a small, semi-detached villa. Sheila, looking fluffily pretty in a pale pink jumper, answered the door and, after Amy had taken her wet shoes off, ushered her into a small sitting room.

When the ritual of serving tea was completed, Sheila produced a book of colour swatches. 'What do you think? I'd like to have the bedroom in blue, but I can't decide. That one's pretty, but I think it might be too dark—they never look the same when they're on the wall.'

They drank tea and discussed colours, and Sheila's new job in a charity shop in Islington. 'I can't believe the things people want to get rid of—beautiful clothes, ornaments, so many boxes, it takes all day to sort them out.'

'What about the people?'

'Oh, they're lovely.'

As Sheila launched into a flood of description, Amy watched her animated face with pleasure. Despite Dr Waterlane's assurances, she'd never have thought it possible that this woman could have been transformed in such a way. Drugs had aided—and would continue to aid—her passage, but she was sleeping, eating, and appeared to be enjoying her new life. In the first dark weeks after Mo's death and Bill's suicide, neither of them had been able to speak about what had happened, and, as Sheila had grown stronger, Amy had skirted round her, not questioning, afraid, quite literally, of sending her mad. She decided that it was better to put unfinished business aside and concentrate on practicalities, rather than going over the past, and Dr Waterlane had warned her that the pace of further disclosure, accelerated to warp speed by the events leading up to Mo's death, would be slow, as Sheila struggled not only to regain her old self but begin to discover a new one, untrammelled by her family and the burden of secrecy she'd carried for so long.

Sheila had never returned to live at Hadley Cottage, and when she learnt that Bill had willed it to her, along with his bungalow and the rents from his fields, she'd been adamant about selling them as quickly as possible and making a new start in an entirely new place. Islington had seemed obvious —Amy would be nearby, and Moira, who'd grown fond of Sheila, had helped with the house-hunting. She and Charlie had supervised the move, and Amy had provided champagne (courtesy of George) and sandwiches for a party in the evening, with the four of them sitting on crates in the cosy little house and Sheila, tipsy, giggling at the daring of it all.

Listening to Sheila talking about the charity shop, and the Starbucks next door—'It seems so extravagant throwing money away on cups of coffee. I always take a Thermos flask'—Amy came to a decision. When Sheila finished speaking, and was sitting back in her chair, contemplating a third biscuit, Amy said, 'There's something I want to ask you.'

Sheila looked up, and Amy, conscious of a deepening of the atmosphere, said, 'I'm sorry. I've wanted to ask for some time, and there just hasn't been . . .'

'I know,' said Sheila simply.

'You don't have to tell me,' Amy ploughed on, 'but I don't want there to be a . . . barrier between us.'

To her astonishment, Sheila said quietly, 'I understand. It's about Bill, isn't it?'

Amy nodded.

'I was going to tell you,' said Sheila, 'but I felt disloyal. He's made all this possible.' She looked round the room. 'But I feel I owe it to you.'

'That day, in the kitchen, what did Bill mean when he said he'd saved you?'

'I think you know,' said Sheila gently. Then,

329

squaring her shoulders as if settling an invisible burden, she continued, 'That was why he was so worried about what was in Mo's diary. He needn't have been, because she never knew the truth about Dad's death. I told Bill about him, you see. It was two or three months after Rosie . . . after she died. I couldn't stand it any more. Mo was so ill, Dad was getting worse than ever with his temper, and Mum wasn't well, either. It was like being broken inside, and I thought I was going mad. Dad made us burn Rosie's things in the garden. He said that if we ever talked about what happened, he'd say it was our fault and we'd all end up in prison, and when we got out he'd come for us and kill us. I didn't care about that, but I didn't want Bill to know, because I was so ashamed. When I went to the farm he'd be there, and he seemed so lonely, and I thought it was my fault. There was one afternoon when I'd got the things from the pig lorry, and said goodbye, but I couldn't bring myself to go home. I don't know why it was that particular day, but I stayed in the farmyard, hiding. Bill thought I'd gone, and then I heard Dad leaving, by the back way, and later, when Bill came out to check something in the sheds, he found me. I'd gone into one of the old Nissen huts, where the bullocks were, and I remember I sat down in the straw. It was warm in there, and the animals didn't take any notice of me—I suppose I must have been in there for a couple of hours, and I knew I'd be in terrible trouble when I got back, for being late, but I didn't care. It was as if I'd just snapped . . . And then Bill came, when he was locking up, and he asked me what was the matter, and I told him about Dad's temper, and hitting us all the time, and that I couldn't stand it any more.'

'Did you know he was in love with you?' asked Amy.

Sheila blushed. 'No! Nothing like that.'

'He was.'

'Yes. Even before Rosie . . . He told me.'

'Do you think that was part of the trouble between them?'

'It might have been. Bill told me they'd grown apart. I don't know. But I never . . . I never *encouraged* him.'

'I'm sure you didn't.' She wouldn't have been sophisticated enough, Amy thought. Despite being raped by her father over many years, Sheila was, in many ways, a complete innocent. 'Did you tell him about the sexual abuse?' she asked.

'He asked me. I don't know why. I suppose he must have guessed from the way I was talking. So I told him. Not . . . details. He asked how long it had been going on, and I told him that, too. Then he said I couldn't go home on my own and he was coming with me. I tried to stop him. He was so angry, and I was frightened. I didn't know what was going to happen, but I thought, if he said something to Dad—confronted him—Dad would kill him.'

'Did Bill take his gun?'

Sheila shook her head. 'He didn't plan . . . I know he didn't. He was talking about the police, and I was terrified. I couldn't believe I'd actually said those things, and after that it all happened so fast, I didn't know what to do. When we got back to Hadley Cottage—we came round the back, through the garden—I went in first. Dad was in the lounge, sitting with the gun propped against his chair, watching television, and I could see he still had his boots on—work boots—and I knew he was going to . . . what he was going to do.'

Amy put a hand on Sheila's arm. 'It's OK,' she said. 'You don't need to explain.'

'He stood up,' Sheila continued. 'He switched off the TV, and then he put his hand on his belt, on the buckle, and I knew what it meant, he was going to take it off. That was the worst, you see, if he started with the belt, and the look on his face . . . Then he stopped—he'd seen Bill come up behind me, and that was the moment everything came apart, and I was so confused.'

Amy felt a pang of recognition. 'You wanted it and dreaded it—both at the same time.'

'Yes,' said Sheila, 'and I was ashamed, too, with Bill there. I realised how it must look.'

'To an outsider.'

Sheila nodded. 'No one else had seen Dad like that, they didn't know. Bill said something, "What the hell do you think you're doing?" or something like that, and Dad looked at me and said, "Get out," so I went to the door, because we always just did what he said, but Bill said I ought to stay. Dad told me to go upstairs. Mum and Mo were up there. Mum said afterwards that he'd told them to stay there when I didn't come back, and they weren't to come down till he said. Then Bill said something about how I ought to hear what he had to say, so I just stood where I was, and Bill said how he knew Dad had been hitting us, and Dad said it wasn't his business. Bill said it was, and Dad said, "I do my job, that's your business."'

'Then what happened?'

'Bill told him he didn't have a job any longer,

332

that he wasn't going to employ a man who beat his family. Dad said it was his family, he could do what he liked, and Bill said he knew Dad had been having sex with me, and he was going to report him to the police. Dad said that they wouldn't take any notice because I was grown up and it was my choice. I think Bill was shocked that Dad could defy him like that, just look him in the eye and say there was nothing he could do, but he said, "You raped Sheila, and if I have anything to do with it, you'll go to prison." Dad said, "Why don't you ask Sheila?" They were both looking at me, and Bill said, "He raped you, didn't he?" It was so hard. Even though I'd told Bill, before, I kept thinking that Dad would kill all of us if I said yes, and that it would be my fault, and what would happen if everyone found out. But at the same time I knew we couldn't go on, and I was terrified of Dad shooting Bill because he had the gun right next to him and I knew it would be loaded. Normally I'd have done whatever Dad said, but with everything coming in on me at once, I couldn't speak. It was terrible.'

'What did you say?' asked Amy.

'I said, "Yes." I'd never wanted sex from him, never. Dad just kept on staring at Bill. They were only about a foot apart by then, and Bill said, "Why did you do it?" and Dad said . . . he said . . .'

'What did he say?'

'He said,' Sheila finished in a whisper, ' "That's all she's good for." '

# CHAPTER FORTY-SIX

Amy gaped at Sheila. 'He actually said that?'

'Yes. Taunting Bill. Then Bill rushed forward and got hold of the gun—Dad tried to stop him, but he wasn't quick enough—and he shot him. Dad was on the floor, and there was a big hole in his chest. I took the gun from Bill. It was double-barrelled, so I knew there'd be another cartridge. I bent over and put the gun right against his chest so I wouldn't miss, and I fired. I wanted to make sure, you see. I didn't want him to suffer.'

'What happened after that?'

'I told Bill to leave, and he did. He said afterwards that he shouldn't have, but it was the right thing. You see, with Mum and Mo . . . it would be different if I said I'd killed him.'

'Why didn't they come down?' asked Amy. 'They must have heard the shots.'

'They were terrified,' said Sheila. 'They thought Dad had shot me. They thought he was going to come up and kill them as well.'

'Did you tell Bill to go,' asked Amy, 'because of what happened to Rosie?'

'I didn't think of it at the time. Not . . .' Sheila tapped her head. 'Not in here. But that was part of it. It's hard to remember, really, what was going through my mind. Bill went, and I stood there with the gun in my hands, looking at Dad. Even though there was blood, and the wound in his chest, I couldn't believe that he was dead. I kept expecting him to get up. I saw the blood on the rug, and on his favourite chair, and I remember thinking he'd be angry about it, and then I looked at him and thought, he'll never be angry any more. But even then . . . I don't know how long I stood there. I suppose it must have been a long time, because Mo came down eventually. I didn't hear her coming, just when she asked, "Is he dead?" She was standing beside me, and then Mum came, and she said, "Is he really dead?" and I must have said, "Yes," because she said, "Are you sure?" They couldn't believe it, either. I suppose I must have put the gun down, and then we were on the floor, beside him, and we cried. For a long time, we just sat and cried. They didn't ask me, "Did you kill him?" Mum said she thought she'd heard a man's voice, but I said it was from the TV. They'd been in the front bedroom—the door was shut, and you can't hear properly. But when she said that, it made me remember the gun, because of Bill's fingerprints, so I went out to the Anderson and fetched an oily rag and rubbed it with that. I didn't want him to get into trouble, and'—she gave a faint smile—'Dad always made us clean the tools for him, so it was right, really, wasn't it? It was Mum who phoned the police. She asked for someone to come because Dad had been shot. We knew we had to do that. They took us to the station and asked questions. That's when I told them it was me.'

'You didn't think of trying to cover it up?' asked Amy. 'You could have said it was a burglar.'

'Oh, no.' Sheila looked shocked. 'We wanted it done properly.'

'Even though you might have gone to prison?'

'It was the right thing,' said Sheila. 'For Bill. I always thought I might have been the one who actually killed him. Bill said he was dead when I fired, but I don't know if that was true. And I didn't care about myself. Just that Mum and Mo would be free, and I thought, whatever happened, it would be better than the life we'd been living. And it was, for a while, only . . .'

'Mo had a breakdown. She never forgave you for Leslie's death.'

'No. And Mum, at the end, when she was confused.'

Amy remembered what Charlie had said about his brother despising his mother because he couldn't protect her from his father—the mind finding ways to accommodate what it couldn't accept. The lies in the head, on the page, in the photograph album. Patti had been the same, creating her version of the past because she couldn't face reality, adding to it until the emotional investment had become too great ever to let go, even when she was dying. She and Mo had been two of a kind, Amy thought.

'Mo stopped visiting Iris, didn't she?'

'Yes. I don't think she ever blamed Mum, but it was just too much for her. She couldn't cope. I am sorry, Amy, about what she did.'

'I know. But you don't need to apologise for her any more.'

'I miss her. And Mum. How they used to be. I think about them all the time. I feel so guilty.' Sheila's eyes glittered with unshed tears.

Amy leant over and took her hand. 'Listen, Sheila, you didn't kill Mo, Bill did. You're just lucky he didn't kill you as well.'

'No. It was because I moved away. He wouldn't have done it, if I'd been in front of her.'

336

'You don't know that.' After a pause, Amy said, 'I saw you . . .' She paused, choosing her words. 'I saw the two of you break apart—Mo moved, too— and then Bill shot her.'

'Is that true?'

'Yes,' lied Amy, looking Sheila straight in the eye. 'He couldn't have done it otherwise. That's what I saw, and that's what I told the police.'

After a moment, Sheila pulled a handkerchief from the sleeve of her jumper, blew her nose. 'I didn't realise. Thank you.'

# CHAPTER FORTY-SEVEN

They went upstairs after that, to look at the colour swatches in Sheila's bedroom and put crosses against the shades that merited testers. 'Why don't you try and match Peter?' Amy asked, looking at the blue knitted rabbit on Sheila's bed. 'He's a nice colour.'

'That's a good idea.' Sheila held the toy beside the strip of pale blue rectangles. 'He's most like that one.'

'I'd better get you the others, just in case,' said Amy. 'I'm meeting Charlie for lunch in ten minutes, but I can bring them round later.'

Sheila said shyly, 'I'm glad you're happy, Amy.'

'With Charlie, you mean?' Amy was surprised. Sheila had never ventured such a personal comment. 'Yes, I suppose I am. We're going to Switzerland in January. My dad's getting married.'

'How lovely.'

'And I finally managed to get the tenants out of

Mum's flat. I'm going to put it on the market.'

Walking towards the gastro-pub on the New North Road where she was meeting Charlie, Amy had no regrets about lying to Sheila. 'I know this sounds terrible,' she said over lunch, 'but I can't help feeling that Mo is better off dead than shut up in some institution.'

'Yeah.' Charlie sighed. 'What about Bill?'

'I was very sorry for him, but he'd have gone to prison, too, wouldn't he?'

Charlie nodded. 'Mitigating circumstances, though.'

'But that would have got Sheila involved. That's the reason he burnt her journals that day, before he went up to Hadley Cottage. Despite knowing the truth, he was still protecting her.'

'What if Mo hadn't been there?'

'I don't know. I suppose Bill wanted to find out where she was—maybe he had some idea of threatening Sheila to get her to tell him. I don't think he really knew what he was doing.' Amy sighed. 'None of it's rational. But you know, in a way, Sheila is free, now.' That single, sideways step, she thought. Away from Mo, away from Bill, for ever. 'She and Bill . . . It was too complicated. She owed him too much.'

'How do you mean?'

'Oh, just over the years,' Amy fudged. 'The house, looking after her like he did.'

Charlie opened his mouth, then shut it again. 'How about another drink?' he said finally.

'Why not?'

Watching him walk across to the bar, she thought, I was right not to say anything. It was Sheila's secret, not hers, a confidence that couldn't

338

be broken. She pictured Sheila in her new bedroom, carefully returning Peter Rabbit to the bed and tucking him under the folded-down sheet so that his head lay on the pillow. He was symbolic, both of the childhood Sheila never had, and, Amy hoped, her future peace of mind.

'What are you smiling at?' Charlie had returned with the drinks.

Amy shook her head. It was too little, and too much, to explain. 'Nothing,' she said. 'Let's drink to Sheila, shall we?'

me